WED FOR THEIR ROYAL HEIR

JACKIE ASHENDEN

THE NIGHTS SHE SPENT WITH THE CEO

JOSS WOOD

MILLS & BOON

First published in Great Britain 2023
by Mills & Boon, an imprint of HarperCollins*Publishers* Ltd,
1 London Bridge Street, London, SE1 9GF

www.harpercollins.co.uk

HarperCollins*Publishers*
Macken House, 39/40 Mayor Street Upper,
Dublin 1, D01 C9W8, Ireland

Wed for Their Royal Heir © 2023 Jackie Ashenden

The Nights She Spent with the CEO © 2023 Joss Wood

ISBN: 978-0-263-30667-5

02/23

This book is produced from independently certified FSC™ paper
to ensure responsible forest management.
For more information visit: www.harpercollins.co.uk/green.

Printed and Bound in Spain using 100% Renewable Electricity
at CPI Black Print, Barcelona

WED FOR THEIR ROYAL HEIR

JACKIE ASHENDEN

MILLS & BOON

To all those who will never pick up a Mills & Boon Modern.
So long, suckers! All the more for us!

CHAPTER ONE

THE CLUB DIDN'T have a name. It didn't need one. Just as the three men lounging on the metal catwalk up above the dance floor didn't need any introductions.

Solace Ashworth knew who they were.

Kings.

They'd once been the three Wicked Princes—or so the media had dubbed them back when they'd been at Oxford university—causing mayhem wherever they went. Now they'd ascended their thrones they were wicked no longer.

Or at least one of them wasn't.

They were all tall and broad-shouldered—clearly, they fed baby kings much better than they did poor nobodies—two of them with short black hair, the third a dark, rich tawny that gleamed gold in the pulsing dance-floor lights.

The tawny-haired man was King Augustine Solari of Isavere, a mountain kingdom between Spain and Italy, and still very, very wicked, or so the gossip columns said.

One of the black-haired men was Sheikh Khalil ibn al-Nazari of Al Da'Ira, an ancient desert kingdom on the Red Sea near Saudi Arabia. He was apparently less wicked than Augustine, though his reputation for ruthlessness was second to none.

It was the third man, though, who held Solace's attention.

He was leaning on the metal rail that bounded the catwalk, long fingers curled around it, staring down at the heaving dance floor beneath him with a single-minded focus that made Solace catch her breath.

King Galen Kouros of Kalithera, a small, picturesque country on the Adriatic coast. Where they were now.

The nameless club was in Therisos, the nation's capital, and a secret venue only open to royalty and their guests. Solace still couldn't believe they'd let her in, but the password she'd paid a lot of money for had worked, and in the silver couture dress she'd also paid a lot of money for she looked as though she belonged here.

Just as well. Because right now, desperate times called for desperate measures and the plan she was about to put in motion was surely as desperate as they came.

A plan that involved the man on the catwalk.

There were many beautiful people in the club tonight, but he was the most beautiful.

Tall and broad, with wide shoulders and lean hips, his was the classic, perfect male form, shown off to perfection by the plain black shirt and black suit trousers he wore. Simple clothes designed to highlight the beauty of the man.

His coal-black hair was worn short, revealing the perfect bone structure of his face: high cheekbones, straight nose, the most beautifully carved mouth.

Solace swallowed. She remembered—

No. She couldn't allow herself to get distracted by memories or by his beauty.

She was here for one reason and one reason only: seduce him, then blackmail him.

Her plan was mad, of course, and very wrong, but she'd been left with no choice. She'd tried contacting the Kalitheran embassy, first via email then by phone, relating her story to them and then requesting help. But they hadn't believed her. Even a personal visit to demand she see someone in authority had involved her being escorted from the premises as a nuisance. She'd briefly considered whether she could get a lawyer to help, but she didn't have the money and she'd heard enough about lawyers not to trust them anyway.

No, all she'd had was herself and this plan of hers.

Getting herself from London to Therisos had been the easy part. Even getting into this very exclusive, nameless nightclub hadn't been the hardest part.

No, the hardest part was going to be getting his attention.

The people on the dance floor were doing a very good impression of acting as if they didn't know who the three men standing above them were, though Solace noticed many sending occasional glances upwards.

Oh, yes, they knew, but the whole point of the club was discretion. Here royalty could relax and be human without fear of media reprisal, even if it was just for a night.

Up on the catwalk, King Augustine, who was standing on one side of Galen, clapped him on the shoulder and said something that made him shake his head. On the other side of Galen was Sheikh Khalil, who stood with his powerful arms folded, his attention also on the dance floor. He'd clearly said something amusing since Augustine laughed and a brief, flickering smile lit Galen's sternly beautiful face.

Solace's heart twisted. She remembered that smile. He'd given it to her once, though she hadn't known who he was at the time. She'd been dazzled by its warmth. No one had ever smiled at her that way either before or since.

You're getting distracted again. Focus.

She gritted her teeth and ignored the ache that lurked just behind her breastbone. It didn't matter what she wanted. It didn't matter that this was going to hurt. It didn't even matter that what she was about to do was very, *very* wrong.

What mattered was getting her baby son back and for him she would do anything, anything at all.

Even blackmail a king. The king who was his father.

Gathering her courage, Solace stepped from the shadows where she'd been lurking and made her way onto the dance floor. Bodies heaved around her, lights flashing. The bass throbbed, so deep she could feel it in the soles of feet, in her chest.

She stood out. She knew she did. She'd made sure of it. The dress she wore was a confection of form-fitting silver mesh with fine silver chains for straps, and it glittered and sparkled in the light.

A dress made for getting attention.

Male heads turned as she began to dance, moving to the music in the way she'd studied through watching countless YouTube videos in her local library. Sexy and sensual, yet not too explicit. She'd prepared for this the way she prepared for everything: as if for a battle where surrender was not an option.

She didn't look up, not yet. He needed to see her first.

Familiar anxiety twisted inside her, but she ignored it with the ease of long practice. If she didn't catch his attention now, she'd think of something else. She'd done it before wearing a catering uniform and a mask; doing it wearing nothing but a silver-mesh dress was surely a piece of cake.

A couple of men were dancing near her now, which made her wary. She knew how being a woman on her own made her a target. She'd been on her own all her life and being thought of as easy prey was something she was intimately familiar with.

However, according to the thread in one of the secret Internet chatrooms she'd managed to gain access to, this club had strict rules when it came to behaviour and those rules were enforced. Sure enough the men didn't come too close, but they looked at her with interest in their eyes. Clearly the dress was doing its job.

But there was only one man whose interest she wanted.

She took a breath and finally looked up.

And froze.

He was looking straight at her.

All the air abruptly escaped her lungs in a wild rush and her skin prickled with sudden heat.

She had forgotten.

She had forgotten how the impact of his gaze was like a gut punch. How he made her feel as if she were going to go up in flames on the spot.

It had happened that night in London, too. She'd been in her uniform and incredibly nervous because it had been her first job with the catering company and a step up from waitressing and cleaning. But she'd been determined to do brilliantly, because the money had been good, and she'd had plans. She'd wanted to go back to high school and finish this time, and then, if she did well, perhaps go to university and get a law degree.

All the staff that night had been instructed to wear

masks to match the guests since it had been a masquerade ball, and they'd been under strict instructions not to draw attention to themselves. She'd been moving through the crowds with a tray of full champagne flutes, pleased that so far everything seemed to be going well.

Then the tall man in the middle of a knot of people had looked up and she'd frozen the way she was freezing now. His eyes had been a dense, dark blue and she'd been caught in them like a rabbit in a trap. And an unfamiliar feeling had swept over her, a sizzling, crackling energy humming in the space between them, making her feel hot all over.

She'd been so shocked that she'd taken an instinctive step back, only to bump into someone standing behind her, which in turn had loosened her hold on the tray, sending it crashing onto the floor...

Solace's mouth was dry and despite the deafening thump of the music she could hear her heart beating loudly in her head.

Above her on the catwalk, his powerful figure had gone very still, his hands gripping the rail tightly.

Galen Kouros was famous, not only for his progressive rule and the work he'd done to improve the lives of his most severely disadvantaged subjects, but also for his spotless reputation, and in the ten years since he'd ascended the throne no hint of scandal had ever attached itself to him. He was the most straitlaced king in Europe. Even the revelation of his baby son, which had caused an initial media fuss, had been swiftly quelled by a sombre palace statement detailing the death of the King's apparent fiancée and the mother of his son, and a request for privacy at this delicate time. Which had been duly given since he was beloved by his people and the media alike.

But that statement was a lie, just as his spotless reputation was a lie.

Galen might be a touch less rigid than his father, but that wickedness he'd once been famous for as a prince was still part of him. And Solace knew because *she* was the mother of his child and there had been only wickedness when he'd taken her in that deserted office the night of that masquerade ball. A wickedness that had left her trembling with desire and desperation, and a need she'd been powerless to resist.

She'd made a mistake that night. She'd surrendered to him and the heat that had burned between them and had earned herself nothing but pain because of it. But she'd learned her lesson and she wasn't going to surrender again. *Never* again, not to anyone. No matter how beautiful or compelling or desirable they were.

Tonight, she was going to do the opposite. Tonight, she was going to be the one with the power and *he* would surrender to *her*. She would use that spotless reputation of his against him and take back the son she'd lost. The son he'd taken from her.

She was a still point in the shifting, heaving mass of dancers around her, steeling herself as she held his gaze, feeling the air between them thicken and come alive with the same burning, sizzling chemistry she'd felt that night at the gala. And that was a good thing, even though it frightened her on some deep level.

But no, she wasn't going to lose herself this time.

This time she had a purpose.

'Come and catch me, Your Majesty,' she whispered to him, even though he wouldn't be able to hear. 'Catch me if you can.'

Then she tore her gaze from his and made her way off the dance floor and deeper into the club.

'That looks like trouble,' Khalil observed coolly from his place on the catwalk beside Galen.

'Pretty trouble,' Augustine agreed.

Galen barely heard them. The woman in the silver dress had disappeared into the crowd, but he was still staring after her, conscious that he was gripping the rail very tightly, every muscle in his body tense.

He'd noticed her immediately. It had been impossible not to. Everyone else in the club was wearing dark shades or black, but not her. She'd stood out in the crowd like the only star in a night sky, glittering and bright in a dress that seemed to be made out of liquid mercury. Her long, straight pale hair had swirled like a veil around her as she'd danced, graceful and sensual. She looked as if she'd been dipped in silver, moonlight in the shape of a woman.

His wasn't the only attention she'd drawn, others had obviously been as taken with her as he was, moving to dance closer to her, and he'd been filled with a wave of possessiveness that had nearly made him stride from the catwalk and down the stairs to join her on the dance floor. Make it clear to every man in the club that she was his.

A ridiculous notion. He'd never been a possessive man and he wasn't about to start being one over a pretty stranger in a club. He wasn't here to find a woman anyway. He was here to meet his friends and that was all.

Except he didn't stop scanning the crowds below him, searching for a flash of silver.

'I take it you're going to go after her?' Augustine murmured.

'No,' Galen said.

'Are you sure? Because if you're not going to then I might—'

'No,' Galen repeated and found he'd pushed himself away from the rail and was now standing on the catwalk eye to eye with one of his closest friends. 'You will not.'

But the expression on Augustine's fallen-angel face was only amused. 'Does that sound like a claim to you, Khal?' he said, not looking away from Galen.

'It does,' Khalil agreed. He didn't sound amused. He sounded cool and unruffled, the way he always did.

Laughter glittered in Augustine's blue-green eyes and probably at Galen's expense, but Galen ignored it. He was long used to his friend's tendency to poke at people to get a reaction. It was useful, or so Augustine claimed. You could tell a lot about a person by how long they held onto their temper.

Galen never lost his, never even let it slip. A loose temper was a sign of a weak mind, his father had often said, which Galen had always thought the worst kind of hypocrisy. Because while Alexandros Kouros had never screamed or shouted, his cold fury had consumed not only his court, but also Galen's childhood into the bargain.

Galen himself tried to be a different sort of king, a less rigid king, but there was only so much he could do given the bitter truth that lay at the heart of his throne. A secret only he knew, that no one else could ever find out.

It was guarding that secret that made him act in ways that made him rather too much like Alexandros for comfort.

Not that he had a choice.

'Not now, August,' Galen said flatly. 'I'm not in the mood.'

Augustine gave him an assessing look. 'Forgive me, my friend, but when are you in the mood?'

'That's none of your—'

'You're in danger of becoming as boring as your reputation, Galen, I told you this.' A light thread of amusement coloured his voice, but there was a hint of steel beneath it too. Augustine was very fond of the iron fist in the velvet glove approach.

Galen was conscious of a flick of irritation. It was his friends' last night in Therisos—they'd both come for a brief, unofficial visit to catch up, which the three of them did every three months or when their schedules allowed—and Augustine had wanted to mark the occasion by visiting the club. It was a chain he'd set up himself, mainly for his own amusement, or so he'd said, but also because he was sick of being photographed everywhere he went and preferred a more…discreet environment.

There were no reporters here and everyone who entered signed an NDA. The perfect place to let your hair down, or so Augustine had said. 'Remember your youth,' he'd also said. 'You could afford to be a little more wicked, Galen.'

But his youth was something Galen had no wish to revisit and being a little more wicked was the one thing he could *not* afford, especially not after the mistake he'd made the previous year. The mistake that had ended with a son Galen had never known he'd had until after he was born.

Galen would fight to the death for Leo, but that mistake? He would not make it again. He *could* not make it again.

'I do not care what you think of my reputation.' He tried to sound as cool as Khal, but it came out sounding more of a growl than anything else. 'I'm not chasing after some stranger just because you think I need to be less boring.'

He's right though. You know what happens when you deny yourself.

Yes, he did. But that only meant he had to try harder.

Augustine shrugged. 'A woman like that isn't going home alone tonight, but I suppose it's your choice. If you don't want her, someone else will.'

Galen knew what his friend was doing, the manipulative bastard. 'I don't care,' he said.

'Do you not?' Augustine raised a brow and glanced over Galen's shoulder at Khalil. 'What about you, Khal? Maybe for yourself?'

The Sheikh, whose mere word in Al Da'Ira was law, looked thoughtful. 'She is…exquisite. Maybe I could—'

'No,' Galen said for the third time. 'Not you as well.'

Khalil only gazed blandly back, his expression inscrutable.

His friends meant well, Galen knew that, but there were reasons he had to behave with the utmost discretion wherever he went. Kostas, his uncle, watched him, waiting for one slip, and while Galen had successfully managed him the past ten years since he'd been crowned, Leo's birth had complicated things, making Kostas even more suspicious than he already was.

Kostas would love to see him have to abdicate and take the throne for himself.

Except Galen would never allow that to happen. It was why he couldn't let go his control over his baser appetites, not even for a moment. He couldn't give Kostas any reason to question him.

The safety of his country depended on it.

But there are no reporters here. No one will tell. And you have not been with a woman in so long. Not since—

Ah, but he wasn't going to think of that night when his son was conceived. Where he'd put at risk everything, including his throne, for passion with a nameless woman at a masquerade ball of all things.

He couldn't allow it to happen again, no matter how hungry his body was.

The woman in silver was exquisite, as Khalil had said, but he wasn't going to go chasing after her. He had a million things to do, a king always did, but one of the things on his list was finding himself a wife. The kings of Kalithera always chose someone from the aristocracy, of a good family since family was important, and he already had a list of candidates. He hoped he'd have chemistry with at least one of them, which would mean he could sate his hunger with her, not some nameless stranger in a nightclub.

'Fine,' Augustine said in a long-suffering tone. 'If you want to deny yourself then on your head be it. But I'm certainly not going to.'

No, but then Augustine wouldn't. He never denied himself anything.

Galen stepped away from the rail. 'Amuse yourself however you like, gentlemen. I have some more work to do tonight.'

Augustine only shook his head, while Khalil gave him a long, expressionless look that Galen knew full well was Khal trying to understand what he was up to.

Well, the answer to that was nothing. He'd had enough of this club, and he was leaving, the woman in silver be damned.

Striding along the catwalk, he came to the stairs and descended into the crowds. His security detail shifted from the various discreet places where they'd been waiting, ready to come with him. Augustine and Khalil hadn't brought theirs tonight, but Galen always had his attend. Kostas would have noticed if he'd left them behind and started asking questions as to why, and Galen didn't want him asking those questions. Since Leo had arrived on the scene, he'd had to be extra cautious. His security were all intensely loyal to him and no man amongst them would have let slip anything, but he couldn't be too careful. If nothing else, last year's catastrophe had proved that.

The spotlights pulsed as he headed towards the exit and a flash of silver caught his eye. He stopped, searching instinctively for the location of that flash.

There she was, standing against a wall in the darkest part of the club, the strobing lights catching the glitter of her dress. It moulded to her figure like molten silver, outlining the most delicious curves he'd ever seen. Full breasts, a neat waist, generous hips...

His fingers itched. He wanted to touch her, run his hands over her, slip the delicate chains holding up that dress off her shoulders and watch as the fabric fell down to reveal all those luscious curves.

But no. Those were old habits. He'd already decided he wasn't going to indulge himself tonight, no matter what Augustine thought. And while she was certainly lovely, this woman wasn't going to make him change his mind no matter how delicious she was.

Yet he didn't move, slowly becoming aware that the woman wasn't alone. A man was with her, leaning over her, and from out of nowhere came a short, sharp burst of territorial anger.

She is your prey tonight.

Prey? Ridiculous. His days of prowling through the

clubs purely for the thrill of the chase and the adrenaline rush of a one-night stand were over, as were the forbidden parties that sometimes turned into orgies and the stupid, drunken stunts he, Khal and Augustine used to pull, causing the kind of mayhem that only three young men with too much money and far too much arrogance could. At least until his father had had a stroke, and he'd been called back to Kalithera, and he'd had to put all of that behind him.

He still remembered going into his father's bedroom the night he'd returned to Therisos. Alexandros had barely been able to speak, but Galen had understood him well enough: the media storm that had erupted after Galen had been at a party with under-age girls had been the last straw. That had proved he was unfit to take the crown of Kalithera and so he was being disowned in favour of Kostas, his uncle.

Galen had always known his father had hated him, the old man had made it quite clear throughout the entirety of his childhood, and even though he'd tried to tell Alexandros that he'd had nothing to do with those girls, Alexandros hadn't listened.

And then Galen had promptly forgotten all about the girls, because then Alexandros had dealt his second, more devasting blow: Galen's mother, who'd died not long after having him, had had an affair with a palace servant nine months before Galen was born. Galen might not be Alexandros's son after all.

The shock had rendered him mute. His entire childhood had been a constant battle to please a man who'd never been satisfied with anything Galen had done, who'd punished him for the smallest infractions and for no reason. Who'd constantly seemed furious with him... It all now made sense.

Not that knowing the truth made any difference. Not when in the end Galen had given up. Given up trying to be good, given up trying to obey Alexandros's seemingly pointless rules. Given up wanting to follow in the footsteps of a man who'd loathed the very sight of him. He'd even given up wanting to be Alexandros's heir...

All that trying had been for nothing. He might be another man's son.

Galen would have found it a relief in its way, if his father hadn't named his brother, Galen's uncle, as the new heir. Kostas had always been a moral vacuum, constantly pandering to his big-business cronies, and had spent years trying to get Alexandros to make Kalithera a tax haven. He'd already influenced Alexandros to pass policies that favoured the rich, ignoring the very real poverty of some of the Kalitheran people.

Alexandros had made no secret of the fact that he thought his so-called son would make an unfit king, and since Galen had found his father's training for the role...difficult, he'd sometimes wondered if there wasn't some truth to that.

Yet even so, he couldn't let Kostas take the crown. It was wrong to take a throne that might not be his, but there was no other heir, and no one else to protect Kalithera.

There was only him.

An imperfect king he might be, but Galen hadn't seen another choice. So when his father had died before he could change the succession, Galen had claimed the throne. Of course, one DNA test would have proven conclusively who he was once and for all, but he couldn't take the risk. If it turned out he wasn't Alexandros's son, he would have to abdicate in favour of Kostas, who would then run Kalithera into the ground.

His uncle hadn't known all of Alexandros's plans to name him the heir, but he'd always been a suspicious man and had known Alexandros hadn't thought much of Galen, and every so often there had been mutterings about Galen's past and how he was unfit to rule. And while Galen had cemented his role as King over the past ten years, he couldn't allow Kostas's mutterings to take hold and foster doubt.

He had to be careful. To behave in such a way as to not draw attention, not put a foot out of line, not to remind his uncle of past behaviour that he'd left behind. Not remind anyone—especially not the media—of the Wicked Prince he'd once been.

And he'd been very successful so far. He'd managed to keep himself and Kalithera out of the headlines for the past ten years. Until that mistake he'd made last year with that woman, that exceptional, lovely woman with clear, piercing grey eyes and the gut punch of a chemistry that he hadn't been able to resist.

It was a flaw of his, one of his greatest, that he found controlling his baser urges so difficult. Which was why he had to try even harder not to fall prey to them.

Yet a similar chemistry was hitting him now, crackling over his skin as he watched her, along with a growing need to stride over to where she stood and take that interloper by the scruff of his neck and jerk him away from her.

As the man leaned further in towards her, she glanced away, turning her head in Galen's direction. Their eyes met and, as he had up on that catwalk, he felt the shock of desire right down low inside him, raw and primal, and he was moving in her direction before he even knew what he was doing.

She saw him before the man standing in front of her

did, her eyes going wide. Her partner, obviously picking up on her shift in attention, looked in Galen's direction too, but after seeing who it was coming towards them he went pale and took a step away from her before disappearing into the crowd.

Galen should have stopped then. He should have turned around and left himself.

But he didn't.

The woman didn't move. She drew him in like a magnet, watching him come closer, her eyes dark and wide. He could see the pulse at the base of her throat beating hard and fast, the light shimmering over the fabric of her dress betraying her quickened breathing. She wasn't exactly beautiful—her nose was too long, and her mouth was too wide—yet there was something mesmerising about her face, something that caught his attention and held it. She seemed familiar in some way, though he couldn't put his finger on why. He'd never met her before, he was sure.

She didn't say anything as he came to a stop in front of her, only looked up at him. Her mouth was full and lovely, her lashes thick and blonde, a startling contrast to her dark eyes. And in those dark eyes a fire burned.

A fire that found an answering spark inside him.

He didn't know what had made him come over to her and he didn't know why he was standing in front of her now, when what he'd fully intended was to leave. This was a mistake, and he knew it, yet he stayed where he was, feeling the flames inside him start to leap.

'Did you want something?' she asked in English. Her voice had a pleasing husk to it that shivered over his skin like a caress. 'I mean, you frightened off that guy for a reason, I presume?' She didn't sound as if she minded her prospective partner being frightened off in the least.

Anger coiled inside him, at himself and what he was doing, and his apparent inability to walk away, and at that tantalising hint of familiarity that he couldn't quite pinpoint. But anger was an emotion he didn't allow himself, so he crushed it. Hard.

'Who are you?' he asked.

Her gaze flickered yet she didn't move. She was leaning back against the wall, almost as if she was trying to put distance between them, yet he wasn't standing that close. She could have moved away if she'd chosen.

'That depends.' The pulse at the base of her throat was beating faster now. He wanted to put his mouth there and taste it. 'Who wants to know?'

Galen ignored the question, taking a step closer as he searched her lovely face, caught in the grip of a compulsion he could hardly explain even to himself. 'You are familiar,' he murmured. 'Have we met?'

'Oh, I don't think so.' Her gaze met his from underneath her lashes. 'I think I would have remembered you.'

And he would have remembered her…oh, yes, he would.

He took another step. 'What is your name?'

'Why should I tell you?' The light shimmered across the silver fabric of her dress, and she raised one blonde brow. 'Your Majesty.'

A challenging woman. Oh, he liked that. He liked that very much. She knew who he was and yet from the heated glitter in her eyes, she was not intimidated by him. Not at all.

It's been a long time. Too long.

Over a whole year and still he thought about that

night at the ball with the beautiful grey-eyed woman. She'd had no idea who he was. With her he'd been just a man and she'd wanted that man so passionately.

As if it didn't matter what a liar you are...

Galen ignored the thought. That night was over and the woman—Solace had been her name, he'd discovered later—long gone. But tonight...well, this woman was right in front of him, and the night was still young, and maybe Augustine had been right. Maybe he did need to let the leash off. He'd make sure Kostas wouldn't know and, besides, he knew from experience that abstinence only made things harder. Every so often it was necessary to let off steam in order to prevent any more mistakes, and if this woman was here and she wanted him...

Galen took another step to test her. There were only inches between them now, and he could smell her subtle scent, warm female flesh and the sweetness of lilies.

She didn't move, only watched him, so slowly he put one hand on the wall beside her head and then, after a moment, did the same with the other, caging her.

There was no alarm in her dark eyes, only that burning flame, that heat. Reminding him that he wasn't just a king, but a man as well, and that man was hungry. No, that man was starving.

Her gaze dropped to his mouth and his body hardened instantly, the warmth of her intoxicating.

Yes. It seemed she *was* interested after all.

Theos, he hadn't felt this intensely about a woman in years. If he ever had.

You did, remember?

No, he was not going to think of her. He would obliterate the memory of her piercing grey eyes and the silver flames that had burned in them with this woman. Now. Tonight.

'Feel free to leave.' He leaned in, inhaling her, his lips almost but not quite brushing hers. 'At any time.'

It was then that he realised she was trembling. Yet it wasn't with fright.

Because her gaze lifted from his mouth, and he felt the moment she locked eyes with him. The impact was almost physical.

Then abruptly she leaned forward and kissed him.

CHAPTER TWO

SOLACE KNEW SHE had to be the one to make the first move. It was vital in keeping him off balance so he wouldn't recognise her, not to mention making sure the power stayed with her. Because she wasn't going to let him take control, not again. Not the way he had that night at the ball, when he'd overwhelmed her first with unexpected kindness, and then with passion. Her life had been turned on its head in that moment, leaving all her careful plans for a future in ruins.

Before him, she'd been a woman who'd finally got her crappy life in order and was starting to think that maybe, just maybe she *could* have all the things she'd wanted back when she'd been a lonely girl in the foster system.

Then he'd come along and shown her the one thing her life had been missing—his touch. And her glittering future had gone up in smoke.

But it was going to be different this time, because this time *she* was in control. This time *she* was going to upend his life the way he'd upended hers, and she was going to take back the one good thing he'd given her: her son.

Galen had come after her as she'd hoped he would, but now she had to steel herself and keep her head, not let the powerful current of their physical chemistry wash her away.

Yet the moment her lips touched his, she could feel that steel begin to fracture.

The way he stood in front of her, looming over her, his arms on either side, caging her in. Surrounding her with his heat and his scent. Blocking out the rest of the nightclub, blocking out the entire world…

It had been like that that night, when he'd held her against the wall in the deserted office, his powerful body between her and the world, making her feel protected and safe. It had been an intoxicating experience for a woman who'd never felt either of those things before, not in her entire life.

He made her feel that way now and she hated it. Because it was a lie. He hadn't protected her, and he hadn't saved her. He'd taken her to heaven and back, then delivered her straight to hell.

It wasn't all his fault. You ran away. Then you signed those papers, remember?

But she didn't want to remember. Not about how she'd run after their encounter or about the papers his representatives from Kalithera had thrust at her that first night out of hospital. Papers that she'd signed, giving up her maternal rights to her own child.

She *never* wanted to remember that, or the black hole of postnatal depression she'd fallen into after they'd taken her baby away, a bleakness that had taken hold of her soul. She'd had no one to talk to, no one to tell her she'd done the right thing giving her baby away. No one to reassure her that eventually the horrifying guilt over what she'd done would one day go away.

No, she was stronger now, she was in charge now,

and she wouldn't let herself get overwhelmed by anything or anyone ever again.

Except then he closed what little distance remained between them, crushing her against the wall, and the steel inside her fractured a little more.

Oh, she remembered this. How he was so hot, like iron, and how glorious he'd felt. He was so much bigger than she was, so much more powerful. He could protect her from harm. And he was so hungry.

All for her.

She'd grown up in a dozen foster homes and apart from Katherine, the one foster mum who'd ever taken an interest, no one had looked out for her, no one had even noticed her. No one had cared.

Now you have a king desperate to have you.

Her senses reeled. His mouth was hot, exploring her with a rough mastery that left her trembling even harder than she had been already.

She'd thought she'd be ecstatic that he'd come after her, and she was. But she was also afraid. Afraid of what she felt and how easily he could overturn her conviction if she let him.

So? Don't let him.

Solace put a hand on his chest and pushed at him, her breath coming in short, hard gasps.

He lifted his head instantly, the expression on his perfect face taut and hungry, but he didn't move away. The look in his hot blue eyes burned.

She'd done her research. She'd watched as many videos of him as she could, at official events and with his subjects, or the occasional, rare interview, and he was always cool and polite and courteous. There had been a distance to him, as if he was keeping himself apart, but there was no distance at all to him now.

Just as there hadn't been any distance fifteen months earlier.

He was not the King now, he was a man, and he burned for her.

She felt dizzy. His warm, woody scent was all around her, and the feel of his hard chest pressed against her sensitive breasts made the low pulse of desire pulse even harder.

'Do you want me to stop?' His gaze was fierce, demanding. 'Because if so, you need to tell me immediately.'

'No,' she forced out, trying to get some air into her lungs. 'I just needed a…a moment.'

He stared at her so intently she felt as if he were seeing inside her head. 'But you don't need one now, do you?'

She did need one now. She needed more than one. She needed to get out of here, get away from him before she lost herself again, yet running wouldn't get her what she wanted.

Besides, you want a taste of him again, don't deny it. A taste of how good he can make you feel.

'No,' she made herself say, both to him and to the voice in her head. 'No, I don't.'

Without a word, he bent, his breath warm on her skin as he brushed his mouth along the line of her jaw. Then he kissed her again, hot and raw and deep, making her go up in flames once more.

Making her remember that night again, and how, when he'd kissed her, she'd lost her mind. She'd never been kissed before, never been touched, or at least not by a man and certainly not for pleasure, and she'd had no idea how good it would feel. That precious half-hour she'd had with him had been…incandescent.

It was incandescent now.

She moaned, the taste of him dark chocolate and sin, the good Scotch she used to steal from that one foster father's drinks cabinet, the flavour of the forbidden, all the delicious things she could never afford to have for herself. It was wrong to want this, especially given who he was and the trap she'd fallen into the last time, but she was finding it difficult to remember why resisting him was so important in the first place.

Because it nearly destroyed you the last time and you can't go through that again.

Everything in her tensed in response. It was true, she couldn't. She had to resist him, she *had* to.

Then his long fingers wrapped around her throat in a firm, dominant hold, and all that tension began to bleed away, as if something inside her had finally stopped struggling and given in to the inevitable.

All her life she'd been on her own. She'd never belonged to anyone. But right here, right now, with his hand on her throat, she felt as if she belonged to him.

The man who took your baby from you.

She barely heard the thought this time as he gentled the kiss, nipping at her bottom lip and tracing the shape of it with his tongue, his thumb stroking the side of her neck.

'I won't hurt you,' he breathed in her ear. 'You're safe with me.' He shifted his hips in a subtle movement, the hard ridge behind his fly pressing against the heat between her thighs, nudging the most exquisitely sensitive part of her and making her tremble. 'But I want you. I want you to come home with me.'

It was what she'd hoped for. She'd spent the blood money the Kalitherans had given her in return for her son on her dress and flights to Kalithera, and not a little of it had also gone to various people she'd contacted who had inside knowledge on Galen's schedule.

She'd planned for this meticulously and it was all coming together. She'd even hoped that their chemistry would be just as strong, because to tempt a man like him, she'd need it to be. And she'd assumed that resisting him herself would be easy, that the lure of her son would be enough inducement not to surrender.

But it wasn't easy. It wasn't.

There was a warm, pulsing ache between her thighs and a different sort of ache behind her breastbone, a longing she couldn't get rid of no matter how hard she tried. He'd seduced her completely once and if she wasn't careful, he might again, and that wasn't how it was supposed to happen.

Does it matter? Why not surrender to him? It's only physical and you would enjoy it.

She would. She could go home with him, be his lover for the night, then take some incriminating pictures and blackmail him with them. Tell him that if he didn't give her son back, she'd release them to the press. And she couldn't take those pictures if she wasn't in his bed. Yet none of that meant she couldn't have a little something for herself. Some pleasure before all the unpleasantness. She was allowed, surely? After all the months of crushing guilt and aching loneliness? All the months of agony?

'Well?' He was exploring the line of her lower lip, brushing soft kisses along it as he shifted his other hand from beside her head, his fingers dropping to slide beneath one of the chains holding her dress up, pulling at it gently so the material tightened over her achingly sensitive nipples. 'Yes or no?' He stroked down over the chain, over the silver mesh of her dress and down, tracing the curve of her breast.

She felt almost drunk, as if she'd swallowed four cocktails in quick succession. Then those wicked fingers brushed across one nipple, sending sparks cascading through her, making her gasp yet again. Only to have his mouth cover hers and swallow the sound, the sensual brush of his tongue against hers making a low moan of need vibrate in her throat.

'Is that a yes?' he murmured, his fingertips now exploring her collarbones with aching lightness.

She could barely speak, having to force out the word. 'Y-Yes.'

He pulled back a fraction and stared down at her. 'You can trust me.'

You can't ever trust him. Not after what happened.

No, she already knew that. But all she was going to trust him with tonight was her body. The rest of her she would keep safely locked away. She just had to remember who this was all for: her son.

Very deliberately, Solace placed her hands on the warm cotton that covered his chest. 'Then take me home, Your Majesty.'

An intense blue flame leapt in his eyes that stole her breath. 'Galen. You may call me Galen.' Then he pushed himself away from her and grabbed her hand, threading his fingers through hers. And without a word, he turned and led her out of the club.

Her legs were shaky, and she almost stumbled a couple of times, catching herself at the last minute. He didn't stop and he didn't turn, obviously desperate to get her away.

And you're desperate to follow. The way you were last time.

But Solace ignored the voice. It wouldn't be like last time. She hadn't known what she was doing back then, but she did now. And this time she had a purpose. This time she'd take the physical pleasure without letting herself become lost in it.

The club's exit was in a different place from its entrance for the added privacy of its patrons, so when she and Galen stepped outside it was into a narrow cobbled street, surrounded by the jumble of whitewashed buildings so typical of Therisan architecture. The street was quiet and empty, bathed in the sulphurous glow of the streetlights, the low hum of the old city—traffic and people and, beyond that, the sound of the sea—murmuring in the background.

A sleek black limo waited at the kerb. Galen's security team came out of the club behind them and moved into formation, walking beside her and Galen as he strode to the car, pulling her along with him. One of the men darted ahead and opened the limo door, and then she was bundled inside, Galen following behind her.

The door slammed shut, cutting off the noise of the city completely.

'Don't worry,' Galen murmured. 'The windows are tinted. No one can see in.' He leaned forward and pressed a button, so the divider rose between them and the driver. 'Now,' he went on as they were finally enclosed in the back seat and completely private. 'Where were we?'

Then he reached for her and pulled her into his lap, positioning her so she was sitting astride him, facing him, her legs spread on either side of his lean hips, her knees pressed into the soft black leather of the seat.

The limo had begun to move, she could feel it, light from outside shining through the windows and flickering over his perfect face. His body was hot and very hard, his expression fierce. The blue of his eyes had darkened into midnight, and they glittered as he swept a glance down over the shimmering silver mesh of her dress.

He dropped his hands to the chains holding it up and her breath caught as his fingers slid beneath them, stroking her skin and making her shiver. 'You're wearing too many clothes.'

Her heartbeat was too loud, the touch of his fingers sending shudders through her. This was happening so fast, and she didn't know how to slow it down. Then again, maybe that was a good thing. Fast didn't give her time to think or to second-guess, or for him to latch onto that familiarity again.

'Then maybe you should do something about it,' she said breathlessly.

That hot blue gaze roamed over her face. 'You like giving orders, hmm?'

'You're talking too much.' She barely knew what she was saying, shifting on his rock-hard thighs, unable to keep still.

'Is that so?' A fleeting amusement glittered in his eyes, only to be replaced by something much more intense. 'I am a king, silver girl. And kings do not obey orders. They give them.'

Then, without waiting for her to speak, he eased the chains off her shoulders.

She made no move to stop him, shivering as the fabric slipped down to her waist, baring her, and then shivering even harder as his gaze swept over her, flaring with hunger.

It sharpened her own, made it bloom inside her like a flower. She'd never thought she'd want a man's attention, but he'd proved her wrong the last time and he proved her wrong now.

She did want a man's attention, *his* attention, so she made no effort to cover herself, even though she'd never been naked in front of anyone before. And when he took her wrists in a firm but gentle grip, guiding them to the small of her back and holding them there with one hand, she didn't protest.

His gaze swept down her body once more and he made no effort to hide his appreciation. 'You're beautiful.'

Unexpectedly, her throat closed. This was different. When he'd had her against the wall in that deserted office, both of them had been too desperate to bother with words. She hadn't known who he was. All she'd known was that his blue eyes seemed to see her soul and his touch had set her on fire.

But now she was half naked and there was time to speak, and she realised a part of her had been waiting for him to either recognise her or discover he'd made a mistake, that he didn't want her after all. Yet apparently neither of those things were true.

No one had ever called her beautiful before.

She'd told herself many times over the years since Katherine had changed her mind about adopting her that she didn't need or want anyone to care. She didn't need their attention or their notice.

Except a part of her did, and that part was unfurling under his gaze like a snowdrop at the first hint of the sun.

As if he could read her mind, his gaze narrowed. 'What is it?'

She turned her head away in an instinctive effort to

hide the traitorous feeling, only for strong fingers to grip her chin and turn her back to face him.

'You don't like being called beautiful?' That blue gaze of his sharp as a spear.

Great. The last thing she needed was an interrogation. This was supposed to be fast and frantic, sex with a nameless stranger he took home for a one-night stand. He was not supposed to be interested in her feelings.

But he was the last time.

Solace swallowed, remembering the horror as she'd stared at the broken glass and champagne covering the floor of the ballroom, knowing she'd be fired. And how she'd gone to her knees, trying to clean up the mess herself, only to hear a deep, calm voice giving orders. And when she'd looked up, those deep, mesmerising blue eyes had been on hers. 'Come with me,' he'd said quietly, holding out a hand. 'This will all be cleaned up. I will see to it personally.' Of all the people staring at her and the mess she'd created, he was the only one who'd helped her. Who'd taken her hand and led her off to the side of the ballroom so she could compose herself.

His gaze had been just as piercing then as it was now. Seeing into her. Seeing *her*.

He'll recognise you if you're not careful and then you'll never see your baby again.

No. *No.* That wasn't going to happen.

'What did I say about talking too much?' She shifted again, trying to distract him. 'You're ruining the mood.'

His eyes widened a fraction, but his grip on her chin firmed. 'Oh? Am I indeed?'

Her breath caught. She didn't know why that had snagged his interest or why he cared. What did her reaction matter? She needed to get him back on track.

She let her gaze drift to his mouth and back up again. 'Sorry, I didn't mean it. I'm just…impatient.'

Whether he believed her or not, she didn't know, the look on his face impossible to read. But his grip tightened, and he leaned in, his mouth brushing across hers in a feather-light kiss. 'I think you did mean it. And I think you don't like me calling you beautiful.' He let go of her jaw and turned his hand over, running the backs of his fingers lightly over the curve of one bare breast. 'I want to know why.'

Solace shuddered at the touch, her skin tightening, heat washing through her. He watched her fiercely, a man used to being given answers when he demanded them. A king used to being obeyed.

'Does it matter? I don't think you wanted to take me home just to talk.'

'That's true, I didn't.' He gently traced the curve of her breast, making her shift and tremble. 'But you intrigue me.'

Her mouth was dry, goosebumps rising wherever he touched, and it was becoming almost impossible to think straight. But he could not find her intriguing. That would lead to him looking at her even more intently and perhaps thinking more about why she was familiar.

She couldn't risk him remembering her, not yet. Not before she was ready.

'I'm not that interesting.' She arched into his hand, encouraging him to keep touching her. 'Please…'

'Hmm. I would disagree.' His fingers opened, cupping her breast with such delicacy she gasped. 'Tell me. How long has it been for you?'

She was shaking now. His palm burned her tender skin and when his thumb brushed over her nipple, she had to bite her lip to stop the cry that threatened to escape. Every thought she had was concentrated on his hand, on his fingers, stroking and squeezing gently, sending sharp, bright electric shocks of pleasure through her.

How long? Why was he asking her that?

'How long since what?' Her voice was uneven and breathy.

'Since anyone took their time with you. Since anyone seduced you.'

'I don't need... I don't n-need seducing.'

He leaned forward again, his mouth brushing over the side of her neck. 'Liar.' His lips were soft and warm on her skin. 'I think you want someone to take their time with you. I think you crave it. I think you're desperate to be seduced, slowly and carefully and with great attention to detail.'

He kissed his way to her throat while his thumb brushed back and forth over her nipple, making her twist and arch in his lap.

'I don't.' She was barely aware of speaking, the words coming out broken and breathless. 'I don't... I don't want that.'

His grip on her wrists loosened, his palm pressing against her back at the same time as his other hand cupped her breast. Then the heat of his mouth closed around her nipple, applying pressure.

Solace gasped as the most exquisite pleasure rushed through her, every thought in her head steadily being eroded by the pull of his mouth and the press of his hand. By the hard ridge she could feel beneath her and the strength of his grip.

There was a reason she was here with him. A very good reason. And there was something she'd planned to do later, something that was bad, but that she didn't have a choice about.

Yet she couldn't remember what that was, and she didn't want to remember. Everything was always a battle, but the past year had been so awful. There had been no escape from the guilt and the regret, and this…him… everything he did was urging her to surrender, to give in to the pleasure.

You weren't supposed to surrender, remember?

No, but she could surrender to this. It was too strong, and she just couldn't fight it any more.

So, she didn't, arching into his mouth, her trembling fingers pushing into his thick, silky black hair.

He must have sensed her give in, because he made a low growling sound as she touched him, and then she was on her back, laid lengthways across the seat, and he was over her, tugging her dress the rest of the way off, leaving her naked but for the tiny, lacy thong and her stiletto sandals.

His gaze was electric, staring down into hers, his long, powerful body settling between her thighs. 'I want you,' he said roughly. 'Now. Here. I can't wait.'

She was panting, the sound loud and gasping in the enclosed space of the car. 'I thought you were going to seduce me.'

'I was.' He bent and nuzzled against her throat, sucking gently, making her shake. 'But you're driving me mad and right now I need to be inside you.'

He wasn't the only one being driven mad. His mouth on her skin and the shift of his hips between her thighs was making her insane. 'Yes,' she said thickly. 'Oh, God, yes, *please.*'

It happened quickly.

He clawed his trousers open and dealt with the protection. Then he shoved aside her underwear and was pushing inside her, sinking deep, making both of them groan.

Her heartbeat had gone wild, her breath coming in short, ragged gasps. The feel of him inside her almost too much. He was big, stretching her in the most exquisite way. She could barely stand it.

'Ah, God, you feel good,' he growled against her throat. 'Hot, tight, wet…everything I wanted.' He drew his hips back, nearly sliding all the way out of her before pushing back in, hard and deep. 'And tonight, you're *mine*.'

That last word echoed in her head, and she clutched at it instinctively like a talisman. Yes, she wanted to be his. She wanted to belong to him. He was everywhere, crushing her into the seat of the car, buried deep inside her, his hands beside her head. And she was back in that deserted office, held against the wall, fireworks exploding behind her eyes, for the first time in her life feeling as if she mattered, at least enough to be given this incredible ecstasy.

It had been good back then, but now, held beneath him, his darkened blue gaze holding her fast, it was… transcendent.

Beneath him, no one could touch her. No one could get to her.

She was safe from the world, and she wanted to stay here for ever.

Then he moved again, and Solace was lost.

She clutched at his back, her nails digging into the black cotton of his shirt, every thought in her head crushed by the weight of the pleasure. She lifted her hips, needing more, and he responded, catching her behind the knee and drawing one leg up and around his waist so he could slide deeper.

She groaned, pleasure crackling through her, lighting her up from inside. 'Oh, Galen…that's so good.' The words spilled out of her in a rush. 'Please, more… Please…'

But he knew, moving faster, driving her into the leather seat as he thrust harder, deeper, devouring her mouth like a starving man. She wasn't alone in her desperation. She could feel the need in him, in his accelerated breathing and the tension in his muscles, in the low, hungry sounds he made as he moved.

And it came to her dimly that there was power in surrendering to him and to this heat they generated between them.

You could destroy him.

The thought was fleeting, ripped away as the storm built inside her, the weight of the pleasure increasing, pulling taut as a bowstring between them. Then he grabbed her hand and pushed it down between them, pressing her fingers against her own slick flesh as he drove himself inside her, and the orgasm burst over her like a monsoon rain. She only had time to hear his low roar of release before she too was lost in the flood.

At first Galen was conscious of nothing but the most intense feeling of satisfaction spreading through him. But slowly, as reality began to assert itself once more, he became aware of something else, something colder and sharper.

He'd lost control.

When she'd kissed him back in the club, everything had gone out of his head. All he'd been able to think about was how quickly he could get her back to the extremely private residence he sometimes used when he needed a break from the fishbowl that was the palace. Once there, he'd been going to draw things out deliciously with a glass of wine and flirt with her a little, because he'd once loved a flirtation and, since he'd decided he was going to allow himself this one night, he was going to allow himself everything. Only then, would he seduce her.

Yet he'd done none of those things. The moment her fingers had pushed into his hair, and he'd sensed her surrender to him, he'd had her on her back and had been inside her in seconds flat.

The anger he'd felt at himself and his own weakness earlier twisted inside him once again, disturbing the heavy post-orgasmic warmth.

Theos, what was wrong with him?

You know what's wrong with you. What's always been wrong with you.

Galen shoved that thought to the darkest corner of his mind. He couldn't afford self-doubt. For the past ten years he'd ruled well enough, and, apart from that one instance last year, he'd managed to keep his own weaknesses firmly under control, conducting himself with restraint whatever the occasion.

The issue was this woman. This woman and the chemistry that burned hot and strong between them. He hadn't experienced anything like it, not since...

She stirred beneath him, giving a little wriggle before pushing at his chest. He shifted to give her some room, propping himself up on one elbow so he could look down at her.

Since that night a year ago.

It was true. Though she was different from the woman who'd caught his interest so completely that night. That woman's hair had been tightly pulled back from her forehead and pinned into a bun, not that he'd taken that much notice of her hair when it had been her grey eyes that had struck him like lightning, setting him ablaze.

The woman who lay beneath him now had pale hair and it was spread over the black leather of the car seat like white silk, and the eyes that looked up into his were dark as midnight. An unusual combination with her pale skin, currently flushed a deep and pretty rose from the pleasure he'd given her.

She'd had pale skin too, remember? And she looked at you just the way this woman is looking at you now.

Yes, but many women had pale skin, and that look of wide-eyed wonder was something he was familiar with. He was a king, after all, and that intimidated people.

Yet he couldn't shake that strange sense of familiarity.

'What?' she asked, the colour deepening in her cheeks.

He didn't reply immediately, still studying her. Where had he seen her? Surely if he'd met her before, he'd have remembered.

He brushed a strand of pale hair off her forehead. 'You don't like me looking at you, do you?'

'I'm fine with it.' Yet her gaze flickered, her lashes sweeping down as if trying to hide her expression.

Interesting. Clearly, she was not fine with it. Which was strange, given the dress she wore was designed to attract attention. And just before, in his lap, she'd been so hungry for him, and impatient, yet when he'd called her beautiful, she'd seemed uncomfortable.

Her kiss was unpractised, too.

The sharp, cold feeling wound deeper. Back in the

club, she'd pulled him in for that kiss and every thought had vanished from his head. Her mouth had been almost unbearably sweet, before turning hungry and desperate after he'd taken control.

He hadn't noticed how hesitant she'd seemed. He hadn't noticed anything except her scent and the warmth of her skin, and how badly he'd wanted to touch her, bury himself inside her.

If she was indeed unpractised, you shouldn't have dragged her into the limo and had sex with her.

Galen shifted uncomfortably. Even before, as a stupid young man determined to push as many boundaries as he could, throw his father's suffocating upbringing back in his face, he hadn't played games with women who hadn't known what games they'd been playing. Only with those who'd wanted what he had: pleasure and nothing more.

But if this woman, this beautiful silver girl, was someone who didn't understand what was going on here, then he'd made another grave error.

You keep making them. One would almost think that your father was right about you all along. That you're unfit to rule—

Galen cut that thought off before it could form.

It was too late to put her out on the street, not that he was crass enough to do that, but he should definitely bring this little episode to a close. Of course, he should never have dragged her into his limo to start with, but, since he had, the correct behaviour now would be to take her back to his residence, give her some refreshments if she wanted them, then get a car to return her to wherever she was staying.

He had to assume she'd been vetted and had signed all the usual NDAs—she wouldn't have been at the club if she hadn't—but he'd get his security to double-check anyway. He had to be meticulous about any indiscretion. He couldn't afford to give his uncle any excuse to drag his past before the media and once again question his fitness to rule.

He became aware that she was watching him from beneath her lashes. 'Thank you,' he said, allowing some warmth in his tone. 'You were a pleasure. But now we'll be going to my residence, and from there I'll see you returned to your accommodation safely.'

She frowned. 'What do you mean I will be returned? I thought—'

'You thought what?' he interrupted, trying not to sound sharp because he didn't want to snap at her. 'Forgive me, but if you were expecting to stay, then I must disappoint you.'

'Why not? Didn't you like it?'

'I don't do one-night stands.' An edge had begun to creep into his voice no matter how he tried to stop it. 'At least not with those who don't know what they're getting themselves into.'

Her frown deepened, the sharp glitter of anger in her eyes. 'A one-night stand usually covers the entire night, not ten minutes in the back of a limo.'

Something inside him stirred, the young man he'd once been, addicted to every adrenaline rush he could get his hands on, the more forbidden the better. Who'd loved a challenge, most especially when the one challenging him was a woman. And even though he'd told himself he wasn't going to do this, he moved over her once again, settling himself between her thighs and pressing her hands down on either side of her head. 'Taking that tone with me,' he murmured, 'will get you into all kinds of trouble.'

A shudder went through her, but there was no fear in her eyes. Only that glittering anger along with something…hotter.

Did she like this? Did she like being restrained by him?

'Perhaps I want trouble,' she said. 'Perhaps that's exactly what I'm looking for.' She shifted as if straining against his hold and his body pinning her to the seat. Yet her movements were languid, sensual, making it clear that she did not actually want to get away from him.

Desire kicked yet again, deep in his gut. He hadn't played this particular game for many years, mainly because when he'd ascended the throne, he'd cut away all his baser appetites as the weaknesses they were, trying to put some distance between himself and his past.

That doesn't mean they've gone away.

Of course, it didn't. If they had, he wouldn't have had Leo and he certainly wouldn't be in this limo right now.

You must try harder.

Yes. He must.

'I don't think you want that,' he said. 'You'll be going back to wherever you come from tonight.'

Her chin came up, challenging him once again. 'What about you? What about what you want? Or are kings not allowed to have anything?'

'You shouldn't argue with me.' He tightened his grip on her wrists, settling more completely on her. 'I am the King of this country.'

'Of this country, yes, but I'm not from here, and you're not my king.'

Her pulse at the base of her throat had quickened and her voice was husky and breathless. She was aroused, he could smell it, and her need sparked his own, along with a dark kind of thrill that wound around him and pulled tight.

He did not want to let her go. He wanted to keep her here, beneath him, the whole night. He wanted to explore this desire, indulge himself completely, and, after all, he'd already had her once. What difference would it make if he kept her?

He was tired of constantly having to hold himself back. Tired of constantly checking himself and making sure nothing he did would cause his past to rear its ugly head. He hadn't had a woman in a year, and he missed it, and not just the sex but physical closeness too.

Surely, one night was allowed. No one would know. No one.

'Do you like to fight, silver girl?' he murmured, staring down into her dark eyes. 'Is that what you want? To fight me? Prove yourself against me?'

Heat flared in her eyes. 'You didn't answer my question. Why should I answer yours?'

Galen was conscious of a building excitement, because that look told him all he needed to know, as had that sharp response. Yes, she liked to fight, and she certainly wanted to fight him.

'Your question,' he said slowly. 'About what I want.' He flexed his hips, pressing the growing hardness behind his zip against the slick softness between her thighs and she shuddered, giving a little gasp. 'Kings are not allowed to have anything for themselves, it's true. But a man can have whatever he wants.'

Her gaze had gone smoky, once more drifting to his mouth. 'And what does this man want?'

'You know the answer to that already.' He shifted once more, making her gasp yet again. 'But I only have a night to give you. There can be nothing more. And afterwards, there will be documents for you to sign. My privacy is very important, and I expect you to honour it.'

'Yes.' Her voice was thick. 'Of course.'

He lowered his head, so he was inches away from her dark eyes, staring down into them, her luscious mouth almost but not quite touching his. 'Are you sure you want this? Because if you have a night with me, it will be *all* night. And we will not be sleeping. If you change your mind, do it now. I won't give you another chance.'

She said nothing, only stared back at him, and strangely, even though he'd always been able to read people like an open book, he had no idea what she was thinking. Then her hips moved once more, making his breath catch. And she shook his hands away, slid her fingers into his hair and brought his mouth down on hers.

CHAPTER THREE

SOLACE WOKE WITH a start, unsure for a couple of moments of where she was.

She seemed to be lying in a massive and very comfortable bed, surrounded by pillows, in a big room with white walls, and large white curtains drawn over the windows. Clearly it was morning since there was a line of bright gold painted along the dark wooden floor from the sunlight shining through a crack in the curtains.

The room was sparsely furnished with an antique chest of drawers thrust up against a wall, a long, low couch sitting beneath the windows and a brightly patterned silk rug on the floor.

It was very much *not* the cheap hostel she'd been staying in for the last couple of days.

Then she became aware of something else: not only was there was an arm circling her waist, a very muscular, heavy arm, but she was also naked.

She stared at the bright line of sunlight on the floor as memories began to filter through, of where she was and who she was with, and what had happened the night before.

The nightclub, the limo, deep blue eyes staring into hers. His hands gripping her, his body pinning her, his mouth...

The king you surrendered to.

Solace swallowed and closed her eyes a moment. Oh, yes, she'd surrendered. She'd surrendered completely, giving herself up to him as if she'd been waiting all her life to do just that, lost in the way he held her in his strong hands. The power of him making her feel as if she could push against him as hard as she could, dash herself against him like a wave against a rock and he wouldn't budge. He wouldn't let her go. There was something comforting in that, something that made her feel safe. She didn't know why.

He was right. You did like fighting him.

She had. And she'd liked the surrender afterwards even more.

Heat washed over her, her entire body prickling at the memory, made even more intense by the hot press of his powerful body behind her.

Remember why you're here.

The thought turned the prickling heat into an icy wave and she had to catch breath.

Blackmail. That was why she was here. She had to take pictures and blackmail the King into giving her son back. She'd forgotten about that the night before. He'd made her forget everything, even her own name, and when she'd finally fallen into an exhausted sleep, all she'd been conscious of was the feeling of being safe again. Of being protected.

A lie. She was never safe and there had never been anyone to protect her. Katherine had once told her that she'd love to be Solace's mum, and that Solace could live with her permanently, and Solace had believed her. But then Katherine had changed her mind and Solace been bounced to another home.

Never trust anyone, that was the lesson. Never trust

what people told you. And most of all, never trust those feelings of safety, because they were lies too.

In the end, all you'd ever have was yourself.

In your case, you can't even trust that.

Shame, sharp as barbed wire, wound around her heart, the line of gold on the floor blurring as her eyes prickled.

Fiercely, she forced the tears back.

She wouldn't be weak again, not as she'd been after the birth of her baby. She'd allowed fear and despair and the overwhelming guilt at what she'd done undermine her and it had taken her six months to pull herself out of the pit of postnatal depression she'd fallen into. She wasn't going to fall into it again. *Never.*

She'd never forget the three people who'd turned up on the doorstep of her grotty flat, literally the day after she'd had her son, either. She'd felt as if she were sitting at the bottom of a deep, dark well, with mile-high walls all around her, unable to get out. And those people, two men in black suits and a smiling woman in some kind of uniform, had seemed…kind.

The woman had explained who she was and that they were from Kalithera, and could they come inside because they needed to talk to her.

So, she'd let them in. And in her tiny bedsit, her baby screaming on the bed since she'd had no bassinet or baby things—he'd come a couple of days early and very unexpectedly—and no money to buy them anyway, the woman had told her that the man she'd been with nine months earlier at that ball was the King of Kalithera. And he wanted his son.

Shock and the fug of birth hormones still flooding her system had made her mute and slowed her thinking, so she'd just stared at the woman, her brain struggling to make sense of everything. She'd still been struggling to make sense of the fact that she'd had a baby at all, let alone the fact that her baby was a king's son.

Both she and the baby were to come to Kalithera, the woman had said kindly, and the King would take care of everything.

It had sounded so good. It had sounded perfect.

But no one took care of everything, she knew that for a fact, which must mean what the woman had told her was a lie. Not so much that her son was the son of a king—the uniforms, the black, expensive car in the street, the air of wealth and authority that clung to all three people made her sure of it—but that she was welcome. Because why? What would a king want with the likes of her? Yes, she was the mother of his child, but she was a poor nobody with no money and no education, and she knew what happened to poor nobodies. They were either taken advantage of or forgotten, especially by people in authority.

Her first impulse had been to refuse, to pick up her baby and hold him tight, send the people away. But then she'd looked around her tiny flat, at the mould on the ceilings and the peeling lino. The lack of a bassinet. The lack of anything resembling baby things because she'd only found out she was pregnant a week before she'd given birth. She'd had no money. No support. She'd known nothing about being a mother. She'd had nothing. What kind of life could she have given her child? He'd had no future with her, none at all.

It had been then that the dark pit had opened up beneath her feet and swallowed her whole.

She'd signed all the documents they'd given her, not seeing any of them, and when they'd told her there would be money in her account, she'd nodded blankly.

It was only after they'd finally gone and her flat had echoed with emptiness and absence, that the crushing weight of what she'd done had flattened her.

A wave of unexpected grief and guilt came, and she had to fight to force it back.

No, she couldn't let that overwhelm her. That was why she was here. She was here to fix the mistake she'd made, to get her baby back however she could.

Taking a calming breath, she gave the room a careful survey.

The night before, the limo had pulled up outside a house in a well-to-do part of the city. She hadn't been paying much attention, too occupied with Galen, and she hadn't paid attention when he'd pulled her out of the car and hurried her up the steps into the house either. Or when he'd carried her upstairs into this bedroom. And especially not when they'd finally ended up in this bed.

But her clothes must be around somewhere and hopefully her clutch, since her phone was in it.

Finally, she spotted a small pile of silver fabric near the door, which must be her dress. The stiletto sandals she'd been wearing lay not far away and in a piece of good luck, right near the bed, was her silver-mesh clutch.

Carefully, she glanced over her shoulder to check on the man behind her.

His face was relaxed in sleep, his breathing deep and even, and for a moment she just stared at him, part of her wondering how someone like her had managed to seduce a man like him. A king. A beautiful, powerful man, from one of the most ancient and aristocratic families in Europe, while she…

She was a nobody of unknown parentage, who'd dropped out of school, who stacked supermarket shelves and cleaned offices for a living. Not that there was any-thing wrong with that—she was proud of the fact that she earned her own money—but it was hardly at the same level as running an entire country.

She wasn't rich, she wasn't beautiful, and she had no power to speak of...

But no, that was being defeatist. She was changing things. She *would* change things. She was going back to school, and she'd apply herself and get great marks. Then she'd work hard and get into university and hope-fully study law. And once she had her degree, she could use it to help people. People like herself.

How she'd do all of that with a child she had no idea, but she'd work it out. First, and most important of all, was getting that child back where he belonged. With her.

Solace slowly leaned over the side of the bed and reached for her clutch.

Behind her, Galen shifted, his arm tightening.

She froze, trying not to breathe. If he woke up now, it would ruin everything.

If only she'd done this last night, it would have been easier. She should have stayed awake until he'd gone to sleep and then taken some pictures. But she hadn't. She'd gone straight to sleep, lying warm and sated in his arms.

You were a fool.

Yes, and now she had to make up for it.

She waited until Galen's breathing had evened out, then reached for the clutch again. This time he didn't move so she was able to grab the bag and extract her phone. Typing in her code to unlock it, she pulled up the camera app and switched it to selfie mode.

It was a good phone, one she'd paid for with the blood money the Kalitherans had put into her account after she'd let them take her baby away. Because her old one was cheap, and the camera was terrible, and she'd needed a good camera if she was going to do this properly.

Putting her head back down on the pillow, she lifted the phone, holding it so Galen's face was clearly in the shot while hers was mostly out of it, leaving only her pale hair and a bare shoulder so people knew exactly what was going on here.

Taking pictures of him was wrong. It was a gross breach of his trust, of his privacy, and she didn't want to do it. She didn't want to blackmail him either.

But she'd exhausted every other avenue she could think of. She had to have her baby back, fix the terrible mistake she'd made in giving him up. Because while she might be a bad mother, she knew what it was like to grow up without one, and surely even a bad mother was better than none at all.

Maybe not. Maybe he's better off here. Maybe he's better off without you.

No, she didn't believe that. She couldn't.

Her hand shook as she fumbled for the button to take the picture, so the first shot was blurry, but through sheer force of will she steadied it and took a few more. Then she lowered the phone and shut her eyes, her heart-beat racing.

There, it was done. The photos would automatically go into her cloud storage, and she could access them anywhere from there. She already had a list of media organisations she knew would be more than happy to receive them.

But taking the pictures had been one of the easier parts of this mission. Now, she had to face the hardest part of all: blackmailing a king.

There was movement behind her, and she only had time to take a sharp, surprised breath before she was pulled over onto her back, her wrists taken in strong hands and pinned to the pillow on either side of her head. An extremely powerful male body shifted between her thighs, holding her down, and then she was looking up into a pair of furious blue eyes.

'What are you doing?' Galen demanded.

Ice flooded through her, freezing her solid.

His gaze went to the phone she had still clutched in her hand and back again. 'You took pictures.'

'I didn't, I—'

His head lowered, blue fire in his eyes, his voice low and very, very dangerous. 'Do. Not. Lie. To. Me.'

Fear wrapped icy claws around her throat and for a second all she could do was lie there, flattened by the force of his rage.

Remember what he did. He might be a king, but you are a mother, and he took your son from you.

True. She hadn't come all the way to Kalithera, bribed her way into an exclusive club, and seduced a king only to cower before him like a kicked dog.

She'd come to take back what he'd stolen from her.

She *was* a mother and, while she might not have the first idea how to be one, she certainly knew how to fight and so she'd fight for her son.

Clinging to that thought, Solace forced away the fear and steeled herself, reaching for her own anger as she stared straight back into Galen's burning blue eyes.

'Yes,' she said coldly. 'I took some pictures. Of you and I.'

His hands on her wrists tightened, his grip just on the edge of pain. 'Why?'

She swallowed, her mouth dry, her heartbeat like a

drum in her head. But when she spoke, her voice was steady. 'To blackmail you with, of course.'

There was no point pretending any more, and in a way it was a relief that finally the moment was here. In fact, she was almost proud of herself. She'd come a long way in six months and her plan had ended up being wildly successful, and soon the awful mistake she'd made would be fixed.

The look on Galen's face was terrible. 'Blackmail me for what? Money? Power?'

'No.' Solace held tight to her own rage. The rage that had dragged her out of that pit and put her feet on the path that had led here. 'I couldn't care less about money or power. What I want, Galen Kouros, is my son.'

Galen heard the words, but they didn't mean anything to him. He was so angry he could barely think. Some of his anger was for her, that she thought she could blackmail *him*, but most of it was reserved for himself and his own monumental stupidity.

He'd allowed his groin to do his thinking for him the night before, and he hadn't done any of the things he should have, such as waited for his security staff to a) do a background check and b) search her person for anything that could be a security risk, such as phones.

But no, he'd decided he was going to allow himself a night of no restraint and so he'd rushed her from the limo straight into his bedroom, no thought in his head but to have her naked beneath him as quickly as possible.

When will you learn? Ten years a king and you still haven't mastered yourself. Alexandros was right about you.

Perhaps. Certainly Leo existed because he hadn't

mastered himself, and, while he'd never regret his son, Leo's existence had also complicated his life to an impossible extent.

Now he'd complicated it even further.

'Your son?' he snapped, fury burning in his veins like wildfire. 'What are you talking about?'

She seemed very calm for a woman in the process of blackmailing him. 'You don't recognise me, do you?'

The familiarity that had tugged at him, their chemistry, the sounds she'd made as he'd pushed inside her... He remembered those sounds. They'd haunted his dreams for over an entire year. They'd haunted him last night, in this very bed, while he'd touched and tasted every inch of her curvy little body.

She was warm beneath him, but he could feel the tension in her, could see it too in the line of her stubborn jaw. Her gaze was dark, and she didn't look away this time, not the way she had the night before.

He let go of her hands and smoothed back her silky pale hair, flattening it tight to her skull. She made no move to stop him, her eyes glittering with defiance.

He stared, studying the lines of her face. It was difficult to tell without the mask, but... No, it couldn't be her. She'd had grey eyes.

'Who are you?' he demanded, the fury in him burning hotter, higher. 'Tell me.'

'You already know who I am.' Her voice was flat, yet he could hear the edge of anger in it.

It's her, you know it is. You knew it the moment you saw her.

Cold washed over him, freezing his anger, chasing away the last remains of the pleasant warmth and satiation he'd woken up with. Before he'd become aware of her lowering her hand and wondered why she was holding a phone.

Before it had penetrated that there could be only one reason.

It was her, it had to be. The woman he'd met at the masquerade ball.

He searched her face, still holding her hair back, and sure enough, there was the line of her lower lip that he hadn't been able to stop himself from licking and nipping, so full and soft. And her eyes looking up into his, full of defiance now, but last night they'd been full of desire. Full of want.

Just beyond the edge of her iris he could see a faint line. Contacts.

His rage leapt, but, with a massive effort of will, he forced it away. If this morning had taught him anything at all, it was that he could not afford to indulge in *any* of his weaknesses. He wasn't a child throwing a tantrum as he had been during his time at Oxford. These last ten years he'd learned how to behave like a king and now he was one. Down to his bones.

Galen let her go and shoved back the sheets, getting out of bed and striding over to where his clothes lay in a heap by the door. He began to dress, pulling on his underwear and then his trousers.

'You will delete the photos,' he ordered as he zipped up his fly. 'And then you will answer every single one of my questions.'

She sat up, wrapping a sheet around her lush curves, her silky white-blonde hair falling around her shoulders. 'It's too late. They're in the cloud. It'll only take me a minute to put them up on social media.'

He couldn't tear his gaze from her pale skin, his body already hardening at the sight of her, but he forced the hunger away. It had no place here. It was sex that had led him into this situation, the physical chemistry that had exploded between them, and he would not let it master him again.

He stared at her coldly, going back over what she'd said now he'd had a chance to fully processes what was happening.

Her son. She'd said that was what she wanted when he'd asked. Not money, not power. Her son.

His son. *His.* Because she'd given him up. She'd signed away her rights and had taken the money he'd authorised his representatives to give her should she not want to come to Kalithera. He'd tried to keep tabs on her subsequently, because his son should know who his mother was, but then she'd vanished without a trace. And Galen had let her, assuming she hadn't wanted Leo anyway.

Yet now, here she was, in his bed, blackmailing him.

Last night was never about you...

Something a lot like disappointment twisted in his chest, but he ignored it.

He could treat last night as yet another reminder of how unsuited he was to the crown he wore, or he could treat it as a warning. He couldn't afford more mistakes, not with Kostas still waiting for an opportunity to take Kalithera from him. And now Galen had not only a country to protect, but a succession to guard. Destroying his son's legacy and putting Kalithera at risk for the sake of his own lusts was inconceivable.

'You cannot possibly think,' he said icily, 'that I'd give my son away just because I didn't want a couple of pictures of myself in bed with you in the media?'

She was already very pale, now she went even paler. But her chin remained at a stubborn angle and still she didn't look away. 'Perhaps you might think differently when the media comes to camp on your doorstep,' she said. 'I don't imagine your reputation will last long after that.'

Deep inside him, past his fury, Galen was aware of another emotion, a reluctant, grudging respect he didn't want to acknowledge. After he'd had the news that she'd had his child, he'd read the file his staff had given him about her. He knew she'd grown up in the foster system and that she hadn't finished her schooling. That she did various low-paid jobs to make ends meet and that her current living situation was not ideal for her, let alone for a baby.

Remembering her grey eyes and wild passion the night of the ball, he'd felt sorry for her and had very much wanted her to come to Kalithera with their son. But his aides had told him she'd refused, no reason given.

He'd been furious about that, furious she'd given up their child without protest, only to disappear off the face of the earth, and he'd assumed all sorts of things about the kind of woman who'd give up her child for money. And he didn't know why she was back to claim Leo now, but one thing was clear: she was a fighter.

Still, if she thought blackmail would work on him then she needed to think again. She'd get no more money from him, if that was what she was after.

'Then your imagination is sadly lacking.' He folded his arms across his bare chest. 'I have the best PR team in the business, and they can spin anything.' It was no less than the truth.

'Oh?' Her cheeks were now flushed, the glitter of anger in her eyes becoming more pronounced. 'You mean like how they spun your son's mother dying tragically in childbirth? Or rather your *fiancée*. Since apparently you were going to marry her after a whirlwind secret romance.' Her tone dripped with disdain.

Galen had never thought he'd be in the position of having to justify the story his PR team had come up with to explain Leo's existence. That had painted him in the light of a grieving single father who'd lost his love tragically.

He hadn't liked the lie, but it had been necessary to stop Kostas from digging too deeply in places he shouldn't and bringing it up with the media.

His team, of course, didn't know the exact reason why it was so important that not a breath of scandal be attached to his name. All they knew was that the reputation of the King had to be protected and so protect it they had.

No one had expected Leo's actual mother—the mother who'd given him up—to turn up in Kalithera to get her son back.

Yet here she was and now he had to deal with it.

'I'm not explaining the decisions of my PR team to you,' he said coldly, ignoring the faint sting of what could not possibly be shame. 'The fact remains that blackmail will not work on me and so you have nothing.'

There were dark circles beneath her eyes, and, through his anger and the cold grip of control, he was conscious of a certain protectiveness.

He'd felt it that night over a year ago, in the deserted office. In the aftermath of passion, he'd held her against the wall with his body, both of them panting, and looked down into her face. There had been wonder in her expression, and desire and not a little awe, and protectiveness had swept through him. She had been a stranger, he hadn't even known her name, yet she'd held nothing back. She'd given herself to him so passionately it was as if those moments with him had been her first taste of pleasure.

Yet then she'd ripped herself away from him and run, vanishing into the crowds before he'd had a chance to talk with her. He hadn't been able to go after her since he'd been the guest of honour, and afterwards he'd been inundated with all the formalities of an official visit.

You knew she was a virgin. You knew. And you left her alone and pregnant with your child.

Guilt caught at him, along with another sting of shame, but again, he forced them away. He hadn't known she was pregnant, not until his security team had finally managed to track her down, following up as a matter of course since they monitored anyone he had an interaction with. As to the virginity, he hadn't known that either, not when they'd barely exchanged a handful of sentences.

'You think I'm bluffing?' she said shakily. 'I'm not.'

'Nor am I.' He met her gaze, held it. 'Go on. Do it. Upload them. My team won't break a sweat explaining them. Though if you are indeed who you say you are, it still won't get you your son.'

She'd gone pale as ashes now, her dark eyes full of accusation and anger. Yet she didn't move for the phone. 'You took my baby from me,' she said instead. 'You took him away. And I want him back. Now.'

He should bring this little scene to a close, that would be the safest thing. He should call his security, get them to delete the photos, and then send her back to London where she came from. Perhaps he'd even send her first class or on one of his private jets—there was no need for jail or anything too heavy-handed. She hadn't actually done anything, after all.

Except…there was a desperate but determined note in her voice that tugged at him. She wanted her baby—their baby—and that fierce look in her eyes didn't seem feigned. His team had told him she'd signed those papers willingly, yet…that didn't gel with the pale woman sitting in his bed. Who'd presumably come all the way from London to seduce him and then blackmail him, purely to get her baby back.

'What do you mean I took him?' he demanded. '*You* didn't want him. You signed all those documents and you—' He broke off as she abruptly shoved herself off the bed and stormed over to where he stood, the white sheet still wrapped around her trailing in her wake.

She stopped in front of him, her dark gaze fierce. 'I *did* want him. But when those…people arrived at my flat, it was the day after I'd given birth and I was shell-shocked. I couldn't take in what they were saying, then they…they said I could come to Kalithera too, but I… I thought it was a lie, so I refused. Then they gave me some documents, and I signed them, but only so my son would be safe. But I didn't want to give him up, I *didn't*.' Her whole body was trembling, her eyes glittering. She looked as if she were preparing to throw herself in front of a truck. 'Why did you take him?' She took another step, their bodies nearly touching. *'Why?'*

He did not know this woman. He'd never known her. Yet he'd spent a year thinking about their one encounter, and last night he'd spent hours enjoying the gift of her body, hours giving her pleasure and letting her give the same to him.

He had no reason to believe what she was saying but…

She hadn't faked any of the orgasms he'd given her, he'd stake his life on that. Her pleasure had been real, and this fury and the pain he could see beneath it... they were real too.

You took her child away from her.

The sting of shame became a thorn, piercing him, along with a guilt that cut even deeper. He knew that fear and anguish himself, had experienced both the moment he'd discovered Leo's existence.

You thought it was only money she was after. But she didn't want to give him up. You should have tried harder to find her. You should have tried harder, full stop.

Oh, he knew. He knew very well how much harder he should have tried. It applied to everything he did, and yet it seemed no matter how hard he tried, it wasn't enough. It would never be enough.

How many more mistakes will you make? Are you sure Kostas wouldn't be a better king?

No, he couldn't think that. He wouldn't. Kalithera *was* better off with him on the throne and, besides, he had to deal with what was happening in the present, not his own insidious doubts.

However, there was too much anger in the room and they both needed a bit of time and space to compose themselves. Certainly, he did.

He stayed still, arms folded, staring down at her. 'We need to talk.'

'I don't want to talk. I want to—'

'You're white as that sheet. You're tired. And you're naked. I think you'd feel better after you've had a shower, got dressed and had some breakfast.'

Her gaze flashed and her mouth opened, no doubt to keep on arguing with him, but he went on before she could. 'Besides, I need to ascertain you are who you say you are and various other things.' Her mouth opened yet again, but again he went on. 'Or would you be happy talking to a complete stranger about the private details of your baby?'

She gave him a furious look. 'You don't need to be so condescending. I'm not a child.'

'I am well aware of that, believe me.' He raised a brow. 'Unless you'd like to discuss our son while you're stark naked and still smelling of sex and me?'

She flushed, yet her stubborn little chin remained lifted.

Good. Anger suited her. He liked that she wasn't so pale and had stopped trembling. Perhaps he should keep her angry. It was better than her fear and anguish. Those he didn't like, not at all.

'You really don't care about those photos?' She was still looking at him defiantly.

'No,' he said with absolute truth. 'But I can't imagine why you'd want to resort to taking pictures of me when a simple phone call would have sufficed.'

'You think I didn't try?' she shot back. 'I didn't actually want to blackmail you, believe it or not, but every call I made to the Kalitheran embassy in London, every email I sent, they all thought I was lying. I even went in there myself, but then they called Security and threw me out.' The acid in her tone bit deeper. 'Apparently when you're a poor nobody, no one believes you when you tell them that you've had their king's child.'

He could well imagine. His reputation was so rock solid that the very idea some strange Englishwoman would have had a night with him and borne his child would have been laughable.

But a nobody? She was hardly that, not having come all the way from England to Kalithera to blackmail him *and* almost succeeding. Naive perhaps, and obviously scrappy and determined. But very much *not* a nobody.

He eyed her, lingering on her silky, pale hair and how it flowed over her shoulders, then further, where her hands gripped the sheet. He'd only have to tug gently, and it would come away, leaving her naked...

Predictably, his body hardened, and he could tell by the way she flushed that she'd picked up on his thoughts. Her fingers tightened on her sheet even as her gaze drifted down over his chest and her luscious mouth opened slightly.

The familiar electricity of their chemistry began to build again, sparks arcing between them, and it took effort to push it away this time, but he managed.

He wouldn't compound the errors he'd made last night by taking her again. Not that it would have been appropriate anyway. She was still distressed and, besides, they had more important things to discuss.

'A nobody? Don't be ridiculous,' he said flatly, crushing the desire flooding through his veins. 'I'll have food brought to you and perhaps more suitable clothes. We'll talk in half an hour.'

Then before he could change his mind, cross the space between them and rip the sheet from her hands, he turned on his heel and went out.

CHAPTER FOUR

SOLACE STARED AT the closed door, her knees weak. She'd stopped physically shaking, but she was trembling still, deep inside. And perhaps some of it was fear, but it wasn't all. Anger made up a good proportion, as did the nagging desire that had licked up the moment Galen's blue gaze had fallen to her shoulders and then to her hand where she still gripped her sheet.

Despite everything, despite the fear and the anger, she was conscious that he was standing very close and wearing only his trousers. His chest was bare and she could see every hard, carved muscle, and all she could think about was how she'd traced those muscles with her fingers the night before, and then with her tongue. His skin had tasted salty and delicious and had felt like velvet…

No. She couldn't be thinking about that, not any of it, not when her plan now lay in ruins.

She swallowed, bitter disappointment turning over inside her, tears stinging her eyes. God, would they ever stop? She was so tired of crying, so tired of fighting. So tired of nothing going right for her, no matter how hard she tried.

But being tired wasn't going to help and neither was crying about it. She'd been naive to think a couple of compromising pictures would be all she'd need to get her child back. Stupid even. Of course, a king would have an entire PR department dedicated to keeping his reputation clean, especially a king like him. After all, she probably wasn't the first woman to try this with him and she probably wouldn't be the last.

Solace turned and went over to the bed, sitting down on it and lacing her fingers together, clenching them hard. Taking a few deep breaths, she tried to calm herself so she could think.

The blackmail hadn't worked and castigating herself over her naivety wasn't going to get her any closer to her son. What she needed was to formulate another plan. The good thing was that now she actually had access to her son's father, so she wasn't starting from zero again. She was here, in his house, and he'd said they would talk.

Perhaps he wouldn't throw her in jail for her blackmail attempt. He'd certainly been furious enough about it, and the really stupid thing was, she understood why. She would have been too.

The other stupid thing was—and she hated to admit this to herself—that part of her couldn't help but respect him for not caving instantly to her demands the way she'd hoped. He'd called her bluff and she'd been fully prepared to grab her phone and do what she'd threatened, but she could see the steel in his eyes. He wasn't going to hand over their child for the sake of a couple of pictures, and that very same part of her, the fierce mother instinct, couldn't help but admire him for it.

He's a king. You really thought he'd give in so easily?

She had, but as she'd already thought, she'd been naive. Not that there was any point going over it again. She had to figure out what she was going to do now.

Half an hour, he'd said, then they'd talk. Which would give her time to have that shower, get dressed and eat something. Because while she hated being told what to do, he hadn't been wrong. Having a conversation about their son while she was pretty much naked apart from a sheet made her uncomfortable. And she did *not* smell of sex and him. Did she?

Well, even if she did she wasn't going to for much longer.

Slipping off the bed, she headed determinedly into the en-suite bathroom. It was huge, with a big, white-tiled walk-in shower and a multitude of jets, plus a vanity of long white marble veined with gold. A bath made from the same material stood near big windows that looked out onto the green of a private garden.

It took her aback, the sight of so much luxury. She'd never seen anything like it.

Her little bedsit had enough room for a sofa bed and nothing else, and she'd thought *that* luxurious after some of the foster homes she'd been in, mainly because it was hers and she didn't have to share it with anyone.

But this…

Your child is heir to all this. Would you seriously take him away from it?

The thought hurt. Because while she was in a much better place than the black hole she'd been in six months ago, nothing she had equalled this. Here he would be a prince, heir to a kingdom, while with her…

He'll be a nobody just like you.

Solace shoved that thought away. She might be a nobody, but a child needed its mother. She'd never had one herself, never had any kind of family, and the lack had been a wound she'd carried with her all her life. It wasn't something she wanted for her son.

But he does have a family. He has his father.

Okay, it was time to stop thinking about that.

She went over to the shower and spent a couple of moments trying to figure out how it worked before dropping the sheet and stepping under the fall of water.

It was glorious. She stood there with her eyes closed, enjoying the warmth, letting the water stream over her and wash away the fear and stress of the past quarter of an hour. She couldn't give in to it; being afraid wouldn't get her son back.

Opening her eyes, she began to wash herself, noticing as she did so small bruises and red patches marring her skin. Galen had left marks.

A wave of heat that had nothing to do with the shower swept over her and she groaned softly, lifting her hands to her face and trying to shove the memories from her head. Thinking about the night before wouldn't help either. She had to formulate a new plan, but what?

How was she going to get her child back? *Could* she even get her child back? He'd given her a glimpse of the steel inside him. He wouldn't give their son to her, no matter what she did. Oh, she could try and manipulate him by playing the mother card and perhaps using their son's future feelings as a weapon against him, but that felt wrong. She didn't want to use their son as a pawn when the battle was between her and Galen. That was selfish.

Taking him away from his father is selfish.

Solace gritted her teeth. Okay, she'd allow that it cut both ways. Taking her child from Galen would leave Galen feeling as she did now, as if there was a hole in her soul, and she wouldn't wish that on him. But then where did that leave her?

If she couldn't take her child back to England, what

else could she do? She couldn't stay indefinitely in Kalithera, not on a tourist visa, and even if she could, would Galen allow her access to her baby? Given the statement his PR department had issued about the fate of his son's mother—presumably to protect his spotless reputation—she could now never be acknowledged as the mother of his child. And she suspected that even if access was granted, it would be limited.

Solace dropped her hands from her face and stared hard at the white tiles in front of her, thinking.

Perhaps she needed to offer Galen something. She had no skills, no useful work experience except stacking supermarket shelves and serving people food, and her education was only of the most basic kind. The only useful thing she had was her body and that, at least, she knew he wanted. Perhaps she could offer to be his mistress? Or maybe, if that wasn't acceptable, she could be her son's nanny? He'd already have one, but maybe Galen would be okay with her helping in some small way.

It felt like begging for something she was already entitled to, and she hated that thought, but she couldn't see any other choice. She had no power here except that which Galen chose to give her, and the only alternative was giving up and going home, and she couldn't do that either.

She couldn't let her own pride get in the way. After all, her feelings didn't matter, only her child did. Perhaps being honest with Galen was the key. Perhaps she'd give him the brutal truth of why she'd signed away her rights as a parent, why she'd given up their son to him. Tell him about the postnatal depression, about her reasons for resorting to blackmail, and about how giving away her baby had torn a hole clean through her heart.

He was a fair man, that was what they said about him as a king. Surely, he'd listen. Surely, he'd give her something.

It went against all her instincts to bare her soul to anyone at all, let alone a man and most especially a man with such power, but what other option did she have?

She would do anything for her son. Anything at all.

Strangely, the decision made her feel stronger than she had for months, a new kind of determination flowing through her. She'd do what she had to for her son's sake and maybe Galen would acknowledge that, maybe he wouldn't, but she'd have tried.

You think that makes up for what you did? You gave him away as your mother gave you away. What makes you any better?

But she shut that thought away as she dried herself off and wrapped herself in a towel.

When she came out of the bathroom, she saw that a small table had been set up in the middle of the room, with plates of toast and eggs and bacon. There were pots of jam and honey, and a slab of creamy butter. A coffee pot steamed gently, filling the room with the scent of fresh coffee.

Solace's stomach rumbled, reminding her that she hadn't eaten since her hurried dinner the night before and she was starving.

Galen's pronouncements about eating and getting dressed irritated her all over again, but while she might be uneducated, she was not stupid, so she put away her irritation, got herself a plate of food and some coffee, and had breakfast.

Annoyingly, she felt better after that and, even more annoying, she liked the dress that had been laid out for her on the bed while she'd been in the shower. It was a simple tiered sundress of thick white cotton that tied at her shoulders, and looked loose and comfortable and casual, as well as pretty.

She liked pretty things yet never had the money to buy them, and she'd have loved the dress if it hadn't obviously been something he wanted her to wear.

Then again, who cared? She liked it and she didn't want to wear the mesh dress again. It felt wrong to wear something so exposing when she was going to discuss her child's future.

Perhaps you should. He might like you on your knees. After all, what else do you have to offer?

Solace's jaw hardened. No, she'd offered her body once and he'd taken it. But she wouldn't do it again. No more manipulation. She'd try honesty and see where that got her.

It won't get you anywhere. It never has before. And would he even believe you anyway?

But Solace ignored the thought, picking up the pretty white dress and going about making herself presentable.

Ten minutes later, a knock came on the bedroom door.

She took a breath, steadied herself, and then went to answer it.

A man in the blue and silver palace uniform stood on the other side. 'His Majesty will see you now. Please, follow me.'

Solace stepped out of the bedroom and followed the man dutifully.

She remembered the hall from the night before, though Galen had been carrying her at the time, and she hadn't really taken a good look around. They'd both been far more interested in getting to the bedroom.

It was a wide hallway with a polished wooden floor

covered by a thick silk runner. The walls were white and hung with various paintings, some abstracts with lots of colour and some more monochrome. The ceilings were high, and windows at the end of the hall let in light.

The stairs were of some dark wood, and swept down to a small but high-ceilinged entranceway. It wasn't as grand as she'd expected from a king's residence, but she rather liked that. It felt more like a home than a palace did, and she liked the spare furnishings too. Nothing was ostentatious or overblown. Just quietly luxurious.

The staff member led her down another hallway to a door that he opened and ushered her through into the room beyond.

It seemed to be a study. Heavy wooden bookcases lined the walls closest to the door, while on the opposite side of the room big windows looked out onto an atrium-style garden, with a square colonnade with white columns around it and a fountain with a lush garden around it in the middle. Also in the room was an enormous antique oak desk with an equally enormous portrait of a man on the wall behind it.

The room was empty.

The man indicated the chair standing before the desk. 'Please sit. His Majesty will be with you shortly.'

He withdrew, shutting the door behind him and leaving her in silence.

Solace sat, her hands clenched in her lap, and stared at the portrait behind the desk.

It was in oils, of a man standing behind a table. He was very tall, his hair more white than black, and wearing formal black clothing. There were medals on his chest and on the table was a crown. He was a handsome man, though unsmiling, fierce dark eyes looked out at the viewer in what Solace couldn't help thinking was a slightly judgmental fashion.

She didn't recognise the man, but the crown gave a hint.

It must be Alexandros Kouros, Galen's father.

There wasn't much resemblance in his face that Solace could see, but the fierce quality of that stare was unmistakable.

Suddenly the office door opened, and Galen came in and all the air in the room disappeared.

He'd changed into a fresh pair of dark grey trousers and a deep blue business shirt that accentuated the colour of his eyes. His hair was damp as if he'd freshly showered and it was clear he'd shaved.

He was absolutely devastating.

Galen strode to the desk and stood behind it, and for long moments he didn't speak, his gaze sweeping over her, his expression impenetrable, every inch of him a king.

'So,' he said at last. 'You will give me an explanation for why you changed your mind about our son, Solace Ashworth, and you will give it to me now.'

Half an hour. That was all it had been. Half an hour since he'd last seen her, after spending all night with her, and yet the moment her gaze met his, he felt the same gut punch of need that he'd felt the night before.

Except this time her eyes weren't dark but the sharp, piercing grey that had haunted his dreams for so long, a crystalline colour like frost on a winter pond. The effect of that gaze was the same too, a sword right through his heart.

She sat on the chair in front of his desk, wearing the dress he'd had one of his staff members do a last-minute dash for—a pretty white thing that made her look pale and lovely—and all he wanted to do was to rip it off her.

It was galling that, even after the night before, the desire for her still dogged him. However, at least he was now in control of it. He wasn't going to let it become a problem, not again.

Conscious of Alexandros's gaze watching from the wall behind him, Galen folded his arms and waited. While he'd showered and changed, his staff had been busy confirming her identity and updating the file they already had on her. And by the time he'd finished buttoning his shirt, that file was in his hands, and he'd familiarised himself with it.

She'd indeed had a difficult life. The kind of life that might have crushed another person, yet it had not crushed her.

She sat in the chair bolt upright, hair lying in waves over her white shoulders, her chin lifted, her stare very, very sharp. The epitome of uncrushed and determinedly so.

It made him even more curious as to what had changed her mind after giving Leo away and why she was here now, six months later, prepared to blackmail him to get Leo back.

'I didn't change my mind.' Anger coloured her voice, he heard it loud and clear. 'I *never* wanted to give up *my* son, I told you that.'

'Yet you did.' He decided to let the 'my son' go for the meantime. 'I've seen the documents. It's your signature on every one of them. You said something about wanting him to be safe?'

Her mouth tightened, small silver sparks glittering in her eyes. 'Okay, you want the story? I'll give you the story. I didn't know I was pregnant. I found out literally a week before he arrived and when he did, he was a couple of days early. I was in shock. My last pay cheque hadn't gone through yet and so I had no money to buy him anything. I was discharged from hospital hours after having him, and I had no support when I got home. I had no idea what to do.'

The silver sparks in her eyes were now flames. 'Your staff arrived the next day. And they told me who you were and whose baby I'd just had. And while I was still trying to get my head around that, they said I had to come to Kalithera with them because my son's father wanted him.' Her jaw line was rigid, her sharp gaze not leaving his. 'I…couldn't think properly. It was like my head was full of cotton wool and I couldn't understand why I was even being asked to come. I…didn't believe them that I'd be welcome. I didn't trust them. But I also knew he couldn't stay with me. He was heir to a kingdom and one day he'd sit on a throne, and I wanted that for him. Because he'd have nothing if he stayed with me. A life of poverty, growing up on council estates, and drugs and who knows what else?'

Her hands were clasped tightly in her lap, her knuckles white. 'I was so tired, so exhausted and all I could think about was how much safer he'd be with them, and so, yes, I gave him up. I gave him up so he could have a better life, and I regretted that decision the moment I made it. I'll regret it for the rest of my life.'

Galen didn't let his shock show. He hadn't known, not any of this. He'd been very clear with his staff about how they were to go about retrieving Leo. They were to do it sensitively and Solace was to accompany them, because he wasn't a monster. He wasn't going to rip away a child from its mother. Yet then they'd told him that she hadn't wanted to come and had given Leo up without protest, and he'd taken that at face value.

You keep making mistake after mistake. You should have gone yourself.

He should have, but he hadn't. Everything about getting Leo had had to be discreet. He couldn't have risked being seen in some down-at-heel street in London, not when the British press were so ruthless. The risk of discovery had been too great. Kostas would have been even more suspicious if Galen had disappeared only to return with a child, and even when the story had come out, he'd asked some difficult questions.

'My staff were under strict instructions,' he said. 'They weren't to coerce you in any way, and they were also to ensure that you'd feel welcome coming to Kalithera.'

'Oh, they explained. They were very clear. But like I said, I was in shock. I couldn't think and they were… impatient.'

Yes, they probably had been. He'd told them not to linger.

'We tried to contact you,' he said, because he had. 'But your phone number was disconnected, and your flat was empty. We had no way of finding out where you were. And I assumed…' He wasn't proud of this, he wasn't proud at all, but she deserved his honesty in return for her own. 'I assumed you'd taken the money and fled.'

Twin spots of brilliant colour burned in her pale cheeks. It was clear whatever confession she was going to make to him, it was going to cost her. 'No, I didn't. My phone died and I couldn't afford another, and I couldn't afford to stay in my flat either. I had postnatal depression and couldn't work.'

Yet more shock hit him. 'But the money—'

'You think I'd ever touch that money?' There was ferocity in her gaze now, a burning fury. 'No. That was blood money, and I didn't want a penny of it.'

You have made a complete and utter mess of this. As expected.

Galen had always hated the strict rules his father had imposed on him as a boy, rules that, no matter how hard he tried, seemed to have been set up precisely so he could fail them. To be good, obey his tutors, be polite and pleasant. Never allow his emotions or his own personal wants and needs to rule him.

Simple rules and yet always there had been something he did that was wrong. He'd laughed when he shouldn't, used the wrong title, run when he should have walked... Small things that his father had treated as huge failures. In the end he'd decided that there was no point in trying when nothing he did was right anyway, and so he'd let his anger at his father consume him.

Then Alexandros had died, and, to protect his country, Galen had had to take the throne, a throne that might not be his. And he'd found himself having to try yet again, to overcome the reputation he'd earned in England, to be the perfect King so no one would ever question his claim. And he'd thought, after ten years of solid rule, that finally he'd laid the ghost of his father to rest. That he might even deserve the throne he sat on...

But you don't, do you?

The thought sat in his head, searing him. In the space of a little over a year, not only had he compromised the integrity of his crown, he'd torn his son from his mother and left her with nothing. She had been done a terrible wrong and he was the cause, and, while her blackmail attempt had also been wrong, he knew what lengths a parent would go to for their child. He couldn't hold that against her.

His own guilt at his role in this was a knife blade. He had to make this right somehow. Yet at the same time, he couldn't put at risk the secret he had to keep.

She couldn't be acknowledged as Leo's mother, not given the story that had already been disseminated about how she'd died in childbirth. If it was found out that, not only was she alive, but also that the palace had lied, well… That would be an opportunity his uncle wouldn't let sit. Kostas would parade the decade-old scandal of that party in London Galen been discovered at, evidence that Galen hadn't been a fit choice of heir. Then he'd no doubt stir up trouble with the old rumours about Galen's mother and the affair she was reputed to have had, causing questions about Galen's parentage and whether he was indeed Alexandros's son…

No, he couldn't allow that, not for his country's sake and not for Leo's.

Uncrossing his arms, he put his hands on the edge of the desk, leaning on them. 'Then what is it that you want, Solace? I apologise for the way you've been treated. None of what happened to you was my intention, and I'll do everything I can to make it up to you. However…' He paused, because on this he would not be moved, no matter what she said. 'I'll not allow my son to be taken out of Kalithera. He is my heir therefore he stays with me, understand?'

'Yes, I understand.' Her back was very straight, and she didn't look away. 'Then I'll stay here with him.'

'And how do you envisage that working? You cannot be acknowledged as his mother, not since everyone thinks his mother is dead.'

'That's not my problem.' There was steel in her voice.

'*You* took my baby away. *You* told the world his mother was dead. I had no choice in any of this, which makes it your issue to deal with, not mine.'

Galen was conscious of that heat building inside him again, the competitor responding to the challenge she'd just laid down, and it was a challenge, whether she knew it or not.

She might have seemed fragile and pale sitting there in her virginal white dress, but her silver eyes were hard and there was nothing but defiance in the tilt of her chin.

A proud, regal woman. A woman who'd been fighting for everything her entire life and now she was fighting for this, for her child.

Their child.

He couldn't imagine the childhood she'd had, with no stability anywhere, not even in her bloodline. It was the opposite of his, where he'd been told from birth who he was and who he'd eventually be. Yet he wasn't a stranger to instability, not when he didn't even know if the throne he sat on was truly his, or even if Alexandros was actually his father.

Not that he could tell a soul about that. It was his secret to bear.

Anyway, what was important now was deciding what to do with her, not getting curious about her, and the simplest thing would be to have her flown back to London and out of his hair. Yet…

He couldn't bring himself to do it. Sending her away would hurt her and he'd already hurt her enough as it was. The right thing to do would be to find a way for her to stay in Kalithera and allow her access to Leo.

Are you sure keeping her here is the right thing to do, though? You know how weak you can be.

Yes, yes, he knew that. But he had himself well in

hand. She might have got under his skin twice already, but there wouldn't be a third time.

Galen pushed himself up from his desk and straightened. 'Naturally, it is my problem. I am King here and I will decide how best to proceed.'

Her gaze was steely. 'If you send me home, I'll fight you. I'm not going anywhere without my son.'

This little warrior was quite a change from the seductive, passionate woman of the night before, and, he had to admit, it intrigued him. He'd seen flashes of this same steel in the back of his limo the night before and it had been…sexy. Especially in combination with her white-hot desire and the way she'd surrendered to him.

An intoxicating combination in a woman, if he was honest with himself, and one he'd never experienced before, not even back in his bad old days of university.

If you married her, it would solve all your problems at once.

The thought came out of nowhere and was so ridiculous, he almost laughed. Because while it was true, he'd been thinking of a wife, he couldn't marry Solace. The Kings of Kalithera married women from important, aristocratic families, not poor commoners. He couldn't break tradition, not given how carefully Kostas watched him, and besides, given the mistakes he'd already made concerning Solace, marrying her would no doubt be a disaster. No, it wouldn't work.

He was going to have to think of something else.

'That won't be necessary,' he said. 'Though I'm not sure exactly how you think you can fight me.'

It was a pointless thing to add, and he wasn't sure why he had, especially when her gaze sparked and she virtually quivered in her seat with suppressed anger. As if she was a hair's breadth away from springing over his desk and strangling him.

'I may look powerless, but I'm not,' she said fiercely. 'I can create trouble for you.'

'You've already created trouble for me.'

'No, *you* created the trouble.' She paused, then spat, 'Your Majesty.'

You need to stop this. Baiting her is a terrible idea.

Especially when the gulf in their stations was so vast. And most especially when he knew all too well that he was only doing it because he found her rage intoxicating. She was like a cornered alley cat, hissing and spitting because she had nowhere else to go, and was no doubt secretly terrified. In fact, him deliberately baiting her was not only cruel, it was also selfish.

So he ignored her sharp retort and looked into her bright silver eyes. 'Would you like to see him?' he asked.

CHAPTER FIVE

SOLACE HAD FELT as if she were going to spontaneously combust with rage. He was so cool and in command standing behind his desk, radiating authority. His voice sounded as icy as his blue eyes, as if nothing at all touched him. So very much not the man she'd been in bed with the night before.

She didn't know what to do.

She wanted to be as cool as he was, as in command and powerful, but all that honesty, laying out all the facts of what had happened to her, had ripped away her defences, leaving her feeling raw and exposed. She wasn't a man, and she certainly wasn't a king, and all she had was her anger, so that was what she'd grabbed hold of. The fire inside her that had propelled her out of the pit of depression and landed her here, in his study, telling a king she was going to fight him.

She'd expected him to send her away, if not taking her directly to jail.

She had not expected him to say in that same cool voice, 'Would you like to see him?'

It sucked the anger right out of her, leaving a cold fear sitting in the pit of her stomach. 'Him?' Her voice shook.

The hard lines of Galen's perfect face softened slightly. 'Our son. Leo.'

It felt as if a shard of glass had pierced her heart, an agony she tried to ignore yet it echoed through her all the same. And before she knew what she was doing, she'd shoved herself out of her chair and walked to the windows, turning away from him to hide the tears that filled her eyes.

Leo. Galen had named him.

You didn't. You didn't even think of a name.

Because she hadn't been able to think. Her head had felt foggy with postnatal hormones and shock. And solving the problem of how she was going to manage with a baby had seemed more important than finding a name for him.

There was silence behind her, then Galen said quietly, 'Leo is short for Leonidas. It is an old family name and it seems to suit him.'

She wanted to tell him she hated it, say how dare he name their child without her, but she didn't hate it. She liked it. A lot. It was only that she'd missed out on so much. He was nearly six months old now... Would he remember her?

He'll certainly remember the mother who gave him away to make her own life easier.

Solace squeezed her eyes shut, forcing away the tears and that terrible thought along with it. Because it wasn't true. It wasn't. She'd had to give him up. She'd had nothing to offer him, nothing at all, while Galen could give him a throne.

Abruptly, she was aware of a spicy, masculine scent, so close. He must be standing right behind her, though she hadn't heard him move.

She didn't want to turn around, not when there were

still tears in her eyes, so she stayed where she was, resolutely turned away.

'Solace.' His deep voice whispered like rough velvet over her skin.

She could feel the warmth of his body and a part of her wanted to lean into it the way she had last night, surrender to him, let his strength hold her up because she felt so weak. But she couldn't. He'd taken her child and she was still furious about that and, besides, she had a battle ahead and she had to stay strong.

No weakness was permitted.

'Please don't come any closer.' She hoped her voice didn't sound as thick as she feared it did. 'And please... don't touch me.'

Another silence fell and then the scent was gone.

She swallowed, biting down on the urge to call him back, to tell him yes, please touch her, because she wanted to feel his hands on her again. Pleasure was always preferable to this pain. Yet that was another weakness she couldn't afford so she didn't.

The sound of papers shuffling came from behind her. 'I have ordered a car. We can be there in twenty minutes.'

Solace opened her eyes, blinking the remainder of her tears fiercely away and forcing the rest of her feelings to the side. Then, once she was feeling steadier, she turned.

Galen was back behind his desk as if he'd been there all along, his blue gaze giving nothing away.

'Where is there?' Solace asked, since that appeared to be the least problematic question.

'A residence of mine on the coast.'

She went cold. 'Not at the palace? But is it safe? He'd be much safer—'

'He has a retinue of twenty armed guards,' Galen interrupted mildly. 'He is more than safe. And the palace attracts far too much attention. I do not intend for him to live in a fishbowl.'

Solace fought down her fluttering panic. Of course, Galen would keep their son safe. Of course, he would. Their child was his heir, after all.

No, not 'their child'. *Leo.*

Another pang of grief hit her, but she ignored it. 'Okay,' she said with some reluctance, because she didn't want to agree with him, but, unfortunately, she did. 'That…seems like a good plan.'

There was something that looked like sympathy in Galen's eyes, and she wanted to turn away from it, but that felt too much like giving in, so she forced herself to bear it.

'He is safe,' Galen said with a gentleness that was almost painful. 'He is happy and well and growing like a weed.'

Tears threatened yet again, and again she forced them away. 'Good,' she said. 'I'm…glad.'

Galen's expression was impenetrable. 'Would you like to go now?'

Her voice seemed to have got stuck in her throat, but she managed a weak, 'Yes, please.'

He nodded and then strode from the room.

Solace was very tempted to sit back down in the chair since her legs felt wobbly, but she gritted her teeth and remained standing.

She was going to see him. She was going to see *him*. The son she hadn't even named. Because one minute she'd been trying to plan for the birth of a baby she'd had no idea she was even having, the next, she'd been in the ER with inexplicable stomach pain.

Except it hadn't been so inexplicable.

She'd had her little boy a few hours later and then had been sent home by the overworked nurses with a sheaf of pamphlets, and that had been it. He'd cried all night and she'd cried with him, because she hadn't had any idea what to do.

The people from Kalithera had arrived the next day.

Solace swallowed again and reached for her anger. It was the only thing that gave her strength, the only thing that got her through the mess her life had become, and that was no doubt about to get messier.

Then the door opened again, Galen standing in the doorway. 'Come. I have a car waiting.' His tone was neutral, his gaze running over her, assessing her.

She didn't like it. It made her uncomfortable. 'Don't look at me like that,' she said. 'I'm not a bomb about to go off, you know.'

If he was offended, he didn't show it. 'Evidently,' he murmured. 'Please, follow me.'

Snapping at him won't help.

Taking a deep breath, she let her grip on her anger loosen a bit then went to the door and followed Galen down the hallway to the entrance way.

Black-suited men waited discreetly outside as she went down the steps to the nondescript car waiting at the bottom.

This time it was Galen who held the door open, waiting wordlessly for her to get in before getting in himself. He shut the door, enclosing them once again in the intimate space of the car.

Her breath caught, the delicious scent of his aftershave surrounding her, reminding her of everything that had happened the night before. Of his hands stroking her and his mouth tasting her. Of him inside her, creating the most intense pleasure between them. Of the weight of him on her and the way he'd held her down, and that terrible feeling of safety...

Prickles of heat washed over her, and she was very, very conscious of the long, powerful thigh almost but not quite touching hers and the seductive warmth of the man sitting next to her. Her mouth dried and she turned her head to look out of the window.

She didn't want to feel this, not now. She'd used their chemistry last night as a weapon, and, while she still could feel the desire coiling tight, it wasn't a weapon she wanted to use again.

Deep inside, threads of the ever-present shame and guilt wrapped around each other, but she forced them away. She'd done what she had to do, the way she always did. And anyway, it didn't matter now. Nothing mattered. Nothing mattered except she was going to see her son.

You don't deserve this. Not after what you did.

Solace closed her eyes, her nails digging into her palms where she held them in her lap, the pain driving the bitter thoughts away.

Then a sudden warmth covered her hands and she opened her eyes with a start, looking down to see one of Galen's large hands covering hers. He wore a heavy gold ring on his index finger, clearly very old and etched with vines and leaves growing around a crown.

His royal signet ring. A reminder of who he was.

She could feel the metal pressing lightly against her skin. It was warm. As warm as his hands were.

For a second, she didn't understand what he was doing. Was this an attempt at seduction and he meant to carry on what had happened between them the night before? But no. His hand didn't move to stroke or caress.

He simply enclosed her icy fingers in his, the way he had that night at the gala after she'd dropped the tray.

Giving her comfort and reassurance.

She didn't want him to touch her like this. It frightened her. Mainly because something inside her desperately wanted his warmth, his touch, his strength. She wanted to be held, to be reassured. She wanted someone to tell her everything would be okay, because she was tired of every day being a battle.

But she knew what happened when she did that, when she trusted where she shouldn't. It always ended up with her suffering and she was tired of that too.

She wasn't sure why this man had the power to make her feel so weak, but she didn't like it and she didn't want it.

As if he could feel her tension, his hand squeezed hers gently. 'Don't be afraid. I'm not here to hurt you.'

'I'm not afraid.' She made as if to pull her hands from his, but he tightened his grip minutely.

'Relax,' he murmured as if she hadn't spoken. 'You're safe. Nothing will hurt you while you're with me. I will not allow it.'

There was a lump in her throat. His grip was very firm, and she doubted she could pull away without causing a fuss, though she could do that, obviously. If she really wanted to. Except…she didn't want to. It would take too much energy and, anyway, she could let herself have this, couldn't she? Just his hand holding hers?

It didn't mean anything, and it wasn't her giving her trust to him. It was a few moments of human contact, nothing major. And maybe it was even true, that nothing could harm her while he was here. After all, he'd told her she was safe the night before too, and she had been. Perhaps in this moment, she could believe him.

As if that thought was all her body needed, her muscles lost their tension and she felt herself sink into the softness of the seat cushions, let her hands beneath his soak up his warmth. But she kept her gaze firmly out of the window, because looking at him was a step too far.

Outside, the narrow streets of Therisos passed by, cobbled and twisted, ancient houses built from white-washed stone all jumbled on top of one another. Stairs and alleyways snaked through the houses and streets—the city was famous for its historic architecture—while bougainvillea cascaded over walls and occasionally the green of a walled garden flashed by.

'I still think about that night,' Galen said unexpectedly, his deep voice quiet. 'That night at the ball with you.'

Shock gripped her. It had never occurred to her that he would still think about it, not once. She'd assumed she'd just been another in a long line of women he'd indulged himself with, despite how incredible it had been for her. 'Oh?' She tried to keep that shock from her voice.

'Yes,' he said. 'It was…remarkable. I wanted to talk to you afterwards, but you ran away.' A pause. 'Did I frighten you?'

His tone was neutral and again, she found herself answering before she could think better of it. 'Not in the way you think. It was more…shock.'

'Ah,' he murmured.

'I hadn't… I don't usually…' She stopped then decided she might as well say it. 'You were my first.'

There was another long moment of silence.

Then Galen said, 'I was going to try to find you, but after the way you ran, it seemed obvious that you didn't want anything to do with me. There were lots of formalities I had to attend to that night as well, and so… I let you go.'

The lump in Solace's throat grew larger and it wouldn't go away no matter how many times she swallowed. What if she hadn't run? What if she'd stayed and he'd found her? She wouldn't have had to have their child alone…

You really think he'd have wanted anything to do with you? Especially when he found out who you were.

Well, he knew now, didn't he?

'It was probably for the best.' She tried to make her voice sound less hoarse and failed.

He didn't say anything to that, but after a moment his grip on her shifted and she felt him take one of her hands and turn it palm up. Then, with his thumb, he urged her fingers to uncurl and gently held them down.

Solace turned her head sharply in time to see him bend to press a kiss right in the centre of her palm.

A lightning strike of sensation went through her, and she almost gasped at the sensation of his lips, warm against her skin. Instinctively, she tried to pull away, but his grip was too strong, and when he lifted his head, there were deep blue sparks in his eyes.

A shudder went through her.

'Why did you do that?' she asked.

'It was a thank you.' His voice was slightly rough. 'For the gift.'

'What gift?'

'The gift of your body.' The sparks in his eyes became hotter. 'And of your virginity.'

Her face went hot. No one had thanked her for anything, still less a man she'd tried to blackmail a mere couple of hours or so earlier, and her instinct was to snap at him to cover her emotional reaction.

But he only smiled slightly, then let go of her hand. 'You'll forgive me. I have several calls to make.' And he reached into his pocket and took his phone out without another word.

Solace quickly turned back to the window, her heart beating fast, though she wasn't sure why. She could still feel his kiss in the centre of her palm and before she could stop herself she'd curled her fingers around it as if to keep the warmth of it close to her skin.

Stupid. She didn't need to be thanked and she didn't need him to kiss her hand either. Yet she kept her fingers curled tight around that kiss as the car made its way along the coastline, past more modern housing developments and a few ancient villages.

Galen had several phone conversations, his deep voice almost hypnotic in its melodic rolling Kalitheran, and she found listening to him a great distraction from the strange ball of anxiety that had settled in her stomach.

Which only got worse as the car eventually slowed, pulling down a twisting, narrow lane that turned into an equally narrow, twisting driveway. Then it pulled up at a large, traditional, Kalitheran whitewashed villa perched on the side of a hill overlooking the sea. Terraced gardens surrounded it, with olives and cypresses, and she could see a couple of other small terraces that faced the sea beneath its terracotta roof.

After the car had come to a stop, Galen got out and held the door open for her. A light, fresh breeze caught the ends of her hair, filling the air with the scent of the sea and the distant sounds of waves crashing against rocks.

A peaceful, quiet place.

Better than your bedsit.

Yes, well. That wouldn't have been hard.

They moved towards the house, walking up a simple white stone path to the front door, which was then opened by a uniformed older woman who gave Galen a small bow. She murmured something in Kalitheran and Galen nodded.

The house was cool and quiet, all white walls and dark wooden floors, and it was peaceful, though the anxiety in Solace's stomach felt as if it were growing thorns and sticking into her, making it difficult to breathe.

Galen led her up a set of stairs and down a small hallway to a plain wooden door. Then he opened the door and went in.

Beyond it was a large room that faced the sea, and probably would have had magnificent views if the white linen curtains hadn't been drawn over the windows, turning the light diffuse and soft. A rustic but beautifully made wooden cot stood near a window, a mobile made of driftwood and shells turning slowly above it.

Solace froze in the doorway, the inexplicable anxiety wrapping around her throat and pulling tight.

Galen had paused beside the cot, looking down at the small form inside it. He smiled and it was as if the sun had found its way into the room despite the curtains, the whole space lighting up. And all she could do was stare at him in astonishment, the anxiety momentarily forgotten in the face of that wonderful smile.

He loves your child too.

The thought resounded like a bell inside her and then was gone, because he leaned down, pulling away the blankets, before scooping up their baby with gentle hands, holding him as if he'd been holding babies all his life.

Then all thought left Solace entirely. Because there he was, cradled in Galen's arms, *her* child. Her baby boy. He'd grown so much.

Leo.

Pain throbbed behind her breastbone.

Galen glanced at her, his gaze luminous. 'Here he is. Come and say hello.'

Her legs felt weak and there was a part of her that didn't want to close the distance, that was afraid. As if once she touched him, he'd vanish. That he wouldn't be real, and this was all a dream. Or maybe that he'd look at her with accusing eyes, knowing what she'd done...

You don't deserve him anyway.

But it was that thought that drove her to move finally, coming over to where Galen stood. And then her arms were full of a warm burden and a little face was looking up into hers.

'He has your eyes,' Galen murmured.

A rush of the most powerful love swept over her in that moment, so intense she couldn't have spoken even if she'd wanted to. He was warm in her arms, and heavy, and he felt exactly as she'd remembered, and it was as if a piece of her soul had returned to her.

She stared down at him, not even noticing the tears running down her cheeks.

She didn't notice, either, when Galen slipped out of the room, leaving her alone with their child.

Galen closed the door of Leo's bedroom quietly and stood there, staring at the dark, polished wood, a fierce wave of emotion tightening in his chest.

An emotion he didn't want, yet had ignited the moment he'd seen the fear on Solace's pale face as she'd stood in the doorway. Then had tightened like barbed wire around his heart when she'd taken Leo in her arms, tears streaming down her face.

Guilt again. Guilt at what he'd taken from her. Guilt that he hadn't tried harder to find her once his son was safely at his side. And something else, something even more powerful that he couldn't name. Something to do with her holding Leo…the mother of his child holding his son…

They both belong to you.

Galen turned sharply from the door and strode down the hallway in the direction of the living area, where he could wait for her.

It was a ridiculous thought to have, like the one he'd had earlier, about marrying her. Yes, his son belonged to him, but Solace? He didn't know her so how could he possibly say? He wanted her physically, that was true, their chemistry was still there and still burning strong. He was going to need a mother for Leo and hopefully more children to secure the succession, so she would be a good choice of wife in that respect, considering she was actually Leo's mother. Also, since he wanted her, the getting of more children wouldn't be an issue.

But as he'd already thought, marrying her wasn't ideal either. Kostas would certainly have something to say about her suitability considering her origins, and how Galen wasn't following tradition. His past behaviour would no doubt be dredged back up, making things difficult, and there would be yet more talk about how unfit he was to rule, and how his contempt for Kalithera was clear in the woman he'd chosen to be his wife.

And then there was Solace's suitability for the role itself. She'd have no idea about what being the Queen of Kalithera meant. How her reputation had to be as spotless as his and she could not be seen to court media attention. There could be nothing in her background that would invite speculation, nothing in her behaviour either. She needed to be someone used to being in the public eye, too, and used to the pressure of being essentially public property.

Galen knew what was at stake. Could he afford to put his crown, not to mention his country in jeopardy for the sake of his guilt? Or even for the sake of Solace's feelings?

It *would* solve a great many of his problems, however.

He could put his PR department to work. Get them to create another story about her and where she came from. Perhaps explain that she hadn't died after all, and he'd reunited with her. It would be a sensational story and it would need to be rock solid to stand up to Kostas's scrutiny, but maybe he could swing it.

Are you really thinking of lying to your people yet again? So many lies...

Galen pushed his hands into the pockets of his trousers, staring out of the window at the rocky cliffs and the sea beyond, his jaw tight. Yes, another lie to fix another mistake. But he now had a debt towards her. He'd caused her a deep and lasting pain on top of a life that had been awful to start with, and, even apart from that, she was the mother of his child, and his child needed his mother.

His own had died not long after having him, and he'd always felt the lack. Especially when all he'd had was Alexandros, who'd actively hated him because he hadn't seen Galen as his son.

You might have been.

Tension crawled across Galen's shoulder blades. That was true. He *could* be Alexandros's son. He'd just never taken a DNA test to find out for certain, because if it was proved he wasn't the true King of Kalithera, he hadn't wanted any record of it anywhere. Better to go on assuming what everyone thought to be true, that he was Alexandros's son and heir, even if deep down he knew he wasn't. His father had hated him for a reason and that reason could only be that he wasn't his son.

Not that thinking about his father was a good use of his time now, not when he had more important problems to consider. Such as what he was going to do with Solace.

He stayed like that, staring out towards the sea, turning plans over in his head, until he heard someone say his name.

Turning, he saw Solace standing in the doorway. She had her hands clasped together and the vibrating anxiety he'd sensed in her in the car, that he'd put his hand over hers to try to calm, had gone. In its place was a determination even more steely than she'd radiated in his office earlier.

Her grey eyes met his, sharp as a shard of glass. 'I am not leaving him. Never, *ever* again.'

Again, he was conscious of the respect she'd earned from him earlier, with her stubborn insistence on fighting for their child, only deepening. It complicated things that she was so set on being with Leo, but all he could think of was how fierce she looked. A small white tiger baring her teeth in defence of her cub. And how he liked that. How it made the desire inside him, that was still there no matter how he tried to ignore it, begin to coil and tighten once more.

He'd thought taking her to see Leo had been the right thing to do, a way to at least start to put right the wrongs that had been done to her, all the while suspecting that seeing her child would only entrench her determination. Sure enough, it had. But he wasn't as unhappy about that as he'd expected. In fact, it had even cleared a few things up.

Yes, why not marry her? He could handle his uncle, and his PR department would do the rest, then his son would have his mother back while he could have a woman in his bed that he had magnificent chemistry with and whom he could have whenever he wanted. This was the one solution that would fix all the mistakes he'd made and put right the wrong he'd done to her.

You think lying to your people to cover up all your errors is any better? It'll only make everything worse. And what will happen if anyone finds out what you've done?

Nothing would happen. Because no one would find out. He'd make sure of it.

And yes, it would mean yet another lie, but there were no good choices here. This solution would ensure Kalithera stayed protected even if something happened to him while his uncle was still alive.

'Good,' he said crisply. 'I wouldn't want the mother of my child to act in any other way.'

Clearly expecting a fight, she blinked in surprise.

Which pleased him. He did like surprising a woman. In fact, now he'd made the decision to marry her, he was very tempted to prowl closer, circle her, see what she'd do. Whether she'd give him a chase or face him, those sharp claws of hers bared. Either would suit him. Either would make him hard.

However, it was not the time or the place, not with his son upstairs, so he remained where he was, his hands in his pockets. 'And if you're to marry me, you'll have to remain in Kalithera anyway.'

Her eyes went wide and this time it wasn't surprise

that rippled over her features, but shock. 'Marry you? What?'

'I think you heard me.' He put authority in his voice, the weight of the crown behind the words. 'I've been considering finding a wife for some time now, mainly because our son needs a mother, but also to secure the succession. However there has been a distinct lack of suitable candidates. At least, there was until last night.' He took a couple of steps towards her, unable to help himself. 'I suspect that you'll do nicely. After all, what better woman to be Leo's mother than his mother herself?'

Solace had gone very pale, her hands in a white-knuckled grip in front of her. 'You can't mean that.'

Galen lifted a brow. 'Why can't I mean that?'

'I'm a nobody, I told you. I don't know who my parents were. I was raised in the foster system, and I dropped out of high school. I... I...have been arrested for shoplifting a couple of times...' She stopped, breathing hard.

'You seem to think that I don't know every single thing about you, Solace Ashworth,' Galen said calmly. 'But I do. None of this is a surprise to me and none of it matters. The press will be told some story about your origins and no doubt we can come up with some reason why the mother of my child is apparently alive and well. They'll be so busy with our apparent emotional reuniting to be bothered about whether it's true or not.'

She took a couple of steps forward, silver eyes glittering. 'No, you can't mean that. I'm not a... I'm not a *queen*.'

He strolled to meet her in the middle of the room, getting closer once again to the fierce passion that burned in her face and the delicate heat of her body.

He shouldn't and he knew it, but he couldn't stop himself. She was irresistible.

'I disagree,' he said. 'You have fought me at every turn since this morning and been nothing but strong and courageous and fierce. Isn't that what a queen is?'

'A queen isn't a nobody,' she insisted. 'A queen isn't a foster kid with no money and no education and no prospects.'

'A queen is whoever I say she is and if I say she's you then she's you.'

'But I don't even know you!'

He lifted a shoulder. 'So? We'll have time to get to know each other. Besides, the most important thing is compatibility in bed, and we have that in spades.'

Her mouth opened then shut and suddenly all he wanted to do was to take her pretty face between his hands and cover that mouth with his own, taste her again. He'd been hoping this morning for more time in bed, at least until her ill-advised blackmail attempt, and now he was reminded again of how good she'd felt in his arms and how sweet her surrender had been.

He wanted more. He wanted to pull the ties of that pretty sundress she wore, let it fall from her body then take her down on the rugs right here in the living room. Perhaps he'd tie her wrists with it. She'd liked being restrained by him. She'd liked it very much.

From the looks of the two spots of high colour that glowed in her cheeks, she wouldn't have protested if he had. Plus, he could tell by how fixedly she was staring at him that she wanted to look at his mouth, the way she did when she was aroused.

But no. He wouldn't touch her yet. She needed to sit with the idea, and she definitely needed more time with their son. That would help clarify things for her.

'I could be his nanny,' she burst out. 'I could be his nurse or—'

'He has a nanny. Not to mention a fleet of nurses. The one thing he does not have is a mother.'

She shook her head. 'No. No, it's impossible.'

It would be interesting to press her about why exactly it was so impossible, but he was conscious that he'd spent more time than he'd intended with her this morning and his schedule for today was already crowded. He needed to return to the palace and quickly.

So, perhaps a week, maybe two for her to get comfortable here. For her to consider his proposal. Not that it was really a proposal, more of a command. Then he would bring her to the palace so they could discuss it further.

Maybe he'd even fulfil his promise of last night to her, of a seduction. In fact, now he thought of it, he couldn't think of anything he'd rather do. He hadn't had the opportunity to seduce a woman in too many years, and, really, it was just the kind of challenge he liked.

'Well,' he said gently, 'since I decide what is impossible and what is not, we will have to agree to differ on that.' He paused, allowing some steel to show in his expression. 'It is also not a request.'

He thought she might take a step back at that, but she didn't. She only stood there, staring at him as if she'd never seen him before in her life. And he could see it then, the legacy of her hard, difficult life. It was there in the anger that glittered brightly in her eyes, and in the stubborn line of her jaw. The bravery of a woman who would not lie down or give up, a woman who'd fought and struggled for everything she had.

Yes, she would make an excellent queen.

'You're crazy,' Solace said. 'I'm not marrying you.'

Galen smiled. 'We'll see.' He stepped back, giving them both some space, because if he remained this close to her any longer, he'd probably do something he'd regret. 'I'll arrange for you to remain here with Leo and you can spend as much time with him as you wish. Though, I must insist on you not speaking with the staff. Your identity must remain secret until this is sorted out. They'll be informed that you're a family member and will need access to him at all times.'

Her jaw had that stubborn line to it again. 'Send them all away. I'll care for him myself.'

It was on the tip of his tongue to refuse since his staff were excellent. But then he paused. Perhaps having her looking after Leo was best. It would mean he wouldn't need to explain why one of Leo's family members had suddenly appeared and also wouldn't have to be concerned about any potential gossip.

'Very well,' he allowed. 'I'll get Maria, his nanny, to leave you all the information about him, as well as contact details for anything you might need yourself.' He turned towards the door. 'I'll send for you when the time comes.'

'Send for me for what? What time?'

He paused at the doorway and smiled. 'The time for you to agree to my proposal.' Then he walked through it before she could speak.

CHAPTER SIX

SOLACE WRAPPED LEO up in his blanket and cradled him in her arms, rocking him gently. She'd just given him his evening feed, a bath and put him in a fresh onesie, and was in the process of putting him to bed.

It was evening, the sunset painting the sky with brilliant oranges and reds and golds, and she stood by the window in his room, watching it as she hummed a soft lullaby.

From the moment she'd first taken him in her arms and his big grey eyes had looked up into hers—Galen had been right, Leo *did* have her eyes—the rest of the world had fallen away. All her fury, all her pain, everything she'd been through, none of it had mattered. The only thing that had was the baby she held. *Her* baby.

Finally, she had him. Finally, he was here where he belonged, safe in her arms. And it had been worth it. In that moment, everything—*everything*—she'd gone through had been worth it.

Galen had left to give her privacy and she'd been desperately grateful to him for that, because all she'd been able to do was hold her son and weep. Weep with grief and guilt for all the moments she'd lost, yet also with dizzying joy that she'd be with him for all the moments still to come. And the relief, the sheer, aching relief that he was safe and well and she was with him again.

Then had followed the happiest week of her life, with nothing to worry about and nothing to do except be with Leo.

She'd spent days lying with him on a blanket in amongst the olive trees, or with him in her arms on the couch in the living room, reading him a book. Or singing. Or showing him white pebbles or flowers or long stalks of green grass in the garden.

She didn't have to worry about money or a job, or how she was going to get nappies or food, or whether the bills had been paid and her electricity was going to get cut off. Everything was provided for her, whatever she asked for was delivered.

Her things from the hostel she'd been staying in had appeared in one of the bedrooms the day after she'd arrived, and, sure enough, Maria, Leo's nanny, had left her a little book full of notes about Leo and his likes and dislikes. What his early months had been like and what kind of baby he was. There were even photos.

Solace had cried over that little book, again for everything she'd missed out on, yet also for what had been given back to her, and it had taken a few days for that to stop hurting. A couple of times she'd demanded frivolous things just to see if Galen really was as good as his word and anything she wanted would be given to her, and indeed they had been.

She'd worried off and on about his ridiculous proposal of marriage and what would happen in the future, and then, because it felt too hard to think about, she'd pushed all of that to the back of her mind, because right now Leo was more important and she wanted to spend her time thinking about him, not the future.

He was such a good baby, calm and rarely fussy, with lots of smiles. The first time he'd smiled at her, she'd thought her heart would burst with joy.

He smiled up at her now as she rocked him, staring up at her as if entranced.

She smiled back, love for him making her chest ache, and then she lifted him for a snuggle. He gave the most delightful gurgling laugh that made tears start in her eyes.

Really, it was a good thing she'd been completely alone with him for the past week given the amount of time she'd spent weeping. She cried more than he did.

Don't get too complacent. This could all come crashing down at any minute.

Oh, she knew that. But a week to allow herself some happiness, to exist in the moment with her child, didn't seem like too big an ask.

Still humming her lullaby, Solace gently laid Leo down in his cot and adjusted his blankets. He generally went down without a fuss, and he must have been extra sleepy today because his eyes closed almost as soon as she'd laid a kiss on his forehead.

She tiptoed out of the room, pulling the door to, and then went down the hallway. She was on the point of coming down the stairs when she heard car tyres crunch on the gravel driveway outside.

Everything inside her tensed.

She'd been alone for the entire week, apart from a security detail so discreet she barely saw them. No one had bothered her. She'd half expected Galen to visit, but he hadn't. She hadn't heard from him for days.

Then only the day before one of Galen's aides had arrived with an invitation for her to come to the palace the next day. It was her summons, just as he'd said.

A car would be sent, along with Maria to look after Leo. It was merely a casual dinner to discuss his earlier proposal, nothing too formal. However, with the summons he'd also sent three dresses that had been chosen with her in mind, since he knew she wouldn't have anything suitable. Dresses that could in no way could be termed 'casual'.

She'd been angry at his high-handedness, all the while sitting on the bed in the bedroom hardly daring to touch the expensive fabric of the dresses laid on the bed. She'd never had such pretty things to choose from before. She'd never had pretty things at all. Everything she had was the cheapest she could buy and there was never anything left over for luxuries.

But these dresses...one in ice-blue silk, another in white satin, a third in tailored black velvet. They were all glamorous and sophisticated, sexy but subtle, nothing like her dress of silver mesh, which was not subtle in the least.

Part of her didn't want to wear the dresses because he'd chosen them and he obviously meant her to wear one, and she hated the thought of accepting his charity. Then again, she loved them, and she didn't know when she'd get another chance to wear something like them again, so why not? It wasn't charity. It was dressing for the occasion. Also, she rather liked the idea of turning him down while wearing something beautiful, because of course she was going to turn him down.

His whole idea was ludicrous. Marry a man she barely knew and not just any man, but a king. And she would become his queen. It was like something out of a fairy tale or a dream, not something that would ever— ever—in a million years happen to someone like her. Naturally, she couldn't trust the idea, not one bit.

Even if a part of her wanted it so badly she ached.

To have a home and a family, and not just any home and family, but one in a palace, with a king for a husband. She wouldn't need to worry about rent or having enough money for food. She'd have her baby with her and a whole garrison of palace guards to keep everyone safe...

And she'd have him. Galen standing between her and the world, standing between her and everything that could hurt her. Galen holding her at night, giving her the most incredible pleasure. He'd made her feel so good...

Her heart throbbed, a tugging ache.

It's too good to be true. You can't trust it.

She knew that. If Katherine, the foster mother she'd wanted to stay with, could change her mind about her for no apparent reason, then why couldn't Galen? He was only offering to marry her because of Leo anyway. He'd never have chosen her if not for that.

No, it was better not to accept anything so out of the realms of possibility as a marriage proposal from him. It was a dream. And the problem with dreams was that you always woke up. Always.

Still, all of that didn't mean she had to forgo a nice dress, and, since they were here anyway, she might as well wear one.

She decided on the ice-blue silk, since it had a lace bodice that left her shoulders bare and a frothy skirt with a hem that fell to her calves at the back while it ended at her knees at the front. There were strappy, high-heeled sandals in ice blue to match, and, with her hair falling loose around her shoulders, she felt like a fairy princess.

It was a shameless indulgence, but why not? Hadn't she earned it?

She waited for the car and when it arrived, she greeted Maria and spent a moment with her discussing Leo's needs for the evening. Maria had looked after Leo since he'd been brought to Kalithera and she loved him too, which Solace had found immensely comforting.

Reassured by Maria's competent presence at Leo's side, Solace then strode from the house and got into the car.

Nerves fluttered in her gut as the car wound up the driveway to the coastal road, but she tried to ignore them. Except the flutter grew more intense the closer to Therisos they got, until it felt as if there were a million butterflies all crowding for space inside her.

She didn't know why, when there was nothing to be nervous about. Except it wasn't only nervousness. She was also conscious of something that felt like excitement fluttering there too, and anticipation. As if she were looking forward to seeing him again, which surely couldn't be right when she hardly knew him.

Except she'd had dreams this past week, of blue eyes and strong hands, and a delicious hot, heavy weight pressing her down. And she'd wake up restless and sweaty, the sheet sticking to her, an ache throbbing gently between her thighs.

You still want him.

Maybe, but that wasn't the same as being excited to see him. Wanting him was physical, that was all, and it certainly didn't mean she was going to agree to marry him.

The royal palace in Therisos was set on a hill above the town, looking out towards the ancient city walls that protected the city from the sea. It was built of white stone and at night was lit up, so it looked as if its towers and terraces floated above the city like a castle out of dreams.

Solace put a hand over the butterflies in her stomach, trying to settle them as the car got clearance from the guards at the palace gates and was driven through, winding up the avenue to the palace itself.

It was imposing, white towers soaring high, topped with the Kalitheran flag moving slowly in the night breeze from the sea.

As she stepped out of the car, a liveried palace servant greeted her and led her up the grand white stairs and into the palace.

Her heartbeat had accelerated, and her mouth was dry, the butterflies in her stomach now numbering in their thousands. But she ignored the feelings. Silly to feel this way about a man she'd only met a couple of times. A man she'd had the most intense night of pleasure with, it was true. Yet he was also the man who'd taken her son from her and that still hurt. Marriage to him was an impossibility and she had no problems telling him that.

She was led through grand halls of plain, whitewashed stone, the walls dotted here and there with paintings of what she assumed were past royals. Galen's lineage, she suspected. An ancient line, ancient blood. Royalty going back centuries.

Solace couldn't imagine her portrait hanging anywhere in these halls. The thought was ludicrous. A hundred pictures of ancient kings and queens, and one of a poor single mother from London.

The servant led her up a wide staircase and down a hall to some huge doors that led out onto a wide terrace, bounded in white stone that looked out towards the sea. Then Solace stopped in the doorway, shocked.

A delicate pergola covered the terrace and fairy lights had been wound all through it, creating a warm, diffuse light. A table stood off to one side, set with a white tablecloth, silver cutlery and crystal glasses. Candles stood around the terrace, on the wall edging it and at various points on the white stone floor, flames flickering and dancing, illuminating the tall figure of a man standing at the edge of the terrace, his back to her.

Galen.

Solace wasn't aware of the servant discreetly withdrawing behind her, or of anything else. Every sense she had seemed to be concentrated on the man on the terrace. On his broad back and wide, muscled shoulders. His narrow waist and powerful legs.

He wore black tonight, the way he had a week ago in the club. Simple clothes that only highlighted his mouth-watering physique.

There was a rushing sound in her head, a trembling that started up deep inside her, that wouldn't go away no matter how hard she tried to force it. The same visceral reaction she always had to the sight of this man, her body wanting his so badly she could hardly stand it.

Slowly, he turned around and the trembling got worse the moment his blue eyes met hers.

He was beautiful. He was devastating. He was a king and far too much for the likes of her, and if she wasn't careful, he would overwhelm her as he had the last couple of times.

She'd thought that after a week of not being around him her reaction to him wouldn't be so intense, but she was wrong. If anything, a week's absence had made her want him more.

The light of a dozen candles flickered over his face, illuminating the perfection of his cheekbones, the straight line of his nose, and the curve of his beautiful mouth.

He smiled and abruptly it washed over her like a wave where she'd seen that smile before: his son had it too.

He will break your heart. They both will.

The thought was fleeting, because then the smile gradually faded and heat leapt instead in his midnight-blue eyes. And she could feel the air between them start to crackle, their chemistry on the verge of igniting like dry tinder.

Galen started towards her, moving like a predatory jungle cat, and she froze, utterly unable to move. Her heartbeat was careening out of control and dimly a part of her was astonished at how quickly she'd gone from being steely and determined, to melting like tar seal under a hot sun. That part of her screamed at her to resist him, to be on her guard, and hadn't she learned that she couldn't trust him?

But before she could even make that choice, he came to an abrupt stop, his hands clenching, his whole body taut. A muscle jumped in the side of his hard jaw. He looked like a man who had himself on a leash so tight it was choking him.

'Solace.' His deep voice was as tight as the rest of him, his eyes blazing a bright searing blue. 'Welcome to the palace.'

She trembled, aching to close the distance between them and feel the touch of his hands, his mouth. Be once again in his arms, surrounded by that wonderful sense of warmth and safety, experiencing that pleasure.

But she couldn't trust him, she couldn't. So, she stayed where she was.

'What—?' She had to clear her throat and start again. 'What's all this? The candles, the lights…'

'It's for you.' He stood rigid, his gaze intense on hers. 'You are here for dinner, remember?'

'You said a casual dinner.'

'It is casual. But I wanted it to be special as well.'

She looked at him blankly. 'Special? Why?'

'It's only been a week, Solace.' That muscle in the side of his jaw jumped again. 'You must remember that I want you to marry me.'

Solace blinked, trying to get her brain working. Marriage, that was right, and she'd been going to refuse. She'd been determined, even. Yet…all these candles, all these lights… It was so pretty. A white tablecloth and fine crystal. Silver cutlery.

He'd wanted it to be special, he'd said.

It was stupid to feel so emotional over some candles and fairy lights, and a nicely set table. It was just… He'd made an effort for her, and no one had ever done that before. No one since Katherine and the princess bed Katherine had been going to buy for her. To go in her new room, Katherine had said. 'A princess bed for my little princess'.

Solace had never wanted anything so badly in all her life. A princess bed just for her. She'd been so thrilled. Then Katherine had changed her mind and hadn't wanted Solace after all. She'd been given no reason, only that Katherine had changed her mind about a formal adoption. So back she had gone to another family, and there had been no princess bed for her.

But now, here, it wasn't only a bed she was being offered, but a man she wanted, a man who gave her pleasure, and a palace, a place of safety. A crown, even. And Leo.

How could she refuse? And it would give Leo what she'd never had: a family.

He took your child. How can you ever forget that?

Maybe she couldn't. Maybe it wasn't possible to forget. And maybe this *was* too good to be true and Galen wasn't to be trusted and she shouldn't agree to it. Or maybe she could put her anger aside and have this anyway, and if it all fell apart in the end, at least she'd have the memory of it. Wasn't that better than the memory of a bed she'd never even got to sleep in?

'Yes,' she said. 'Yes, I remember.'

His blue gaze roamed over her as if he couldn't help himself. 'Well? What is your answer?'

There was only one answer she could give, and she knew it. But it wouldn't hurt him to make him wait for it.

'I don't know yet.' Her chin lifted and she gave him a challenging look. 'Convince me.'

Something in Galen's eyes flared, as if he'd been waiting for her to say that all along, and he strode forward, crossing that aching distance between them and stopping in front of her. 'And how do you wish to be convinced?' The rough edge in his voice left no doubt in her mind about what kind of convincing he wanted.

Luckily it was exactly the sort she wanted too.

She met his gaze squarely, letting him see the intensity that blazed inside her. 'I think you know.'

He didn't wait. He lifted his hands and took her face between them and she didn't pull away. And when he tipped her head back and covered her mouth with his, her own hands lifted helplessly, her fingers threading in his hair.

And everything fell away.

There was nothing in the world but this kiss, full of heat and desire and longing.

Nothing in the world but the warmth of his body and the delicious spice of his scent.

He is everything you dreamed about in the lonely darkness. Everything you've ever wanted.

Perhaps that was even true. He was certainly everything she wanted right now.

His mouth on hers was hungry, exploring her, tasting her as if she'd been lost to him for years and now he'd found her again, he was hell-bent on familiarising himself with every single part of her.

She couldn't resist him, not even if she tried. Though she wasn't going to try. They were like magnets, helplessly drawn to each other, unwilling to be torn apart.

His fingers pushed into her hair, tipping her head back further, the kiss deepening, turning hotter and more feverish. Stripping everything away, all her anger, all her fight. Yet for some reason, tonight her passion didn't make her feel exposed or vulnerable. No, tonight there was a strength in it. Because, for all his power, he was as much a slave to this white-hot chemistry as she was. Just as helpless. In fact, the whole reason she was even here right now was because of his inability to resist her.

You've always had that power over him.

She liked that idea very much.

Galen tore his hands from her hair and lifted her up in his arms, and then she was being carried over to a bench covered with thick cushions. He put her down on the edge, then pushed her knees apart so he could kneel between them. And he kissed her, his hands stroking over her neck and her shoulders, tracing the lines of her collarbones and then pulling at the delicate ice-blue lace of her dress, easing it away and down.

'Galen,' she whispered against his mouth as he tugged the fabric down to her waist, his fingers stroking the curves of her bare breasts, making her shiver.

His lips moved from hers, following the path of his hands, down her neck to the hollow of her throat, tasting her. 'Yes, silver girl?' he murmured. 'What do you want? Tell me.'

But she couldn't think of why she'd said his name. Maybe it had only been for the pleasure of it. And as for what she wanted… 'Don't stop,' she whispered. 'Please.'

He gave a soft laugh. 'Oh, believe me, I have no intention of stopping.' As if to prove it, his hands settled lightly at the small of her back, making her spine arch, and then his mouth was on her breast, sucking and teasing her nipple, biting gently and making her moan.

Then he pushed her against the back of the seat, spreading her thighs wider, her dress up around her hips. He pulled her to the edge, tearing off her lacy underwear, and then his fingers were pressing apart the delicate folds of her sex. He bent, his breath against her sensitive flesh, and then his tongue exploring her.

Solace cried out, her fingers buried in his hair as the bonfire of pleasure built inside her, making her shake. His hands held her thighs firmly apart and down, pinning her to the cushions, holding her there so he could taste her lightly at first then deeper, with firm strokes of his tongue.

The pleasure built so quickly she was on the brink of ecstasy before she even knew what was happening, her whole body shaking. He kept her there for what seemed like eons, drawing out the moment endlessly, until she was writhing on the cushions, desperate for him to finish it, saying his name over and over like a prayer.

Then his strong, capable hands tightened further, and his tongue pressed hard and firm on the place where she needed it most and she was flying up into the night sky, only to burst like a firework in a bright explosion of glory.

Galen felt Solace's body shake, his name a desperate cry that echoed in the night air and he allowed himself the deep, primal satisfaction that came with it in response.

This was not how he'd planned for this night to go. He hadn't thought that everything would completely vanish from his head the moment he turned around and saw her standing in the doorway.

Yet it had.

Her hair had been loose over her shoulders, and she was wearing one of the dresses he'd picked out for her personally, the blue one, which happened to be his favourite. And it looked as fantastic on her as he'd thought it would, the lace showcasing beautifully her pale shoulders and neck, while the uneven hemline made the most of her pretty legs.

She'd looked ethereal and lovely, and the kick of desire had taken him utterly by surprise. It shouldn't have. He should have known that need would be lying in wait, ready for the moment when their eyes would meet and it would flare into life, burning through every good intention he had.

He'd wanted to seduce her, first with food and conversation, and then, when he'd got her agreement to the marriage, because of course she'd agree, he'd seduce her with his body. Show her exactly how good being married to him would be.

A foolproof plan, he'd thought.

Until he'd taken one look at her and that plan had burned to the ground.

He'd tried to stop himself. God knew, his whole life had been nothing but try and try and try. But when it came to her, no matter how many warnings or assurances he gave himself, that this time he'd stay in control, that this time he'd resist, he always forgot every single one the moment he laid eyes on her.

She'd given him that direct look, and it had been full of heat. Then challenged him to convince her, and he'd been lost.

He hadn't understood how hungry he'd been for her until her fingers had pushed into his hair and she'd kissed him back. And he was hungry still, even now, kneeling between her silky thighs with the delicious, sweet flavour of her on his tongue. He needed more than this taste. He needed to be inside her and right now.

She'd sagged back against the bench, her face flushed, her mouth slightly open, and the sight of her only honed his hunger to a sharper edge.

'Solace.' Her name came out as a growl, but he didn't try to stop it as he rose to his feet. It was meant to be a question, yet he couldn't quite get out the rest. There was nothing but demand left in him.

Her silver eyes were lit up by the candles and the fairy lights above, and he felt something tighten behind his breastbone that had nothing to do with the other tightness he felt down below his belt.

She was so very lovely, a woman made of starlight and silver, and delicate-seeming. Yet there was heat inside her. Heat and a strength that he found just as sexy as the rounded shape of her breasts or the slick softness between her thighs.

And also an aching vulnerability that made him want to gather her up and hold her in his arms, protect her from everything that might harm her. He wasn't sure why he was feeling such things about a woman he didn't know, but he felt them. It was as if his body already knew her, and his mind was taking its time to catch up.

Her gaze focused on him and then unexpectedly she lifted her arms, and the painful tension inside him relaxed. Then he was pressing her down on the cushioned bench, settling between her warm thighs, and he was surrounded in the delicious, lightly musky scent of aroused woman.

He pushed a hand down between them, stroking her, making her gasp and sigh once again, her hips undulating against his. Her hands were pressed to his chest, her fingers curled into the fabric of his shirt, and she lifted her head, finding his mouth. Such a sweet kiss. She was so passionate, all that ferocity and anger turned into heat. It was glorious and he wanted it.

His childhood had been so cold, Alexandros demanding and exacting. He'd never touched Galen, not once. Not a hug or even a handshake. There was no closeness, no warmth, only a thinly veiled loathing that sometimes Galen felt like a poison deep in his heart.

But his life would never be cold if she was in it. There would be arguments and fights aplenty, yet then there would also be passionate reconciliations…

She would fight for you if she were yours. She fights hard for the things she loves.

And she did. She'd fought for Leo, coming all the way to Kalithera with her blackmail plan. He hadn't met a woman like her. Even the few he'd managed discreet liaisons with had all tried to turn themselves into what he wanted them to be, but not her. Never her. She wasn't afraid of him and even when she'd seduced him the week before, she'd been nothing but herself.

Galen undid his trousers, suddenly desperate, then reached for her hand, pushing it down between them. 'Put me inside you, silver girl,' he ordered. 'I want you to do it.'

There were sparks in her eyes, the pretty flush in her cheeks creeping down her throat. 'I don't take orders.'

'You'll take mine,' he murmured. 'And you'll like it.' Then he flexed his hips, pressing into her hand.

She gave a little moan. 'Galen…'

'You know what to do.' He bent and bit the side of her neck gently. 'So do it and put us both out of our misery.'

Her fingers tightened around him, the slight pressure driving him half out of his mind, then she was guiding him to her and easing him inside, her slick, hot flesh parting for him so sweetly.

She shuddered beneath him as he pushed in deeper, her gaze on his, glittering like stars. And he was caught by how intense this moment was, how it always was with her and only with her. She'd looked at him like this that night at the gala, just like this. With wonder and pleasure and a certain kind of awe that made the man in him want to growl with satisfaction. She'd looked at him like this that night in his limo too.

Perhaps she would always look at him this way and perhaps the expression on his face would always be the same.

There was a connection between them on some deep level he couldn't articulate, that went beyond merely physical. Maybe even beyond the blood tie they had in Leo. He had never believed in such things, but he believed when it involved her.

'Well?' he demanded roughly. 'Are you convinced

yet? Marry me and we'll be together every night, just like this.'

'Galen…' She shifted, arching up, trying to get him to move. 'Please…'

'Only if you say yes.' He kept still, though it took everything he had, holding her brilliant gaze with his. She'd used their chemistry to get what she wanted and now it was his turn. He would have this. He would have her in his bed and his people would have a queen, and, most importantly, his son would have his mother. 'I will have you, silver girl. You are mine.'

She gave a breathless sigh and then, as she had in the limo the day he'd taken her to see Leo, when he'd put his hand over hers and had felt all the fight slowly melt out of her, she melted beneath him now. Her hands pulled him down, her legs tightening around his waist. 'Yes,' she murmured against his mouth. 'Yes, I'll marry you.'

Satisfaction filled him and he bent to kiss her hard, allowing himself to move at last. He drove himself into her, feeling her grip him, so hot and so tight, keeping him exactly where he wanted to be.

He pulled her hands from his shirt and held them down beside her head, because he liked restraining her, liked her wriggling and writhing pinned beneath him. And he knew she liked that too, because her eyes were dark with desire and her thighs gripped him the way her sex gripped him, as if she didn't want to let him go.

He drove harder, faster, taking them both higher, until he was drowning in pleasure, drowning in the feel of her body and the sounds of her gasps in his ears, in the heat that was being generated between them.

The orgasm came like a tidal wave, roaring through him, sweeping away all thought and all awareness, crushing him utterly beneath the relentless onslaught of pleasure.

It took him long moments to gather himself together again and shift to give her space to breathe. But he kept his fingers around her wrists, though he loosened his hold. He wanted her to remember what she'd promised him, because, even after that, he did.

'You had some hesitations about marrying me,' he said after some time had passed. 'I want to know why.'

Her eyes were closed, blonde lashes lying still on her cheeks. 'Does it matter?'

'Yes, of course it matters. Ours isn't a marriage of convenience, Solace. It will be a true marriage and, since we aren't familiar with each other, I think we should start getting acquainted.'

Her lashes lifted, her eyes still darkened with the aftermath of pleasure, and she studied him a moment. Then she said, 'Yes, I have hesitations, though it isn't any mystery as to why. You know all about my background, Galen. Why do you think I'd have doubts about marrying a king?'

'I think many people in your position would have no doubts whatsoever. Not when they can have all the power, money, social standing they desire.'

She shook her head. 'Money is useful, I won't deny that, and power…well, I've never had any so I can see the attraction. And as for social standing, I don't care about that at all.'

Galen stared down at her, aware of his own growing curiosity. Her file had given him, as she'd said, knowledge of her background, but nothing else. He wanted to know more. He wanted to know where she'd found her backbone of steel and the flames of her anger, and the drive he could sense in her.

She hadn't let her background crush her and he wanted to know why not.

'Then why?' He searched her face. 'Is it because you and I don't know each other?'

'No.' She let out a slow breath. 'I've told you already. I told you last week. I'm a nobody, Galen. I don't know who my parents were, yet you have a whole line of portraits of your ancestors that go back hundreds of years.'

If only she knew. Luckily, she didn't. Yet he didn't think that her unknown parentage was the issue here, or not the main issue. There was something else going on.

He studied the shifting emotional currents in her gaze. 'What are you afraid of?'

Instantly she scowled. 'I am not afraid, I'm just not the type—'

'Don't lie to me,' he interrupted. 'I can see the fear in your eyes.'

She looked away, her lashes sweeping down, her body tensing beneath him. It was clear she did not want to talk about this and maybe, at a different time, he wouldn't have pursued it.

But she was going to be his queen, which meant he needed to know. He needed to know everything about her, her dreams and her hopes, and, yes, her fears too.

'If you think I'm going to let this go, you're mistaken,' he said.

'I don't have to tell you if I don't want to.'

He released one of her wrists and took her chin in his hand, turning her to face him and holding her there. 'Yes,' he insisted. 'You do.'

'I don't—'

'Remember what I told you in the nightclub? About being able to trust me?'

Her gaze sharpened like a spear. 'You took my baby,

Galen. You took him away from me. And that hurt. It *hurt*. How can I ever trust you after that?'

That spear slid beneath his skin, a sharp pain stabbing deep.

There had been many misunderstandings in the aftermath of Leo's birth, but, ultimately, he was the one who'd made the mistakes, starting with the fact that he hadn't worn a condom. Then he'd taken Leo away, thinking the worst of her, that she'd given him up in favour of money. Then he'd lost track of her so that she'd had to spend six months desperately trying to get her son back, all the while suffering postnatal depression.

She had lost everything because of him.

You took a crown that wasn't yours to take and then you took a child...

The spear slid deeper, into his heart.

She was right not to trust him. In her place, he wouldn't trust him either.

'I know,' he said. 'I know. And you have every right not to trust me. But...' He paused and held her gaze, letting the intensity of his regret blaze in his. 'I'm sorry for what I did, Solace. You will never know how sorry. I shouldn't have taken him from you, and I shouldn't have assumed the worst of you. I shouldn't have let you fall through the cracks and be forgotten. And I can promise you now, my word as a king, that I will *never* take Leo from you or you from him, not ever again.'

Her silver gaze cut him into shreds and he let her. He'd never let anyone study him so completely before and it wasn't comfortable, but he let her. He had the sense that if he didn't, she might not ever give him her trust and, if this was going to work between them, he needed it. And that a clear demonstration was required.

'People say things,' she said. 'People say things all

the time about how they can be trusted, and they always lie.'

The tight feeling in his chest tightened even more. 'What people?'

'Foster parents. Social workers. Government officials. I...' She broke off as if afraid of saying too much.

'You what?' He could feel the tension in her jaw, as if she was trying to pull away from his fingers, so he tightened his grip. He didn't want her to pull away. That would only delay this conversation and he didn't want to delay it. He was hungry for knowledge, everything about her, everything her background report hadn't said.

The look in her eyes now was pure defiance, her defensive anger leaping. 'I don't know you, yet you want to marry me, and I don't understand it. I don't trust it. No one has ever wanted me before so what makes you any different?'

Galen was conscious of a small, bright ache behind his ribs. As if part of him knew exactly what that felt like. Because even though he hadn't known the reason until later, he'd never forgotten the way Alexandros used to look at him. There had been no love there, only fury. Galen had never been a son to Alexandros, only a cuckoo in the nest.

Sometimes it still puzzled him why Alexandros hadn't tested his paternity the moment Galen had been born, but Alexandros had always been a proud man. Perhaps he'd never wanted anyone to know that he'd been cuckolded.

Or perhaps he just wanted a reason for his hate. Perhaps you were really his son after all, and he hated you anyway...

Galen stopped that thought dead in its tracks. No, he

wasn't Alexandros's son. It was the only logical reason for his father's loathing.

Regardless, he didn't want Solace to feel unwanted the way he had, because it wasn't her fault. Just as it hadn't been his fault his mother had found pleasure with someone else. His parents' disastrous marriage wasn't something he wanted to repeat himself. Not when he knew intimately how it could affect a child.

As he looked at her, at the anger in her eyes and the fear beneath it, he realised that her feelings about this mattered very much. She mattered. She was Leo's mother and the woman he'd chosen to be his queen and he wouldn't have her feeling somehow less due to something that had happened in her past. Because whatever it had been, she hadn't let it crush her. He'd genuinely never seen anyone so strong.

'Listen to me,' he said, and it was a command, with all the weight of his authority. 'You are the woman who left behind everything she knew to blackmail a king for the sake of her child.'

'I was naive. I should have—'

'Yes, you were naive. But you were also brave and fierce and resourceful.'

'I gave away my child!' Her voice shook, real distress in her eyes. 'My own mother gave me away without a thought and I just did the same thing. What kind of mother does that? What kind of person does—?'

Galen lowered his head and stopped her words with his mouth, a kiss to take away her pain. He could feel her trembling against him, but he didn't move. He let the warmth and weight of his body hold her fast. He remembered how she'd relaxed in his hold that night in the club, when he'd put his hand around her throat, and sure enough, after a long moment, he felt the trembles shaking her lessen gradually, until she was completely relaxed beneath him.

Her mouth grew soft under his and he lifted his head. She'd closed her eyes, her breathing a little too quick.

Of course, that was what scared her, her own self-doubt, and he knew all about that, didn't he? But she didn't need to doubt herself. She was a testament to her own strength and courage, and she needed to believe that.

'You weren't well,' he said, his voice flat and certain. 'You'd just had a baby that you'd had no idea you were going to have. And you thought that what you were doing was best for him. And when you realised you wanted him back, you went out and did exactly that.' He brushed his mouth across hers in a feather-light kiss. 'You were on your own, with no support. You did the best you could with what you had, and you put him first. Every decision you made was for him. That's the best kind of mother, silver girl. You're a tigress. And a tigress is exactly what a queen should be.'

She let out a long breath, and then, finally, her eyes opened again. 'I don't...' Her voice was soft and hoarse. 'What if you change your mind?'

This was a very real fear, he could see it in her eyes, and it puzzled him, because once he made a decision, he stuck to it. But...perhaps she didn't know that? And perhaps, at some point in her life, someone had changed their mind and it had hurt her?

'I won't change my mind,' he said with utter certainty. 'Kings generally don't. Why would you think I would?'

She stared at him for a long moment, the shifting emotional currents in her eyes unreadable. Then she said softly, 'It doesn't matter. Not now.'

'Solace—'

But this time it was her turn to interrupt. 'Kiss me, Galen.' Her hands lifted to his hair, her touch gentle. 'Make me feel good. Please.'

Her honesty laid him open. How could he refuse? Perhaps he didn't need to know everything now. The rest could wait.

So, he kissed her and then he made them both feel so good they forgot the rest of the world even existed for the rest of the night.

CHAPTER SEVEN

SOLACE SAT ON the hand-knotted silk rug and stared at the open folder she'd set on the floor in front of her. There was a neat stack of papers in the folder, the apparent life story Galen's PR team had given her that she was supposed to memorise.

Leo was kicking on a blanket beside her, the living area full of the happy sounds he was making.

She'd much rather have been playing with him, but Galen had been very clear that she was to know all the facts that were given in that stack of papers. She was supposed to know this woman's backstory backwards, so it was instinctive. So it was hers.

It wasn't hers, of course. It was a lie.

Galen had told her not to worry about her origins, that his PR department would 'put together' something for her that would explain where she came from and how they met. How the news of her apparent death had been a cover for something tragic that had happened in her past, but now she was happy and healthy, and she and Galen were to be married.

He'd said such an elaborate backstory was necessary to spare her and Leo as much of the ensuing media circus as possible, as well as to protect the palace. His office could hardly admit to lying about Leo's mother

death and so another explanation needed to be con-
structed.

Solace accepted that, but she didn't fully buy into it.
Galen's commitment to his reputation seemed excessive in her opinion, so she'd busied herself with research
on his rule, since now she was going to be his queen.

She hadn't known what to expect, perhaps a distant
king, a bit too rigid, a bit too staid, and one out of touch
with his subjects, but that wasn't what she'd found.

It was clear his people adored him and what she saw
on TV and on the web, at official functions and royal
walkabouts, and other events where he met his subjects,
was a warm, generous man who greeted his citizens
with genuine pleasure.

He took an active role in his parliament too, making sure the direction of his country was about putting
his people first. For example, he'd done an immense
amount of work tackling the poverty that had become
entrenched during his father's rule, though plenty of
the ruling classes had been unhappy about it and had
made no secret of the fact.

Galen had argued with them and then, when they'd
blocked his policies, he'd overruled them entirely, which
was something the King of Kalithera could legally do.

She admired that. She liked that he wasn't afraid to
fight for people who had no one to fight for themselves.
People like her, which meant she knew how much that
mattered.

But it did make her wonder why, if his people were
that important to him, he'd decided to essentially lie
to them.

He's altogether too fascinating.

Solace frowned at the papers in front of her, trying
not to pay attention to the complicated tangle of her

emotions whenever she thought of him. The intense physical desire and the constant knot of tension she'd always carried around with her relaxing whenever he was near. The curiosity she had about him…

Perhaps agreeing to marry him had been a mistake.

Too late now. Especially now you've told him everything.

She swallowed, remembering that night at the palace a week ago, where she'd lain under the reassuring weight of his body, warm and sated and relaxed in the aftermath of their passion. He'd told her that she could trust him and had given her a vow, the strength of an iron conviction in his blue eyes. She'd believed him. More, she'd *wanted* to trust him, and so she'd told him things she'd never thought she'd reveal to another person, about Leo and giving him up, and how, her own mother uppermost in her thoughts, she was afraid that doing so made her a terrible person.

But there had been no censure in his eyes. No blame. He'd been so very matter of fact about how she'd been unwell and vulnerable, and the blame was his. It had been his responsibility and he'd failed her. Then he'd given her a list of all the reasons why she'd make not only an excellent mother, but an excellent queen.

It wasn't what she was used to. Validation had never featured strongly in her life; she'd had to do it for herself.

Solace shifted a paper, staring sightlessly at the pile, memories of what had happened afterwards replaying in her head.

Of how he'd made her feel as good as she'd asked him to on that couch, and later, he'd gathered her in his lap at the table and fed her titbits while asking her every single detail of her life. And as if a dam had cracked and broken, out it had all come, the foster system and her chaotic childhood bounced from one family to the next. Her failed schooling and the menial jobs which were all she could get, and her dreams of going to university and being a lawyer and helping kids like she'd once been.

The only thing she'd kept back was about Katherine and the princess bed because it had felt like too stupid a thing to mention.

Through it all, Galen had listened attentively and asked questions, making his genuine interest clear, before telling her she could continue her education right here in Kalithera. He'd also pointed out that while she couldn't be a lawyer as Queen, that didn't mean she couldn't get a law degree and that her position would enable her to do more for kids like her than being a lawyer could.

She hadn't thought of that, and it pleased her more than she'd expected.

All in all, it had been a magical evening. For a night she'd felt safe, the low level of stress and anxiety that were always at a constant hum in the background quietening completely. That night she'd slept in his arms, in his bed, and even though they'd barely slept, she'd still felt rested the next day. The following morning, he'd taken her back to the little house by the sea, where Leo was.

She was to stay there until she was officially announced as his fiancée. He visited when he could, spending time with her and Leo, though he did not touch her again, which confused her. He'd said he wanted to wait until after they were married and that they needed to be discreet. His uncle, apparently, was a stickler for protocol and had taken an interest in Galen's more frequent visits to the house. Galen didn't want him going to the press before their engagement could be made public.

Galen was all about discretion, about how no gossip or scandal could be attached to the throne, though he hadn't been clear why this was important. Perhaps it was supposed to be obvious. Perhaps the reasons for the whole lying about her origins thing was supposed to be obvious too.

She didn't like it. Just as she didn't like the way Galen seemed to avoid questions about himself. She'd asked him a few times about his life and his background, what it was like growing up a prince. But he always seemed to evade answering. He'd distract her by talking about Leo, or about some aspect of protocol, or their future as the Kalitheran royal family. And his evasions always worked, because having a family of her own was a dream she'd never let herself have, and the thought of having a family with him seemed more and more attractive.

What about love?

The thought made Solace frown. Love had never been part of her childhood growing up and she'd never seen any evidence of it in the families she'd been placed with. Those families had all been dysfunctional in some way, love seeming to be given and withheld randomly from her perspective.

Having Leo had changed her thoughts on that, though, since she loved Leo regardless of what he did. She'd love him fiercely and without reservation until the day she died, but that was because he was her child. She couldn't imagine loving anyone else like that.

But don't you want to be loved like that?

Solace flicked the cover of the folder over the stack of paper, her heart beating fast. No, absolutely not. How could she? To be loved you had to be someone that someone else wanted, and, even if you were, being yourself wasn't enough for them to keep wanting you. People changed their minds, they just did.

Love wasn't something she could trust, full stop. Besides, she'd grown up fine without it and, also, she had Leo. He was all she needed.

'Solace?' The voice was deep and very familiar.

She looked up and saw Galen standing in the doorway. He was beautiful today, as he was every day she saw him, dressed in a perfectly tailored dark charcoal suit and crisp white cotton business shirt, and her heart gave a funny little leap in her chest.

She smiled, getting quickly to her feet and taking a few steps towards him before she realised what she was doing and stopped. 'Galen,' she said breathlessly, conscious of how much lighter the room seemed now he was here and how much her hands itched to touch him. 'I wasn't expecting you today.' There was an odd ache behind her breastbone, a yearning almost. She didn't understand it.

'I know. I had some time free this afternoon and thought I'd come and visit.' If he'd noticed her breathlessness, he gave no sign, strolling over to where his son lay on the blanket and bending to pick him up. Leo squealed with delighted laughter as Galen tossed him playfully up in the air a couple of times before settling him in the crook of his elbow.

Leo loved being with his father and it was clear from the brilliant smile on Galen's face that he loved being with his son.

But she knew that already. All the times Galen had visited, he'd attended to his son's needs, whatever they were, without hesitation and with absolute authority, whether it was feeding him, changing him, playing with him, or putting him down to sleep.

It made her heart melt to see them together, and as she looked at him now, smiling down at Leo, a tiny part of her couldn't help imagining what it would be like to have him look at her that way.

He never will. Why would he? Why would anyone?

Yet as soon as the thought had entered her head, Galen looked up and smiled, and her heart clenched tight as if he'd put his fingers around it and squeezed. 'I'm also here because I need to talk to you.'

Despite his smile, Solace tensed. The sensation, which for years had been second nature due to the precarious nature of her life, felt foreign now and even more unpleasant for it.

You're becoming too used to the good life. It'll all come crashing down at some stage and you know it.

No, he'd promised that he wasn't going to change his mind, that she could trust him, and he'd meant it. And so far, he hadn't done anything to betray her trust. He hadn't broken his word and sent her away, hadn't forbidden her to see Leo. Hadn't told her he didn't want to marry her after all.

'Oh?' She tried to sound casual. 'What things?'

Something in her tone must have given her away, because he frowned slightly. 'Don't look so worried,' he said. 'It's nothing.'

'I'm not worried,' she responded automatically.

He gave her a dubious look, then turned his attention to his son, rubbing his little tummy to make him giggle, before putting him back down on the blanket.

Straightening to his full height, Galen gave her an assessing look. 'I haven't changed my mind. If that's what's concerning you.'

Solace could feel a blush threatening, which was annoying. She wasn't especially comfortable with him knowing her well enough to be able to tell what she was thinking. It was a new experience for her, and she wasn't sure she liked it. 'I wasn't thinking that,' she said with some dignity.

The look in his blue gaze made it clear that he knew exactly how much of a liar she was, but, strangely, he didn't press her the way he normally did. Instead, he put his hand in the pocket of his trousers and brought out a small velvet box. 'I came here to give you this.'

She stared at the box, her heart giving another jolt. It looked like a ring box. 'I—'

'But before I give it to you, I need to know why you were lying to me just now.'

Okay, so she hadn't escaped after all. *Now* he was going to press her.

Solace forced her gaze from the box to his face. 'Only if you tell me why you felt the need to lie about my background.'

An expression she didn't understand flickered briefly over his perfect features and then was gone. 'It's to protect you from any unwanted attention, I told you. And to protect Leo too. The press can be persistent.'

'You told me my background didn't matter,' she pointed out.

'And it doesn't.'

'Yet you want to lie to your people about where I came from? With that nonsense cover story?'

The lines of his face hardened. 'You have a problem with it?'

'I have a problem with lying in general.' She hesitated. 'If you're so obsessed with not having any gossip or scandal attached to the throne, then why not just tell the truth? Or were you lying when you said my background didn't matter?'

'To be clear, *I* don't care about your background.' His gaze was now distinctly chilly. 'But the media will. The Kings of Kalithera marry aristocracy, it's traditional, plus I've a certain reputation to live up to, a reputation I've had to work at building. What do you think the media will do if they discover that the heir to the throne is the product of a one-night stand?'

'Why is your reputation so important though?'

He was silent, then after a moment said, 'Years ago, at Oxford, I didn't exactly cover myself in glory. I preferred partying to studying, drank too much, had many…liaisons. The media were all over it and the people here were less than impressed. They weren't supportive of me being King and I couldn't blame them. I've worked hard to show them those years are behind me, and I don't want them to think I'm backsliding now.'

She hadn't known that. She hadn't known anything about his past, but this put his reluctance to court media attention into context.

'Okay,' she said slowly. 'But you didn't seem to mind a media firestorm when I threatened to upload my pictures on the Internet. So, why are things different now?'

'Because I'm going to marry you.' There was a faint edge to his voice. 'You'll be bound to the same rules I am, since any scandal attached to your name will then reflect on me.'

'Yes, but it's been years since you were at Oxford, Galen. And your people love you. Why would you care about that now?' Pushing this would no doubt end up making things worse with him, but she couldn't let it go. If this was going to be an issue at some point in the future, she had to know now. 'And what if people find out about me anyway? You can't hide everything for ever. Surely if it got out that you lied about me, that would cause an even bigger scandal?'

'Oh, you can hide a great many things and for years, believe me.' His cool blue eyes were sharp. 'Are you worried about it getting out? Because I can assure you, it won't. The cover story my team put together for you is specifically designed to generate very limited interest. Enough to explain your miraculous reappearance from the dead, but not enough for anyone to investigate further.'

There it was again, that strangely 'off' feeling. As if he wasn't quite telling her the truth. Because maybe his people hadn't wanted him on the throne before, yet they certainly did now. He'd proved himself, surely? After over a decade on the throne?

She shook her head. 'I still don't understand. Do you not trust your people, Galen? Is that why you feel the need to lie to them?'

'I've told you why. I don't need to explain further.' His expression had become icy and hard; he looked every inch the proper king he was supposed to be. Very much *not* the man who'd taken her hands on the night of the ball, the man who'd seduced her thoroughly in the back seat of a limo, who'd pinned her beneath him only the week before. It was as if that man didn't exist.

But he did exist, didn't he? Behind those icy blue eyes and his cool and contained front, there was a different man, a passionate man. A man he was hiding from her, she was sure of it. She just didn't know why.

Solace came over to him and looked up into his perfect face. 'There's something you're not telling me, Galen? What is it?'

'Nothing that concerns you.' He seemed like a

stranger now, as if the warm, passionate man she'd known didn't exist. 'And I suggest you leave the subject alone in future.'

Her chest ached and she realised with a kind of shock that it hurt he wouldn't tell her what the issue was. Almost as if she wanted him to trust her just as much as she wanted to trust him.

Have you ever thought that he might not trust you? Trust is a two-way street, remember?

Except she hadn't remembered. For too long her life had been only about survival, having to focus solely on her own needs, because who else would? Having her son to care for felt like a natural extension of that, but Galen?

He wasn't a child, but a man with thoughts and feelings of his own. Another person. A person she wanted to trust, but of course that went both ways.

Do you want him to trust you?

She looked up into those cold blue eyes. A mask he wore, she knew, a front. But there was a man behind that front, a man she wanted very much to know if only he'd let her. And yes, she did want him to trust her.

'I'm going to marry you, Galen,' she said with some determination. 'And while it's true that I don't know much about marriage, I do know that any relationship has to start with trust. You told me I could trust you. So how about you do me the same courtesy?'

His expression didn't change. 'The subject is off-limits, Solace.'

If he thought that was going to put her off, he had no idea who he was dealing with. 'I see, so is that the marriage we're going to have? You dictating what we can and cannot talk about? And me meekly accepting it?' She lifted her chin. 'What kind of example does that set for our son? What kind of dysfunction will that lead to? Because, believe me, I've seen dysfunctional families. I've lived in them. And I won't have that kind of life for Leo. I won't.' She let him see her certainty, just so he knew what he was dealing with. 'So, if that's the kind of path you want to head down, then I'm telling you now that I won't marry you.'

At first Galen was conscious of nothing but shock. Then a wild fury burst up inside him that seemed totally out of proportion with a mere refusal.

She could *not* refuse him now. She'd agreed to the marriage, and he'd swung his whole PR team into action to put together a decent story of her origins and their love affair for the media. Enough to make sure Kostas didn't start making any trouble.

He'd started looking at his diary for possible wedding dates—asap of course—and had already postponed a visit to Isavere to see Augustine and Khalil, since Augustine was playing host that month. Both his friends had demanded an explanation, but he'd been vague. He hadn't wanted to tell them about Solace just yet. What he wanted, though, was a honeymoon, because he'd restrained himself from taking her for the past week and he was so hungry for her he could barely think.

Perhaps that had been a mistake. Perhaps he shouldn't have kept his distance. Part of it had been wanting to make sure Kostas didn't start paying too much attention to his visits to the little house where Leo was, and wondering why he was going more than usual and staying for longer. And part of it was wanting to test himself. It wouldn't be necessary, not once they were married, but the challenge would do him good. Because marrying her didn't change the fundamental problem: he wore a crown that might not be his and his past was still an issue while his uncle remained a threat.

He'd also thought she'd need some time to adjust.

Except he hadn't wanted her to adjust so far that she'd changed her mind about marrying him after all.

Trust. Why was she talking about that? She'd given him hers that night in the palace and he hadn't betrayed it. He never would. But surely she couldn't expect him to tell her everything? He couldn't tell her his secret. Even one other person was one person too many, and, when it was his country's safety at stake, he couldn't be too careful.

'No,' he said, iron hard, trying to crush the possessive fury that threatened to strangle him. 'You cannot refuse. You will be marrying me and that is final.'

But she kept shaking her head. 'You can't make me, Galen.'

'I can make you do anything I please,' he snapped, before he could think better of it. 'I'm the King.'

'Really?' she snapped back, grey eyes going silver with annoyance. 'I would never have guessed.'

For a moment anger burned in the air between them, made even worse by the seething sexual chemistry that the past week of abstinence had only built to fever pitch.

She looked stunning today in her casual, light blue skirt, and plain white T-shirt. Pretty and virginal and delicious, making him want to chase her, tear those clothes from her and take her on the floor. Uncover the passion that lurked just under the surface of her skin. That was what he wanted, not her naming all those doubts he'd firmly shoved to the back of his mind.

But she wasn't wrong about marriage or setting examples, and he knew all about that. He'd never witnessed Alexandros's marriage to his mother, but he could guess.

Once he'd asked Alexandros about his mother, but his father had cuffed him and told him never to speak her name in his presence again. Galen had only learned about her from his nannies, and they'd told him that Queen Katerina had been too young, too wild and too passionate for Alexandros, and he'd been too cold and proud for her. It hadn't been a love match. What it had been was a disaster from start to finish, they'd said.

Galen didn't want a marriage like that.

Dysfunctional, Solace had said, and she wasn't wrong. His family—though could he even call one father who'd loathed him a family?—had been extremely dysfunctional.

Is that what you want for Leo?

No, of course it wasn't what he wanted for Leo. But while he'd been able to mention having to rebuild his reputation after his time at Oxford, he hadn't been able to tell her the real truth. He couldn't tell a woman who wanted only safety and stability how precarious his throne was, and how all it would take was one test to bring it down.

You are so certain of what that test will say.

Yes, he was certain. The answer lay in the fury he felt hammering away inside him, in the insatiable need for her that pulsed in his blood. All the base, toxic emotions, anger and jealousy and lust. The emotions that his father had hated, that Galen had tried so hard to get rid of. And all because he'd hoped for one kind word, one smile. One sign that Alexandros hadn't really hated him as much as Galen had feared he did. But he'd never got that sign and he knew why: he was never Alexandros's son.

But what if you are? What if you're his biological son and he hated you anyway?

No, Galen didn't believe that. He couldn't. Alexandros was all ice, while Galen seemed to be only fire. Plus, his father had made it sound so easy, all the things Galen had to do, all the rules he had to obey. Yet none of it had been easy and he'd never seemed to do it right. 'One would think you were someone else's child,' Alexandros had told him coldly once, after he'd got the line of kings wrong, 'not mine.'

Galen turned away before he said something he'd regret. Leo was fussing, picking up on his parents' tension, so Galen bent and scooped him up, shamelessly using him as a distraction. 'Leo's tired,' he said flatly. 'I'll put him down.'

'He's not quite—'

'I know his schedule.' He was already heading for the door. 'I know what he needs.'

He looked down at his son as he stalked upstairs. All of this was for Leo, that was what he had to remember. Yes, he had to protect his country from Kostas, but Leo was the future.

And a legacy of lies that he'll be forced to continue when he grows up.

Ice settled inside him. What a throne he would leave his son… Mistake upon mistake, lie upon lie, and Leo would have to carry the burden, despite none of it being his fault. But what else could Galen do? The truth would expose Kalithera to Kostas and he wasn't prepared to risk that.

You could tell her. It's not a solution, but at least you won't be bearing this alone.

No, he couldn't share this. It wasn't a burden he'd

ever sought, but it was his, nonetheless. She'd been through too much. He couldn't ask her to carry this too.

She is strong, though, you know her strength. And she deserves to know what's at stake.

Taking Leo into his bedroom, Galen prepared him for a nap, laying him down in his cot. Then he stood there a moment, stroking his son's downy forehead a couple of times to settle him.

Perhaps she did deserve to know. So many people had let her down in her life and she had reason to question him. And he couldn't in good conscience keep refusing to answer, not if he wanted their marriage to be successful. He'd just have to consider what answer he could give, because the bare truth wasn't it.

Leo was blinking sleepily and looking as if he was ready for his nap, so Galen turned silently and went out, stalking down the hall and down the stairs, trying to wrestle his recalcitrant emotions into submission before he saw her again.

Yet the moment he stepped back into the living area and saw her standing by the window, the sun shining on her pale hair, his desire and his anger and his possessiveness roared back into life.

He didn't know what it was about her that made him feel this way. It was more than a physical response and it always had been, and whether it was her strength or her passion, or courage, or even the way she relaxed in his hold, trusting him completely, he didn't know. What he was sure was that he felt it and it seemed that no amount of trying to control it worked.

He shoved his hands into his pockets to keep them occupied, his fingers closing automatically around the box that contained the Star of Kalithera, the diamond ring that had graced the finger of many a Kalitheran queen.

Solace had drawn herself up, her chin lifted, looking as if she were Queen already.

'You're right, I'm not telling you everything,' he said, carrying on their conversation as if he hadn't left the room. 'But it's a secret that has the highest of stakes and it affects the throne. It affects Kalithera. It affects our son. And the fewer people who know about it, the better.' There, that was as much as he was prepared to give her.

'But I'm our son's mother, in case you'd forgotten, and you can't tell me?' She folded her arms, her grey eyes uncomfortably direct. 'I gave you my trust, Galen. Why can't you give me yours?'

Galen gritted his teeth, the edges of the ring box digging into his hand. 'I have. But this is a secret that threatens national security. I don't know what more I can say.'

'You could be honest with me,' she said in the same relentless tone. 'And I'm not talking about whatever your secret is. I'm talking about all the other things you avoid. You know everything about me, Galen. Everything. I didn't want to tell you about my postnatal depression, but I did. I didn't want to tell you about any of the other things either, how I wanted to be a lawyer, all those pipe dreams I had. Yet I did.' The silver in her eyes glittered. 'But I know nothing about you, except you were once a hell-raiser at university.'

'You know about me,' he argued. 'Everything you could want to know is on the Web—'

'I know all about the King. But nothing about the man.'

He didn't want to talk about it. He didn't want to go

into his cold, lonely childhood and all the things he'd done wrong that his father had never let him forget. Little things that had become big things, because the older he'd got, the more he'd realised that nothing he did would ever change Alexandros's opinion of him.

So, whatever he'd been told to do, he'd done the opposite, until Alexandros, disgusted with him, had sent him to Oxford. A mistake. Because there he'd found like minds in Augustine and Khalil, and there he'd allowed his anger and pain free rein in the form of drunken parties that had turned into orgies, endless nights in the clubs in London, too much alcohol and too much of other things. Getting into trouble with the police on the odd occasion, because he just hadn't been able to stop himself from pushing all the boundaries. And the more the press had made sensations out of everything the 'Wicked Princes' had done, the more he'd wanted to do them.

He'd been a selfish young man back then. Everything he'd done in a mindless knee-jerk reaction to Alexandros's active loathing. Goading him, pushing him, seeing how far he could take it before Alexandros finally repudiated him.

And then that party at one of his friends' houses in London had happened. There had been too much alcohol involved, too many party drugs, and when the police had finally broken it up, they'd discovered a whole lot of underage girls. The girls hadn't been invited, they'd sneaked in, and Galen hadn't known how old they were at the time. He hadn't had anything to do with them, but, as far as the press went, it had been the story of the year.

Alexandros's stroke had had nothing to with the media storm that had broken afterwards, or at least that was what the doctors had told Galen, but that had been the last straw as far as Alexandros had been concerned.

'You are not my son,' he'd said. 'And I will not have you on the throne. You are unfit to be King and you always have been.'

No, he did not want to tell Solace that. Not any of it.

Yet he had to give her something. He'd promised her a life, and he wanted her in his bed. He wanted her at his side as Leo's mother. She had to marry him and if she was going to then he wanted her to be happy. He did not want to repeat his parents' marriage.

'Very well,' he said flatly. 'My mother died when I was born, and my father was a cold and distant man. My childhood was unpleasant—I was rather a handful, and he didn't know how to deal with me, so when he sent me away to Oxford, it was a relief. I was called back to Kalithera after he had a stroke and when he died soon after, I ascended the throne. Is that what you wanted to know?'

She frowned, her silver gaze searching. 'What do you mean "unpleasant"?'

Galen found he was squeezing the ring box even tighter, a familiar hot fury coiling in his gut. A fury he'd been trying to deny for years without success, which didn't make sense. It had been years—*years*—since Alexandros had died and he had proved himself. He should not still be so angry with him.

'Alexandros was very strict,' he said. 'There was a level of behaviour expected and he punished me when I didn't meet those expectations. And I didn't meet those expectations very often. I was...rebellious and headstrong, and he was...exacting. He...did not like me.'

A look of fleeting shock passed over Solace's face

and she took a step towards him, then stopped. 'But he was your father. Why would he not like you?'

He gave a short laugh. 'Because nothing I did was good enough for him, nothing was right. And he always made it very clear that I wasn't the son he wanted.' The shock had gone from her expression now, leaving behind it a concern that felt like a needle sliding beneath his skin. 'It was years ago,' he went on roughly. 'There's no need to look at me like that. It wasn't as if I was starving on the streets.'

She took another step towards him. 'It doesn't matter. That's a terrible way to handle a child. And I should know. I had plenty of foster parents who treated me that way.' She gave him another of those direct, searching looks. 'Why did he do that to you? Who did he want you to be?'

He couldn't tell her the truth. That it didn't matter that Galen might actually be his son, what Alexandros wanted was for Galen not to exist.

'I don't know. Someone else.'

'But—' Solace began.

But nothing. He was done with this conversation. The more they talked about himself, the closer they got to the truth and he wasn't going to tell her. He couldn't.

'I think that's enough about me for one day.' He pulled out the ring box once again. 'Here. I need to give you this.'

But she didn't look at the box. She kept her direct grey gaze on him instead. 'You're very angry with him, aren't you?'

He could feel a muscle twitch in his jaw. 'My father is dead. I am his son, and I am the King now.' He flicked open the box. 'Hold out your hand.'

She didn't move. 'No.'

His impatience rose and along with it, his frustration. 'Your hand, Solace.'

The look in her eyes was sharp as a blade and there was no escape. 'You told me that I could trust you and yet you won't trust me.'

'It is not a matter of trust. I can't—'

'Then what kind of future can we have? What kind of future are we going to give our son?'

She was so definite. So certain. The only woman who'd ever confronted him like this—the only *person*. And he could feel his grip on his temper loosening, the hot, suffocating emotions that had always lurked too close to the surface all boiling up.

He was so tired of having to keep a grip on them. So tired of lying, of having to protect a secret that wasn't even his. So tired of trying to be better than a man who hated him and who hadn't wanted him on the throne.

So tired of trying to put his past behind him in order to be a good king.

There was only one way to deal with his anger and that was to turn it into pleasure and let it burn the way he'd so often done at Oxford. But it wasn't some random woman he wanted to burn with him, he wanted Solace.

He'd *always* wanted her. Even when he hadn't known anything about her, not even her name, he'd wanted her. Those silvery eyes behind the mask, the way she'd looked at him, not knowing he was a king. The way she'd wanted him just as badly as he'd wanted her…

She'd haunted his dreams for over a year and he'd thought at first it was just physical. But it wasn't. It never had been.

She'd seen something in him that no one else did, maybe the hot-headed, restless, stubborn boy he'd once been, and she'd matched him.

She was as passionate and stubborn as he was, which would have made it a marriage made in heaven if her blunt honesty hadn't cut through the web of lies he'd surrounded himself with.

He wanted to close the space between them, wanted to hold her down and restrain her, feel her melt against him in total acceptance, because that was what she'd always given him. She surrendered to him as he was, not a king, but a man.

But there was no surrender in her now.

He could make her, render her incoherent with pleasure. But it wouldn't mean anything if he had to take it from her. She had to give him her surrender willingly.

Abruptly the expression on her face changed, and she was the one coming to him, crossing the space between them, the look in her eyes full of a compassion he'd never seen before.

She lifted her hands and laid them on his chest, her silver eyes glittering as she looked up at him. 'I'm sorry,' she said. 'I don't want to force anything from you. You don't have to tell me if you don't want to.'

The apology went through him like a sword. He was used to digging in, to being stubborn, to resisting, and, used to the fight, he stared down at her, for a second lost.

But he saw the flames in her eyes suddenly leap, the heat between them building, and he didn't think.

He lifted his hands, plunged his fingers into her hair and took her mouth as if it were water and he were a man dying of thirst.

CHAPTER EIGHT

Solace had taken one look at the rigid lines of Galen's face and had known that one of them had to give in. At least in this moment. Because whatever secret he was keeping it had clearly trapped him and was torturing him.

There had been fury in his eyes and yet he'd been so still, as if frozen, rigid as a board while a volcano of emotion erupted behind his eyes. And all she'd been able to think about was how, if she wanted his trust, forcing him to give her something he'd told her he couldn't wasn't the way to go about it.

Trust was slow to earn, and she knew that all too well. He'd taken some steps to building it with her, but she needed to take some steps too. It wasn't all on him, no matter what had happened with Leo, and it couldn't be, not if she wanted this marriage to work.

Plus, while fighting him was exhilarating, that couldn't be the whole of their relationship. Someone had to take the first step towards a compromise, and it was clear to her that he either wouldn't or couldn't. Whatever this secret was, keeping it was hurting him, she could see it in his eyes, and it wasn't until this minute that she realised she didn't like that. His pain mattered to her. In fact, it made her hurt too.

His father and his 'unpleasant' childhood, for example. Because she knew what it felt like. His upbringing might have been a thousand times more privileged than hers, but that didn't make it a happy one. And it was clear it still affected him on some deep level.

He'd always been kind to her, right from that first encounter, and, despite the pain involved with Leo being taken from her, she couldn't keep throwing that in his face. They had to move on from it somehow, and he was trying to make it right. He deserved her kindness as much as she deserved his.

So, she'd crossed the gap between them and laid her hands against his chest, told him she'd never force anything from him that he didn't want to give, and in that instant she'd seen shock leap in his eyes, then a wild, rushing heat.

Then he was kissing her, his mouth on hers hot and demanding and feverish, and she could taste the need in him. Some part of her recognised it. The need for connection, for closeness, and she understood. His childhood sounded as if it had been as barren as hers, so of course that was what he wanted.

But he'd done so much for her already and it was time for her to reciprocate.

Solace tore her mouth from his and pushed him back over to the couch. He went without resistance, dropping down on it. Then she went to her knees in front of him, leaning forward between his powerful thighs, reaching for the buttons of his suit trousers.

His fingers wove their way through her hair. 'I promised myself I wouldn't touch you,' he murmured. 'I promised myself I'd be good.'

'You don't have to be good.' She undid the zip of his trousers, her fingers already shaking as blind need began to rise. 'I want to do something for you, Galen. You've done so much for me, now it's my turn.'

His grip in her hair tightened. 'But this marriage, Solace? What about that?'

It had always been something of a bluff. She'd never been going to refuse, not when it would leave her in the same position, having to choose between staying for her son and leaving for herself. And she'd have to leave, because she couldn't take Leo away from Galen. Not only when it would condemn Leo to the kind of life she'd had herself, but also it would hurt Galen immeasurably.

She couldn't do that. Just as she couldn't walk away from him. And it wasn't to do with his power or the fact that he was a king or because of their chemistry. It wasn't about the kind of life he could give her. It wasn't even because he was Leo's father.

It was him. She wanted to stay with him because when she was in his arms, she felt safe. When he looked at her, she felt as if she was worth something for the first time in her life. And when she spoke, he listened. She wasn't invisible with him.

With him she was seen.

'I'll marry you, Galen,' she said, then reached inside his trousers and found him, hard and ready and hot in her hands.

His body was tense, all his muscles rigid, and he murmured something sharp and bitten off as she slowly drew him out. His skin was smooth and velvety, and her mouth watered as she leaned forward to taste him.

He tightened his fingers convulsively as she licked him, tracing the long, hard line of his sex with her tongue. Then he growled her name as she took him into her mouth, taking him deep. His hands firmed and she let him guide her, because this was for him, after all, and she wanted to give him everything she could.

She let him direct her, sucking him hard and then

softer, slower, her own fingers digging into his rock-hard thighs, dizzy and drunk on the taste of him.

She didn't stop. She took him to the edge and when the climax hit him, it came hard and fast, his grip on her hair painful, his low, masculine growls of satisfaction making her own need build.

But she didn't care about herself, not this time, because there was so much satisfaction in giving him what he needed. She hadn't realised until now how good that would feel. So much of the time she had to put her own needs first, but taking care of his, taking care of him, satisfied something deep in her soul she hadn't realised was there.

After a moment, Galen loosened his fingers in her hair and pulled her up into his lap, holding her with her head against his broad chest, and for a while they sat like that, content in the silence.

Then Galen said, his voice a low rumble in her ear, 'Nine months before I was born, my mother had one night with one of the palace staff. She and my father were trying for an heir at the time.'

Solace went very still, staring at the white cotton of his shirt.

'She died a few days after I was born due to complications from the birth. There were rumours about the affair, but no one knew for certain. No one except my father. A simple paternity test would have solved the issue of who my actual father was, but Alexandros was a proud man. He couldn't stand the thought of anyone knowing his wife had been unfaithful, and he needed an heir, so he claimed me as his anyway.'

He was very warm, the tension gone from his muscles, an arm around her waist. She could hear the beat of his heart. It was fast.

So…what did all of this mean?

'Alexandros never had me tested,' Galen went on. 'He didn't tell me that there was a possibility he wasn't my father until I was called back from Oxford after his stroke. That's when he…disowned me. He told me about my mother and her affair, that it had always been clear to him that I wasn't his son and my behaviour at Oxford proved it. Then he told me he was going to pass the crown on to my uncle, Kostas.'

Shock rippled through her, but she stayed silent. It was clear he still had things to say.

'Kostas never cared about the people of this country. It was all about big business and making the rich richer while making the poor even poorer. I couldn't allow that to happen. I couldn't allow him to rule and so when Alexandros died before he could formally change the succession, I took the throne even though it might not be mine by right.' He paused. 'Everyone assumed I was the true heir and so I let them keep on believing that in order to protect Kalithera. Kostas doesn't know the truth but Alexandros must have let slip something because he'd always been deeply suspicious of me. I cannot afford to give him any reason to question me or my rule, especially not considering my past, because if I do, if I have to take that test and it finds I'm not Alexandros's son, then the throne will pass to him.'

Slowly Solace shifted her head and looked up at him. 'But you don't know for sure that you're not Alexandros's son?'

Galen's deep blue eyes were impenetrable. 'No. But if I'm not, I'll have to abdicate in favour of Kostas. He's already tried to block a number of the policies I've put in place to help tackle the poverty we've had here, and he's made no secret of the fact he wants to turn Kalithera into a tax haven.' His expression hardened. 'I won't have it. I won't allow my country to be turned over to big business and criminals, and if I have to lie in order to protect it, I will.' Anger glittered in his eyes now, the strength of his conviction finding an echo inside her too. She knew what it was to fight for something, to do anything you could to protect the things that mattered, that you cared about.

But still, that this would be the secret he was hiding had never even occurred to her, and she could see now why he hadn't wanted to tell her. This affected not only the stability of his throne, but his entire country.

She studied his beautiful face. 'You don't have to take the test, surely?'

His expression betrayed nothing. 'No, I don't. But if questions about my paternity were asked and I refused to take a test, it would create doubt in people's minds. There would be questions about my right to the throne, especially considering my past, and Kostas would take advantage of that. And of course, if they'd question me, they'd definitely question Leo.'

The shock spread out, ice water in her veins.

Of course. This affected Leo too.

'Galen—'

'That is why I cannot have any press looking too closely at me. It's not just about what happened in Oxford, it's about Kostas too. He's tried to use my past against me before, to discredit my suitability to rule, and I cannot give him any more ammunition. That's why I had to bring Leo here. I cannot have a son of mine, my DNA, living anywhere but with me. I have to go on as if I was Alexandros's son, even if I'm not, because that's the only way I can protect this country and the people in it.'

She put a hand on the cotton of his shirt, feeling the

warmth of his hard chest beneath it. 'But you might actually be his son, in which case none of this is necessary.'

His expression hardened. 'But I might not. In which case the throne goes to Kostas and everything I've tried to do for my people will be undone.'

It was a terrible problem, she could see that now. For anyone else, a simple test would have cleared up any questions, but not in this instance. A simple test would certainly give answers, but it also might lose him everything. Of course, he couldn't take it.

'You can't let that happen, can you?' she murmured, looking up into his face. 'That's why you have to lie about me?'

'I've never wanted to lie, believe me,' he said bleakly. 'But for the past ten years it's been more a lie of omission than anything else, at least, until...' He stopped.

But she didn't need him to go on. She knew already what he was going to say.

Until Leo had been born. Until she'd turned up, complicating everything.

Pain twisted in her gut, her throat closing. 'Oh, God. Leo and I must—'

'No,' he interrupted, unexpectedly fierce. 'I will never regret Leo. *Never.* And you...' His blue gaze burned. 'I will never regret you, either.'

The pain eased, but the lump in her throat didn't go away, no matter how many times she swallowed. 'But you have to lie to your people for me.'

Galen touched her cheek gently, but the intensity in his gaze didn't falter. 'You are worth every lie I have to tell. Every single one.'

Her chest ached with a sudden tightness, and she had to look away from the intensity in his eyes, concentrating instead on her thumb moving across the fine cotton of his shirt, stroking him. 'You don't think you're Alexandros's son, do you?' It seemed obvious since if he truly believed he was, then he wouldn't have gone to all this trouble to play games with the truth. And he would have taken that test.

He didn't even hesitate. 'No. I do not.'

'Can I ask why?'

He didn't answer immediately, reaching down for her hand where it lay on his chest and taking it in his. 'Alexandros didn't just not like me, he hated me. I could see it in his eyes every time he looked at me. And just in case I didn't understand why, he told me before he died that I was no son of his.' Galen paused a moment. 'That trouble I had at Oxford was a party I attended that ended up in the press. There was alcohol, party drugs, plus some under-aged girls somehow got in, and the fact that I was there was made into a big deal. Alexandros was furious and told me that was the last straw, that no son of his would ever have been involved in that.' Galen shook his head. 'He said I'd never make a good king, that I was unfit for it, which is why he was going to pass the crown to Kostas.'

Solace felt something inside her shift and tighten at the echo of pain she could hear beneath the words. 'You wanted to be his son?'

A flicker of anger crossed his face. 'Once, I did. Once, I wanted to follow in his footsteps. And I'd have done anything to get him to look at me with kindness, just once, but...' Galen glanced at her. 'There are only so many times you can try pleasing someone determined to resent your very existence. So, no. No, I didn't want to be his son.' A muscle flicked in his hard jaw. 'Sometimes I think it wasn't my behaviour he wanted to correct, but my very existence.'

Her throat constricted with a terrible sympathy. 'It's

not your fault, Galen. You do know that, don't you? It wasn't fair for him to take it out on you. You can't take responsibility for the mistakes your parents made.'

His gaze met hers. 'And yet that is all I'm doing now, is it not? I didn't want the crown in the end. I wanted him to disown me, I wanted him to admit that he hated me, that he'd never wanted me, and that's exactly what he did.' Galen let out a breath. 'Sometimes I wonder if I only took the crown to spite him. Because he was so desperate for me not to have it.'

Her hand in his felt warm and so did he, and she wished she could give him the same kind of reassurance that he gave her. 'No,' she said quietly. 'That's not why you took it. You took it because you wanted to protect your country and do right by its people. That's what being a good king is.'

There were shadows in his eyes. 'But I'm not a good king, Solace. I'm not…suited for it. I did everything I could to throw the crown in my father's face and when he disowned me, I instantly took it back.'

'Yes. To save your country.'

'Or was it more to spite my father? Perhaps that I could do a better job than my uncle is just another lie I tell myself.'

She stared at him. 'Do you really believe that?'

He said nothing, but he didn't need to. She could see the truth in his face.

'No,' she said again, more fiercely this time. 'No, it's not true. I did my research about your rule, I saw what kind of king you are. You're compassionate and kind, and you care so much about your people. You want to do the best for them, and you're prepared to fight for them.' She took her hand from his and laid her palm against his cheek, feeling the warmth of his skin. 'Your father was wrong, Galen. You're a good king. You're an excellent king. And the only standards you should be meeting are your own.'

'Solace…'

'Listen to me. I don't know who my father is, or my mother. And I'll never know since they didn't want to be found. So I had to decide who I wanted to be. I think, in the end, all you can do is decide that it doesn't matter what your background is or where you came from. Or who brought you up and how. All that matters are the choices you make, and only you get to decide who you are.' She stroked her thumb across his cheekbone. 'Don't let one man's wrong opinion of you determine who you get to be, Galen. You are more, so much more than that.'

He gave her a long look and didn't speak. Then slowly, he nodded. 'I shouldn't have told you all of this, you know.'

'So why did you? What changed your mind?'

'You've been so very honest with me and so I wanted to be honest with you.' He caught her hand against his cheek. 'You were right about trust. I want this marriage to work, and we have to start somewhere.'

In spite of herself, Solace's heart gave the oddest leap. She smiled. 'I want it to work too. And speaking of trust, I won't tell anyone else what you told me, Galen. I swear on Leo's life.'

He nodded then opened his hand and bent his head, dropping a kiss into the middle of her palm. 'I know you won't. Now… I'd better do what I came here to do.' Reaching into his trouser pocket, he brought out the ring box and flicked it open. Sitting in it was the largest diamond Solace had ever seen.

Galen took the ring out of the box and slid it gently onto her finger.

It fitted perfectly.

CHAPTER NINE

A WEEK LATER, Galen sat in a chair and watched Solace turn slowly in front of the mirror the designer had brought into the living area, unable to tear his gaze from her.

She wore a gown that had been made for her by one of Kalithera's best designers—Galen was a firm believer in locally made products.

It was strapless, with a fitted silver bodice that then frothed out into a cloud of silver skirts down to the ground. The silk shimmered and the whole thing had been hand-beaded, so the gown sparkled as if it had been dusted with diamonds. It left her shoulders bare, her pale hair falling down her back, and she looked like an angel. She looked like a queen.

It was the gown she'd wear for her formal presentation as his bride, a tradition that all Kalitheran rulers followed when they got engaged.

Galen had been reluctant to give one for himself, considering the stakes, but since it was part of tradition and it would cause more comment if he *didn't* present her, he couldn't afford not to do it. So, he'd ordered the ball to be arranged and quickly.

Their marriage needed to happen as soon as possible since he wanted Solace with him at the palace. But since she hadn't been formally presented yet, her presence would have caused a lot of unwanted gossip and so she had to stay in the little house by the sea with Leo.

He hadn't wanted to tell her the truth about his paternity, yet that day he'd tried to give her his ring, when she'd gone on her knees for him and given him so much pleasure, the words had just spilled out. He'd been carrying them for so long and he was tired of it.

In fact, there were a great many things he was tired of, and even though he'd told himself he didn't want to share the toxic relationship he'd had with his father with her, he'd told her anyway. And once he had, he couldn't remember why *not* doing so had felt so important.

She'd understood too, and after he'd told her he'd felt as if a weight had lifted from him. His burdens had always been heavy ones and he was used it, but it was good to share the load a little.

Afterwards, he'd wondered if she'd see him differently once she knew that his throne might not be his. That she'd view his kingship, too, in a different light, after he'd told her about his father's belief that he was unfit to rule.

Yet she hadn't. She'd laid her hand on his cheek and told him he was a good king, an excellent king even, and there had been conviction in her eyes. As if she believed everything she said.

He hadn't known that was something he'd needed to hear until she'd said it. He hadn't known it would matter to him, but it did. And so did she.

There didn't seem to be much point in testing himself by keeping his distance from her, so he didn't, and those few hours he could spare with her were precious and not just for the pleasure they both took from each other, but also for afterwards, lying in each other's arms and talking. Her telling him about the shock of her pregnancy and those six months where she'd struggled. While he shared his own shock at finding out he had a son. And other things too, plans for their little family and whatever the future might hold.

She was nervous about the ball, though. It put her under pressure, and he was well aware of the fact. He'd drilled her in her backstory personally, making sure she knew it backwards and forwards in the hope it would make her feel more comfortable when the time came. And he'd promised her that he'd be at her side the whole night, especially with Kostas likely to be there. He wouldn't leave her to manage on her own.

He understood her nervousness. She hadn't been brought up for this. It was alien to her, as was Kalithera, its politics and its language. She could get away with not knowing any of that, since he'd kept as much of her own story as he could in the fiction they'd crafted for her, but if there was an error or inconsistency...

The palace would be exposed and potentially the throne along with it.

Solace's grey eyes caught his in the mirror for a second, then she hurriedly looked away, a stain of pink in her cheeks.

Galen sat forward. 'Would you excuse us?' he said to the designer, who inclined her head and vanished through the doorway.

Once she'd gone, Galen rose from the chair and crossed to where Solace stood, coming to stand behind her. 'Do you like the dress? You look unsure.'

She let out a breath. 'No, I love the dress. I just...feel a bit like an imposter in it.'

He met her gaze in the mirror and held it. 'You're beautiful in it. You're a queen.'

The expression on her face eased. 'I had a foster mother once, Katherine, who was going to adopt me and she said that when I was finally her daughter, she'd get me a princess bed.' Solace glanced back at her reflection. 'Except she changed her mind, and I never got that bed. And now look at me.' Her voice had gone husky. 'I never thought…'

That this was a painful memory for her was obvious. That she'd offered it to him without him asking or pressing for more made his breath catch.

This was her trust, he understood, and it was rare and precious, and it made his heart ache.

'You never thought that you were that princess all along, hmm?' He settled his hands on her waist, the beads pressing against his palms. 'And not only a princess, but a queen-in-waiting.'

Her hands came to rest over his, her eyes shimmering with tears. 'It's silly to feel so much about a stupid bed. But to this day I don't know why she changed her mind about the adoption. Whether it was something I did or said… All I remember is that I didn't get the bed.'

It wasn't only about the bed, he could see that. Solace had been promised a mother, being part of a family, and then this Katherine had changed her mind. There must have been some reason for it, and hopefully a good reason, but right now Galen didn't care what that reason was. Whatever it had been, it had hurt her.

'It would not have been something you did.' He let the conviction ring in his voice the way it had rung in hers a week ago. 'I can guarantee you that right now. Because who wouldn't want you, silver girl?'

A tremulous smile turned her mouth. 'Some people might not.'

'Those people are fools. Also, you don't need Katherine. I'll get you a princess bed. I'll get you as many princess beds as you desire.'

The pain in her eyes faded, to be replaced by something else, something much warmer, the smile losing its tremulousness and deepening. 'I don't need a princess bed, Galen. I don't even need a crown. You make me feel like a queen already.'

His breath caught at that smile, at the look in her eyes, making him feel as if someone had punched him in the stomach.

She feels something for you.

The thought crossed his mind like a comet, trailing flames and sparks, and it shocked him. Because somehow it had never occurred to him that emotions might factor into any of this. His own, certainly not. But hers? He'd had no idea.

It changed things. It changed things completely.

This marriage wasn't based on emotion, but necessity. He hadn't thought about feelings.

Except you feel something for her too, you can't deny it.

Galen let her go and turned away abruptly, unable to bear her gaze. He took a couple of steps towards the door, then stopped. His heart was beating faster than it should and he had the strangest urge to stride back to her, pull her into his arms and keep her there, never let her go.

No, he didn't feel anything for her. Or at least nothing beyond friendship, but her… She felt something for him, and what it was, he wasn't sure, but one thing he did know: he didn't want her to feel it. Because while he could give her a crown and a home, create a safe and stable space for her and their son, if it was love she wanted, he couldn't give her that.

How could he? When he didn't even know what love was? His mother had died having him and his father had hated him from birth. No one had ever shown him, no one had ever taught him.

Perhaps there's a reason for that. And it's not because you were potentially another man's child, but because you're someone no one can love.

Cold seeped through him. All his life, his father's hatred had never wavered and maybe the reason was him. A wrongness in himself, that he'd been born with, that made him impossible to care for.

He'd tried over the years to compensate for it, to learn how to be a decent king, He'd made mistakes—he was even continuing to make them—and perhaps he could even learn to be a decent husband and father. But he had to face the fact that he'd never be able to compensate for that wrongness, that lack of whatever it was that would have made his father love him.

He had no examples to follow, no rules or guidelines to keep him on the right track. And he couldn't afford mistakes, not with Solace and not with his son. He had to be perfect for both of them, because they both deserved perfection.

Except he wasn't perfect. And he'd fail, the way he'd failed with Alexandros. He'd make mistakes and he'd hurt them.

Then she'd finally see that wrongness in you, and then she'll end up hating you too.

The cold turned to ice. He couldn't allow that. He couldn't allow their marriage to turn toxic because of him. It was better she felt nothing for him, because it would turn to hate in the end, and that would hurt not only Solace, but Leo too.

'Galen?' Her voice came from behind him, soft and puzzled-sounding. 'Is there something wrong?'

Unfair of you to bring her into this mess you created and give her such a heavy burden of responsibility to carry. Especially considering you cannot give her what she so desperately needs.

The ice spread through him, freezing him solid. Because regardless of how she felt about him, Solace herself needed to be loved. No one in her life ever had, and the closest she'd got to having it had been Katherine, who'd changed her mind.

Another impossible situation.

And yes, it was impossible. He'd never been loved himself, he had no idea what it felt like, so how could he give it to her? He 'd be condemning her to a loveless marriage, because how could he change his mind and not marry her? Do to her what Katherine had done to her?

He took a breath but it felt as if he couldn't get enough air. It made his chest hurt, as if someone had wrapped barbed wire around it. He didn't want to turn around and meet those sharp grey eyes of hers, the ones that looked deep into his soul. She'd be able to see what was there, or rather the lack of what was there. She'd know. He could pretend with everyone else, but he couldn't pretend with her. That would be one lie too many.

He'd promised he'd marry her, and he couldn't break that promise, not when he'd given his word. He couldn't break that trust. But she had to know that was all she'd ever have from him. Their marriage would be based on mutual respect and the bond they shared as parents, but that bond didn't include love. Maybe it never would.

Galen turned.

She stood in front of the mirror with her back to it, her gaze soft. There was a small crease of concern between her fair brows.

She was so beautiful. Dressed all in silver and looking like spun starlight.

His chest ached, the barbed wire digging in. She was going to make such a wonderful queen. A better queen than he was a king.

His expression must have given him away, because she came over to where he stood, her dress glittering with every step she took. 'Something's wrong.' She stopped in front of him, the crease between her brows deepening. 'What is it?'

She could read him so well, she always had. And he couldn't keep it from her. She'd taught him about honesty and now he had to give it back to her.

'This marriage between us,' he said, keeping his voice very level and measured. 'It isn't one of the heart. You do understand that, don't you?'

'I'm not quite sure what you mean.'

'I mean, we're not marrying for love.'

'I know.' Expressions flickered across her face, gone so fast he couldn't read any of them, but she clasped her hands, the beginnings of a hopeful smile curving her mouth. 'But… I hope that eventually, given time, we might—'

'No,' he interrupted, the ice inside him creeping into his voice no matter how hard he tried to stop it. 'That's what I'm trying to say, Solace. Love will *never* be part of it.'

For a second there was shock on her face and a bright flare of what could only be anguish in her eyes. Then it was gone, nothing but the guardedness he remembered from when she'd first tried to blackmail him returning. 'Can I ask why?' Her tone gave nothing away.

'Because love was never a part of my life,' he said

bluntly. 'I know what it isn't, but I couldn't tell you what it is. And I feel that you should know that before we marry.'

Her chin lifted in that challenging way she had and she gave him a look that was almost regal. 'And why did you feel that I should know that?'

Tension pulled his muscles rigid, and he found himself wishing that he could take her in his arms and kiss her senseless so she wouldn't ask him these questions. So they wouldn't have to have this conversation. But it was too late to take what he'd said back and so he went on, 'Because I want you to be clear what I can and cannot give you. I can promise you the life you always wanted and a crown too, as well as a family. But love will not be a part of it.' He took a silent breath, because he could see only one way out for her. 'I won't break my promise to you. I gave you my word that I wouldn't change my mind, and I haven't. But the choice to go through with this marriage is yours. And if you decide not to, then I understand.'

Solace stared at him, and he couldn't have said what she was thinking. Then, abruptly, anger sharpened in her gaze. 'I see. You haven't got the guts to break it off yourself, so you're going to make me do it?'

This time the shock was his, echoing through him, cold as a north wind, a growing anger coming along behind it. 'No, that's not what I said. I don't want to get out of it.' He took a step towards her. 'I mean to marry you, believe me. But I needed you to know that if you're looking for love from me, you won't get it.'

He stood there radiating tension, looking impossibly gorgeous in dark trousers and a shirt of midnight blue.

His eyes, though, had gone dark, the lines of his beautiful face rigid.

She didn't understand why they were having this conversation. His proclamation about love had seemed to come out of the blue. Or perhaps not. She'd told him about Katherine and the princess bed, because the words had just fallen right out of her. It had felt natural to tell him, and when he'd looked at her in the mirror and said that people were fools not to want her and that he'd buy her a princess bed, there had been nothing but conviction in his eyes.

Her heart had tightened in that moment, as if someone had wrapped their fingers around it and squeezed hard, and so she'd told him he made her feel like a queen, because it was the truth. And more than that, she felt like *his* queen.

Yet then he'd pulled away.

She'd been too honest, hadn't she? She'd let her feelings show, feelings that had been building inside her for the past week they'd been together, that had coalesced that moment he'd looked into her eyes in the mirror and told her she was a queen.

She could feel it inside her now, a longing, an ache. And she knew that continuing to argue with him about this was betraying herself even further and that he would know. But suddenly she didn't care.

This marriage with him was something she'd come to want, but not only for Leo. All her life she'd wanted safety and stability, a home, a family, and he was going to give her that. But now, as she looked at him, so impossibly beautiful, the dense blue of his eyes full of shadows, she knew that wasn't enough.

She wanted him. She wanted to love him and be loved by him in return. And she was going to argue for it, because the objections he was giving her didn't make any sense. 'Why not?' she asked.

A muscle flicked in his hard jaw. 'I told you. How can love ever be a part of our marriage when I have no idea what love is?'

'I don't believe that. You think anyone ever loved me growing up? You think any one of those families ever cared about me? No, they didn't. But I know what love is, Galen, because I love our son.' She took a step towards him, wanting him to understand. 'And you can't tell me you don't love him. I see your face when you look at him, when you smile at him. Whether you know it or not, you love him just as much as I do.'

'Is it love, Solace?' His voice was cool. 'Or is it because he's my heir and I'm supposed to feel that way?'

He couldn't possibly think that. *Why* would he think that? He was Leo's father, and she could see the love in his eyes when he held Leo in his arms. He had to feel it just as she did.

Why would he? When he was brought up by a man who hated him?

She'd been brought up by people who hadn't cared about her, too. Except…there had been times where she'd seen moments of caring in a playground, where a mother would comfort a crying child. Or even in the street, a husband pulling his wife in for an embrace and a kiss. Brief moments, enough to wonder what it would be like to have those for herself.

But Galen wouldn't have had those moments, not in the insular world of the palace, with a father who'd never seen him as a son and never treated him like one.

'It's not duty,' she said. 'I'm his mother and I can tell you I don't feel it's duty.'

'Be that as it may, the bond between a child and parent is different.' He seemed to be retreating from her, withdrawing into a distant kind of formality. 'I'm not trying to be cruel, Solace, I hope you know that. I just… I've made so many mistakes with you.' His eyes had darkened into the same midnight as his shirt. 'I don't want to hurt you any more than I have already.'

'You think I'm not hurt now?' Even two weeks ago, she'd never have admitted that. But things were different now and she wanted him to know that this mattered to her.

'I'm sorry.' There was a fine edge of pain in his voice. 'But that's why I had to tell you. Better you know going in exactly what you can expect from me.'

'Which is nothing.' It hurt. It hurt more than she thought possible. Because she hadn't known what she'd wanted until now, not truly. Hadn't known what she craved with every part of her, which was him.

Anguish glittered in his eyes. 'I'm sorry,' he said again. 'I'm trying to do the right thing for you.'

'What if the right thing for me is you loving me?' She couldn't help herself, the words came right out. 'What if the right thing for me is us loving each other?'

'Solace—'

'Don't we deserve that, Galen? We had no one growing up, no one who cared, but now we have each other. We want the same things so why can't we have them? And why can't we give them to our son?'

His eyes were almost black now, as if the shadows were consuming him whole. 'You deserve it, silver girl. And so does Leo, that goes without question. But…it took me years to learn how to be a decent king and I've made so many mistakes. I'm still making them. And it will take me years to learn how to be a decent husband too, if that's even possible. I'll fail you, Solace. At some point I will, and I'll fail Leo too, and I cannot… I just cannot bear that.' He was holding himself so rigidly he looked as if he might shatter at the slightest touch.

She had been angry with him just before, but it had all gone now, leaving behind it an aching sorrow. All those years he'd spent trying to please the one man who should have loved him, who should have encouraged him to be the passionate, caring, protective man that he was. And who instead had hated him, setting him up for failure time and time again. Making him doubt himself and his kingship. Turning his caring nature against him so that he had to lie, so that he had to be someone he was never meant to be.

'You haven't failed, Galen,' she said thickly, emotion clogging her throat. 'I don't know what it will take for you to believe that, but you haven't. And you won't. It was you who were failed. Your father—'

'My father thought I wasn't his son, Solace.' His voice was bleak as midwinter. 'He saw nothing in me to make him change his mind, nothing that made him want to at least try to be a decent father.'

'That wasn't your fault. That was all him.'

'And what if it turns out that I am his son after all?' His voice had become rougher. 'What if my own father just hated me? Because there's something…wrong in me.'

Pain welled up inside her. 'No. There is nothing— *nothing*—wrong with you.'

'How can you know that? There has to be a reason.'

She was aching to cross the distance between them, to put her hands on his broad chest and lean against him, soothe him, warm him, reassure him, but she didn't know if he would welcome it, so she stood where she was. 'I was never given a reason for Katherine to change her mind. And you told me she was wrong. You said, "Who wouldn't want you?"' She swallowed. 'So, I'm telling you now, I don't know why your father treated you the way he did, but he was wrong, Galen. He was *so* wrong. Because there's nothing wrong with you. You are the most special man I know. You're a wonderful father and an amazing king who feels so deeply about his country.' Something slipped down her cheek, a tear she hadn't quite managed to blink away. 'Those aren't failures. Those aren't mistakes. They're triumphs. And that's who you are. You're a triumph and you don't have to be anyone else.'

He looked at her for one long, aching minute.

Then without a word he turned and walked out.

CHAPTER TEN

GALEN WAITED IN the small antechamber to the palace ballroom, listening to the music and buzz of conversations from the guests in the ballroom itself.

It was Solace's presentation ball and he'd kept the guest list to a minimum—a mere five hundred people. But he'd put all his effort into making sure this ball was the most magnificent the palace had ever put on, filling the room full of flowers and delicate lights and music. There was a fountain in the middle and serving staff circulating with the best champagne and the finest food. The atmosphere was one of joy and happiness and excitement, and, since he'd been practising his smile for the past week, he was sure no one would know how hollow he felt inside.

He hadn't seen Solace since that day at the house by the sea, where he'd confessed so many things he wished he hadn't, all those terrible doubts spilling out of him. He'd said too much. And she'd only looked at him with that intense silver gaze and told him there was nothing wrong with him, told him everything he was... A triumph, she'd said.

But he didn't recognise that man. It wasn't him.

He'd had to leave in the end. He'd had to turn around and walk out of the door, because he couldn't bear it.

He wanted so badly to be all the things she'd told him he was, but he never would and one day she'd see it too.

All week he'd been waiting for word that she'd changed her mind and left Kalithera, and half of him had debated cancelling the ball in preparation. But he hadn't heard a thing since he'd walked out on her, and so he had to assume that she still wanted the marriage to go ahead.

He couldn't imagine why, not after what he'd told her.

He looked down at his watch. She was a little late. What if today was the day she changed her mind? What if she left him standing here? He hadn't given her any reason to stay, and if she decided to take Leo and go back to London, well... He'd decided he wouldn't stop her. It would be no less than he deserved.

His fingers felt cold. Everything felt cold.

Abruptly the door opened, and his heart leapt, but when he turned from his contemplation of the empty fireplace it was to see Augustine stride in with Khalil close behind him.

Of course, he'd invited the pair of them, but they should be in the ballroom with the rest of the guests.

Galen told himself he wasn't disappointed and frowned as Khalil shut the door firmly. 'You two shouldn't be in here.'

Augustine shrugged. 'You know I'm always where I shouldn't be.'

'And I don't take orders,' Khalil added casually.

'Also...' Augustine strolled over to the fireplace where Galen stood '...where is the welcome, lovely to see you and thanks for coming?'

Galen stared coldly at them. 'You should be with the guests in the ballroom. I'm waiting here for my fiancée.'

'Ah yes,' Augustine murmured. 'The fiancée you neglected to tell us about.'

Khalil came up to stand on Galen's other side, giving him an enigmatic glance. 'You don't look like a man about to get married,' he observed.

'And what does that look like?' Acid had crept into his tone and he didn't wait for Khalil to reply. 'It's a royal marriage, what do you expect?' He glanced at Augustine. 'She's the daughter of a perfectly respectable—'

'She is not,' Khalil interrupted in his cool way. 'Do not bother with the palace lies. We know the truth.'

'Indeed, we do,' Augustine agreed. 'Though it's exceptionally irritating to have to find out all of this ourselves since our supposed friend neglected to tell us.'

There was a stunned silence.

He hadn't told his friends, not the truth about Leo's origins and not about Solace. It had felt too complicated, and it led too close to his own secret, and both men were far too sharp to be fobbed off with the same lies. It was easier to not bring it up at all.

Galen turned to face the empty fireplace, putting his hands on the white marble mantelpiece and leaning against it. He said nothing. What could he say? If they knew everything?

'Why are you marrying her?' Augustine asked, his tone absolutely neutral.

'Because she had my child,' Galen bit out. 'And I need a wife. And she's—'

Fierce and brave and beautiful. Sharp and cool on the outside, but so soft and hot on the inside. Honest and determined and resourceful...

'I think you do not want to marry her,' Khalil said. 'I think you—'

'I'm marrying her,' Galen growled and shoved himself away from the mantelpiece, giving his friends a furious look. 'I promised her I would and so I am.'

'And you're obviously very happy about it,' Augustine observed. 'Congratulations?'

'It wasn't supposed to be about emotion,' Galen said, not even realising he'd been going to speak until it came out. 'It's a royal marriage. No feelings should be involved.'

'No,' Augustine murmured soothingly. 'Of course not.'

Khalil watched him with enigmatic dark eyes. 'Then why are you so angry about it?'

'Because she deserves more than I can give her,' he snapped. 'I promised her I'd marry her, and I don't want to break my word, but I'm condemning her to a loveless marriage and she needs more from me than that.'

Augustine and Khalil stared at him.

'But you do not love her,' Khalil said.

'No, but—'

'Why not?' Khalil tilted his head like a bird of prey, eyeing him. 'Is she somehow unlovable?'

'No, of course not.'

'Then I fail to see the problem.' Augustine waved a hand. 'Just…give her the love she deserves.'

'What? You think it happens on command? That it's that easy?'

'If you say she's worth it, then I don't see why not.'

It was clear neither of his friends knew what they were talking about, and Galen opened his mouth to tell them that, when the door opened again and this time it was Solace who came in.

He felt as if someone had hit him over the head.

She was dressed in the beautiful silver gown she'd

worn the last time he'd seen her, only this time her hair had been pinned on top of her head in a soft bun, tendrils around her ears. A delicate platinum tiara set with diamonds glittered on her brow and around her throat was a matching diamond collar. There were small diamonds in her ears, and she glittered and sparkled as if she'd been set with stars.

She looked every inch a queen and she was here. She hadn't left. She was *here*.

'You're mad,' Augustine muttered. 'It is that easy. I'm in love with her already.'

'Indeed,' Khalil said, his voice getting deeper, a definite appreciation vibrating in the word.

Possessiveness turned over inside Galen. Solace was *his* queen, not theirs. 'Out,' he ordered. 'Now.'

Solace lifted a brow as the other two sauntered towards her.

Augustine paused beside her. 'Allow me to—'

'You can introduce yourself later,' Galen growled. 'Get out.'

His friends glanced at each other and, for some reason, both smiled. Then they left the room, closing the door firmly after them.

Solace came over to him and stopped. Then she lifted her hands and smoothed the black fabric of his jacket, making sure the decorations and awards pinned to the breast were lying flat. Then she fussed with the black bow tie he wore, touching him as if she had every right, as if he were hers already.

His chest ached and ached. It hadn't stopped aching since he'd left her a week earlier. He felt as if something inside him, a part of him, had broken beyond repair and now the jagged edges were grinding together, causing him agony.

'What are you doing?' His voice was rougher than it should have been.

'Making sure my fiancé is presentable.' She looked up at him, grey eyes shining. 'Did you think I wouldn't come?'

'I…' He couldn't finish. His voice refused to work, his fingers icy.

'Of course, I came,' she said, as if there had been no doubt whatsoever. 'But I'm not here for the crown, Galen. I'm here for you.'

'Solace, I can't—'

'I know,' she said simply. 'You were clear. There's something wrong with you. You don't want to fail me, and you don't know what love is, I get all of that.' She reached for his cold hands and gathered them in her small ones, her skin so warm against his. 'But like I told you last week, you haven't failed me, and you haven't failed Leo either. You haven't failed your country. And I can show you that there's nothing wrong with you. I can teach you. Perhaps it will take time, but I don't care. I have the time. Also, and most important, I know what love is.' She lifted his hands and brushed a light kiss over his knuckles. 'And I love you. Our marriage won't be loveless, Galen, because I can love enough for both of us.'

Just give her the love she deserves,' Augustine had said. '*If you say she's worth it, then I don't see why not.*'

He stared down into her lovely face, into her grey eyes, and, as they had over a year ago, as they did every time he looked into them, they pierced his soul.

And it came to him like a revelation straight from God that if there was anyone in his life he trusted, it was her, and if he didn't trust her to teach him about love, if he didn't trust her vision of who he was, then his father had been right all along.

That all he was was an unfit king and a hated son.

Except Solace shouldn't have to teach him. Solace shouldn't have to love for both of them.

'There's nothing wrong with you,' she'd told him, before listing all the things that were right about him, all the good things. 'Your father was wrong.'

Why would you believe him when you have her?

He didn't know. But right now, with her small hands holding his, he knew if he didn't trust her vision of him, if he didn't trust her with everything in him, then that would be one mistake he'd regret for the rest of his life.

Because you love her.

He couldn't breathe, the moment drawing out, suspended for an eternity as he looked into her eyes, a feeling rushing through him, raw and powerful and relentless. Growing bigger and wider and deeper with every passing second. The sweetest, most welcome kind of agony.

But it wasn't new. He'd felt it before. He'd felt it the very instant he'd seen her in that ballroom fifteen months earlier. And it had been there all this time, waiting for him to recognise it for what it was. He'd given it so many names, lust, desire, need, obsession, yet none of them had felt right. None of them encompassed its true nature.

It was love. And he'd been running from it for far too long.

He was tired of running, just as he was tired of all those other things he'd been doing for years now, and especially tired of the self-doubt his father had instilled in him over the years.

Because there was no self-doubt now, not about this. Not about her.

He loved her and he was never letting her go.

'No,' he said quietly. Then stronger. 'No.' And he adjusted their hands so hers were enclosed in his, his fingers no longer feeling quite so cold. 'You've done everything on your own for far too long and that ends here. It ends tonight.'

There was uncertainty in her eyes. 'What do you mean?'

She'd told him once he had to decide for himself who he was, and he knew now what that was supposed to be.

He was supposed to be her husband. He was supposed to love her.

'I don't know how it's supposed to feel,' he said roughly. 'But when I'm with you I can't think of anything else. When I'm with you all I want to do is touch you, kiss you. All I want to do is stay as close to you as possible and talk with you, listen to you laugh. Watch you smile. I want to know everything about you, every single thing, and I would kill anyone who hurt you. And I want to take care of you for the rest of your life and make sure you never know a moment's pain.'

Her eyes filled with sudden tears. 'Galen...'

He brought her hand to his mouth and kissed it, holding her shimmering gaze with his. 'And if that's love then I love you, Solace Ashworth. I have loved you since the moment I met you.'

Her hands were shaking. Everything was shaking. This was the last thing she'd expected.

She'd spent the past week half in tears, weeping over him, and half in a fury. A dozen times she'd packed a bag, determined to walk out and leave him, only to get to the front door and stop, because of course she wasn't going anywhere.

She couldn't walk away from him. He had no one. He was the world's loneliest king and if she left him, she knew she'd never forgive herself.

She was in it now, and of course she knew why.

She'd fallen in love with him body and soul.

Leaving him was impossible.

Which left her only one option. To stay and to show him exactly what love meant by loving him every day for the rest of their lives.

She could do it. She could be his queen. She could be his wife and live with him, and, in the end, she would show him.

Love had driven her from London to Kalithera, and love would keep her here, because love was her strength and it always had been.

So, she'd stayed and tonight had dressed with extra care, embracing that fire in her heart, and even though when she'd seen him standing by the cold fireplace, so impossibly beautiful in his evening clothes, the heavy gold signet ring of state on his finger, and yet, despite his friends, so alone, she'd nearly burst into tears.

But she wouldn't. She'd show him her strength. Show him that she wasn't going anywhere.

She'd expected to cry later, after the evening had ended, not now.

Except she couldn't help it, there were tears on her cheeks, ruining her make-up, and she couldn't stop them.

He loved her. He really did.

'Galen,' she said again, but he'd bent to kiss her now and his mouth was hot and sweet, the kiss telling her everything he hadn't said. That he was sorry, and he'd missed her, and he was so hungry for her he might die.

She leaned into him, feeling his warm arms wrap around her, holding her tight. 'Don't let me go,' she whispered against his mouth. 'Don't ever let me go. I love you, Galen Kouros, and I want to spend for ever with you. Promise me.'

'I promise,' he murmured. 'You're mine for ever, silver girl.'

Then, because they had duties to fulfil and from now on there always would be, he pulled back and wiped away her tears, helped her fix her make-up, and then they went to the ballroom doors to be announced.

The evening went off without a hitch, and she was note-perfect with her story. Even Kostas couldn't find anything to be suspicious about.

Not that the majority cared. All they wanted to know was where she got her gown from and all they wanted to say was how beautiful she was, and lucky Galen to have caught her, and how in love they both seemed to be.

He didn't let her go all evening, not once.

It was the most magical night of Solace's life.

After it was over, even though it wasn't quite the done thing since they weren't married, Galen picked her up and carried her to the wing of the palace where his private rooms were and took her into his bedroom.

And right in the centre of the room was the biggest four-poster bed, piled high with pillows and hung with gauzy curtains.

A princess bed.

Solace had no words. She couldn't even speak.

But when he took her in his arms and carried her over to the bed, putting her down onto it, she pulled his mouth down on hers and showed him exactly how much it meant to her with all the passion in her soul.

And all the love in her heart.

They were married the following week, in a small, private ceremony, attended only by two kings and one very small boy.

And they lived happily ever after.

EPILOGUE

Twenty years later

GALEN SAT AT his desk in his office, staring at the email from the DNA company. He hadn't opened it yet and he didn't know if he wanted to. He didn't even know why he'd done the test, though, to be fair, he'd been thinking of his children and the legacy he would leave them. He didn't want them to feel the same uncertainty he had.

Then again, did it even matter after so many years? Kostas had passed away not long after he and Solace had married, taking the threat that had been hanging over Galen's throne with him. And Galen's four children were happy and healthy and thriving, so maybe it didn't.

At that moment, the door opened, and his wife came in, looking stunning in one of his favourite dresses, a simple white one with ties at the shoulders he could undo whenever he wanted to. Her hair was loose and there was a stormy expression on her face.

He loved it when she looked like that. It meant she wanted to argue about something, and he adored it when they argued. Especially when making up was so sweet.

'I have something to tell you,' she said, frowning.

'Oh? Wait, you're pregnant again?'

'No, of course not,' she said crossly. 'I'm way past that.'

He pushed back his chair and held out his arms imperiously.

She let out a little breath, jutted her chin a second, then finally came around the side of his desk and settled herself in her favourite place: his lap.

He put his arms around her, feeling her relax against him, the tension leaving her. 'Are you sure you're way past that?' he murmured.

She gave him a light swat then put her head on his chest and sighed. 'Don't get your hopes up.'

'My hopes are firmly centred on the conceiving part, it's true,' he admitted, settling her more comfortably against him. 'What is it you want to tell me?'

'You know, I can't even remember now.' She smiled and looked up at him. 'You still make me forget whatever it is that's bothering me almost immediately.'

He smiled back, the special smile he saved just for her. 'We don't have any immediate duties, do we?'

She always knew, because she seemed to know their schedules off by heart. She was a master organiser and a powerhouse when it came to getting things done, and as a queen she was formidable. She'd done much for the disadvantaged, especially children, and his subjects adored her.

Heat leapt in her eyes. The familiar heat that had always been between them and that still burned as brightly as it had years ago. 'No, I don't think so. And Xander is off trying to kill himself on that wretched skateboard of his.'

Xander was their youngest and the only one still at home. Leo was at Oxford—his choice—and doing extremely well studying mathematics. The twins Elena and Io were in the first year at university—Cambridge, so they didn't have to be near their brother—Elena studying physics and her sister medieval English literature.

Meanwhile, Xander, who wasn't at all academic but loved doing anything physical and especially loved it if it was dangerous, was busy turning his parents' hair white.

Galen loved them all to distraction, but he especially loved it when they were not around so he could do whatever he wanted to his beautiful wife.

'Excellent,' he murmured, then leaned forward and quickly deleted the email.

'What was that?' Solace asked.

'Nothing important,' he said, then he kissed her, and they both forgot about it.

Because that email didn't matter. It didn't matter who his father had been, or what his DNA was.

He knew who he was now. A king, a husband, a father, a lover.

With her, he'd found a home.

With her, he'd found a family.

With her, he'd found love.

With her, he'd found himself.

And there was nothing else he needed.

* * * * *

THE NIGHTS
SHE SPENT
WITH THE CEO

JOSS WOOD

MILLS & BOON

CHAPTER ONE

LEX STOOD IN the arrivals hall at Cape Town International airport, an iced coffee in one hand and a battered Thorpe Industries sign in the other. She kept meaning to make another one but, between her part-time jobs, ferrying her sisters to their after-school activities, supervising homework, making dinner and studying towards her degree, time was short.

The little things tended to fall between the cracks—such as signs.

Lex blew a copper curl out of her eyes and, when it refused to budge, she used her baby finger to pull it back and tuck it behind her ear. She'd pulled her too-long hair into a loose braid but it was already falling apart. She needed a hair cut, a facial, a massage, two million dollars...

Lex looked at the electronic board and then at her phone, checking the time. The incoming flight from London had landed fifteen minutes ago, so she could expect the passengers to start walking through any moment now.

She'd picked up many Thorpe Industries employees over the past couple of years and wondered who she'd get this time. Sometimes she'd get a talker, wide-eyed and excited about being in Africa, and she'd be peppered with questions, which she answered as best she could. Sometimes she got someone glued to their phone, who either spent the trip back to their hotel or to Thorpe Industries' headquarters looking at their tablet or taking and making calls and answering emails.

She frequently had to resist the urge to interrupt their scrolling or incessant work-based conversation to tell them to look out of the window, to take in the world-famous Table Mountain—sometimes covered by its cloud table cloth, sometimes not.

She wanted to point out the endless sea curling around the land, wild in winter, calm in summer. She wanted to remind them that they were in one of the most beautiful cities in the world, to take the moment, to haul in a breath, to pick up their heads and look at something besides their screens. But she kept her mouth shut and drove, because that was her job, and it was one she needed.

Flexible, well-paying jobs were not easy to come by.

Lex sipped her coffee, hoping that the extra hit of caffeine from the double espresso would soon kick in. Last night she'd fallen asleep at the dining room table, somewhere around two. Studying for her degree in Forensic Psychology was something she only got to after Nixi and Snow went to sleep and, invariably, when she was exhausted. She was passing her modules, but she wished she had the time to do better, to dive deeper into the subject. She didn't like being average, or not living up to her potential, but there was only a finite number of hours in the day.

You're doing the best you can. It's all anyone can ask of you. It's all you can ask of yourself.

But it still felt as if she were walking a tight rope above a sky-high canyon, about to plunge onto the jagged rocks below. Right now, the rope was tight and steady, and she knew where to put her feet. If the wind picked up or someone else jumped on the rope, she'd lose her balance and do a rope-free bungee jump.

Life had to keep ticking along just as it was, with no interruptions or distractions.

Lex noticed that the passengers from the London flight were starting to trickle into the arrival hall. Lifting her sign, she sipped her coffee, wondering whether the tall blonde wearing white linen trousers would be her pick-up, or the geeky-looking guy wearing horn-rimmed glasses. No, these were the first-class passengers and, while she'd had one or two pick-ups who were that far up the corporate ladder, most of her pick-ups either flew business class or economy.

The airport was busy and there was always something, or someone, to capture her attention. Two little boys of no more than four or five, were bouncing up and down, thoroughly over-excited at the thought of seeing Daddy, Mummy or Grandma. A thin woman stood opposite her, her arms tightly folded, staring at the ground, looking as if she'd rather be anywhere but here, meeting the person coming off that plane. There was a lull in passengers coming through the tunnel and Lex shifted from foot to foot, turning her head to look behind her.

Taller than most, at six two or six three, and dressed in solid black, he immediately caught her attention. Lex cocked her head, enjoying the view of his broad shoulders and narrow-hipped swimmer's body. The sleeves of his V-neck jersey—cashmere. she was convinced—were pushed halfway up tanned and muscled forearms. The fine material skimmed his wide chest and hugged big, muscular upper arms. He wore a pair of black trousers that didn't disguise the length and strength of his legs. Trendy black-and-white trainers covered his big feet and he carried an expensive-looking bag and a sleek laptop case.

He was breathtakingly, knee-shakingly sexy. *Hot*.

Lex was currently single and would be for the short- and, she presumed, medium-term future. Even if she had time for an affair—which she didn't—most men backed away when they realised her love life had to be scheduled around the needs and demands of her half-sisters. Even if it was just a short-term fling, men didn't like not being at the top of her priority list.

Even if she wanted a relationship—and she didn't—her mum had jumped in and out of relationships her entire life so she was cynical about love and humans' ability to commit—having a guy in her life would be impractical and unworkable.

Even a short-term affair would be tricky but, wow, with someone like Gorgeous Guy she'd make the effort to fit him into her day. Or night.

He stopped, pulled a smart phone from the back pocket of his trousers and scowled down at it, his thick eyebrows pulling together. His hair was a rich, dark sable, cut short to keep the waves under control. She couldn't tell what colour his eyes were, but his nose was long, his jaw chiselled and his cheekbones high. He wasn't pretty-boy handsome but, man, his sheer masculinity stopped traffic. Lex grinned as a woman turned back to look at him, not watching where she was going, and bumped into a luggage trolley she hadn't noticed.

Lex didn't blame her. Gorgeous Guy deserved a second or third look.

Unable to look away, she watched as he raked his hand through his hair, obviously frustrated. He jabbed a finger at his phone and lifted it to his ear, scowling. He

looked Italian—maybe Greek or Arabic? His national-
ity didn't matter. He would be classified as a hottie from
Cartagena to Canberra and everywhere in between.

And she had to stop gawking at him before he noticed her open mouth and glassy eyes. Honestly, she
should get out more if she was this affected by a random handsome guy in an airport terminal.

Pull yourself together, Satchell!

Unfortunately, yanking her eyes off him proved
harder than she expected. She was about to—she
was!—when he turned his head and his eyes collided
with hers. Despite being across the room, she felt the
heat of his gaze as his eyes moved over her face and
down her long body. It was easy enough to figure out
what he was thinking: bright-red hair, long and curly,
tendrils springing out around a heart-shaped face, every
inch covered in distinctive freckles with a small nose,
a wide mouth and green eyes. A tallish, too-thin redhead dressed in black jeans, biker boots and a battered
black denim jacket over a long-sleeved white T-shirt.

He didn't drop his eyes or walk away and a hot slap
of attraction hit her, causing the world to shift under
her feet. A million tiny needles hit her over-sensitised
skin and she felt light-headed and weird. Why did all
the colours and sounds in the airport seem amplified?
Maybe she was having a stroke because all her nerve
endings felt as if they were on fire, sending bolts of current up her arms and straight to her heart.

Or maybe this was pure animal attraction. She tipped
her head to the side. She'd heard of the phenomenon but
had never experienced it, not to this degree anyway.
He picked up his overnight bag and started to walk...

And, good grief, was he heading in her direction?

Was he seriously going to initiate a conversation…with her? What? *Why?*

She was way out of practice with guys and didn't know how to flirt any more. Lex shuffled from foot to foot, her heartbeat loud in her ears. She couldn't get enough air into her lungs and, despite having taken a few sips of icy coffee, her mouth felt as if it hadn't experienced liquid for weeks. What would he say when he reached her. How would she respond? Lex darted a quick look over her shoulder… Maybe someone behind her had captured his attention and she was reading the situation wrong, but…nope. He was definitely focused on her.

And, standing in a busy airport, she felt naked, emotionally vulnerable. As if he knew her or could easily discover her secrets. That he knew that, beneath her insouciant exterior and her 'I've got this handled' attitude, she was floundering and second-guessing everything she did.

And, sometimes, who she was.

Damn, he was still heading her way, his eyes still locked on her face. Why couldn't she look away from him? What was wrong with her?

As he approached, Lex realised his eyes were a topaz-brown colour, a gorgeous mixture of gold and amber tinged with hints of green. Lex, feeling off-balance and more than a little shocked—he was now just a few feet from her—felt her sign fall to the floor. His cologne, a masculine combination of sandalwood, lime and something herby, drifted over to her, along with the hint of expensive soap. He'd showered recently because the tips of his wavy hair were wet, but he hadn't bothered to shave, as thick stubble covered his lower face.

Up close he was even more impressive than he was

from a distance and Lex tightened the grip on her coffee cup.

Be cool, Lex. Don't do, or say, anything stupid.

Lex tipped her head back to look up into his eyes as he opened his mouth to speak.

'I'm Cole Thorpe…'

But, before he could finish his sentence, a loud jangle emanated from the back pocket of her jeans, causing her to jump. The ring sounded like a foghorn—she'd made it that loud so she could hear it ring from every corner of the house—and Lex squeezed her plastic coffee cup so hard that the lid popped off. She watched, horrified, as a long stream of cold coffee flew into that hard face and down that wide, cashmere-covered chest.

Oh.

Oh, *help!*

Cole was used to walking off his private jet and straight into a car that would whisk him away to his next destination, a seamless transition that he'd made five hundred times or more. His arrival in Cape Town had been anything but standard.

And, so far, deeply annoying.

Had his long-term virtual PA been in charge of his travel arrangements, he would already be in a car, halfway to Thorpe Industries, Cape Town. But, because Gary was on paternity leave, Cole was making do with another virtual assistant he'd found through some agency. So far she was proving to be a shade up from useless. In capitals. And by the end of the day, if he remembered, she'd be gone and he'd be onto temporary assistant number four. He had too many balls in the air for inefficiency and needed someone who could make his life easier, not harder. And, really, what was so difficult about making sure he had a ride from the airport to Thorpe Industries' Cape Town headquarters?

After hanging around in the airport for fifteen minutes—a complete waste of time—he'd reached someone at Thorpe Industries who'd told him that the driver's instructions were to wait at International Arrivals. She had a sign, he was told, but you couldn't miss her...

His driver was a woman, and would probably be dressed in black. She also had red hair. Once he started looking for her, Cole found her almost immediately, only to find her eyes already on him. For the first time, his feet felt glued to the floor and his lungs didn't seem to be taking in enough air.

She was tall, maybe five-eight in those clunky, ugly boots, but to say that she had red hair would be like saying the sun was yellow. It was a deeply unimaginative description for such an unusual shade. Long and curly, it wasn't red, orange or auburn, but a cacophony of colours, reminding him of the fallen maple leaves that carpeted the ground at the end of autumn in the Bukhansan National Park in South Korea. And those freckles...

They ranged from pinpricks to tiny dots, each one perfect. Hers wasn't just a spray across her nose, or on her cheeks, but her entire face was covered in a Milky Way of cinnamon-coloured tiny stars.

Heart-stopping stunning.

Her hair and her freckles captured his attention—how could they not? Her body was slim but curvy, and she had dark-red, perfectly arched eyebrows over bright eyes—green or blue?—and a wide, sexy mouth. Without her freckles and red hair, she'd be another attractive woman, but her unusual colouring made her stand out from the crowd. And that wasn't easy in a busy airport.

She was also, apparently and weirdly, his driver. Cole

looked down at the sign she held in her hand—it was upside down—and winced internally. She was the first woman he'd been attracted to in months—the last six months had been hectic and his sex life had dropped way down his list of priorities—and she worked as a driver for Thorpe Industries.

He didn't play where he worked. Ever.

Tucking his phone into the back pocket of his jeans, he swung his bag up so that it hung off his shoulder and started to wind his way through the crowds to the redhead. She watched him approach, her eyes wary. Then her lips parted and her tongue appeared between strong, very white teeth. He was old enough and experienced enough to know that his immediate, and intensely inconvenient, attraction to her was reciprocated.

After everything that had happened these past few months, this was not what he needed.

Slowing down, Cole told himself to take a breath, to gain control. He was tired, stressed, overworked and he was overreacting. She was just another woman, nobody special. He didn't believe in special and he didn't have time for an affair. He had a hedge fund to manage, a company he didn't want to sell and a life to resume.

He'd be in and out of Cape Town in a week…maybe two.

Forcing his feet to move, Cole walked towards his driver, telling his stomach to unknot, his throat to loosen and his lungs to take a breath. He couldn't let her know that he found her compelling, let her suspect that it felt as if she'd slid her hand through his ribs and held his heart in a tight grip.

Normally very cool and completely collected, Cole had never been sideswiped by attraction before, and he was stumbling around in unknown territory. But he only had a few feet to pull himself together…

Three, two, one…

He took his final steps up to her and introduced himself, only to be interrupted by the sound of a foghorn piercing a dark, stormy night. He braked, the redhead squeezed her takeaway container of coffee and a stream of the cold, sticky liquid hit his cheek and lips and slid off his chin to fall to his chest and then the floor.

He stood there, shocked and, well, wet, wondering what else could go wrong. Then tears started to roll down the redhead's face.

He could handle a long flight, being inconvenienced, having to track down his ride and being smacked in the gut by a very unexpected attraction…but a woman's tears?

Nope. They were enough to drop him to the floor.

As her phone went silent, Lex closed her eyes, praying that this was a nightmare, that she hadn't just started crying in front of her boss, the brand-new owner of Thorpe Industries, the man who, indirectly but ultimately, signed off on her pay cheques.

What on earth was wrong with her? She never cried. Why in front of him? And why right now?

Lex scrabbled in her tote bag for a pack of tissues and pulled out a small pack, her shaking fingers unable to pull back the tab to the opening. A tanned hand gently took the packet and pulled back the tab, allowing her to pull a couple of tissues from the pack. She wiped her eyes, thankful she seldom wore make-up. Streaks of mascara down her cheeks did not pair well with wet eyes and the post-box-red of her skin under her freckles.

Oh, how she longed for the floor to cave in beneath

her feet. Anything would be preferable to standing here, feeling like a complete, over-emotional wreck. The last time she'd spontaneously cried was when Joelle had bleached her hair and she'd ended up looking like a half-ripe apricot. She'd been thirteen. She was now more than double that age and should be in control of her emotions.

The problem was that she normally was.

So why was she crying? What was wrong with her? She'd known sad, and she was a long way off from feeling that overwhelming emotion. Sure, she was tired, but she'd learned to function on minimal sleep. Was she stressed?

She was a woman in her late twenties trying, with the help of her sister Addi, to raise her young half-sisters, study, stretch their income further than it was supposed to go and keep their rag-tag family together. She was studying psychology. She knew that stress always found a way to express itself, sometimes when the person was least expecting it. It rolled through the body, looking for a way out, and sometimes it was released through tears.

And exhaustion inhibited the body's ability to self-regulate and made it more prone to emotional outbursts. Yes, she tended to shove her feelings down, telling herself she didn't have time to deal with them, that she'd process all she was feeling later when she was less tired, when she was alone. However, she never had time, was infrequently alone and there was a good chance that all those pesky feelings had piled on top of each other and spilt over and out.

But why did she have to cry in front of Cole Thorpe, her boss? Was it because, subconsciously at least, her attraction to him made her realise that she was still a woman, still capable of feeling sexually aroused and knowing there wasn't a damn thing she could do about it, even if she'd wanted to? Was it because seeing him, knowing that she couldn't just accept a potential offer to join him for a drink or dinner later, made her remember all she'd sacrificed for her sisters, all that she couldn't have?

Had it made her see that she wasn't a normal single woman, that she had more responsibilities than most, that she sometimes felt trapped, and felt guilty for feeling that way?

Possibly. Probably.

She could figure out the reasons for her tears later—they were so stupid!—but right now she needed to rescue this situation, preferably before Cole Thorpe fired her. If he did that, she'd have a very decent excuse to cry and another huge reason to stress. She desperately needed this job: it worked around her big sister-substitute mum duties.

Lex sniffed and lifted her eyes to see a black jersey being pulled up to reveal a washboard stomach and a muscled chest. Her mouth fell open as a steady hum started in her womb and the space between her legs buzzed, getting warmer by the second.

His sweater came off and he impatiently tugged down the black T-shirt that had ridden up his chest. She couldn't help noticing his bulging arms as he dragged his jersey over his coffee-splashed face and chest. Then he dropped to his haunches, snapped open his leather bag and pulled out another sweater, pale-grey this time, and pulled it over his head. He shoved the black jersey into a corner of his bag and stood up.

From start to finish, his swapping of jerseys couldn't have taken more than a minute, but Lex felt as if she'd watched the longest, sexiest movie in her life. And she wanted to hit rewind.

He was her boss, and Lex needed to stay employed, so maybe, instead of ogling him, she should apologise profusely and try and act like the professional she knew she could be. But, after having shared some serious eye contact, tossed her coffee over him and burst into tears, there was a good chance that she might have over-cooked her golden goose.

Lex held out her hand, gave him an embarrassed smile and cleared her throat. 'I'm sorry. For tossing coffee over you and crying.'

He put his hand in hers and gave it the briefest shake before dropping it as if it was a Cape Cobra. 'And you are?'

She'd forgotten to give him her name. *Great.* 'I'm Lex Satchell.'

He nodded, picked up his overnight bag and slung it over his shoulder. 'I've seen enough of this airport, so I'd like to get out of here. Where's the car?'

It was hard to think around him. 'Uh, we need to go down a floor. It's not far but, if you prefer, you can wait in the pick-up zone. I'll take your bag to the car.'

'I've got legs. I can walk.'

He had very nice, very long, very strong legs… *Stop it, Lex!*

'Let's go,' he added, his tone brusque. 'I want to check in at my hotel and drop in at Thorpe's Cape Town headquarters today.'

So did that mean she wasn't fired? Or was he just waiting for her to deliver him to wherever he wanted to go before he canned her? Lex started to ask him but he took off towards the escalator, moving quickly.

Lex followed his broad shoulders, feeling dazed and

disoriented. He was implacable and unreadable, and she suspected she wasn't the first, and certainly wouldn't be the last, person who'd wonder which way was up around the inscrutable international businessman.

CHAPTER TWO

COLE SAT IN the back seat of the Thorpe Industries SUV, diagonally behind his sexy driver—his *driver*, Cole mentally reminded himself—dark sunglasses over his eyes. He had to stop looking at her, but his eyes kept bouncing from her lovely profile to her slim shoulder, to the one hand he could see on the steering wheel. She drove with cool competence, easily manoeuvring the big car in busy traffic. Her eyes darted between the rear view and side mirrors, and he found it hard to believe that the cool, remote woman behind the wheel was the same one who'd been crying just twenty minutes before.

Judging by the mortification in her green eyes, crying wasn't something she did often. Or at all. What had set her off? They'd been trading glances, and he'd seen the awareness of him in her eyes. He'd introduced himself, her phone had rung and she'd tossed coffee over him. Had she been scared he'd yell at her, lash out at her, fire her? Was that what had caused her to become emotional?

His curiosity burned a hole in his stomach lining, and he fought to keep the urge to demand an explanation behind his teeth. She was his employee. He had no right to that knowledge and the best way to show her respect was to pretend nothing had happened.

But he couldn't. Partly, yeah, because of that curiosity—an anomaly in itself, because people generally weren't interesting enough for him to dive into their psyche—and partly because he wanted to comfort her, to make everything that upset her go away.

The urge to take her in his arms and shield her from the world terrified him. He'd never been protected, and even as a child he'd been expected to take, and deal with, life's vagaries, disappointments and lack of fairness. He didn't coddle people—didn't know how—so his need to protect and remedy whatever ailed her confounded him.

Cole swallowed his sigh and turned his head to look out of the window, catching a glimpse of a low-income suburb on the side of the road. He was now in the southernmost city in Africa, last week he'd been in Chicago, two weeks before he'd been in Hong Kong. As well as visiting Thorpe Industries' regional offices, he was also managing his internationally acclaimed, billion-dollar hedge fund.

His candle was now a stub the size of a thumb nail.

Cole slipped his index finger and thumb under his sunglasses and pushed them into his closed eyelids, and an image of his older brother meditating in his orange robes flashed behind his eyes.

Did Sam ever think about crisscrossing the world in the Thorpe private jet, wearing five-thousand-dollar suits or the long work days and the responsibility of being the CEO of Thorpe Industries demanded? He'd walked away from his privileged life of being the highly educated, driven, feted first-born son of Grenville Thorpe—the famous industrialist—to join a Buddhist monastery and Cole wondered if he regretted his decision.

Cole dropped his fingers and opened his eyes, but the events of the past six months rolled through his mind in a series of snapshots. His father's death a year ago had been a shock, not because Cole felt any grief for the man he'd never known, but because Grenville dying of a heart attack had put a mortal dent in his plans to take revenge on the father who'd ignored him all his life.

For five years before Grenville's death, or more, he'd been quietly and surreptitiously buying up Thorpe Industries shares and had amassed a big block of shares in the multinational company his father had owned and operated. He'd been a few months off staging a hostile takeover—his father wouldn't have been able to ignore him or that—when Grenville had died of a heart attack on his yacht off the Amalfi coast. Sam, his brother, had inherited all of Grenville's assets and Grenville's shares in Thorpe Industries.

Cole, unsurprisingly, hadn't been mentioned in the will.

Since Cole hadn't had the same desire to ruin Sam as he had Grenville, he'd stepped back and re-evaluated his plans. His only aim in acquiring Thorpe shares had been to look his father in the eye as he'd told him that he'd no longer be ignored or dismissed.

But death had whipped his revenge out of his hands.

Then Sam, on the six-month anniversary of their father's death, had swapped his Armani suits for orange robes, his single life as one of the world's most eligible bachelors for abstinence, and material abundance for one meal a day and sleeping on a thin mat, covered only by his robes. Cole had had no problem with Sam reinventing his life—that was his choice—but what had possessed Sam to transfer every asset he owned, and everything he'd inherited from Grenville, including his controlling interest in Thorpe Industries, to Cole? How dared he? What on earth had his brother been thinking?

Cole would have asked him but Sam, according to his London-based lawyer and point of contact, was currently unavailable. Sam was fine. He stood by his decision to transfer everything to Cole, he had no interest in the outside world and was living his best life.

Cole had wanted the company, the lawyer said, so Sam had given it to him.

Yeah, but he hadn't wanted Thorpe Industries like this—it meant nothing without the sweet taste of revenge. Now it was, simply, a pain in his backside.

Cole flipped his phone over and over, thinking that Grenville had to be doing cartwheels in his grave. His worshipped firstborn—not an exaggeration—had renounced everything, including his name, and his despised and shunned second-born son now owned all his worldly possessions. Despised? No, that was wrong. You had to care about someone or something to despise them, Grenville hadn't been able to gather enough energy to hate him. He'd been discounted and discarded, not worthy of his father's notice.

Cole's phone buzzed and he looked down at the screen, sighing when he saw the identity of the caller. He ignored the call and allowed it to go to voice mail. Somehow, along with his company, apartments and all his material possessions, Cole had also inherited the responsibility of Sam's long-term girlfriend, Melissa. He now owned the aristocratic blonde's apartment and he'd continued Sam's tradition of paying her a hefty monthly allowance.

Cole didn't mind her having the apartment and cash. She and Sam had been together for a long time and she'd expected to marry him some day. She deserved some sort of compensation for the trauma his brother had put her through. But, over the last couple of months, despite sharing nothing more than a few dinners and attending a mutual friend's wedding together, the press had started linking them together, treating them like a couple.

Not on, Cole decided. He'd had a couple of serious relationships in his early and mid-twenties, all of which had fizzled away. He wasn't good at being part of a couple, he pushed people away when they asked for emotional intimacy. He'd been raised by an unemotional mother, had been ignored by his father and had had little contact with his brother. He was better on his own, was used to his solitary life, and when he got back to London he'd present Melissa with an exit package of a couple of million and ownership of the flat. That would ease the sting of severing her ties to the Thorpe family.

Hopefully, getting rid of Thorpe Industries would be as easy. Early on, he'd decided that dismantling the company and selling its assets to local business people was the most logical and efficient way to rid himself of the Thorpe empire.

While he could get a lot from spreadsheets and balance sheets, Cole knew that the best way to gather information was to get his boots on the ground, to make his own assessments. He'd spent many weeks crisscrossing the world, visiting all Thorpe companies and inspecting the assets he'd received from Sam. He'd put Sam's London and Hong Kong apartments on the market, sold his yacht and private helicopter and his art collection was due to be sold at auction in a few months. Cole intended to put a portion of the proceeds he realised into a fixed-term investment in case Sam decided he didn't want to be a monk any more, but the rest he intended to distribute to various charities. He had his own apartments, art and car collections—he wasn't into yachts—and he didn't need his brother's pass-me-downs. He had enough of his own money. He didn't need Sam's or his father's.

His African assets were fairly straightforward and he didn't foresee any complications.

Lex looked in the rear-view mirror and caught Cole's bleak expression—she should think of him as Mr Thorpe but, because she'd seen his ridged stomach and his bare chest, she couldn't. She wished she could ask him what was bothering him, why he looked as if he carried the weight of the world resting on his impressively wide shoulders.

He looked so damn lonely...

Despite knowing it wasn't her place—drivers didn't speak to owners of companies—Lex knew she was going to say something, although she knew not what. All she knew was that she was desperate to distract him and needed to pull him back from whatever dark place he'd wandered into. It wasn't her place or part of her duties, and he might tell her to mind her own business, but nobody should look that...that *desolate*.

But she already had two black marks against her—tossing coffee and crying—and she didn't want to give him an excuse to hand her another one, so her question couldn't be personal. So, what should she say? Ah, just around the next bend was a decent view of Table Mountain: she could point it out and ask him if he'd visited Cape Town before. The city was an innocuous, friendly subject.

Cole Thorpe, despite having all the money in the world—that was a limited-edition luxury watch on his wrist—looked as though he needed a friend.

Lex was about to speak when her phone rang. She expected it to be the receptionist at Thorpe Industries again—her call precipitated the Toss Coffee Over Your Boss incident—but, when she looked down, Lex recognised the number of St Agnes primary school and her heart lurched. Getting a call from her half-sisters' school was never good.

If the call had come from anyone else, she would've ignored it, but a call from the girls' school shot her anxiety levels sky-high. She answered the call via Bluetooth, knowing that Cole would hear the conversation. Damn, another black mark. She was racking them up today.

Within twenty seconds she established that the girls were fine but Nixi's teacher was calling to remind Lex that she'd promised to supply the school with twenty-four cupcakes for their bake sale.

'And we need them here by lunchtime,' she was told.

Cupcakes? What cupcakes?

'I'm sorry, what cupcakes?' Lex demanded, her stomach sinking to her toes. The school frequently made last-minute requests—or, truthfully, she processed the necessary information late—but two hours to produce two-dozen cupcakes was terrifying on another level.

'I sent a reminder a week ago.'

Lex winced. Yeah, her inbox was full to overflowing and she could easily have missed it. 'Look, I dropped the ball,' she told Ms Mapton. 'Even if I could get to a bakery to buy them, I don't think I'll be able to get them to you in time.'

'Just do your best, Ms Satchell,' Ms Mapton told her before disconnecting the call.

She'd try but she didn't see how she'd fit a cupcake delivery into her day. She didn't know whether Cole needed her to ferry him around any more today and, if he did, she'd have to postpone her French lesson student. She also had an assignment to email off before five this afternoon, as yet unfinished. But Cole's claim on her time came first: her part-time chauffeuring gig for Thorpe Industries, which she'd acquired through Addi, paid well and it wasn't one she could afford to lose.

That was if he didn't fire her today.

Lex turned her attention back to her cupcake problem. How had she dropped this ball? If she didn't deliver the cupcakes, she knew her sisters would be disappointed, which would be quickly followed by resigned acceptance. Snow and Nixi were so used to being disappointed by Joelle, the mother all five sisters shared, that being let down wasn't anything new or strange.

Cupcakes. What else was this day going to throw at her?

Lex slipped the SUV into the fast lane to overtake a fuel truck. She considered calling Addi, who worked at Thorpe in the hospitality section, but knew her older sister was in meetings all day and wouldn't take her call. She'd ordinarily ask Addi's assistant Giles, who was also a family friend, to do the cupcake run, but she couldn't—not with their boss of bosses listening in.

She didn't want to paint a bullseye on Addi's back because it was her job that paid the bulk of their joint expenses while Lex provided the day-to-day care the younger girls needed. Without each other's contribution, the younger girls would've been split apart and placed in the foster care system, because neither she nor Addi could look after them on their own. Addi's salary made it financially possible for them to stay together, and Lex being present for the girls gave them the emotional stability neither she nor Addi had had growing up. But, lately, because Addi went to work early and walked in late, Lex frequently felt like a single parent.

She couldn't believe so much time had passed since they'd taken responsibility for the girls. At twenty-three, she'd been single, and she'd just met someone she thought might be the one to change her mind about love, trust and commitment. Addi had been engaged, counting down to her wedding in three months, and Storm, their middle sister, had just left school. Then, after not hearing a word from their mother in seven years, Joelle had rocked up with Nixi and Snow—sisters they'd never met, sisters they hadn't known about. She and Addi had been busy taking in that bombshell news—Joelle now had five daughters from five different men—when Joelle had asked them to look after the girls for a weekend.

They were still waiting for Joelle to return to the country.

As a result of Joelle's daughter-dump, Addi's wedding had been postponed and then cancelled. Lex's love interest had done a runner and, yet again, her suspicion that 'love' always melted when came into contact with a little heat was confirmed. Addi's father had bolted when Joelle had told him she was pregnant with Addi—Lex didn't even know who her dad was. Joelle invariably skipped out on a person or situation when times got tough, and Addi's fiancé had broken up with her just two months after their half-sisters' arrival in their lives.

She got the message: love couldn't be counted on to see you through the tough times. Determination, persistence and grit were the traits needed to deal with the reality of a stunningly fickle mum and raising her two half-sisters.

Love was outstandingly unreliable and, frankly, useless.

The onboard GPS broke into her thoughts by telling her to take the next exit and Lex shook herself out of her introspective reverie. She was normally too busy to look back, and she rarely allowed herself to think of the past and the rough hand she and Addi had been dealt. It was what it was, and no amount of thinking, or wishing, could change reality.

Enough now. She was tired and stressed and that was why she was being bombarded with memories of the past. And, at twenty-eight, she couldn't operate on three hours of sleep night after night and be expected to be Positive Polly.

Two more years of studying, she told herself as she took the exit. Then she'd have her degree in Forensic Psychology and, with the girls being a little older, she could look for a full-time job. She could maybe even think about having a fling, some fun.

Until then, she just had to keep trying her best. It was all she could do. But sometimes Lex felt that her best wasn't nearly good enough and she was letting her sisters down, just like her mother had let her down, time and time again. But she, at least, was showing up, climbing into the ring, doing her best.

She was doing all she could, in the best way she knew how. All she could do was keep putting one foot in front of the other and trudging on.

'Do you have kids?'

Lex looked in the rear-view mirror and her stomach flipped over when her eyes connected with Cole's. Was that disappointment she saw? No, she was just projecting her attraction onto him. Rich, handsome guys who operated in nose-bleedingly high social circles didn't waste their time, energy or emotions on women who were anything less than stunningly beautiful or incredibly talented—possibly both.

But his question broke the tense silence between them and for that she was grateful. 'No, the cupcakes are for a bake sale at my sisters' school.'

'And why did you get the call? Where's their mum?'

Lex stopped at a traffic light and her grip on the steering wheel tightened. 'Me and my sister Addi—she works as a VP at Thorpe in your hospitality and leisure sector—are raising our half-sisters together.'

She saw what she thought might be respect, possibly approval, flit across his face. 'Did one or both of your parents die?'

Their deaths would have been so much easier to explain than Joelle's deep selfishness and lack of responsibility. The traffic light turned green, Lex accelerated and slammed on the brakes when a passenger bus cut in front of her, far too close for comfort. She hit her horn, the bus accelerated away and a brief wave was the only apology she got.

'Cape Town drivers are the worst,' she told Cole, seeing the stone gates for the Vane Hotel up ahead. 'But we are nearly there.'

'Pity,' Cole murmured.

And what, Lex wondered as she steered the car through the gates to the Vane, did he mean by that cryptic statement?

CHAPTER THREE

LEX DROVE UP the winding drive to the Vane Hotel and Cole immediately noticed the city's famous mountain behind the sprawling hotel, now understanding why it was said the Vane had the best views of Table Mountain. Despite Thorpe Industries owning a boutique hotel on the Waterfront, Jude Fisher, who was a friend of the owners, had recommended this hotel to him, saying that, in a city that boasted incredible hotels such as the Silo and Mount Nelson, the Vane was the best of the best, boasting six-star elegance and facilities, and staying there was an experience not be missed.

Lex pulled up under the portico and Cole released the catch to his seatbelt and pushed a hand through his hair. He was about to exit the car when Lex hit the button to drop her window and asked the valet to give her a minute. The valet hesitated, nodded and stepped back.

Lex turned round in her seat and her extraordinary eyes slammed into his. 'Are you intending to go to Thorpe Industries today? Shall I wait, or when should I return?'

He shook his head, recalling her question. 'My assistant has organised a hire car for me. I prefer to drive myself,' he told her, desperately trying to ignore the prickle of attraction flying up and down his spine. Maybe he could cancel the car and get Lex to drive him round Cape Town. He loathed not being behind the wheel but wouldn't mind spending more time looking at her unusual but gorgeous face.

It was an idea...

It was an asinine one. He'd long held the belief that having a driver was both pretentious and a waste of money since he could drive himself wherever he needed to go. And being in the close confines of a car with someone he wanted more than he needed to breathe was a recipe for disaster.

She was his employee, for goodness' sake. He didn't cross that line—ever. That was asking for complications he didn't need or have time for. But the thought of not seeing her again while he was in Cape Town was a knife through his temple, a kick to his head.

He wanted to know why she was raising her sisters, and how that had come to be. He wanted to taste the skin on her neck, kiss his way down her spine and hook her naked thigh over his hip. He wanted...

Seriously, Thorpe? Cole took the opportunity to run his hands up and down his face, trying to wake up his brain cells. What was wrong with him? And what was it about this woman that fascinated him so? He'd known many beautiful, stunning women, and had slept with quite a few of them, but none of them made him feel as if he were sixteen again, disconcerted and enthralled.

She's just another woman...

He could repeat that mantra until the sun rose in the morning, but it wouldn't make a jot of difference. There was, as they said, something about her that called to him on a deep and dark—scary—level.

And that, more than anything, was why he had to

stay away from her. 'So you won't need me to drive you anywhere?'

'No.' Unfortunately.

He thought he saw disappointment flash in her eyes, possibly panic, and was tempted to change his mind, to put up with the frustration of being driven simply to see her again. Maybe the time difference and jet lag were messing with his mind and his emotions. Then Cole silently cursed when he remembered that he'd got a solid six hours of sleep last night as the plane had flown south and that there was only a two-hour time difference between London and Cape Town.

But those eyes in that face, and her raspy, deep voice, enthralled him. He could look at her, listen to her, for the longest time.

A porter and a car valet approached them and Cole exited the vehicle, with Lex half a second behind him. He saw a well-dressed woman exit from the lobby and knew she was his personal concierge. He was about to thank and dismiss Lex when his phone rang, the call coming in being from one of his biggest investor clients. She wasn't someone whose call he could ignore.

He looked at Lex and nodded to the concierge. 'Tell her who I am and grab my laptop bag from the boot and take it up to my room. Wait with it until I get there.' His state-of-the-art laptop was his life and he never let it out of his sight. It held all his personal, business and client information, yet he instinctively trusted Lex to transport it to his room.

Of course, he could've just held it while he took his call. It wasn't as if it was heavy. Not wanting to interrogate that thought, he turned away and answered his call.

Ten minutes later he stepped into the impressive art deco style lobby, the concierge approached him and offered to show him to his room. He took his hotel card, asked for directions to the penthouse suite and declined her company. It was a hotel suite, not interstellar travel.

On the top floor, in the east corner, he stepped into a hallway and saw Lex standing in the open door to his suite, his laptop bag over her shoulder. On hearing his footsteps, the porter appeared in the doorway, a polite smile on his face. 'Would you like me to unpack for you, Mr Thorpe?'

Cole slipped him a tip and told him that he'd manage. When the porter was out of sight, Cole looked at Lex and stepped inside the hallway to his suite, his eyes drifting over the sophisticated lounge to the massive windows dominating the space. His room was high up, so he looked over old oak trees directly at Table Mountain.

'That's got to be the best view in Cape Town.'

He turned to see Lex standing next to him in the hall, her eyes on the view. He'd never been to the city before, but he thought she might be right. It would be hard to beat.

After another minute of silence, with both of them looking at the incredible view, he turned back to face Lex. She'd transferred his laptop bag to her hand, and he reached for it, their fingers brushing. Cole couldn't believe that such a small touch could hold so much power, and he tensed, unable to pull his eyes off her truly lovely face. Her green eyes darkened and underneath the freckles he saw a pink flush, some distinct heat in her cheeks. The tip of her pink tongue touched her upper lip and she rocked on her feet...

'Mr Thorpe, I...' She started to speak but her words faded when she noticed their fingers entangled as they both gripped the handle of his laptop bag. She stared down at their hands, but she didn't pull away, as he'd expected her to.

He should break the contact now…immediately. She was his driver, his employee, someone he should not be this close to—ever. But he could no more break their contact than he could stop his heart from beating.

'You should move back,' he told her, his voice rough-sounding.

'I should,' she agreed, sounding bemused and dazed. 'I want to, I know I must, but I can't.'

He released a groan and inhaled a solid hit of her scent, something fresh and unisex, light and lovely. Instead of pulling away, his thumb slid over her knuckles. Passion flared in her eyes, her breath hitched and she tipped her head back, lifting her mouth. What else could he do but lower his mouth to hers?

He was an inch from her mouth, and anticipation hummed through his veins, when she slapped her hand on her chest and pulled back. His eyes connected with hers and he saw panic and a healthy dose of anxiety.

'Are you married?' she demanded.

'No.'

'Engaged, seeing someone, sleeping with someone?' she demanded.

He hadn't had sex in months. He'd been too busy to think about taking a woman to bed. The only woman he had any contact with on a personal level was Melissa, but there had never been anything between them. Okay, they'd kissed once, but that had been at her instigation, not his. She was connected to him through Sam, not because he wanted her in his life.

'No,' he told Lex, desperate to taste her.

'Are you sure about that?'

'Yes, damn it. Can I kiss you now?'

'We shouldn't. I work for you,' Lex told him, the expression on her face yearning. She wanted his mouth on hers as much as he wanted his there. If he pressed her, he knew she'd admit that their attraction, their desperation to see each other naked, was all that was important right now.

'Tell me not to kiss you, Cole,' Lex begged.

'I can't,' he whispered, bending his knees a little to meet her mouth.

He was about to make contact when voices coming from the passage—there were two penthouse suites—pulled him back to the present. The door to the suite was open and anyone walking past would get more than an eyeful. Cole stepped away from Lex and a cold dose of reality slapped him in the face. He was in Cape Town to work—Lex was his driver, for goodness' sake.

He didn't do this. He wasn't the type of guy who hit on female employees, not if they were directors, managers or cleaners—or chauffeurs.

He owned the company. He paid her salary.

He. Wasn't. That. Guy.

At the sound of the lift door opening behind him in the hallway, Cole dropped to his haunches to pick up his laptop bag.

As three people passed his open door, he turned his back to them and gripped the handle of the laptop bag, hauling in long, deep gulps of winter air.

'Thanks for the lift,' he told Lex.

She nodded. He noticed that her braid was loose, and he wondered how it would look spread out on his pillow. 'It's my job.'

He took a deep breath and she nodded once before turning away and walking down the hallway to the lift. When the lift doors closed, he bent over and put his hands on his thighs, bent over and took a couple of long, steadying breaths. He couldn't remember when he'd last felt so shaky and off-balance.

How—in the name of all things holy—had things got out of hand so quickly?

Before her younger sisters had arrived, Lex had had a lover or two and thought she knew what attraction was.

She'd been so very, very wrong...

She liked men, liked how they made her feel, but nothing prepared her for the intensity she and Cole shared. As soon as his fingers connected with hers, she'd felt as if she was being tugged towards a portal and, had he kissed her, he would've propelled her into another universe where nothing existed but them.

Despite their non-kiss, she still felt shaky, off-balance and, hours later, her heart was still bouncing off the walls of her ribcage. A million butterflies had taken up residence in her stomach and she felt as though she could sleep for a week or run an ultra-marathon.

In other words, she didn't feel like herself.

Lex stood on the small veranda off the lounge of Addi's and her cottage, a blanket wrapped around her shoulders, the laughter of her sisters drifting in from where they were gathered in the kitchen. As they did every few minutes, her thoughts drifted back to what might've happened in the hotel room. Alone with Cole, she'd been oblivious to anything but him, entranced by the desire in his warm eyes, desperate to feel his mouth on hers, his big hands moving over her body.

When he looked at her, he made her feel powerful. Feminine. Lovely.

After she'd walked away from him, and when her heart rate had dropped to a pace where she thought it wasn't about to explode, she'd left the lift and taken a slow walk through the hotel to where the valet had delivered the SUV, hoping that the freezing wind would cool her burning cheeks and shock her back to reality. It hadn't, and for the rest of the day she'd been less than useless.

And she'd completely forgotten about the cupcakes… Snow and Nixi were still unimpressed.

Lex sighed, pulled her blanket tighter around her shoulders and sat down on the sofa tucked under the eaves. She pulled her legs up and rested her cheek on her knee, feeling both tired and, oh, so wired. Up until today, she hadn't known how intense physical attraction could be, how it could cause one to act irrationally. If she'd had any warning of the way Cole would flip her inside out, she would've run a mile, because she was very familiar with the effects of unbridled desire: she'd been living with the fallout of it all her life.

Her mother Joelle was a very sensual woman, someone who never hid the fact that she loved men, loved the way they made her feel and that she was built for excitement, not monogamy. Joelle ran from man to man, chasing that constant sexual high. If what Lex had experienced with Cole was the same high Joelle chased, then she sort of got it. Why wouldn't she want more of that as often as she could get it?

Lex didn't have a problem, per se, with how Joelle lived her life. She couldn't care less how many men she had, who she slept with and why. It was her body, her life, her choice…

But Lex hated the fact that she and her sisters were the random casualties of her mother's war against societal norms, being sexually constrained and being expected to stay in one place with one man. As young girls, she and Addi had been introduced to so many men and shunted into the spare bedroom of Joelle's latest boyfriend's flat, house or hovel. They'd keep their heads down and pretend to be invisible but within a few weeks, sometimes a few months, they'd be on the move again.

Only Storm's dad, Tom, bless him, had managed a few years before he'd called it quits with Joelle, taking Storm with him. After their split, life had continued as normal—a series of strange houses and strange men—until their mid-teens, when Joelle had convinced her Aunt Kate to allow Addi and her to stay with her for the long summer holidays, telling her aunt she had work in Thailand.

Joelle hadn't returned in the New Year and had only come back six months later. It was hard to tell who'd been happier—she and Addi, or Joelle—when Aunt Kate had informed Joelle that the sisters had a permanent home with her. But, thanks to years of instability and having experienced Joelle's rapid and impulsive decisions to move them on, Lex had known that anything and everything could change and had refused to get her hopes up only to have them come crashing down again.

It was only when she and Addi had inherited this, Aunt Kate's, house on her death shortly after Lex's twenty-first birthday that she'd felt that they had a permanent base and security, a place that was theirs. Nobody would ever again force them to move, kick them out or throw their stuff onto the pavement. They would never again be at the mercy of someone's charity, used as a bargaining piece to stay: *'You can't kick us out! I have children!'* Nor would they be blamed for the demise of another of Joelle's relationships: *'If I didn't have you two, he'd still love me.'*

Of course, history had repeated itself when Joelle had returned five years ago with two more daughters in tow.

Lex often thought about Joelle, how easily promises, plans and words of love tripped off her tongue.

The words came as freely as a stream flowed down a mountainous slope, yet she always walked away, every single time. Despite doing everything she could to become what Joelle wanted, from changing her hair colour and covering her freckles, her mum always walked away.

And, if her mother couldn't love her enough to stick around, how could she trust anyone else to?

'Lex? Are you okay?'

Lex lifted her head to see Addi standing in the doorway to their sitting room, her ultra-short blonde hair ruffled. She carried a wine glass and handed it to Lex, before sitting down next to her. Lex pulled the blanket from her shoulders and draped it across their legs, snuggling up to her older sister. They'd spent their childhood like this, cleaved together, standing up to a world ruled by volatile adults and trying to follow rules they didn't understand.

'Are the girls watching TV?' Lex asked.

'Yes,' Addi answered. 'Are you okay? You've been out here for a while.'

'I…' Lex started to tell Addi about the almost-kiss, but stopped when she realised she was drinking alone. Sharing a glass at the end of a day was what they did, a tradition.

'Are you okay?' Lex asked. Now that she looked closely, Addi looked exhausted. She had blue circles under her eyes, her pale skin was tight across her cheekbones and her normally quick-to-smile mouth was full of tension. 'Have you heard anything about your job?'

Addi shook her head and Lex could see she didn't want to discuss her work situation. 'You know I'm not that worried if I get retrenched, Lex. Just last month I had two calls from companies wanting to headhunt me. I'll pick up something very quickly. Let's not talk about that now, okay?' Addi rested her temple on Lex's shoulder. 'Storm called and she wanted to know how we felt about her taking the girls with her to visit Hamish and Callie at a beach house they've rented in Durban for the upcoming winter holidays.'

Hamish was Storm's older half-brother by her father Tom's first marriage and was married to Nixi's and Snow's paediatrician. They had two sons, roughly the same ages as Nixi and Snow.

'And how do you feel about that?' Lex asked her.

'I think they should go,' Addi told her. 'Durban is divine in winter, so much warmer than here. The kids will have a blast. And who better to look after them than an orthopaedic surgeon, a paediatrician and their sister, who is an experienced au pair? And you need a break, Lex. You are exhausted.'

She was, and the thought of not having to worry about the girls for three weeks made her feel both guilty and thoroughly over-excited. 'I'm okay with them going,' she told Addi.

Lex placed her glass on the table next to her, not really in the mood for wine, trying to think of a way to introduce Cole Thorpe into their conversation. For some stupid reason she didn't understand, she wanted to know whether Addi had met Cole yet and what she thought of him.

'So I picked the big boss up earlier...' she said, silently cursing herself. Why was she torturing herself like this? She should just put him out of her mind. 'I tossed my coffee over him.'

Addi looked horrified. 'Oh, Lex! Please tell me you're joking?'

She wished. 'You're friendly with Trish in Human Resources, Ads. Have you heard that I'm going to be fired?'

'No, as far as I know, you're still on retainer as Thorpe's part-time driver.'

Okay, good. Phew.

'He's a good-looking guy,' Addi mused.

That was like saying an asteroid strike was a slap. 'Have you met him?' Lex asked, irritated by the hint of anxiety she heard in her voice. Addi was a brown-eyed blonde, completely ravishing, and men routinely fell over themselves to get her to notice them.

'He called a firm-wide staff meeting yesterday afternoon, introduced himself— told everyone that he's here to inspect the operation, to look at the assets and tour the companies under the Thorpe umbrella, to consider his options.'

'Did he mention selling?'

'No, but it's common knowledge that he's in negotiations in the US and in the East to sell those assets. He'll probably do the same here,' Addi stated, sounding calm. 'I think you should look for another part-time job, Lex.'

She had been, but there weren't many that paid as well and were as flexible as her Thorpe Industries gig.

'Why can't he just leave us alone?' Lex muttered. If he'd stayed in London, she wouldn't have to look for work again and she wouldn't be sitting here feeling jumpy, weird and out of sorts.

'There's weird tension in your voice every time you talk about him,' Addi commented.

You should see us together, Lex silently replied. Electricity hummed and the air shimmered.

'Did something happen while you were driving him?'

Her, 'No,' wasn't a lie. All that had happened in the car was that their eyes had occasionally collided in the mirror. She couldn't remember one thing about the drive from the airport to the CBD. It had been as if she'd been on autopilot. It was a miracle she hadn't crashed the car.

She never kept secrets from Addi but she couldn't tell her she and Cole had nearly kissed in his hotel room. She didn't understand it so she couldn't explain it.

She took an overlarge sip of her wine. Yes, he'd ignited a spark—or a raging fire—within her but it didn't mean anything. It couldn't. It was just one of those strange, inexplicably random things that happened that were never to be repeated. Their eyes had connected across a busy airport, she'd liked what she'd seen, and so had he. Lex skipped over the embarrassing memory of tossing coffee on him and her tears, pausing the movie playing in her head on the scene where he'd swapped his wet jersey for a dry one, giving her a super-quick peek of his simply marvellous, muscled, powerful torso.

And, yes, they'd indulged in some serious eye contact in the car—she'd never seen eyes his colour before, a light golden-brown—but after parking the SUV she'd pulled herself together and told herself to do her job. She'd done as he'd asked and had taken his laptop bag up to his penthouse suite, desperately thinking of how she could persuade him to let him drive him.

Then their fingers had touched—their *fingers* for goodness' sake!—and all hell had nearly broken loose.

Or heaven. Or something.

Addi scooted away from her, her eyebrows raised. 'Is there something you're not telling me, Lex Satchell?'

I nearly kissed our boss and, given half the chance, would do it, and more, again. But need like that scares me, because every bad decision Joelle made was born out of passion and rooted in her obsession over a man. But I liked it. I like him.

Lex shook her head and looked away. She was making a big deal about nothing. She wasn't even going to see Cole again. He'd hired a car, but he didn't like being driven around by a chauffeur, so driving him had been a one-time thing. It was a one-and-done situation. She should stop thinking about him and move on.

'What aren't you telling me, Lex?'

Lex remembered the fear on Addi's face earlier and tossed her sister's question back in her face. When Addi wrinkled her nose and looked away, Lex knew she'd hit a target she hadn't known existed. Anxiety washed over her, pushing ice into her veins. 'Addi, what aren't you telling me?'

Addi stood up and stretched, placing her fists on her slim hips and arching her back. 'I'm going in. It's freezing out here and I'm getting cold.'

Lex was about to push when her phone beeped with a loud notification. She frowned and opened the message from the unknown number.

I have a dinner engagement. Pick me up from the office in an hour fifteen. CT.

Her stomach rolled over and her knees melted, just a little, at the thought of seeing him again.

Oh, Lord, she was in so much trouble here.

CHAPTER FOUR

ON THE MOTORWAY, Lex hit a puddle, eased off the accelerator and flicked her windscreen wipers onto a higher setting. She darted a look at Cole, who sat in the passenger seat next to her, his expression as remote as the endless, empty Skeleton Coast. When he'd sent her the text message earlier telling her he required her services this evening, her heart had bounced around her chest and she'd wondered if, like her, he couldn't stop thinking about their almost kiss.

She mentally slapped herself. Cole was a guy in his mid-thirties, someone who'd probably had a few serious relationships, many affairs and more than a few one-night stands. He hadn't given their encounter any more thought than the brand of fuel she put in her car.

She might not have been able to think of anything else, but he was far more experienced and sophisticated than she could ever be.

Sitting next to him and wishing he'd kiss her again, hoping that he was seeing her as a woman, not an employee, was an exercise in sheer stupidity. 'Thank you for making yourself available,' Cole said. 'I know it was short notice.'

'It's my job and not a problem. Why did you change your mind about driving yourself?'

'I haven't,' Cole replied. 'I wasn't happy with the hire car my assistant organised and had it returned. Somehow, the message that I required a replacement car was lost along the way.'

Lex grimaced at the annoyance she heard in his voice. She was glad she hadn't been on the other side of the phone when Cole demanded to know why he didn't have a car at the end of the day. In casual clothes he was impressive and sexy but, dressed in a deep-grey suit and a patterned tie in metallic shades of copper and gold, he looked powerful and remote.

Yet she wasn't intimidated. And her attraction to him had nothing to do with the fact that he wore ten-thousand-dollar designer suits, sported an outrageously expensive wristwatch and splashed designer cologne on his face—she really wouldn't mind burying her nose in his neck and staying there—but everything to do with their very combustible chemistry.

She still, rather desperately, wanted to know how his mouth tasted and whether, when she was plastered against him, her body would stop missing his. How could she miss something she'd never experienced? She had no idea, but she did.

The Chauffeur's Inconvenient Attraction to the CEO... Her life could be the title of a romance novel.

'I was out of line earlier and I apologise.'

Lex grimaced and turned her head away.

Be cool...pretend it didn't mean anything. Do not let him know that you've thought of nothing more since leaving him yesterday.

'It wasn't...optimal,' she agreed. Optimal? Where had that word come from?

'I want to assure you it was an aberration.' *Wow*. And how was she supposed to take that statement? Was she an aberration? Was almost kissing his driver an aberration? Kissing at all?

She stopped at a traffic light, turned to face him and lifted her arched eyebrows. In the dim light of the inside of the car, she saw colour touch his cheeks.

'I never lose control like that,' he admitted, shoving his hand through his hair and looking genuinely confused. She thought about pointing out that nothing had happened, that they hadn't actually kissed, but honesty had her admitting that, had they not heard those voices in the hallway, they would've kissed. And, possibly, done more.

'Are you tired? Overworked? Stressed?' Lex asked him instead, interested, despite her irritation—an *aberration?*—in what made him tick.

'All of the above,' Cole replied, 'All the time. It's my default mode.'

His deep sigh filled the car. 'It's been a very long, tough six months.'

What did that mean and how did it relate to what had almost happened between them? Did he only kiss strangers when he was stressed?

'I apologise, Ms Satchell.'

The traffic light turned green and Lex pulled away. They could discuss this to death, but she suspected she wouldn't get any satisfactory answers, so maybe it was better to put this behind them. Yes, she wanted him but that was her impetuosity talking, her long-neglected libido. It was time to be sensible and sober, to remember what was important—kissing him again wasn't, working as his driver was.

And this was the perfect opportunity to raise the subject. 'Cole—Mr Thorpe—I need to ask you whether I can get back to work as your driver.'

'I told you, I prefer to drive myself.'

Lex swallowed her growl. Fine, she got that he liked driving himself, but he didn't understand that his wanting to haul himself around Cape Town was making a serious dent in her income. She was paid a piddly retainer, but she earned the bulk of her money when she put in the kilometres behind the wheel. Driving Cole around would be an excellent way to bring cash to their communal table. And she wasn't too proud to tell him that. She needed money, and his being independent was blocking her from getting it. She wasn't asking for charity. She was asking him for the opportunity to do her job.

'Thorpe Industries only pays me a small retainer to be on call, but I only earn decent money when I drive. So your independence is affecting my earnings,' she said, keeping her tone as business-like as possible. He didn't need to know that the girls needed new winter pyjamas, that she needed to pay for next term's module and that her car desperately needed some work.

She felt his gaze on her face, but Lex kept her eyes on the traffic, watching for any sudden moves by impatient truckers or taxi drivers. He did, of course, have the right to drive himself. Nothing in her contract with Thorpe Industries stated that the owner or employees were obliged to use her services. But, damn, she hoped he would because, A, his was a very nice face and body to drive around and, B, she hoped he was nice enough to put aside his needs, wants or preferences so that she, or anyone else, could earn a reasonable wage. It was just the decent thing to do…

'Pick me up from my hotel at seven tomorrow morning,' Cole told her, his voice gruff. 'When I get to the office, I can give you my schedule for the day, but I usually end quite late.'

Lex did a mental fist-pump as she turned down the road to where Snell's, the restaurant, was situated. Looking for parking, she was grateful Storm was on leave from her au pair job, as she could do the school run for the next week or so, and then it would be the winter holidays. Surely Cole would be gone by mid-July? Lex reversed the car into an empty parking bay— her parallel parking skills were on point tonight—and briefly closed her eyes. Cole was prepared to let her drive him so she didn't have to worry about her income for the next few weeks. *Yay*.

Now all she had to do was stop thinking about his big body, his mouth and how his hands would feel on her body, on her breasts, between her legs.

Lex pulled up to the blackened windows of the restaurant and peered through the darkness at the small gold plaque on the side of the closed door. Snell's. It was a good indication that you were a fine-dining restaurant when all you needed as advertising was a twelve-inch black square with gold writing.

'Thank you,' Lex told him when she switched the ignition off. She nodded at the restaurant. 'I hope you have a good meal.'

He looked at her, his expression a little annoyed. 'What will you do while you are waiting for me?' he enquired.

In the boot was a bag containing her laptop and her study notes. She'd noticed an all-night café attached to a brightly lit garage on her way in and she'd thought she'd wait there and study until Cole was ready to be picked up. But she was just a car door down from the restaurant entrance and there were security guards outside and at each end of the brightly lit street. She would be perfectly safe waiting for him right there.

'I'm going to stay here and, when you're done, I'm going to drive you back to your hotel.'

Because that was her job for now. It wasn't for ever. In two years she'd have her degree and would look for work in her field. Time flew by quickly and, one day, working as a chauffeur—and as a maid and as a coffee barista…she'd done both—would be a distant memory.

'One of the reasons I hate having a chauffeur is that I loathe knowing people are waiting around for me,' Cole muttered. He undid his seat belt and Lex reached for her door handle, about to hop out and run around the car to open the door for him. His hand on her arm stopped her progress and she felt an electrical buzz skitter up her arm. 'I've agreed to you driving me, but if you open one door for me I will fire you.'

Her lips twitched, amused and surprised by his lack of snobbery. She tipped her head to the side, knowing this was a battle she wouldn't win. 'I'm going to get out of the car and get a laptop bag from the boot,' she told him. She lifted her hands in mock surrender. 'I promise I won't come anywhere near your door.'

'Smarty pants,' Cole muttered. 'Stay there.'

Since the heavens were dripping again—this time it was a fine, persistent drizzle—Lex opted to wait in her warm seat, and within a minute Cole opened her door and dumped her laptop bag in her lap. 'Will you be okay?' he asked. Lex swallowed at the concern in his voice. When had someone, outside of her sisters, last wondered whether she'd be alright? She couldn't actually remember.

She nodded, conscious that the rain was darkening his grey suit to black and dampening the waves in his hair. 'Cole—sorry, Mr Thorpe—I'll be fine. Go inside, *please.*'

He narrowed his eyes at her and poked his index finger into her thigh. 'Calling me anything but Cole would be another fireable offence.'

All righty, then. Cole slammed her door shut and walked over to the black door, and the security guard whipped it open for him. But, instead of walking inside, he reached for his wallet and pulled out what looked to be a high-denomination note. He nodded at the car, then at her, and when Lex saw the bouncer nodding in agreement as he took Cole's money she knew she had her own private security guard.

Sweet, she thought. And thoughtful. Two things she hadn't expected Cole Thorpe to be.

'Snell's was voted as the world's fiftieth best restaurant in 2021,' Jude said, sitting opposite him.

It was good to be with Jude, Cole decided as he looked around the restaurant, taking in the surprisingly warm industrial space with a busy, open kitchen in the middle of the long restaurant. They'd attended university together in London and Jude had gone on to inherit the Cape Town based Fisher Holdings, a well-respected hospitality and leisure empire.

Cole looked up at the cloud of steel discs hanging from the ceiling, and idly wondered how many of the world's best restaurants he'd eaten at over the past ten years. Twenty? Thirty? More?

He'd eaten sushi made by the master Jiro Ono at Sukiyabashi Jiro, eaten duck at Noma, Copenhagen, and Massimo Bottura's 'Five Ages of Parmigiano Reggiano' at his restaurant in Modena.

But the worst of it was that he knew, without thought

or hesitation, that no meal he'd ever eaten would hold the complexity of Lex's mouth. She would be, as the French said, *bonne bouche*, a delicious mouthful. He wanted, more than anything else, to feast on her.

He understood sexual attraction—at thirty-six, he should—but he couldn't work out how she'd slipped under his skin with such ease. She'd invaded his thoughts and, because he couldn't stop thinking about her, he felt a little panicky and angsty. And annoyed.

He didn't have time for distractions, damn it. Why here? Why now? Was his reaction to her a consequence of the stress he'd been under lately and the denial of his revenge against his father? Were his emotions, frustration and disappointment, leaking out of the steel vault he'd locked them into and masquerading as need and interest? It had been such a weird time lately that anything was possible.

Not recognising himself, frustrated by his strange thoughts—he never gave any woman this much space in his head, ever—he tossed back his whisky. When he opened his eyes, he saw Jude looking from his glass to his face and back to his glass again. 'Tough few days?' he asked.

Cole dug his thumb and index finger into his eye sockets, rubbed hard and shook his head. 'No more than usual,' he lied. He'd only nearly kissed—ravished—his chauffeur an hour after he'd met her. And, despite never having employed a driver, he now had one.

Jude called the waiter over, ordered the tasting menu and leaned back in his chair, his eyes on Cole's face. They'd become friendly while playing for the same university based social rugby team seventeen years ago and somehow, despite their insane schedules, had remained friends. As students, they'd taken a skiing holiday every

January and they'd kept up the tradition, carving out time to do something they both loved. When they'd been young, they'd saved hard to spend a week on the slopes. These days, they still stayed out all day, alternating between snowboarding and black diamond runs, but instead of returning to a youth hostel they enjoyed private suites and had immediate access to steam rooms and experienced masseurs to work out the kinks seventeen years had put into their muscles.

'Did you ever get hold of your brother?' Jude asked.

Cole shook his head. 'No, and I've been told not to expect him to make contact. As I've recently discovered, he's been practising Buddhism for years and often expressed a wish to join a monastery. Nobody took him seriously until he did.'

Jude leaned back in his seat, his narrowed gaze penetrating. 'Are you very sure you want to get rid of the Thorpe assets, Cole? You are dismantling your family's century-old business.'

His family—the one he'd never been allowed to be a part of? His first memories were of being confused about why his father wouldn't pay him any attention, why he only ever focused on Sam. His parents had divorced when he'd been four, and he'd spent his childhood wondering what was wrong with him, and why Sam had got to spend time with their mum while he'd never seen his father.

He'd frequently asked his mum for an explanation and had been told that his father was 'funny that way', and that once his mind was made up nothing would change it. When he'd mentally divorced himself from his father, he'd vowed he'd make a fortune to rival that of his father's, and that he'd do it for himself, by himself. But he'd still craved their attention. What better way to get that than by taking control of their empire?

Taking away Thorpe Industries had been the only way he could think of to make them notice him but they'd both dodged that bullet.

Damn them.

Cole picked up the menu and scanned it, frustrated. Up until his father died, he'd had a plan, a reason to work long hours, to push himself. He'd wanted to be in a position where his father and brother couldn't ignore him, where they'd have to look at him across a conference table and know that he held all the power, their financial lives in his hands. They would've been forced to acknowledge him, deal with him and respect him.

But, by dying and stepping aside, they'd both robbed him of that opportunity and him of his purpose. He felt like a leaf on a river in a flood, swept away and out of control, aimless.

'So, I've been looking through your South African-based assets,' Jude told him. 'I'll buy all your hospitality interests, except the ski-lodge.'

'Why don't you want the ski-lodge?' Cole asked. The waiter had picked up two plates from the pass and he hoped they were destined for their table. He was famished.

'Firstly, it's a ski-lodge in Africa, dude. Yeah, it's in the mountains, very remote, and the area gets snow in winter, but it's never guaranteed.'

'Surely they have snow machines?' Cole suggested, leaning back so that the waiter could deposit his plate in front of him.

'They have them. Look, judging by the photographs, it's a stunning place. Your father spent a king's ransom renovating it. But to recoup those costs, your hospitality division had to stratospherically hike the accommodation costs. South Africans who can afford to pay those rates can afford to fly to Gstaad or Aspen, Whistler or Verbier, where there are numerous runs, guaranteed snow and world-class facilities,' Jude explained. 'Frankly, I don't understand the decision-making behind the ski resort at all but I've heard it was your father's pet project.'

Cole frowned. Why, when he had businesses around the world, would Grenville have cared so much about a ten-bedroom boutique hotel in a remote part of South Africa?

And why, if he didn't care about his father, Thorpe assets or the family empire, did that puzzle arouse his interest and curiosity?

It was eleven-thirty when Cole tapped on the driver's window of the company SUV. Lex turned her head and looked at him through the rain-splattered glass, and it took her a while to switch from whatever she'd been reading to her job as his driver. She hit the lock to open the passenger door and Cole ducked around the hood of the vehicle, clutching his fancy takeout box. It was raining harder now, and he felt icy drops hit his hair and roll down the back of his neck. Africa was supposed to be about sunshine, but all he'd experienced was wild and wet weather, and more was on the way.

Fabulous.

He climbed into the passenger seat and balanced the box on the dashboard, shoving his hands into his hair to dispel the rain drops. Without asking, Lex punched the button to start the car and warm air hit his face and chest. 'Thanks.'

'How was dinner?' she asked as she closed her textbook. He looked down to see that it was a battered copy, something to do with the evolution of neuroscience. An array of sticky notes poked out from its pages and Lex slipped the book and her equally old laptop into her bag. Zipping it up, she placed the bag behind his seat. She'd pulled her long hair back into a messy bun, and he reached across and removed a pen from behind her ear and handed it to her.

'Thanks,' she replied, blushing. She tossed it into the console and pulled on her seatbelt.

He saw her glance at the box before looking away.

'Back to the hotel?' she asked.

'In a minute,' He reached for the box, flipped open the lid and handed it to her. Lex took it with a puzzled frown, looking down.

'What is this?'

'You picked me up at six, which means you probably haven't eaten,' Cole explained. He reached into his jacket pocket and brought out a set of chopsticks, which he handed to her. 'Peter Snell boxed it up for me—it's a selection from his tasting menu.'

Lex's mouth dropped open and it took all of Cole's determination not to bend down and cover that luscious mouth with his. 'He's a Michelin-starred chef,' she stated.

'So?'

'You asked a Michelin-starred chef for a takeaway?' Lex asked, stupefied. 'For me?'

What was the big deal? He'd asked, Snell had said yes, here he was.

Cole waved the chopsticks in the air. 'Do you want these or not?' he asked, hiding his smile when Lex snatched them out of his hand. She slid them between her fingers and lifted a piece of pastry-wrapped fish to her mouth.

'It's tuna, obviously. But what's between the fish and the pastry? It tastes citrusy but I can't identify it.'

'Yuzu and enoki mushrooms, I think.' He pointed to the other dishes. 'Veal, Jerusalem artichokes, scallops and some orange-chocolate-chilli thing.'

'Oh, yum.' Lex took the second bite of tuna before darting a horrified look at him. 'Sorry, I can eat this later. Let me get you back to the hotel.'

'Eat, Lex. I'm not in a hurry. All that waits for me at the hotel is more work.'

Lex waved her chopsticks in the air. 'You're going back to the hotel to work? It's after eleven.'

He pushed his chair back and stretched out his legs. He linked his hands across his flat stomach and rolled his head around. 'Says the woman who was working up until ten minutes ago.'

'Mmm, that's because I have an assignment due.' She opened the lid to the artichoke dish and stared down. 'I've never eaten artichokes before.'

'They are delicious,' Cole assured her and watched as she took a cautious bite. She'd surprised him tonight, in so many ways. She'd been so up and honest about needing work, so unembarrassed about telling him that she needed to drive to earn money. He admired her put-it-out-there attitude. She didn't seem to care what he, or anyone else, thought about her.

When he'd told her that he didn't need her to drive him, he hadn't given a thought to how his arbitrary decision might affect her. He did what he liked, what suited him, and hadn't given her needs a second thought. He felt ashamed of himself, annoyed by his self-serving attitude.

He had to do better, be better. Think more about people and how his actions affected them.

Though maybe a part of him not wanting Lex to drive him was because he knew that in the confines of a car, surrounded by her smell, hearing her rich voice, he'd be constantly distracted by what he wanted to do to her in bed—or on a desk, or up against a wall. He didn't like being distracted or frustrated—who did? He'd thought it better to put her, and his fantasies, out of sight and mind.

Hah! No chance of that now. 'What are you studying?' he asked.

'Psychology—specifically forensic psychology,' she told him, her attention on her food. She'd already demolished half of the food and didn't look like she was going to stop any time soon. He didn't mind. All that waited for him was spreadsheets and emails, and boring ones at that. He'd much rather sit in a stationary car in the rain with Lex than be alone in his hotel room.

And that was strange because, after an evening spent in a busy restaurant, even if he did eat with someone he knew well, he normally couldn't wait for the quiet of his hotel room.

'Why psychology?' he asked, intrigued by her. It was obvious that she was intelligent, but she worked as a driver and she needed flexible work hours. Where were her parents, and why was she raising her sisters? Was that why she hadn't finished her degree years ago?

Lex inspected the perfectly round medallion of veal. She grimaced and raised her eyes to look at him. 'Veal is baby cow, right?'

He smiled at her squeamishness. 'Think of it as coming in a polystyrene tray wrapped in plastic,' he told her. 'And, trust me, you want to taste that, it's the best dish on the menu.'

'Good enough for me.' Without hesitation, Lex popped the veal into her mouth. She chewed, tipped her head to the side and incredulity crossed her face. He wondered if the same look of wonder and contentment would cross her face when she orgasmed. He thought it would, but at double the intensity. And he was desperate to see her do exactly that.

'So, psychology?' he prompted, dragging his thoughts off his vivid imaginings of Lex's long, pale body, her hair bright against the white sheets of his bed. He felt his trousers getting smaller and counted to ten. Then to twenty.

He. Paid. Her. Salary.

Nope, the sexy image wouldn't be dispelled.

Holy Batman.

'Oh…right.' She stared out of the window again, as if she was trying to find the right words. 'Initially, I studied it because I wanted to try to work out why certain people in my life acted the way they acted, did what they did. Then I realised it would take me a lifetime to understand if there was any sense to be made, so I switched to forensic because the criminal mind fascinates me.'

'So, no criminals in your family?' he asked, joking.

'Not that I know of,' Lex replied. 'Criminally stupid, sure. Actual miscreants? I don't think so.' She looked down at her supper and blew out her cheeks. 'I am so full.'

She only had the orange-chocolate-chilli tart left to eat. And, if she didn't, he would. It was the perfect end to the meal. 'You've got to try it,' he told her. 'It's stunning.'

She looked at him, placed her hand on her stomach and popped the bite-sized confection into her mouth. She chewed, looked up at the ceiling and chewed some more, looking undecided and underwhelmed as she did so. Oh, come on! How could she not like it? It was delicious.

'Well?' he demanded when she swallowed and put her chopsticks into the box and closed the lid. She took the handkerchief he pulled from the inside pocket of his jacket and delicately wiped her mouth, then her fingers, on the cool cotton.

'Not terrible,' she told him, and it took him a few beats for him to realise that her tongue was firmly in her cheek and she was teasing him.

He put his hand on the back of her neck and shook her very gently. He couldn't keep his lips from inching upwards into a smile. 'That's probably the best dessert you've ever eaten.'

As soon as the words left his mouth, he realised that he sounded as if he was putting her down, highlighting the financial differences between them. He hadn't meant to. It had been one of the best meals of his life too.

'Absolutely,' Lex replied, shrugging. 'There's no question that it's the best meal I've ever eaten. Thank you for arranging that for me.'

He'd lost track of all the exceptional meals he'd eaten in his life, but watching Lex eat bits and pieces from Patrick Snell's tasting menu from a box in a car in Cape Town was his best food experience this decade. Possibly ever.

Damn it. He was in a world of trouble here. And his honest, direct driver had put him there.

Brilliant.

'Let's get you back to the Vane,' Lex said, starting the car.

And, when they got there, it took all his willpower to leave the car without asking her to join him upstairs.

CHAPTER FIVE

COLE WAS EXHAUSTED, thanks to lying awake in his hotel room and fantasising about his heavily freckled, redheaded driver. He'd spent the past week reading too many profit and loss statements and balance sheets and his brain was fried. He'd been working twenty-four-seven for months now, and he knew himself well enough to know that he needed a break, to step back and away for a day, maybe two.

A weekend of doing nothing more intellectually stimulating than breathing would be the best way for him to rest and recharge. Yesterday, Lex had asked him if she could have the morning off and he'd agreed, taking the keys to the company vehicle from her hand. He pulled the SUV into its designated parking space in the underground garage and sighed. The car smelled like Lex, and he was once again bombarded by the image of her red hair, recalling the passion in her green eyes as he'd lowered his head to kiss her. He could almost feel her elegant hands in his hair, the feel of her long legs around his hips.

Why couldn't he get the memory of that kiss-that-never-happened out of his mind?

He definitely needed a break. Or a lobotomy.

Cole grabbed his laptop bag, exited his car and

slammed the door shut, mentally running through his schedule. He had virtual meetings all morning but he was free from lunch onwards. He was planning to leave the city for the weekend and had asked his assistant to book two nights at one of the upmarket safari operations in the area. He knew there were a couple just a few hours' drive from Cape Town.

Could he ask Lex to drive him and take her along? Would that work, was that even an option?

No, of course it wasn't, for all the reasons he'd previously thought of and, possibly, a hundred he hadn't considered.

Cole felt an icy wind swirl around his neck and heard the unmistakable sound of a car with a hole in its exhaust. He turned and watched a yellow hatchback roll up the ramp. Through a windscreen sporting a crack in the top right-hand corner, he caught a glimpse of red hair and a pale face behind the wheel. A cool blonde sat next to Lex, and another blonde and two little girls, one with hair as red as Lex's, sat in the back.

Were these her sisters? *All* of them?

Standing next to the lift, partially hidden by a concrete column, Cole winced at the sound of squeaking brakes—her brake pads needed replacing—and he watched the older blonde, dressed in a black power suit, exit the car. Lex switched off the engine and the little girls left the car, taking turns to hug the first blonde. Lex stood between her door and the frame, looking at them over the rusty roof.

'Bye, Addi,' they said. Right, so the blonde was Addison Fields, and she worked in his hospitality and leisure division.

'I might as well drive Storm and the girls straight from here to the airport, Addi,' Lex said as Addison hugged the second blonde, whom he assumed was Storm. 'It's a bit early but there's no point in going home first and leaving again in fifteen minutes.'

'We're going to the beach, we're going to the beach,' the little redhead chanted, spinning around in circles. Cole shivered, unable to understand her excitement. It was wet, windy and cold, weather that only Arctic penguins enjoyed.

Storm chivvied the small girls back into the car and the three women stood in a circle, their voices carrying over to him.

Lex, who faced him, smiled and it was like a fist ploughed into his sternum. Her joyous, wide grin could power a small city. 'Five years, guys. It's been five years since I've had a break. Am I mean to be this excited?' She bit her lower lip, suddenly looking deflated.

Storm rubbed her arm and Addison shook her head before speaking. 'No, babe. You know you're the best sister ever and you've been with them constantly since the day they arrived. I go to work and don't spend a lot of time with them. You do. Take these three weeks and enjoy them, Lex, because, honey, you deserve it.'

Cole recalled his mother telling him that children were expensive, time-consuming and limited your freedom.

His mother, so warm and affectionate.

'What are you going to do with all your spare time, Lex?' Storm asked her.

Have an affair with him? Cole wished.

'I'd love to take a road trip and just drive and drive and drive, but I have to ferry Cole Thorpe around. The money is too good for me to take a holiday right now. Besides, my car is shot, and fuel prices are crazy. So, in between driving him, I'll just nap, study and binge-watch box sets.'

'Maybe we could take a day trip up to Lamberts Bay,' Addison suggested.

Lex smiled. 'I'd love that,' she answered, but Cole knew that wasn't what she wanted or needed. She wanted the open road, the freedom of driving. It wasn't about the destination but the journey: the sound of tyres on the tarmac, the growl of an engine, the silence and vastness of an uninhabited landscape.

'I'm sorry about booking my car in for a service today. If I knew that the girls were flying to Durban today, I would've scheduled it for another time.'

Lex shrugged. 'Their holiday was a last-minute arrangement, how were you to know?'

Addison sent a doubtful look at the yellow car. 'But I hate you doing long trips in your car, Lex, or being on the highway.'

Lex wrinkled her nose. 'I know, I do too, especially in this weather. The tyres are smoother than I'd like.' She hesitated before speaking again. 'I know it's expensive, but I think we should put them in a cab.'

Cole cranked his head to look at her tyres and noticed that they definitely needed replacing. In wet weather, they would slide all over the road.

'I'll pay for it,' Storm offered.

Addison shook her head. 'Honey, you paid for the flights to Durban, and you're going to be entertaining the girls for the next three weeks. You need to save your money. I think the house credit card has a little room on it, Lex.'

Lex nodded. 'Okay, cool. Let me just park and I'll order one.'

This was ridiculous. There was a perfectly good SUV

sitting right there, with a full tank of fuel, doing nothing. He saw Lex's eyes widen as he stepped out from behind the pillar and her gorgeous mouth dropped open.

'Good morning, Lex,' he said, deliberately formal.

Her face pinkened under her freckles. 'Uh…morning.' He walked up to Addison, holding out his hand. 'I presume you are Addison Fields? I'm Cole Thorpe.'

Addison looked a little dazed but she put her hand in his. 'I'm sorry we haven't connected personally before now, Mr Thorpe.'

'I hear Jude Fisher has been running you ragged,' he replied. He looked down at the two little girls who were looking at him with wide eyes through the back window.

'Sisters?' he asked, aiming his question at Lex.

'Yep. This is my middle sister, Storm, and Nixi and Snow are in the car,' she told him.

Cole looked down at the little girls, who couldn't have been more different in looks if they'd tried. The older was a dark-haired, dark-eyed beauty while the younger had Lex's red hair, complexion and eye colour. This was what Lex's little girl would look like, he realised—all long limbs, pale skin, red hair and freckles.

Addison bit her lip, looking embarrassed. 'I know I'm late, Mr Thorpe, but I'll be up in a minute. I just need to sort something out.'

In other words: *shoo*. But nobody told him where to go or what to do. He looked at Lex and nodded to the SUV. 'There's no need to order a cab.'

Lex's eyebrows raised in silent disapproval of his eavesdropping. He shrugged. 'Voices travel in empty spaces. Use the company car to take your family to the airport, Lex. The roads are slick and it's the safest option in the rain.'

Lex lifted her nose in the air and her mouth thinned. He knew that she was about to refuse but Addison beat her to the punch. 'Thank you so much, Mr Thorpe, that's incredibly generous of you. We'll contribute to the cost of the fuel.'

He appreciated the offer. 'That's not necessary, Addison. I am aware of how hard you've been working lately, and I'm happy to help.'

Still looking at Addison, he asked her whether she was free to meet with him shortly. 'I've been meaning to catch up with you and chat about your future with Thorpe Industries.'

He saw the flash of fear in her eyes and immediately looked at Lex and saw the same scared expression on her lovely face. Storm just bent her head and looked at the grubby floor. The realisation that the three women were terrified Addison was going to lose her job hit him with all the force of a sledgehammer, and he was reminded that his actions had real-life, real-world consequences.

Judging by the fact that they were debating whether to hire a cab or not, money was very tight.

'Half an hour?' he asked Addison before looking at Lex and handing her the keys to the SUV.

'Drive safely, Lex. It's horrible out there,' he told her, sounding serious.

'Yes, I know.' She nodded, swallowed and nodded again. 'Thank you. I appreciate you letting me use the car.'

She didn't like him knowing they were in a jam but wasn't too proud to express her gratitude. He was already deeply attracted to this woman. He didn't need to like her as well.

He heard the lift open behind him and nodded. 'Have

a good trip, ladies. Addison, I'll see you in half an hour. Lex, I'd like to see you when you get back too.'

'Me?' Lex responded, confused. 'Why?'

He couldn't tell her that he needed to know that she was back safely, that he needed to see her face, so instead of answering he stepped into the lift and hit the side of his fist against the button to close the lift doors.

He glanced at his watch as the lift took him to his penthouse office. He didn't have any trips scheduled for today, and after hearing that Lex needed some time off last night he'd given her the rest of the weekend off, telling her he wouldn't need her again until Monday morning.

Right, he had a couple of hours to work out a reason for wanting to see her again. He was a smart guy. He was sure he could find something to tell her that she would believe.

Because telling her that he wanted to know that she was safe and that he'd missed seeing her face this morning, that he wanted to kiss her again—that he wanted to spend the weekend with her, preferably in bed—was out of the question. It was a shock to realise that, even if sex was off the table, he wouldn't mind her company, seeing her blinding white smile, exploring her bright mind.

What? Was he catching feelings for this woman? Was that the strange sensation he was experiencing? If he was, he'd better stop. And he could. He could gather up his emotions and shove them behind the sky-high wall he'd built. He'd done it often enough before and could, and would, do it again.

After meeting with Addison—and reassuring her that he'd talk to Jude about him taking her on when he acquired his hospitality portfolio—Cole had a pounding headache and a craving for a decent cup of coffee. The only down side of having a virtual assistant was that he had to track down and make his own coffee.

On crazily busy mornings like this one, not having coffee delivered was a pain in his butt.

Cole leaned back in his leather seat and looked out of his window onto a spectacular view of Lion's Head. Or, it would be spectacular, if the famous landmark wasn't obscured by driving rain. A cold front had moved in and another, bigger one was on its way.

He wasn't going to see the African sun for a while.

He thought back to his meeting with Addison. Shortly after sitting down opposite him, Addison had expressed her sympathy for his dad's passing and told him Grenville had hired her a few months after she'd finished her degree, a wet-behind-the-ears kid with no experience, and had become her mentor.

His father had taken a chance on Addison, a stranger, but hadn't given him the time of day. It shouldn't still hurt but it did. Addison wasn't the first person Grenville had looked after and mentored—there was a young woman in India, and a few people in the States, who hadn't stopped singing his praises.

Grenville had been able to see the potential in other people but had never offered his youngest son what he so readily gave to others. Did Grenville know that he'd graduated from the London School of Economics with a brilliant degree, that he'd got his MBA in record time? That he was the youngest hedge fund manager employed at Hershel and Grimm, one of the oldest, most respected investment firms in the world? Did he know he'd left them after a year and had taken most of their clients—their choice, not his—with him? That he had been a millionaire by thirty, a billionaire a few years later? Grenville had evidently cared far more for other people than he did for his own son.

It was that simple.

Why? What had he done? It was painful not to know. But being ostracised had made him tough, made him resilient, and, damn, it had made him determined to show his brother and father what he could do, what he'd achieved. Had his father lived, they would've been forced to acknowledge his achievement, to accept that he'd far exceeded the low bar that had been set for him. That he was their equal in every way that counted.

He felt cheated, like a child who'd reached for his stack of presents on Christmas day to have them whipped away and replaced with a chunk of coal. He'd so badly wanted his father's approval, a hint of respect, because if he couldn't have his love—and that had never been on the cards—he'd have settled for respect and approval. Love: it was such a stupid emotion. He'd been right to walk away from it, to stop looking for it. It caused nothing but heartache. It was far easier to live his life emotionally unconnected.

His eyes fell onto the Rossdale Ski Lodge folder, and he picked it up and banged its corner on his desk. He felt jumpy and irritated, and unable to focus.

Unfortunately, his inability to concentrate wasn't something new.

Since his dad's death and Sam's disappearance, it felt as if all he'd done was react. He was a guy who called the shots, he didn't take them.

Right, focus, Thorpe.

What was he going to do about Rossdale Ski Lodge, the asset Jude didn't want, and the acquisition and the refurbishment of which puzzled both Jude and Addison?

He understood why. The cost of the renovation and

refurbishment had meant that they'd had to charge exorbitantly outrageous nightly rates, and the lodge had had just a handful of customers in the eighteen months it had been open. It was run by a couple who were paid a huge salary to do nothing.

He needed to see the place for himself, to try and figure out what his father had been thinking when he'd purchased the property. He wouldn't get that information from balance sheets and spreadsheets so that meant a trip to the far-away property. Cole pulled up a map and grimaced when he saw that it was more than a twelve-hour drive to reach the lodge.

It would be quicker to hire a private plane, then a helicopter. That was likely how his father had tackled the journey.

Cole reached for his phone, thinking there had to be someone in this place who could get him a cup of coffee. He was about to call down to Reception when he heard knocking and a bright head appeared between the door and its frame.

His heart settled and sighed, and he waved Lex to come inside. When he saw that she carried two mega cups of coffee and a brown grease-stained bag, he nearly wept with joy and briefly considered proposing to her.

The thought made him smile and, funnily enough, didn't make his skittish heart want to bolt for the hills. *Weird.*

Cole had to stop himself from lunging across the desk to take the cup she held out. He lifted the mug to his mouth and took a hit of the hot, rich liquid. It was black and strong, just the way he liked it.

Lex took the seat opposite him, amusement turning her eyes lighter. 'Wow. A little addicted, are we?'

'A lot addicted,' Cole replied. 'Thank you, you have no idea how much I needed this.'

'I'm beginning to get the idea. You wanted to see me, I wanted coffee, so I picked up one for you as well.'

He couldn't remember when someone had last brought him a cup of coffee, or anything else, just because it occurred to them. It was a small gesture, but to Cole it felt as if someone had handed him a winning lottery ticket.

Cole nodded to the paper bag. 'And that?'

Lex smiled. 'That is a thank you gift for letting me use the SUV. I know this tiny bakery, and they do a limited run of the most fabulous chocolate croissants in the city. I called the owner and begged her to keep two for me. You loved the dessert from the other night, so I thought you'd enjoy this too.'

Cole reached for the bag, opened it and closed his eyes as the delicious smell of butter, chocolate and pastry hit his nostrils. He'd run eight miles on the treadmill and done a weightlifting session in the hotel gym this morning and eaten only bran and yoghurt for breakfast. He deserved something sweet and artery-clogging.

He broke off a piece of the croissant and nodded in approval when she did the same. He popped it into his mouth and closed his eyes at the hit of sweetness and spice.

As he ate, he tried to keep himself from launching across the table to find out what the combination of Lex and croissants tasted like. He watched as she unwound her scarf and shed her battered but still chic bomber-style leather jacket. Today's tight long-sleeved T-shirt was a pretty mint colour and her skinny jeans disappeared into knee-high boots.

'Did your sisters get off okay?' he asked.

'Yes. Snow cried a little, but she was fine by the time I left.'

Cole stood up, walked around the desk and perched on the edge of it, facing Lex, his thigh just an inch or two from her knee. Giving into temptation, he stroked the pad of his thumb across her cheekbone. 'Why do your younger sisters live with you, Lex? Where's their mother?'

Those incredible eyes met his and he saw a flicker of pain cross her face. 'In Thailand. She's been there since we were teenagers. We've had them for five years,' Lex answered him, and he didn't hear a hint of rancour or resentment in her voice. 'Nixi was three, Snow two.'

So she'd been their mother, father and sister and the pillars of their world for five years and would be for the rest of their lives. She would've been twenty-three or twenty-four when they'd dropped into her life. He rubbed the back of his neck, unable to understand how nonchalant she sounded, as though taking in two small children was what young adults did every day.

'And your father? Their father? Or fathers?' he demanded, unable to make sense of the dynamic.

Lex lifted one shoulder and he suspected her blasé expression was well-practised. 'My mum has a very relaxed attitude towards sex, and obviously contraception. And her lovers' names.'

Lex hesitated before continuing. 'She put the name of Addi's father on her birth certificate, and she married Storm's dad. My father was a guy called Seamus, but she's not completely sure if she got the right guy on the right night.'

'I don't get it. Weren't you angry? Frustrated? Bitter?'

'At what? Not knowing who my dad is or being left to raise the girls?'

'Either,' Cole replied. 'Both.'

'I can't be mad at my biological father. He doesn't know about me and never will. I was the result of a random hook-up between two very drunk, possibly high, people.' Lex shrugged and picked at a tiny thread on the cuff of her shirt. 'As for raising my half-sisters, how would being angry help? Nixi and Snow were already feeling lost and uprooted, they didn't need to know that they were unwanted too.'

His family hadn't given him a fraction of the love and care Lex—and the other sisters—showed those two little girls. They'd had all the money in the world but had been emotionally bankrupt. The sisters, from what he gathered, were short on cash but long on loyalty. He couldn't form the words to tell her how he was overwhelmingly impressed by her, that he admired her courage and intensely respected her, but she might get the message if he kissed her. So he did.

Lex sighed and her breath hit his lips, holding a hint of coffee, croissant and mint mouthwash. Cole fought the urge to take the kiss deeper, to haul her up so that her body was flush against his, her head tipped to take his deep, long and sexy kiss. Lex's fingers came up to rest on his jaw, rough with stubble. Her lips softened, he tasted her sigh and then her tongue came out to brush against his, spicy and delightful.

Her mouth was a revelation with soft, unpainted lips, as smooth and soft as expensive ice-cream. All he could think of was getting closer to her, to having his hands on that soft skin. Forgetting where he was, who he was, he stood up, pulled her to her feet and pushed her so that her back was to the wall next to his desk. He crowded her with his body, chest to chest, his knee between her thighs. He gripped her hips, enjoying her slim but curvy body, but he needed to know whether her skin was as soft as he imagined. He pulled her shirt from his jeans and slid his hand under her fabric, sighing at the silkiness of her skin. Lex wound her arms around his neck and kissed him, as hot for him as he was for her.

Cole felt his erection straining the fabric of his trousers, hot, heavy and desperate. He placed his hands on Lex's hips, easily lifting her so that their mouths were level. In a move that was as natural as it was unexpected, she wrapped her legs around his legs and rocked against him, releasing soft little sounds in the back of her throat.

Lex's elegant hands slipped under his shirt and he shuddered as her fingers danced up and down his spine, and dipped behind the waistband of his trousers. Needing to know more of her, to know everything, he placed his hand on her breast and drew his thumb across her nipple. Would it be as pink as her lips? Would she like it if he captured it between his tongue and the roof of his mouth…?

Damn, he needed a bed, but there was a desk just a foot or two from them…

There was a desk…and they were in his office and, because he didn't have a gatekeeper sitting at the secretary's desk next door, they could be interrupted at any second. And the last thing he wanted was interruptions.

So he pulled back, blew out a long stream of air and led her back to her chair, which she sank into with a long sigh. Cole reached for his coffee, resumed his previous position facing her and stretched out his legs.

'Another aberration, Cole?' she asked, looking him dead in the eye, and Cole felt pinned down. Damn, she was so direct.

'I don't understand.'

'You called our almost-kiss at the hotel an aberration,' Lex explained.

That hadn't been a good choice of words. Cole pushed his hand through his hair. 'No, but kissing you was...is...ill-advised. I'm your *boss*, Lex. I'm never anything but professional and the fact that you can make me lose my head is baffling.'

'If it's any consolation, I can't afford to put my job on the line by making out with my employer,' Lex told him. 'If you do sell your Cape Town assets, both Addi and I will lose our jobs, so I need to make bank while we can.'

While he had more money than most—a *lot* more money than most—he did understand the pressure of only having himself to rely on, of knowing that if he didn't make it work, nobody would do it for him. He couldn't promise Lex a flexible job, but he could reassure her about Addi. 'As I told Addison earlier, if I sell the hospitality sector to Jude Fisher I'll make Addison's job a condition of that sale. She won't have to accept Jude's offer, but he'll have to employ her for at least a year if he wants to buy my assets.'

She looked at him as if he'd hung the moon and stars. Damn it, he could get used to seeing that expression on her face. 'Thank you, Cole. That's... Wow, an incredible offer.'

It was and now he had to sell it to Jude. But, if he'd read his friend's expression correctly whenever Addison was mentioned, it wouldn't be a difficult negotiation.

He just wished he could do something for Lex. He could write her a cheque but knew she'd never, in a million years, accept his charity. No, she needed to drive to earn money, and a germ of an idea started to percolate and bubble. If she drove him to Rhodes, where his ski-lodge was situated, she would earn a packet, far more than she usually would. And he'd be able to give her that road trip she seemed to want so much.

Cole stood up, his mind running a million miles a minute. He'd been planning to fly into Rhodes, in and out, but he could spare a few days out of his crazy schedule. He'd been running fast and hard for months, and a road trip would be as good for him as it would be for her. He felt a tingle on the back of his neck, a warm heat invading his veins. Was that excitement he felt? It had been so long, he didn't recognise it any more.

Lex looked down at his half-eaten croissant and he saw the longing on her face. He pushed the packet in her direction. 'Help yourself.'

'I shouldn't, I had a slice of pizza at the airport, but I will,' she replied, ripping off a piece and putting it into her mouth. Even when eating she was sexy.

Taking his seat again, he placed his elbows on the desk and looked at her. 'I need to get to Rhodes in the Eastern Cape. I'd need two days to get there, right?'

To her credit, Lex didn't blink at his change of subject. Neither did she demand to know why he'd kissed her or feel the need to analyse their encounter. 'Yeah. It's too long a drive to do it in one stretch. I mean, you could, but it would be crazy long.'

'Where would I stay the first night?'

'Colesberg, I guess.' Lex looked puzzled. 'But why drive if you can fly? It's so much quicker.'

'I'm not crazy about small planes or helicopters,' he lied. And it was a whopper. He adored anything with an engine and, one day, he intended to get his helicopter licence. But if he flew into Rhodes to see the ski-lodge he wouldn't have the excuse to take Lex along for the ride.

Cole asked himself what he was doing, what on earth was he thinking? Was he really going to take four, five days out of his schedule to drive to this ski-lodge so that he could give this emerald-eyed, tired, sometimes sad, sometimes feisty woman the road trip she so wanted? But suddenly he couldn't think of anything more he wanted to do.

Yes, he wanted to give her the break she needed, the road trip she'd said she wanted, to take her away from Cape Town and the demands of her busy life. It wasn't a Mediterranean beach holiday, but she would be getting away, doing something different. It was shocking to realise how much he wanted to whisk her away from real life.

But long hours in the car, being in close proximity, would either ratchet up their attraction or make them want to kill each other. If the latter happened, and he knew it wouldn't, he had the means to hire a helicopter to fly them back to Cape Town.

But what if they landed up in bed? The chances of that happening were sky-high because she was as physically attracted to him as he was to her. They were dry kindling meeting a spark…and with one kiss they could set Table Mountain on fire. But sex was sex, work was work, and he'd never let his personal feelings colour his views, so Lex's job would never be in jeopardy because of what they did outside of work hours. He knew that, but did she?

Strangely, he wanted her more than he could remember ever wanting anyone ever—he wanted to spend a long, lazy time exploring her body, running his hands through her hair and sliding inside her to know how she felt from the inside out. And he desperately wanted to take her away from her responsibilities and give her time to breathe, to relax.

Man, he sounded like a saint, and he wasn't. He didn't even come close. He wasn't being uncharacteristically unselfish. The thought of peace, quiet and hours without talking was deeply alluring. He craved the silence of saying nothing, of allowing his mind to wander, to slow down, to be less than pinprick-focused.

But would she say yes? Would she even agree to his crazy proposition?

No. Maybe. He could only ask. Thank goodness they were alone so that, if Lex shot him down in flames, no one would notice the fireball.

'So, you asked to see me and here I am,' Lex said, crossing her slim leg over her knee. 'Do you need a ride somewhere?'

It was a perfect opening. 'Yes, I do.'

'I wondered how long you would last driving yourself. Cape Town traffic is hellish and, being spread out between the mountains and the sea, it's fairly hard to navigate.'

He'd driven in some of the most dangerous cities in the world and Cape Town was a doddle compared to Manila, Seoul or Mumbai. But he'd allow her to keep thinking he needed her help, especially if he ended up getting his own way. Sometimes, the end justified the means.

'Are you about to tell me that you need me to drive you this weekend?' Lex asked, and he heard the note of excitement in her voice. Then she flushed and looked away. 'You should know my rates triple if I work Saturday afternoon, or on Sundays.'

Cole was pretty sure he could afford whatever she charged. 'Noted.' He wondered what she'd spend the extra money on. He hoped she would buy a new set of tyres for her car and get her brake pads fixed. He heard his phone buzz and saw a notification from Petra, his temporary assistant.

I have booked two nights for you at the famous Aquila Game Reserve, they are expecting you this afternoon.

Right. Damn. He swiped his finger across the screen, punched four on his speed dial and put his phone on loudspeaker. Petra answered immediately. 'Are you happy to go to Aquila Game Reserve, Mr Thorpe? It's one of the best in the country, with incredible amenities. I've booked you a suite—'

'Please cancel the booking.'

He heard her gasp and didn't blame her. He was acting like a spoiled billionaire who couldn't make up his mind. 'My fault, not yours—my plans changed unexpectedly.'

He heard the breath she sucked in. 'Right, okay. But I cancelled your current hotel booking, they've packed up your clothes and they are waiting for you to collect your luggage. The SUV you rented is also waiting for you at the hotel.'

Being picky about his cars, he'd wanted something with a little more grunt, so he'd instructed Petra to find him something hot and exciting to drive.

'Tell the lodge to keep the deposit and I'll rebook for another time,' Cole told her. 'Please book two rooms in Colesberg, and make a booking for two at Rossdale Ski Lodge for two of their best rooms for Saturday and Sunday night.' He looked at Lex and watched her green eyes widen.

There was a good chance she'd say no, and there

was always the chance that their crazy attraction would bubble over and scald them both. But that was a chance he was willing to take.

Was she?

CHAPTER SIX

'I'M GOING ON a cross-country road trip to Rhodes, in the Eastern Cape. Would you like to come with me?'

Lex blinked, not sure she'd heard him clearly. He couldn't possibly be asking her to travel halfway across the country, could he? Why? And what, *exactly*, did he want from her? If he assumed, from one hot encounter, that she was going to provide the additional service of warming his bed, boss or no boss, she'd throw the dregs of her coffee in his face.

There were a few very big steps between one hectic kiss and her hopping into bed with him. And that was a journey she hadn't taken for years, five or more to be precise. Acquiring two sisters had played havoc on her dating life and libido.

He saw something in her face or eyes that had him straightening his back, his mouth tightening. 'I'm offering you a job, Lex. It's a twelve-hour drive to Rhodes, and I will need to spend part of that trip working—I do have an international company to run. I will pay you double your normal rate and will cover the costs of your food and accommodation.'

Right, okay. But they couldn't ignore their kiss and their crazy, hot attraction.

'I'm not naïve, Cole, it would be disingenuous to think we'll keep our hands off each other.'

'I love your in-my-face honesty, Lex.'

After a lifetime of dealing with her mother's lies, half-truths and evasions, it was the only way she knew how to operate. 'I prefer honesty to sugar-coated BS.'

'And here it is—I do need to go to Rhodes, I need to inspect this ski-lodge and try to figure out what to do with it, and why my usually sensible father lost his head when making decisions about this property,' Cole said, keeping his tone even. 'It's a long drive to do on your own and you are the Thorpe driver kept on retainer to drive.'

She was.

'But you are also the woman I can't stop thinking about, and I desperately want to see you naked.'

And there it was, in black and white. 'I'm shocked by the attraction between us. It's strong and intense. And unexpected,' Cole said, spinning his phone on the table before stopping it with his index finger.

Unexpected—that was one way of putting it. She would use other adjectives. Earth-shattering would be one. Other-worldly would be another.

She opened her mouth to speak, but Cole beat her to it. He leaned forward, his hard expression lightening just a fraction.

'Should I have kissed you? The answer is obvious—no. But I did—we did—and we can't change that. Do I want to kiss you again? Yes, of course I do. I know how good we can be together. If one kiss can cause so much heat, then there is no doubt that we would contribute to global warming if we got naked together.' He lifted one powerful shoulder in a shrug. 'We seem to have chemistry. I have no idea where it came from, but

I'm not a teenage boy at the mercy of my hormones. If you say no, then it's no.'

He lifted his hands and spread them. 'And nothing that happens between us would affect your job with Thorpe Industries. Yes, if you come with me, there's a good chance we'll end up in bed. But that will always be your choice, and I promise not to pressure you. It will be your call and it's not something you need to decide right now.'

'It's not?'

He frowned. 'No, of course not. Look, if sleeping together is off the table, that's fine and we'll still go to Rhodes as friends. If sex happens, great, and if you decided to sleep with me again, I'd be honoured. If it happens and you don't want to do it again, I'll back off, no questions asked. You hold all the power here, Lex,' he added.

Cole rubbed the back of his neck, as if he were uncertain of his words, whether they were the right ones. 'All I'm asking of you, at this moment, is to come with me, Lex. Step away from real life and let's go on a road trip, forget about reality for a while. Just you and me, the sky and the road. Let's go on an adventure.'

Man, when he put it like that…

Lex asked Cole to give her a moment to think, stood up, walked over to the window and laid a hand on its cold pane. She wasn't naïve. She knew that there was an excellent chance of her ending up in Cole's bed and in his arms. He'd be her first lover in five years, and probably her last for a long time, because when next would she meet a man she felt so attracted to, someone she could imagine being naked with? The men she met were usually married, and the ones who were divorced but single had the heavy baggage of kids of their own and ex-wives. Cole was hot, single and he wanted her.

But he wouldn't push her into doing anything she wasn't comfortable doing. If she decided she was only there in her capacity as a driver, he'd respect her decision and would behave like a gentleman. She trusted him.

And that was strange, because she didn't trust anyone aside from her sisters.

She didn't have to decide about sleeping with him now. He wasn't asking that. All he was asking was to go on a road trip with her. He was offering her the opportunity to leave Cape Town, and her responsibilities, behind.

The girls were away, she didn't have any assignments due or any upcoming exams, her French student was away and Addi would love to have the house to herself.

There wasn't any reason to say no—except, somehow and in some way, she knew that any concentrated time she spent with Cole would change her somehow.

She didn't know how, just that it would.

Lex looked back to see that Cole was working on his laptop, giving her the time and space she needed. And she couldn't ignore the fact that driving Cole to Rhodes would earn her more than she usually made in six weeks. It was an extraordinarily good deal and it was the opportunity to do what she most wanted: get on the road, drive and clear her head.

She frowned at Cole, wondering if he was taking the long trip for her. No, that was silly, why would he put himself out for her? Sure, he'd kissed her, but he wouldn't change all his plans, take days out of his very busy schedule, to give her the road trip he'd heard she wanted. It was madness to think that way. No, it was just a coincidence. She liked to drive and he needed a driver because he was scared of small planes and helicopters. She squinted at Cole, thinking that such a big, powerful, rugged man didn't look as though he'd be scared of anything.

They couldn't be more different. He was a billionaire who lived in London and had houses and companies around the world, someone who socialised with celebrities, politicians, the pretty and the powerful. She was a twenty-eight-year-old woman who was all but broke, who was trying to give her sisters the stable childhood she'd never had and part-time student who couldn't find enough time to finish her degree. Why was he even attracted to her and she to him?

It made no sense.

Sure, he was a great-looking guy, masculine and attractive rather than simply handsome, with a face and body that demanded a second or third look. And, for some strange reason, he found her, with her intensely freckled face and bright hair, attractive too. And, yes, she really wanted to spend the next few days with him.

But it was dangerous. With him, she felt there was a barrier between her and the world, and whoever wanted to take a piece out of her would have to go through him first, and that Cole would put up a huge fight. She felt protected and feeling that, liking it, was incredibly risky. She was the protector, not the protected.

Lex pushed her hand into her hair and bit down on her bottom lip. She hadn't been looking for him, for any of this. She'd been content in her isolation, in being with the girls, in her woman-dominated world. Because Joelle hopped from one man to another, from one situation to another, she'd learned to protect herself by standing still, by not letting anything or anyone touch her, because she was terrified of letting someone in and having them walk away. She'd mentally distanced herself from anyone but her sisters, keeping her world ultra-small.

But Cole tempted her as no one had before, luring her to explore the world outside her bubble. She felt as if her eyes were opening, her fists were unclenching, her wings unfurling. She didn't like it.

'It'll be okay, Lex, I promise.'

She turned to look at him and saw the almost tender expression on his face, the warmth in his eyes.

'Are you in or out, Lex?'

'I'm in.'

She'd all but agreed to the possibility of having an affair with a London-based billionaire boss. She hoped she'd made the right decision.

After what seemed like hours of travelling on a dirt road that hugged the curves of a series of mountains, they rolled into Rhodes, a tiny town comprised of a series of pretty Victorian cottages, with Lex behind the wheel. It was only four in the afternoon, but the day was already sliding into twilight, not helped by the massive mountain looming over the town and the low-hanging, dark clouds.

They'd left Cape Town yesterday afternoon and it had taken them for ever to get out of the city. They'd shared the driving and it had been after eleven when they'd rolled into Colesberg. They'd both been exhausted by the long drive in the driving rain and had been unable to do anything but murmur a quiet goodnight before retreating to their separate rooms.

They hadn't kissed again, and Lex missed his lips and wanted his arms around hers. She was deeply conscious of every move Cole made, every breath he took.

She looked at his hands, one holding his phone, the other resting on his thigh, eager to have them on her body, his mouth on hers.

Would they make love tonight?

She hoped so.

They had limited time together—she didn't want to waste a minute of it.

On the main street, one of what seemed to be just a few streets in the town, cars were parked nose to nose and bumper to bumper. Down the street, an empty lot held a stage and they noticed a group of people swaying to the sounds of a band. Everyone was dressed for winter weather, except one old man who simply wore a jacket over his pair of shorts. He also wore flip flops on his feet.

Unbelievable.

Seeing a car coming up behind them, Lex indicated to turn left and braked to allow an elderly couple cross the road, both wearing matching yellow beanies. They passed the hood of Cole's car and then, without discussion, turned to walk up to her window. Lex pushed the button to allow the window to drop and pulled up a smile.

'Hi there,' she said, resting her elbow on the windowsill. Damn, it was cold out there.

'Hi, are you the people heading up to Rossdale?'

Lex greeted the couple and nodded, asking them how they knew. 'It's a very small town and all the residents were asked to look out for a fancy car due in around about now.'

'Why?' Cole asked. He leaned towards her window and his face was inches from hers, so close that she could see each long, individual eyelash, a scar on his upper lip and that his eyes held flecks of green. He smelled of the woods and the sea, as fresh and clean as the icy air. Talking about being cold, she wished they'd wrap up this conversation because she was freezing. And, damn, was that a splodge of mushy ice on her windscreen?

'The couple who manage the place left earlier this morning on their way to a doctor. They think Bheki cracked his ankle.' The woman pulled a bright sticky note from her jacket pocket and handed it to Lex. 'They got to town and realised they left their work phone at the resort, so we've been on the lookout for you. Here's the code to the front door. Lerato will try to be back some time mid-morning. You're the only guests.'

Cole pulled back and looked at Lex. 'We can look for a place to stay in town and take a drive up there in the morning.'

That sounded like a plan. She couldn't wait for a hot bath, to get into something warm and to have a decent meal, maybe soup or stew, in front of a roaring fire. A glass of red wine would be her reward for getting them here safely.

'Oh no, dear, you can't do that. The town is full and everyone is booked up.'

'It's either the ski-lodge or a few more hours' drive.' The old man tapped her windowsill. 'You'd better get going, there's snow coming in.'

The couple stepped back from the car, linked arms and ambled across the road and through a cast-iron gate into the brightly lit hotel on the corner.

Lex glanced at Cole, to find his eyes on hers. 'So, what's our next move?' he asked her.

They could either leave, drive to the next town to try and find accommodation or drive up to the very empty lodge. The answer was obvious, but Lex appreciated him asking her opinion. 'The ski-lodge. We're guaranteed a bed there.'

'But we'll be alone,' Cole pointed out.

She got his subtext and knew he was reminding her that there would be no one around to dilute their attraction, or who'd require them to be circumspect. They'd have to face each other and the desire bubbling between them. There would be no place to hide, to run.

His topaz eyes glinted in the low light of the car and Lex shivered, not from the cold but anticipation. She patted his thigh, hoping to lighten the tension in the car. 'It'll be good for you to make your own bed and your own coffee and not be waited on hand and foot.'

Cole covered her hand with his and lifted it to brush his mouth across her knuckles. 'I'll have you know that I make my own coffee all the time,' he quietly told her, his tone low and sexy.

He turned in his seat and grimaced at the clouds building behind them. 'If we're going to go, we should go now. I don't want us driving on an unknown road in the dark during a snow storm. And, damn, I could murder, a whisky.'

'Me too.'

'I like mine in a crystal tumbler, on two cubes of one-inch ice and served on a silver tray.'

It took a moment for her to realise he was teasing and, when she did, she slapped his thigh before starting the car and heading out of town into the night. She flashed her cheekiest smile. 'Thanks, I look forward to you pouring me one.'

Despite the gloom, Rossdale Ski Resort was more impressive than Cole expected it to be. Built of weathered dark timber, steel and stone, it looked modern but still held a hint of old-world charm.

Having been involved in a few construction projects himself, Cole didn't want to think about how the original builders had transported the wood and stone up the ten-kilometre road he and Lex had just navigated. The road was narrow and there was the occasional drop-off. If a vehicle left the road, it would land on rocks or in the stream below. Lex, looking cool and confident, had navigated the road with ease, allowing the four-by-four slowly to inch its way up the icy road.

They were on a plateau now, and a couple of buildings sat on the only flat piece of land in the immediate area. The boutique hotel looked like what it was—a three-storey smallish hotel set on the edge of another, gentle slope. Off to the other side, at the bottom of the steepest slope, sat another building, the offices, a small pub and a shop which hired out snow equipment. A smallish snow lift stood at the bottom of the hill.

The slopes looked pretty decent and would give some good skiing if they received a couple of feet of snow. He wouldn't get to ski, he reminded himself as Lex pulled the vehicle into an empty parking bay—one of many. They weren't going to be here long enough.

He watched Lex remove her hands from the steering wheel and then flex and bend her fingers before shaking them out. They were trembling, he realised.

Capturing the hand closest to him, he gently squeezed her fingers before lifting her hand so that he could kiss its tips. 'Hey, are you okay?' Under her freckles, in the cool light of the car her skin was now ashen.

'Just glad that's over,' she told him, emotion in her green, green eyes.

'Glad what is over?' he asked, following her gaze

to look over the back seat. 'Are you talking about the road?'

'Well…yes,' she admitted. 'I'm used to urban roads, dodging potholes, passenger buses and pedestrians, not negotiating slippery tracks on the sides of mountains.'

'Have you ever driven a four-by-four before?' Cole asked her.

'I've never driven on a dirt road before,' Lex admitted.

Damn it. If he'd known that he would've taken the wheel at the bottom of the hill when Lex had asked him whether he wanted to drive. He'd wanted to say yes but hadn't wanted to offend her by suggesting that he didn't trust her driving.

'You did well,' he told her, dropping her hand. He looked to the left, to where the triple-storey stone-and-wood structure sat in the ever-descending darkness. 'What do you think?'

Lex leaned forward to look past him and he caught the scent from her hair, lemon and berries, fresh and sweet. 'It looks amazing.'

Cole left the warm car and turned up the collar of his leather jacket, frowning when a splatter of ice hit his nose and then his cheek. He cursed as he walked to the back of the vehicle to pull out their bags.

'The temperature is dropping rapidly, and we need to get a fire started,' he told her. 'Get your pretty butt out of the car, Lex, and let's get inside.'

Lex exited the car and tried to take her bag from Cole but he wasn't having any of it. Putting the strap of his bag over his shoulder, he held her overnight suitcase in his other hand and grabbed her free hand, tugging her through brittle grass to wide stairs leading to a massive front door. Next to the door was a panel and Cole keyed in the code, intensely relieved when the door clicked and opened an inch. Placing his hand on the solid timber, he pushed it open, followed Lex into the house and found himself on a narrow gantry overlooking the double-height common room. Cole dropped the bags and, using the torch app on his phone, found the light switch. One minute they stood in near darkness, the next the hallway was flooded with light.

They had power and, most importantly, he was with Lex. So far, so very good.

CHAPTER SEVEN

LEX DID A full circle of the main house, taking in the wall lined with vintage skis as decor, and the benches where people could sit down and remove their shoes. Not wanting to have to mop the floor, she toed off her muddy trainers and winced when the cold floor permeated through the thin layer of her socks. Ignoring her tingling toes, she looked over the railing into the great room below. The room was huge, with two fireplaces at each end and leather couches and chairs grouped around the room, some facing the double-height window that ran the length of the room. In daylight they'd have extraordinary views of the mountains, slopes and valleys spreading out below them.

Wow, she thought, placing her hand on the railing that stopped the guests from tumbling to the slate floor below. She was impressed.

Cole also removed his shoes and she followed him down the passage, looking around him as he opened doors. An office, a beautifully appointed bedroom, another bedroom and what was obviously the master suite with the same incredible views of the mountains. There was another set of steps that Cole told her led to the third floor.

'I'm betting this layout is duplicated on the other side

of the hall,' he told her as they walked out onto the gantry again. 'Let's see what's downstairs. We also need to get some heat into this place, and I bet we'll find the controls in the kitchen.'

'And food,' Lex said.

'Hopefully,' Cole agreed. She walked down the wide, quite steep wooden stairs, appreciating the way the designer had managed to give the house an essence of sophistication while still keeping the rustic ski-lodge vibe.

'Is this a new build?' she asked Cole.

He looked around. 'Sixty percent of it is. From what I recall from the file Addi handed me containing all the paperwork relating to this place, there was an old farmhouse, double-storey, on this spot. My father kept some walls, removed others and added a floor. Damn, this place looks so familiar,' Cole added.

She stared at his broad back, taking in the way he cocked his head to look at the old stone wall above one huge fireplace. 'I thought you said that you've never been here before,' Lex said, coming to stand next to him.

'I haven't but I feel like I know this house.' Cole pushed a hand through his hair, shook his head and sent her a strained smile. 'Sorry, I'm being ridiculous. I must be hungry and tired.'

Maybe. Or it could be that he did know this house. Maybe he'd seen photos of it, had heard it described or had visited here as a child and was never told.

But she knew that Cole wasn't interested in discussing his memories or feelings with her, so she slipped past him and walked into the back of the lodge, past the massive dining table, a twenty-four-seater with brightly patterned cushions on the bench seats.

The kitchen was adjacent to the dining area and she

stepped into the vast room. It was huge and beautifully designed with large tiles and marble counter-tops. The wine fridge and all the appliances, including an espresso machine, were built in. She looked around, saw an AC control panel and scanned the menu for heating, jabbing her finger against the button. She adjusted the temperature, heard a faint buzz and hoped that within a few minutes—ten or twenty—they wouldn't feel like polar bears walking into an ice shack.

'Great, heat,' Cole said, placing his hand on the counter-top of the free-standing island. 'I don't suppose you've found any food yet?'

'Still looking,' she told him, heading over to the fridge. She opened the doors. As she'd expected, it was filled with fresh vegetables and salads, cheeses and a huge variety of condiments. *Excellent.*

But no milk, she noticed. And that meant no coffee for her, which was problematic.

Curious, Lex walked to the end of the kitchen, saw the entrance to the utility room and stepped inside to see three washer-dryers. Seeing another door, Lex popped it open and released a fist pump, taking in the full to bursting shelves.

There was pasta of all types, cans of Italian plum tomatoes, herbs, spices and various other foods. There were bottles of capers, Asian sauces and spices, vinegars and salad dressings. Seeing a chest freezer in the corner, Lex lifted the lid and saw a series of carefully and beautifully packaged ready meals, soups, stews and curries. There were also frozen beef fillets and tuna steaks, and all types of frozen sea food and—*yay*—frozen milk.

And enough boxes of hand-crafted Belgian chocolates to satisfy Cole's sweet tooth.

She could work with what she'd found.

'Woohoo!' she shouted. 'Cole, we have food—Oomph!'

Lex bounced off Cole's hard chest and the plastic bottle of frozen milk dropped to the floor. It rolled away and Lex ignored it, caught up in the intensity of Cole's yellow-brown eyes. He placed his hand on her hip to steady her and the heat of his hand burned through her clothes into her skin. She didn't need an external source of heat, she just needed to be close to him.

'We've got food,' she told him, annoyed to find she was repeating herself.

The corners of his mouth kicked up. 'I heard. I think the entire valley heard.'

'Sorry, I didn't know you were behind me,' she murmured.

'And yet I am very aware of you, all the time,' Cole stated, his hand coming up to hold the side of her face.

Lex knew she was at a crossroads. She could either stand here and pretend to play it cool, hoping he'd kiss her, or she could give him the green light by making the first move. She was so tired of pulling back, of hiding her attraction, trying not to let him see how much he affected her. She wanted to stop censoring herself, to be herself, for Cole to know the real her for the few days they were together.

She'd promised herself that she'd be completely honest, consistently authentic in her words and her actions, and she wanted him for as long as she could have him. They only had a finite amount of time and, quite frankly, they'd wasted too much of it already.

She also knew there was nothing more between them than a blazing attraction. There was no possibility of a relationship, of a happy-ever-after. She lived in Cape

Town and he was based in London but travelled continuously. She wasn't prepared to watch someone she cared for walk away from her, and Cole would definitely do that. And, because she was co-raising her sisters, she couldn't follow anyone anywhere, even if she were asked to do that.

He was her employer. She was his employee.

But none of that mattered, not in this isolated, fabulous boutique hotel on the edge of a mountain deep in rural South Africa.

In this place, it was just Lex and Cole. And Lex very much wanted to get to know Cole in the most earthy, primal way possible. She wanted to be with him—have sex with him—and if she didn't wring every bit of magic out of every second with him she'd regret it for the rest of her life. She couldn't think of anything worse than being old and grey, thinking, *I wish I'd slept with him. I wish I knew what that was like.*

'I'm so attracted to you,' she murmured, her hands on his chest.

'Ditto,' he replied. 'If craving you could be called attraction.'

He craved her? Good to know.

Lex tipped her head back and sent him a long look. Gathering her courage, she swallowed and machine-gunned her next sentence. 'Will you take me to bed? Will you make love to me?'

'Are you sure that's what you want?' he asked her, holding her chin in his big hand.

Lex nodded. 'Very.'

'And you understand—'

'That you can't give me more—not that I asked you to—and that us sleeping together won't affect my job and it's a brief fling in the mountains?' Lex interrupted him. 'Yes, yes and yes.'

Cole wouldn't let her look away. 'It's just that I don't want there to be any misunderstandings later.'

Lex released a very frustrated sigh. 'I get it, Cole. So, unless you want me to sign a damn contract, will you please—I cannot believe I am asking this again—take me to bed?'

She caught the amusement in his eyes, underneath which was a river of desire and anticipation. 'It would be the greatest pleasure of my life, Lex. What's Lex short for, by the way?'

'Yamilex,' she replied, licking her lips. 'It's Arabic.'

'Lex suits you better,' he told her, before pushing a long red curl off her cheek with his finger. She wished he'd kiss her, simply take her mouth so that she'd forget how to speak and think. It had been so long since she'd lost herself in a man's arms and allowed his mouth and hands to spin her away. Lex wound her arms around his neck and pulled a half-smile onto her face. 'So... question.'

'Mmm?'

'Are you planning on seducing me in the pantry? Because I'm pretty sure this luxurious lodge comes with a bed or two.'

Cole wrapped his arms around her waist, lifted her and held her close against his body. He told her to wrap her legs around his waist, and she did, unable to stop herself from placing her lips against his mouth, from sliding her tongue inside his warm heat. He stumbled, just a slight misstep, and he tightened his hold on her.

'I always knew men couldn't do two things at once,' she teased him.

'In a minute, and once I get you horizontal, I'll

prove just how wrong you are,' Cole promised her on a sexy growl, walking her out of the pantry and into the kitchen.

When he stepped into the great room, Lex noticed the warmth. He'd lit the fire in the bigger of the two fireplaces and the hiss and crackle of dry wood burning made her smile. That sound, along with rain hitting a tin roof and a howling wind roaring around the house, was one she associated with winter.

Then Lex looked out of the double volume window and gasped. Sleet had turned to proper snow and huge, soft, powdery flakes fluttered down, bright and white against the last of the day's light.

'Cole, it's snowing!' she squealed, pointing to the window. He gave the snow a cursory glance and nodded.

'Yep, well, that's not unexpected.'

'Let's go outside!' she suggested, sliding down his body and hopping from foot to foot. 'I've never seen snow before and I want to know what it feels like.'

'It's cold and wet,' Cole told her, sliding his hands up and under her jersey, his fingers tap-dancing on her ribs and sliding over her breasts. 'I, on the other hand, am hot and dry.'

Right. She really wanted to make love to Cole but… 'The snow might stop and I want to catch a snowflake on my tongue,' Lex told him in an agony of indecision.

'You're kidding, right?' he demanded, incredulous.

She shook her head and winced.

'It's going to snow all night, Lex,' he told her, sounding desperate.

'I know that you think I'm mad, but once me, Addi and the girls, on hearing that the snow would last all day in the Ceres area, drove three hours to find puddles at the end of our trip. The girls cried. Addi and I cursed.'

She wrinkled her nose. 'In Africa, when you see snow, you go outside *immediately*. It's a *rule*.'

No matter how tempted she was, no matter how she burned for him, how she couldn't wait for him to make her sigh and scream, she wanted to stand in the snow. The bed, couch, the wall—wherever he wanted to have her—would still be there in ten minutes but the snow might not. 'Ten minutes, Cole. Please?'

Cole looked up at the ceiling and shook his head. 'I cannot believe that we are having this conversation.'

'In the snow versus sex battle,' Lex told him, sounding serious, 'snow is probably always going to win.'

'You Africans are seriously weird.' Cole walked over to the side door leading out onto the patio and opened the door. 'I'm giving you five minutes to catch your snowflake and then I'm getting you naked.'

That sounded like a truly excellent compromise.

Lex caught a snowflake on her tongue and, as soon as she did, Cole covered her mouth with his, tangling his fingers into her hair and twisting his tongue around hers, the snowflake dissolving instantly.

Not expecting to be out for long, they'd left the house in just their jeans and jerseys, and Cole felt the snow landing on his shoulders, in his hair, his body temperature steadily dropping. He knew they should go inside, but Lex's joy in what to him was such a banal weather event had a tiny stream of what he thought might be joy running through his system. For as long as he lived, he'd remember standing out here with her. The vision of Lex catching snowflakes on her tongue, her arms spread out wide, would remain with him until he died.

He felt her shiver and knew that they should return inside as neither of them wore shoes. His socks were wet, and hers would be too, but there was just one thing he needed to do before they went inside.

It was his most recent fantasy, but they didn't know each other well enough for him to ask her to strip in a snowstorm. Pity.

Without warning, Lex whipped her top up and over her head, and she gasped as a couple of snowflakes hit her bare skin. 'Cole, it's freezing!' Lex moaned, hopping from foot to foot.

'You're the one who took her clothes off, you crazy woman. Why?'

Her blazing eyes met his. 'Because you looked like you wanted me to,' she replied. 'And I want you to do whatever you were thinking of.'

'You kill me, Lex,' Cole told her, reaching for the front-facing clasp holding her bra together. 'I just wanted to see you standing in the snow naked. Or half-naked. Lex, you are so very beautiful,' he murmured.

Her torso was long and slim, her breasts bigger than he'd expected and tipped with blush-pink nipples. Freckles covered her skin, fine and the colour of golden syrup, a few shades lighter than the ones on her chest and shoulders. He wanted to kiss every one, but for now he'd be content to lick a snowflake, just one, off her nipple. He felt as if he was commanding nature when a snowflake landed on her breast and slid down her skin. As it hit her nipple, Cole ducked his head and suckled her, his tongue hot against her freezing breast.

He felt her hand come up to grasp his head, her fingers sliding into his hair, and he heard her moan, low, sexy and sweet. Knowing that he couldn't keep her out here for one minute longer, he swung her up in his arms and walked her into the house, kicking the outside door closed with his heel.

Cole walked straight to the area in front of the fire, sighing when the warm air enveloped them. Lex's feet hit the Persian carpet and she turned her back to him, holding her hands out to the fire, utterly unselfconsciousness to be standing half-dressed in front of him. He liked that she wasn't shy, that she felt comfortable with him and trusted him enough to take care of her.

And take care of her he would.

Cole dropped her jersey and bra to the floor, bent down, lifted her foot and slid her wet sock off, tossing it to the side. He removed her other sock and, standing up, toed off his own. Then he ran his hands over her slim shoulders and down her long arms to tangle his fingers in hers. Dropping his head, he rested his forehead against hers.

He wanted her, more than he thought was possible. If he was an imaginative man, he'd think she'd cast a spell over him, that he now understood why men crashed onto rocks at the call of a siren, why they launched a thousand ships because of a lovely face.

At this moment there was nothing he wouldn't do to have her under him, to be inside her, making her his.

But ten minutes in the icy cold might've changed her mind. 'Is this what you still want, Lex?'

Instead of replying, she undid her belt, popped the buttons on her jeans and shimmied the fabric down her legs, before kicking them away. She wore plain white panties, and through the fabric he caught the suggestion of a tidy strip of red hair.

Wrenching his eyes up, he took in her flat stomach, her rounded hips and those stupendous legs. She pulled a band from her hair, shook her head and red curls fell over her shoulders and down her back. He picked one up and gently pulled it straight. If her hair was straight, it would fall to the middle of her back. For some reason, Cole couldn't imagine Lex with straight, smooth hair. It didn't suit her open, vibrant personality.

She was everything lovely, as wild as a summer thunderstorm, as unexpected as a blizzard in Africa—complicated, intriguing, different.

He couldn't wait to explore every inch of her fabulous body, but it was her mind that intrigued him more.

It shouldn't, but it did.

On shedding her jeans, Lex expected Cole to yank her into his arms, lower her to the leather sofa behind them and, well, get busy.

But, instead of hurtling towards the finishing line, Cole just looked at her, taking in her curly hair, her breasts—smaller than she liked—and her too-long legs. His eyes passed over her panties and moved up again, stopping to inspect the small tattoo she had on her right hip. Three, each an inch high, adult elephants encircled two, tiny baby elephants. He paused, and Lex knew he was curious about the artwork.

It wasn't the time for questions and, needing to touch him, to feel connected, Lex reached for his jersey, gently pulling it and the T-shirt he wore underneath up his torso, revealing his wide chest and ridged stomach. After dropping his garments to the floor, she skimmed her hand down his shoulder, down his muscled arms. Her fingers drifted over the back of his hand, slipped between his fingers and he lifted her knuckles to his mouth. His eyes, containing flames of yellow and gold, collided with hers.

'Are you sure about this?' he quietly asked.

She could no more have said no than stop the clouds from releasing snow. 'I'm sure.'

Cole's fingers fluttered over her lips, her cheek-bone, the sweep of her jaw. His gentle touch was unanticipated, as sexy as his take-me-away, lust-drenched kisses. She hadn't imagined that such a remote, emotionally unavailable and mentally tough man could be so tender. Cole held her head in his hands, his thumbs sliding over her eyebrows and across her cheekbones.

'I adore your dots, Lex,' he told her, his voice rough with desire.

'Kiss me, Cole,' Lex whispered, raw need in her voice. He lowered his head and his mouth skimmed hers, once, twice, before he covered her lips, feeding her kisses and keeping the tempo sexy and slow.

As they kissed, Lex revelled in the freedom to touch his long, hard body. She trailed her fingers over his chest, down his sides, and walked them across those hard abs. She explored the long length of his sexy hip muscles and ran her finger under the band of his jeans, relishing his groans of appreciation. A slap of power hit her. She could make this man want. She had the ability to make his big body quiver with anticipation. She stroked the tip of her finger along his erection from base to tip and was rewarded by the sound of him sucking in a harsh breath.

'Lex...'

Cole cupped her breasts in his hands, groaning as he buried his face in her neck, sucking on that spot where her neck and shoulder met.

'I need you now,' Cole told her as he hooked his thumbs into her panties and pulled them down. He stared at her thin strip of soft hair, and she gasped as he ran his finger over it. 'So pretty.'

Lex, unable to help herself, widened her legs and

heard his harsh gasp as he slid his hand between her legs and his index finger brushed ever so gently over her super-sensitive bundle of nerves. Stars and fireworks exploded on her skin, sensitising her from tip to toe. Her thoughts fled, and she forgot to breathe as his hot finger slipped inside her, followed by another. His thumb swept over her again and Lex felt sexual pressure building. It had been years since she'd been with a man, but she didn't recall sex being this out-of-the-world experience, this exhilarating.

'Cole...'

He'd never in all his life seen anything as sexy as Lex standing in front of the fire, about to orgasm, with snow falling outside. A part of him wanted to watch her as she fell apart, see how her face changed when pleasure hit her, see the wonder in her eyes, watch her skin flush pink under her freckles. But a bigger part of him wanted to be fully and wholly connected with her this first time.

Scooping her up, he laid her on the couch, taking a moment to appreciate her. She looked like femininity distilled: long hair, wild eyes and smooth skin. It took all he had not to rip off his jeans and sink into her, to discover her. Her eyes slammed into his and she lifted her hips in a silent plea to be taken, to be completed. For him to give her what she craved. Before Lex, with those women whose faces and names she'd obliterated from his memory, he'd never taken the time to savour. To discover slopes and valleys, dips and curves. What made a woman scream and what made her sigh.

He couldn't wait to see her fall apart but, first, protection... Digging into his back pocket, he yanked out his wallet, dug around in it and pulled out a condom. Dropping his jeans and underwear, Cole rolled on the condom and placed one hand on the back of the couch, the other on the cushion next to Lex's head, and lowered himself down, keeping his eyes locked on hers. He took a calming breath, knowing that he needed control. But in Lex's eyes he saw impatience, passion, and heard her unspoken plea to be taken on her lips. Her legs fell open and he brushed her entrance, pushing in just a little. Man, she felt amazing.

She whimpered and then sighed his name.

The tips of her long and elegant fingers meandered over the stubble on his jaw. She painted fire on his skin as her fingers skimmed down his neck and danced across his shoulder blades, down his spine and over his butt. Unbelievably, he hardened even further. Unable to wait, Cole lowered his weight and pushed into her with a long, controlled slide.

He covered her mouth with his and the world faded away, entirely focused on where their bodies met. She met him stroke for stroke, her breath deep and sexy in his ear. He held himself rigid, knowing that if he didn't stop she'd be left unsatisfied. *Not acceptable.*

But heat and demand roared through him and his control was on a knife-edge. This was original sin mating, wild, basic, organic, the way it was meant to be. He couldn't wait. He had to move, take, plunder…harder, faster, higher. His breathing increased and his heart threatened to explode…

He heard a whimper, then her groan. Lex clenched around him and his orgasm rocketed through him, chasing hers up, around, through that star, hopping across the moon and sliding down that meteor shower.

When his tour of the galaxy ended, Cole buried his

face in Lex's sweet-smelling neck, trying to make sense of their intense physical connection. She, the sex they'd shared, was the best he'd ever had. Why here? Why now? And why, when it was so very inconvenient?

CHAPTER EIGHT

THIS PLACE LOOKS so familiar.

Thinking back to what he said earlier, Lex dressed in Cole's jersey, swung her legs across his thighs, the backs of her bare legs rubbing against his jeans. Much to her dismay, he'd pulled on his T-shirt.

But, since he'd found a bottle of excellent red wine and two glasses, she was prepared to forgive him.

Lex turned to look behind her and smiled when she saw that it was still snowing. A layer of white covered the brown grass and the patio and she was tempted to get up, get dressed and go and play in the snow. Maybe she could persuade Cole to have a snowball fight with her. Or to make a snowman.

Cole took one look at her face and shook his head. 'I would rather suck my eyeballs out with a straw than go outside,' he told her. Snow wasn't the novelty to him that it was to her.

Lex pouted but Cole remained unmoved.

'I checked the weather forecast earlier and they are predicting more snow tonight. I'm hoping for a few feet so that I can test out some of the slopes.'

'You can ski here?' As soon as the words left her mouth, Lex realised what a stupid question that was. Of course people could ski—it was a ski-lodge. She waved her words away. 'I mean, won't the slopes here be a bit tame for you? In the car, you mentioned that you take a skiing holiday every year, and I can't imagine you doing anything other than the hardest, steepest slopes. What do they call them again—black runs?'

'Why do you assume that I'm good at it?' he asked, amused.

'Because you have an athlete's body.' And because she couldn't imagine Cole being anything but good at things. He was one of life's golden people, both sporty and intellectual. She couldn't see him tolerating failure at anything. He liked control too much to allow that to happen.

'If we get enough snow, I could teach you to snowboard tomorrow.'

Lex shook her head. 'I have the grace and balance of an elephant with an ear infection.'

He laughed. 'You can't be that bad.'

She really was. Lex looked down at his big hand on her thigh—he'd pushed his jersey up to find bare skin—thinking how tanned his hand looked on her pale skin. It was wide, with long fingers ending in short, clean nails. She had a thing about hands, men's hands in particular, and she approved of Cole's.

She especially approved of where he'd put them on her body. They'd made love twice already and, as much as she'd love to indulge in round three, they needed to rest and recuperate, and they needed sustenance. Lex thought about getting up and getting some food, but she was so comfortable sprawled across him.

She recalled Cole's statement about him remembering this house. 'Your father did extensive renovations to this house. It can't possibly look the same, so I'm wondering what's tickling your memory.'

He looked up at the beams crisscrossing the ceiling of the room. 'I feel like I recognise that wall, the fireplace, the slate floors.'

'Did you come here with your father as a child?'

Cole shook his head. 'My father only bought this property about ten years ago and I never went anywhere with my father.'

Lex heard the thread of ice in his voice, a great deal colder than the snow falling outside. '"Never" is a strong word,' she murmured.

'But accurate,' Cole said, seemingly unaware that his grip on her leg had tightened. He wasn't hurting her but the tips of his fingers sank deeper into her flesh. 'My father and I didn't have a relationship. At all, ever.'

Lex skimmed her fingers up and down his bare arm. 'I know how it feels to have a parent who disappoints and lets you down.'

Cole scooted down the couch and rested the back of his head on the couch. 'Oh no, my dad was a great father. Involved, interested, present.'

'But—'

'Just not to me,' Cole clarified.

'I don't understand,' Lex replied.

Cole lifted his hand off his head to push his fingers through his hair. Since she'd done the same earlier, his waves were more pronounced than normal. 'I have an older brother: his name is Sam. He's older by seven years. My father adored him and worshipped the ground he walked on. My parents divorced when I was three or four and I went with my mum, Sam stayed with my dad. Our lives separated from that point onwards.'

They'd split up their family—one child for you, one child for me? To Lex, it sounded so cold and calculated. She'd do anything and everything she could to keep her sisters together, to be a family, but Cole's parents had casually ripped his apart.

'How was your relationship with your mum?'

She hoped it was great and that, unlike her, he'd had one parent he could rely on.

He rolled his shoulders. 'Not bad, I guess. She was there, physically. She fed and clothed me and did those things that mums were supposed to do. I went to boarding school when I was thirteen and, from then on, I only saw her a couple of times a year.'

'Where is she now?'

'She died when I was twenty,' Cole replied in a flat voice.

Lex winced. 'I'm sorry.'

Cole shrugged. 'Sadly, I didn't miss her that much. She was pretty distant and emotionless, to be honest.'

Lex grimaced. He made it sound as if he'd been raised by a robot. Joelle had her faults but the last thing she could be called was emotionless. 'So how often did you see your father? He must've had visitation rights.'

Cole's expression tightened. 'He had them, but he never used them. I don't think I made this clear…from the moment my parents split up, I never had any contact with my father. No calls, emails or visits.'

Cole stood up and headed over to the fireplace, tossing some logs onto the already roaring fire. Lex saw the devastation in his bleak eyes and her heart contracted.

She felt intensely sad for him. While Joelle had, on the whole, been an indifferent mother, they had known affection when Joelle had remembered. Her father had never been in the picture, and Lex knew nothing more about him than his first name. And Joelle wasn't even a hundred percent sure about whether she'd remembered the right guy at the right house party.

Cole's situation with his dad was far more heartrending. He was constantly reminded that his father didn't want him, and all his life he'd watched his brother have a relationship with their father that he'd been denied, with no explanation. Her heart ached for him.

'How often did Sam see your mum?' she asked.

Cole took his time answering her. 'Once a month, if I remember correctly. Sometimes he spent a week of his school holidays with us.'

That was so sad. Sam had had both his parents while Cole had only had one. 'Do you know why your dad…?' She couldn't find the right phrase to use. Hated him? Neglected him? Cut him out of his life? What type of monster ignored and neglected a child for all of his life?

Cole shook his head. 'I have no idea. I asked my mum, but she always changed the subject or brushed me off.' He lifted his hands and linked them behind his head. 'Not knowing is the killer.'

She instinctively knew what he meant. 'Because it's far better to be hurt by a truth than comforted by a lie,' Lex said.

'Exactly.'

'Being truthful, being authentic and knowing the truth, seeing things clearly, is important to me,' Lex told him. 'I'm really big on seeing things how they are and not how you want them to be.'

Lex waved her words away, conscious she was talking about herself when they'd been talking about him and his childhood. 'Do you think you could be the result of an affair your mum had?'

'It would be an easy explanation except that I am the carbon copy of my father,' Cole replied, blowing her hypothesis out of the water. Cole shoved both his hands into his hair and tugged. 'Why are we talking about this? Surely there's something else we can discuss?'

Lex knew he was done with the heart-to-heart and that she wouldn't get any more from him tonight. And that was fine. These intense discussions were dangerous. It was one thing to explore his body, to find out what made him groan and gasp, but discovering what made him tick, what circumstances had shaped the person he was, was dangerous.

She couldn't afford to become emotionally attached to him. That wasn't something she wanted to do, not when she knew he'd be walking away from her. This was a brief affair, one that would end when they got back to Cape Town.

If they weren't making love then she had to keep their conversation light, skimming the surface. Lex looked up at him through half-closed lids, an expression she'd seen Joelle use a hundred, a thousand, times. 'I've got an idea...' she drawled, dropping her voice in an attempt to sound sexy.

Expectation dashed across his face and his eyes flickered with interest. 'I'm listening...'

She ducked her head so that he couldn't see a hint of her smile. 'There's a freezer in the pantry with some frozen meals. You could take two out and shove them into the microwave to heat.' She arched an eyebrow. 'You do know what a microwave is, right?'

'Funny girl,' he muttered, fighting to hide a smile. He walked over to her, held out his hand and hauled her to her feet.

Then he grimaced. 'At what temperature and for how long?'

Lex rolled her eyes. 'Billionaires, useless at everything but making money,' she teased him.

Cole patted her butt and sent her a satisfied smile. 'I'm good at two things,' he informed her. When she raised an eyebrow, he grinned. 'Making money and making you scream with pleasure.'

She couldn't argue with that.

The next morning, Lex woke up in the massive empty bed in the biggest of the guest rooms and rolled over, looking for Cole, before remembering that he'd murmured something about…something. Then she'd gone straight back to sleep but, judging by the fact that Cole's side of the bed was still warm, he couldn't have been gone for more than ten or fifteen minutes.

She really hoped he was making coffee.

Lex stretched, pointing her toes and flexing her fingers. Despite having had no more than a few hours of sleep—they'd made love three times during the night but had spent even more time kissing, touching and indulging in some very heavy petting as they'd taken a shower before bed—she felt energised and, yes, happy. Content.

Pretty damn wonderful.

She should enjoy every moment of feeling like this— it was a one-time deal. In a couple of days, she would go back to the predictability of her life, consumed by her need to give her sisters the stability she'd never had. When she returned, she'd go back to putting their needs first.

Here, in the mountains, with the snow still falling and the wind howling, it was all about her pleasure, her wants and needs. And Cole, judging from the way he'd made love to her last night, was determined to give her everything she needed…

Sexually, that was.

He couldn't give her what she craved, what she dreamed about. He'd never be able to make space for her in his life, and space for her sisters, to put her needs first, to be the person she could trust and rely on to be there for her—but that was okay. She was asking a lot and even if he, or any other man, offered, she doubted she'd be brave enough to trust him to do as he promised.

She had love issues, trust issues, being disappointed and being abandoned issues.

Frankly, she was a lot to handle.

Irritated with the longing she felt somewhere deep in her heart, she flung back the covers, walked over to the free-standing club chair and pulled Cole's long-sleeved T-shirt over her head. After shoving her arms into the too-long sleeves, she buried her nose in the neck band, inhaling his scent. She had to find out what cologne he used—it was super-sexy and, oh, so Cole. She closed her eyes, lifted his shirt over her mouth and breathed deeply again.

'Are you having a relationship with my shirt?'

Her eyes flew open to see Cole standing in the doorway, holding two cups of coffee, amusement dancing in his eyes. He wore black, straight-legged track pants and a fresh, long-sleeved cream T-shirt that fell down his chest and over his stomach. It also highlighted the muscles in his big arms.

She dropped the neck of the T-shirt, wishing she could control her blush. 'I just like the way you smell,' she admitted.

'Good to know,' he told her, walking towards her and holding out a mug. Lex gratefully accepted the mug and wrapped her hands around it. She jumped a little when Cole dropped a kiss on her head, unused to casual affection and surprised to realise how much she liked it.

Feeling a little embarrassed, Lex walked over to the tall window and looked down the valley, which was covered in a thick layer of snow. It looked like a Christmas card, the snow a glittering white carpet. 'Wow.'

'There's a better view from the adjoining sitting room.' Cole nodded to the door to her right. Lex walked through into a room with two glass walls forming the corner of the room and giving them a one-eighty-degree view of the valley spread out below them. A white lounging bed sat diagonally across the corner, and Lex could see herself lying there with a blanket over her knees, watching the snow drift past. Or sleeping with a puppy tucked into her legs, or lying there naked, her hand on her belly, swollen with a baby…

Longing swept over her, not so much for the gorgeous room in a lovely hotel, or for the view. It was a longing for what she couldn't have, what she wouldn't have for years, if ever: peace, tranquillity, quiet…*stability*. Time on her own, a life of her own. A baby and a place of her own…

What was wrong with her? It was a room—one of the nicest she'd ever seen, but still a room—and not a dream chamber!

Cole walked into the room and sat down on the edge of the lounger, and when she joined him there he put his free hand on her knee. 'That's some view,' he admitted. 'This is a very pretty place.'

Lex leaned into him just a little. 'My sisters would love this,' she admitted. Yes, she'd told herself she wouldn't think about them, but they were a huge part of her life and she couldn't help it.

They were a part of her and always would be.

Cole half-turned to face her. 'Tell me how you came to have them, Lex. In fact, go back further…'

'That's a long story,' she murmured, wanting to open up but scared that she'd tell him more than she should, more than she'd told anyone before.

He lifted his coffee cup. 'This is a big cup of coffee and I'm not going anywhere until it's done.'

Well, then. She looked out of the window and wondered where to start. 'I told you how they came to live with us, how much of a free spirit my mum was.' She wrapped her hands around her mug and sipped. 'We bounced from house to house, depending on what boyfriend was willing to house her, her blonde-haired angel and her red-haired brat. Life with Joelle was...unstable.'

Cole held up a hand. 'Wait, back up. What did you mean by that "red-haired brat" statement? Did your mother not like your looks?'

'Not liking my looks was a very tame way of putting it,' Lex said, trying to keep her tone level as old hurts washed over her. Still after all this time, despite the work she'd done to come to terms with Joelle's cruelty, she felt small and vulnerable.

'Tell me, Lex.'

'When I was five, she told me that my face looked like someone had thrown dirt at it and stained it. By six, I suspected I was ugly. By seven, thanks to Joelle's comments, I believed I was.'

'The last thing you are is ugly, Lex,' Cole informed her, his voice hard and tinged with anger. Not at her, but at her mother and her casual cruelty.

'I know that now. But, when you are a young child with bright-red hair and a face full of freckles, when you look so very different, it's easy to believe what you are told. Especially when your mother constantly tells you how pretty your blonde sister is, and how angelic she looks. I was bullied at school. I had no friends and I wanted to be anyone but me.'

'Go on, Lex.'

Lex tapped her finger against the cup. 'So, one summer holiday, Joelle decided that it was time to dye my hair. We had no money, so she bought a cheap dye kit which turned my hair neon-orange. Tom, Storm's dad, sent me money to go to the hairdresser and the choice was to either dye my hair blonde or shave it off. I went for blonde and I remained a blonde for the next decade or so. I also used foundation to cover my freckles. My efforts paid off because my mum started calling me pretty.'

Cole released a low growl, picked up a bright curl, wound it around his finger and rubbed the ends between his fingers. 'Obviously that phase ended. What changed?'

She lifted her mug to her mouth, took a sip and smiled. 'Actually, that relates to your original question about how Nixi and Snow came to live with us.'

'I'm listening,' Cole assured her again and everything about his body language said that he was. His eyes didn't leave her face and his hand on her thigh was a connection she badly needed. 'Long story long…when I was sixteen and Addi seventeen, Joelle dumped us with a great-aunt and forgot to collect us, which was a blessing in disguise. Addi and I adored Aunt Kate and we loved living with her. Shortly after I turned twenty-one, Aunt Kate died of a massive heart attack, but she left her house to Addi and me.'

'Giving you the stability, you craved,' Cole murmured.

How did he know that? How was she able to hear what she didn't say?

Feeling bewildered, she continued. 'We rented rooms in the house to other students and their rent paid our living expenses. Aunt Kate also had a small life insurance policy, but it was only enough to cover the fees for one of us to attend university. Addi is a lot more academic than I am—she's quite brilliant, in fact—so we decided that she would study full-time and I would work and study part-time. Then, when she got a high-paying job, she would help me to pay for my degree. That was the plan...'

'But?'

'But Joelle returned to Cape Town with the girls. Suddenly we were responsible for two little girls who were confused and lost. Luckily, Addi had just graduated and was offered a great job by your dad. She had the money to support us, but there wasn't enough to pay for day care. I had plans to go to university full-time, but someone needed to look after the girls, to do the cooking and the cleaning.'

'And you were how old?' Cole asked.

'Twenty-three.'

'That's young to take on that much responsibility.'

But what else could they have done—sent the girls into foster care, or back to Joelle? Keeping them had been the only decent option.

'Finish the story, Lex.'

Lex shrugged, confused. 'That's it.'

He shook his head. 'You haven't explained how you went from being a bottle blonde to embracing your red hair and freckled face.'

Oh, *that*. 'As you saw, Nixi is olive-skinned with black hair—I think her father might be from India or one of the island countries. Snow looks like me. You do know that red hair is a mutant gene, right?'

'You are not a mutant,' Cole empathically stated. 'I think your hair is gorgeous, as are your freckles.'

Lex smiled at his immediate, and sweet, response. 'Anyway, to get red hair and freckles, and if neither parent is ginger, they both need to carry the gene and pass it on. So, Joelle is partly responsible for my much-hated hair, a fact I occasionally remind her of.'

'So you do speak to her?'

'We only started speaking to her again a few months after the girls came to live with us. We nag her to talk to Nixi and Snow, so that they have *some* contact with her. We don't have much to say to her, and Addi tends to do the communicating, because I lost it with her about eighteen months ago.'

'What happened?'

'I caught Snow putting my foundation all over her face and over everything else. She told me she hated her hair and that she wanted to cover her dots, like I did. My heart stopped—because she's beautiful, so beautiful, Cole.'

'As are you,' he softly murmured.

Lex had to ignore him or else she'd never get her words up and through her tight throat. 'Joelle told her, just like she told me, that she had dirt on her face and that her hair was ugly. I was so angry, Cole. I told her she was beautiful, that she was unique and lovely and wonderful—' Lex heard her voice crack. 'She just looked at me and asked me why she should believe me when I covered my freckles, when I dyed my hair.'

Cole sucked in a sharp breath. *'Sweetheart.'*

'I realised that I couldn't let Joelle destroy her as she destroyed me and that I had to walk the walk as well as talk the talk. I washed the foundation off my face and went to the store, grabbed a bottle of dye that was closest to my natural colour and dyed it back to red. And I promised Snow, promised myself, that I would never be anything but authentically me.'

'That's incredible, Lex—you're incredible.' The sincerity in his eyes and on his face made her throat close up. 'And is your sister embracing her looks too?' he asked.

Lex released a low chuckle. 'She's a flaming diva, in every way that counts. And she isn't being bullied at school, and I'm grateful for that. But that could be because she's Nixi's sister.'

'She's popular?'

'She's eight, so whatever popular means at eight. Nixi is a strong character. She's either going to become a world leader or lead her own gang.'

Cole's deep laugh filled the car. 'They sound...interesting.'

'Interesting, frustrating, stubborn. Sweet.'

He squeezed her knee again, keeping the pressure until she looked at him. 'Just like their half-sister. And Lex?'

Her heart, stupid thing, missed a couple of beats at the warm flames she saw in his gold eyes. 'I'm very glad you're not a blonde any more. You wouldn't be you without your bright hair and million-plus dots. Oh, and I also think your body is pretty fabulous and I love...' He stopped speaking to pull back the band of the shirt she wore to kiss her shoulder.

What did he love...what? He wasn't about to say something weird, was he? They'd only slept together once and this was supposed to be a brief fling, not anything serious. But what if he did? How would she answer? What could she say?

He lifted his head to grin at her. 'I love the fact that

you know your way around a microwave. You wouldn't happen to know your way around a frying pan, would you? Because the housekeeper can't get back because of the weather. I saw bacon in the freezer and pancake mix in the pantry...'

Breakfast.

He was talking about food.

Getting a bit ahead of yourself there, weren't you? Idiot.

CHAPTER NINE

THE NEXT DAY, Cole stood by the huge windows of the great room, his hands wrapped around a cup of coffee, and stared at the white landscape in front of him. It was exceptionally cold, and the clouds hung low in the sky, threatening to dump another batch of snow onto the three or so feet they'd received the night before.

Cole wasn't familiar with winter in the Eastern Cape, but this amount of snow seemed excessive. He heard movement in the kitchen and the sound of Lex singing. It took him a while to recognise the chorus because Lex couldn't hold a tune. Sitting down in one of the huge leather chairs, he rested his ankle on the opposite knee, happy for some time on his own.

What had possessed him to spill his secrets to Lex, to run his mouth? He'd told her more about his family situation than he'd told anyone, and he felt angsty and irritable. She was someone he was having an ultra-brief affair with—she wasn't a girlfriend. She barely qualified as a friend.

So why then had he rambled on and on?

Cole rubbed the back of his neck, wincing when his cold fingers touched the skin under the collar of his shirt. Lex was temporary, a transient attraction...

Why was he spending so much time convincing himself that she meant nothing to him, reminding himself she was leaving his life? Was he doing that because a part of him—the same part that had trusted her with his hurt and confusion around his family—wanted her to stick around, to be a part of his life going forward?

He couldn't sustain a relationship with her. He knew he'd bail when he got into waters that were deeper than he liked. A decade ago, he'd had a series of relationships, none of which had worked out. He simply wasn't any good at them, and within a couple of months he felt as if he had a noose around his neck, all the life and air being squeezed out of him. Some of his previous lovers had offered everything they had, love and acceptance, fidelity and adoration, but it had never felt as though it was enough.

Cole knew, with complete certainty, that he was the problem, not them. He was unable to receive love and, because his failures hurt other people, he'd vowed to keep his relationships shallow and short.

He ran at the first demand of commitment and the tiniest hint of emotional intimacy as soon as a woman started asking for more. The chances were high that he'd do the same thing if he tried to have a relationship with Lex.

He knew that however much he was offered—a woman could hand him her heart on a velvet cushion—it would never be enough. They'd never be able to fill the hole his father's neglect had left in his life.

And, even if Lex was the one person who could make him feel whole—which was a stretch, but this was a mental exercise and not a lifelong commitment—a relationship between them could never work.

He'd always avoided single mothers and couldn't see himself being a stepdad. He hadn't been given the opportunity to be Grenville's son and had no reference point on how to be a father. And, if continuing his affair with Lex were an option, he'd have to share the little time he had with Lex with her sisters. Not ideal.

Ifs, buts, whats, hows... He sighed. A couple of days, that was all they had, the only commitment he could make.

Lex crossed the great hall to him and held up her phone. 'I don't have any signal,' she told him. 'And the power has just gone out.'

That wasn't a surprise. Power and communication were always the first to go in weather events.

'This place will have a generator,' Cole told her. 'There is no way that my father would spend millions on decor and not have a backup plan if the lights went out. It should come on in a few minutes.'

He'd barely finished his sentence when the rumble of the generator drifted over to them and the lights in the great room flickered on.

Lex sat on the arm of his seat and, thinking she was too far away, Cole wrapped his arm around her and pulled her onto his lap. She sat at right angles to him, her back against one arm of the chair, her legs draped over the other. Happy to have her close, he ran a hand over her bright head.

Lex took his mug out of his hand and took a sip. 'It's so beautiful. It looks like someone sprinkled icing sugar everywhere. The girls would love this place and would adore the snow.' She handed him a small smile. 'I feel a bit guilty that I am here without them.'

Cole picked up his phone, researched some flights and distances, did some mental calculations and looked at his watch. 'It's shortly after nine. If we all hustle, we could probably get them here by mid-afternoon.'

Lex stared at him, a frown pulling her eyebrows together. 'What are you talking about?'

'A private plane from Durban to East London, a helicopter from East London to here. We could send them back tomorrow.'

Where were these words coming from? Hadn't he just admitted to himself that he wasn't prepared to share his time with Lex with anyone else? But he'd seen the yearning on her face and had instinctively wanted to make her happy.

Her mouth fell open and he used his knuckle to lift it close. 'If they want to see snow, I can make that happen.'

'It would cost a fortune!'

He shrugged, prepared to spend whatever he needed to. 'Well?' he asked, when she didn't say anything.

She wrinkled her nose and, after another minute of thinking, shook her head. 'It's a lovely offer, Cole, and I so appreciate it…but we couldn't put you to that trouble and that expense.'

'I'm offering,' he pointed out.

'Thank you, but no.

'I appreciate you thinking of them—it was very sweet of you,' she added in an ultra-polite voice. She didn't sound like herself at all. And sweet? He was anything but.

Lex rolled off his lap and stood up, jamming her hands into the front pockets of her jeans and hunching her shoulders forwards. She wore a russet-coloured jersey and fluffy socks on her feet.

He sat up, reached forward and hooked his finger in the band of her jeans, pulling her to where he sat. He pulled her back down to his lap and sighed when she sat on his thighs, her back ramrod-straight, her hands between her knees.

Why did she look so miserable, so guilty? He remembered hearing that she hadn't had any time away from them in five years. 'It's okay to say no, Lex.'

She turned her head to look at him. 'This is the first time I've had concentrated time on my own since they arrived five years ago. This is my little holiday, my time to decompress, to simply be. I don't want to be interrupted by someone asking me for milk or juice or how snow is made. I don't want to have to supervise meals and bath times and read six stories before they go to sleep. I just want to be here, with you, isolated and quiet. For a few days, I just want to be me,' she told him.

Fine with him. He didn't have a single objection to anything she was saying.

'But I feel so damn guilty for turning down such an amazing opportunity for them to be overawed by the helicopter ride, to play in the snow. They've had so little, Cole—we haven't been able to give them much.'

He stroked his hand up and down her slim back. 'No, only a stable house, food, the chance to go to the same school every day and sleep in the same bed every night.'

He leaned down to kiss her temple. 'And don't forget love and affection, Lex—you've given them a lot of that. They are very lucky girls.'

He'd been raised with every toy, been given the best education and had always worn designer clothing but he'd have swapped all of it in a heartbeat for a kiss goodnight, someone to read him a story, to nag him about bath and bed times. Lex had no idea how valuable her gift to her sisters was.

Lex released a huge sigh, the tension flowed out of her body and she leaned sideways to rest her head on his chest, curling into him. 'I feel so damn guilty, Cole,' she whispered.

'For what, sweetheart?'

'For resenting them, for being angry because I've sacrificed so much for all of them. For being jealous of Addi,' she added, so quietly he almost didn't hear her.

He encircled her body with his arms, keeping her clasped to his body. 'Do you want to explain that, Lex?'

'No.'

It was an honest and forthright answer and not unexpected. 'C'mon, Lex,' he coaxed her, partly because he was curious about this woman, but also because he sensed she needed to talk to someone.

'When we were young, I loved her to death and she was my best friend—but I was angry because she was born blonde and beautiful and I wasn't. She's so very smart and so effortlessly lovely.'

Sure. But Lex's sister hadn't generated a spark of desire in him while Lex sparked an out-of-control wildfire.

'When we were kids, I always felt like I was a step or two behind her, constantly trying to catch up. I thought that would change when we became adults but, even then, Addi always came first.'

'Give me an example,' Cole prompted.

'How many do you need?' Lex asked with a snort-laugh. 'She got her degree first. I went out to work. I was going to go to uni when the girls arrived, but I had to stay home and look after them while Addi went out to work. I haven't had a moment to myself lately because Addi's been haring around Africa staying in your fancy hotels as she shows Jude Fisher around.' She pulled away but he wouldn't let her.

'Go on.'

'I feel like I'm the one who's made the majority of the sacrifices, who's always got the short end of the stick.

I gave up my career, my love life, my student life, my degree, to look after the girls. Sometimes I feel like Cinderella, and that my sisters have had an easier ride than me. That I am the one who's always going to be expected to make the sacrifices.'

She pushed away from him and pushed the balls of her hands into her eye sockets. 'And I hate feeling like that, hate feeling cross and resentful and jealous. I love them, Cole.'

'Of course you do,' he told her. 'You can still love them and feel angry, Lex. You are allowed to feel two emotions at once.'

She nodded. 'But I sound like I'm whining, and I hate whiners. You have to play the cards you are dealt and simply get on with it. But, now and again, I'd like to be at the top of the list of priorities, Cole. Just once.'

He stared at her lovely profile and his heart rate kicked up just a little. She'd done so much for so many people and she was beating herself up for some very normal feelings. She was, bar none, one of the strongest people he'd ever met. He could juggle numbers, make billion-dollar decisions without turning a hair and fly down steep ski-slopes but, if two half-siblings dropped into his life, he wouldn't know what to do with them or how to raise them.

And he was thirty-six, not in his early twenties. She'd have his respect for ever for doing the hard stuff. And, yeah, she was occasionally allowed to feel resentful and jealous. He was just surprised she didn't feel those emotions more often.

He watched as she pushed her hands into her hair and twisted the curls, making some sort of messy bun on the top of her head which she secured with the hair band she wore on her wrist.

She sighed and looked out at the snow. 'Despite wanting to be here with you, on our own, I'm still very tempted to take you up on that offer to give the kids a helicopter ride, to allow them to play in the snow. It would be a dream come true for them, and they'd remember it for the rest of their lives.'

He forced a grimace. 'I might've got a bit carried away with that offer, sweetheart. I don't think the helicopters would be able to fly when there's a chance the weather will close in.'

It wasn't a complete lie. The reports said that another system was moving in and more snow was expected.

'Are you just saying that to make me feel better?' Lex asked, looking suspicious.

Of course he was. He'd do anything, say anything, pay anything to take the misery out of her eyes. 'No.'

She smiled at him, sliding her hand up and down his chest. 'Liar. But thank you.' Lex settled back down and they both stared out of the window, enjoying the snow-covered slopes, the stillness of the morning punctuated by the low hum of the generator. This lounge, and the deck outside, was a great place to sit and watch the skiers while enjoying a cup of *glühwein* or whisky-laced hot chocolate.

Cole gestured to the ski-slope to their left. 'I'm going to tromp down there shortly. I can't come to a ski resort I own—or temporarily own—and not ski. There's a rental shop within the office buildings. I'll find all the equipment I need there.'

'You're going to have to figure out how to get the ski lift working or else it's going to be a long, wet hike up that hill,' Lex told him, smiling.

'I'll figure it out,' Cole told her. 'When I'm done, maybe I can teach you how to ski.'

Lex sent him a look full of humour-coated desire. 'I

could think of something I'd much rather do with you than learn to snowboard.'

'That's so incredibly tempting.'

Cole ducked his head to kiss her but pulled back at the last second. They'd had two intense conversations—one last night, one a minute ago—and they needed some distance, a little bit of space. This was getting too deep, too fast, and it pushed him out of his comfort zone.

'If I kiss you properly, I'll be tempted to take you upstairs instead of hitting the slopes.'

Lex sat up and he could feel her pulling back as her many shields came up. 'I'm sorry I dumped on you. I know that wasn't part of our no-strings fling.'

He frowned, puzzled by her statement. He'd opened up to her, had exposed himself, and he didn't feel the need to apologise. Why did she? 'We can be friends as well as lovers, Lex.'

She wrinkled her nose and shrugged. 'I guess.' But she didn't look convinced. He felt the need to reassure her. 'There isn't a rule book we need to follow.'

She patted his chest and climbed off his lap. 'It would be so much easier if we did,' she quietly said before pulling up a smile. 'I'm going to have a nap while you play in the snow.'

His eyes sparked with interest and Lex smiled, her good humour restored by the interest she saw in his eyes.

He wanted her, she wanted him…nothing more, nothing less.

It was one sentence and the only rule they needed to follow.

Who needed a book?

Cole came to a controlled stop at the bottom of the run and placed his hands on his thighs, pulling in deep breaths of icy air. He turned and looked up the slope, called, according to the map in the shop, Charlie's Run, and nodded, satisfied. His thigh muscles burned from the three treks he'd made up the ski-slope through the snow carrying his board but flying down the slope was always worth it.

Cole bent down to release his feet from the snowboard and wondered who Charlie was and why the name popped up all over the resort. The small pub with a deck overlooking the ski-slopes was called Charlie's, this run was called after Charlie and the subsidiary company of Thorpe Industries that owned this ski resort was called Charlie On The Mountain. A stupid name for a company but, obviously, one that had held some significance for Grenville.

Was Charlie the name of a lover, an old friend, a dog his dad had loved? Because he had no insight into his father's life, and had never met the people who were important to him, he didn't know.

But he could ask. Cole pulled his phone out of a zippered pocket in his ski-jacket and opened up his email application, banging out a quick message to Sam's lawyer.

Who is Charlie? Why is everything at the ski resort Grenville owned named after him? Can you ask Sam and get back to me?

There were rules about how much contact Sam had with the outside world and Cole knew that he might not get an answer. And, if he did, it might be in a few weeks' or months' time. Or never.

Cole picked up his snowboard and tucked it under

her arm, debating whether to climb the slope again. He loved to exercise, loved the hitch in his breath, feeling his muscles burning and perspiration rolling down his spine—and his body felt tight after all that driving.

Sex was great, but it wasn't great exercise.

Sex with Lex was better than great, he admitted as he pushed his hand through his damp hair. Did he have time for another run? he wondered, glancing at the bank of black clouds in the distance. They were calling this system the biggest snow event of the past fifty years and those dark clouds moving in held more snow. He had maybe an hour left before it started to snow again. This would be his last ride for today.

Besides, he couldn't wait to get back to Lex.

Despite only catching a few hours' sleep last night, he'd slept well, and deeply. He generally preferred to sleep alone but he loved having her in his bed. Wrapping his arm around her waist and anchoring her to him felt right, completely natural.

When he'd woken up, she'd been in the same position. Having her there, her butt tucked into his bent legs, his hand holding her breast, was where she was meant to be. But then she'd wiggled and all thoughts had been obliterated as his body had come to attention and his brain had shut down.

She was as alluring out of bed as she was in it. He'd been surprised by her opening up this morning, pleased but surprised. But, as soon as they'd ended the conversation, she'd pulled back and he'd sensed that she regretted being so open and honest about her thoughts and feelings. Why? She'd had a rough few years, and she'd played the game with the chips she had. If she occasionally felt bitter, edgy, resentful, she had the right. She'd made huge sacrifices for her sisters.

He admired her and respected her more. He was a child of extreme privilege, and had had every opportunity. While he'd worked extremely hard to set up a successful company, he'd been afforded the time to get his degree, and had been able to give his entire focus to his studies, and afterward to his company. He'd always had money, but Lex was juggling her sisters, her degree, a part-time job and making ends meet.

And she felt bad because occasionally she felt guilty about taking some time for herself, resentful about what she'd been forced to sacrifice. She was, frankly, one of the strongest, best people he'd ever met.

At the top of the slope, he slipped his feet into his mounts, tightened the clasp and rocked the board back and forth. Instead of seeing the snow-covered slope, he saw Lex's lovely face, her bright hair on his white pillow, her slim, sexy body, and thought that he couldn't wait to get back to her, to lower her to the rug in front of the fire. Or to simply share a cup of coffee or glass of wine with her, happy to listen to tales of her busy, girly life.

Cole sighed, annoyed with himself. They were having an affair, he reminded himself. A temporary fling, something that was only built to last a few days for as long as they were here at Rossdale—or maybe, if he could talk her into it, for as long as he was in South Africa. There was nothing between them but sex…

But, damn, a small part of him wished there could be.

Cole rocked the board, the snowboard slipped over the lip and he started to gather speed. He was at a pretty high altitude, he realised, that was why his brain was scrambled. There wasn't enough oxygen to power his brain. When he got back to Cape Town, things would go back to normal.

He hoped.

Because if they didn't, he was in big trouble.

CHAPTER TEN

'WE HAD AN extraordinary amount of snow already, and they are forecasting more tonight,' Cole told Lex as he poured her a glass of red wine.

They were in the kitchen and Cole stood next to her at the kitchen island, watching her as she threw together a simple pasta dish of garlic, capers and anchovies.

'When I got back this afternoon from snowboarding, I jumped onto my computer and managed to find the town's social media page,' Cole continued. 'Rhodes is cut off and no one is getting in or out for the next few days. They've had reports of damaged homes and businesses already and, apparently, there's more to come.'

Lex bit her lip. They were higher up the mountain and were probably going to see more snow than everyone else. Would the ski-lodge be able to cope with what was coming? Cole placed a hand on her butt and gave her a reassuring pat. 'We might not be leaving any time soon but we'll be fine.'

Lex lifted the glass of wine to her lips, thinking that he was good at reassurance. He'd managed to convince her that exposing the fear and resentment about raising her sisters, and the sacrifices she'd made, was normal.

It was nice to unburden herself, to feel emotionally connected to a man, but she couldn't allow it to happen again. He'd been there this time, but he wouldn't be there in the future. She couldn't make opening up, sharing her inner world, a habit. Cole wasn't going to stick around.

Even if he did live in Cape Town and wanted more from her, he'd run when confronted with the day-to-day reality of her life. She was her sisters' primary caregiver and they'd be a huge part of her life—the biggest part—for the next ten to fifteen years. Cole, or any other man, would have to be able to accept the package deal: Lex and her four sisters, two of whom would live with her until they were grown.

Yeah, her baggage would fill one of those massive cargo planes that carried tanks and helicopters—Cole wasn't even interested in a relationship, so he would never be prepared to help her carry hers. And, that being the case, she shouldn't open up to him, let him in.

It would make saying goodbye a thousand times harder than it needed to be.

No, she couldn't watch another person she loved walk away from her—not again. Her heart had been kicked around enough, thank you.

'We have wood, food and lots of fuel for the generator,' Cole reassured her, pulling her back to the present.

'I'm not worried,' Lex told him. Well, she wasn't worried about the snow storm. Allowing herself to get close to him, to feel more than she should? Yeah, she was worried about that.

'What else did the local media have to say?' Lex asked him.

Cole straightened and frowned. 'They have people missing and a town that is packed to capacity, people who are stranded.'

Lex's head snapped up. 'They have people missing?'

'Yeah. Two shepherds haven't checked in, and they can't contact them on their phones. They're assuming their batteries have died.'

'Have they sent their S and R team out?' Lex demanded.

'Search and Rescue? It's a small town, Lex, they don't have the resources. But I did call the number I found online and spoke to a guy who's coordinating their disaster management team. I offered to hire a helicopter to search for them and said that I would cover the costs to bring in an S and R team.'

Or course he had. Whether it was a life-or-death situation, or giving her sisters a treat of playing in the snow, he was so quick to offer his help, to use his money. Lex respected that. What was the point of having so much money if you didn't use it to help others?

'That's good of you, Cole. What did they say?'

Cole frowned. 'They appreciated the offer, but all helicopters and planes are going to be grounded shortly. The authorities don't want anyone flying, as the next cold front is moving in very quickly.'

So, even if she'd wanted to take Cole up on his very generous offer to bring the girls here to play in the snow, the weather wasn't playing ball, which allowed Lex to release the last vestiges of guilt at denying her sisters an awesome treat.

It was still going to be Cole and her alone in this big house. Excellent. Then she remembered that men were caught in the snow and felt ashamed of herself.

'The coordinator said that he was hoping the shepherds got to one of the huts they have at higher altitudes. If they did, there are enough supplies in the huts to keep them warm and fed,' Cole explained.

'And the sheep?' Lex asked. She couldn't stomach the idea of the animals freezing to death.

'I asked about them too, and apparently the herders love their animals and the huts have enclosed shelters to house the flock. Apparently, they are hardy men who know these mountains and how unpredictable the weather can be. He was cautiously optimistic.'

Lex nodded, relieved.

'How old is this place?' Lex asked him, changing the subject as she stirred the sauce.

'The original structure is over eighty years old,' Cole told her, resting his arms on the island. 'Maybe Charlie was the original owner of Rossdale Ski Resort.'

Cole explained how so many things at the resort were named after 'Charlie' and that he'd been wondering who this Charlie person was.

'It could be anyone,' Lex told him, wrinkling her nose.

Cole grimaced. 'I know. But the name is everywhere, so I'd like to know why my father felt the need to name everything after this person.' He explained that he'd sent an email to his brother's lawyer but wasn't expecting a reply soon, if one came at all.

'You don't sound very optimistic,' Lex commented.

Cole stared into his ruby-red wine. 'Sam and I have a complicated relationship. I saw him when he visited our mother, but I veered between worshipping him—he was a lot older and cooler—and being incredibly jealous and resentful because he had a relationship with Grenville and I didn't. We haven't had contact for fifteen years so the chance of a quick response, or any response, isn't good.'

Lex grimaced. She knew how important siblings could be and couldn't imagine her life without her sisters. Addi was her first and last best friend. They were a solid team, and they had each other's backs, no matter what. The sky could fall in and sea levels could rise but she and Addi would build a boat, make a plan…together.

'Why is that?'

Cole didn't elaborate on his comment so Lex gently kicked his ankle with her sock-covered foot. When he couldn't look at her, her heart plummeted to her toes. 'What happened with your brother, Cole?' she asked.

He walked around the island and picked up the cork to the wine bottle, tossing it from hand to hand. 'We were never close but we did keep in contact after he left school and went to uni,' he explained. 'Then one day—I was in my late teens—he stopped answering my calls, nor did he return my emails. I went over to his flat and I sat on his steps every afternoon for two days until he appeared. I demanded to know what his problem was.'

Lex placed her elbows on the island, morbidly fascinated. 'What did he say?'

'Nothing. He told me that a relationship between us was impossible.'

'Why would he do that?'

'Because my father ordered him to and Grenville's word was law. If Sam wanted to be his son, inherit his fortune, be the next Thorpe to run the family business, then he had to cut me out of his life.'

'But why? That makes no sense.'

'It made sense to Grenville. And, when Grenville died, I was not mentioned in his will. He left everything to Sam.'

Wait, hold on. Lex knew that he owned Thorpe Industries. She'd seen the company memo stating that Sam Thorpe had retired and that Cole was now the main shareholder and CEO of Thorpe Industries, the holding company with hundreds of smaller businesses under its wing. How had that come about if his brother had inherited everything from their father?

Cole explained about Sam renouncing his material possessions to become a monk and how he'd passed all his assets over to him.

'I was on my way to acquiring their company, about to launch a hostile takeover. When I had their attention, when they had to deal with me, I was going to demand answers from my father and have that showdown I thought I needed. All I ever wanted was for them to see me, acknowledge me.' Cole stared out of the window into the stygian night. 'But my father pre-empted me from having any sort of closure by dying, and then Sam pulled this crazy stunt of passing everything over to me. I wish…'

His voice was laced with pain, making his words sound scalpel-sharp. 'What do you wish, Cole?' she asked softly.

He placed his hands on the island and stared down at the tiled floor. When he spoke, his words were so low that she had to strain to hear them.

'I wish I knew what I did to make him hate me so.'

There was pain in his voice, also confusion, frustration and impotence. How did one understand a situation that had never been explained, created by a man who was now dead?

Cole straightened, shrugged and reached for the bottle of wine to top up their glasses. He lifted his eyes and she saw that they were as hard as agates. He'd emotionally retreated behind an impenetrable shield. 'So, I got an interesting email today. A client of mine is having a garden party at his sixteenth-century chateau in

Burgundy next weekend to celebrate Bastille Day and I'm invited.'

She blinked, not sure she'd heard him correctly. They'd been having an intense conversation about his brother and now he was talking about a garden party in France?

What?

'Why don't you come with me?' he asked.

Okay, had she stepped into a strange metaverse? He was acting as if they hadn't just had a deep conversation about his past and his family, and she wondered how he could switch subjects so quickly. 'We were talking about your brother, Cole,' she pointed out.

His shrug was annoyingly nonchalant. 'Now we're not. So, will you come? We can fly from Burgundy to London, and you can see where I live. I might be able to fly back with you on Tuesday, depending on my schedule.'

She stared at him, expecting to see another head emerging. 'I can't go to France, then London, with you.'

Cole lifted his glass and sipped. 'Why not? Your sisters will only be back the following Saturday so it's not like you have to be back for them.'

It was the craziest idea she'd ever heard. She couldn't just fly off on a whim. It wasn't what she did, who she was. She wasn't the girl who jetted off on private planes to attend garden parties at French chateaux. She worked, she studied, she looked after Nixi and Snow—she didn't *jet*.

'And, you know, even if your younger sisters were due home, why couldn't you take that time for yourself?'

She jerked up, her spine steel-rod straight. 'Because that's my job—that's what I agreed to do.'

'When you and Addi worked out your division of duties, was there a clause that said you couldn't do anything for yourself any more, that you couldn't do anything fun?' Cole challenged her. 'I'm not asking you to marry me, Lex, I'm asking you to come to a weekend party with me, to visit my home.'

He was moving the goalposts and she didn't like it. They were supposed to be having a road-trip fling. It wasn't supposed to last beyond this time in Rhodes. And, damn it, she was also mad because she was so tempted to say yes, to run away, to feel young, impulsive and free again. But she was terrified that, if she did, she'd never be content to return to the life she knew, the life she'd carefully created to give her sisters the stability she'd never had.

'You can't keep putting your life on hold for your sisters, Lex.'

'Why not? Why can't I do exactly that?' she demanded, her voice rising. And how dare he say that? He hadn't walked in her shoes. He didn't know what motivated her to make the choices she had.

'You're putting them first because nobody put you first, Lex. You're making sure that their lives are as wonderful as you can make them because nobody did that for you.'

Oh! He was right and she hated him for saying what she barely could admit to herself. She was trying to be all and do all for Nixi and Snow to make the little girl who still lived deep inside her feel better about herself, to feel worthy.

'It's not fair on you.'

Fair? Ah, now there was a statement she could fight. 'You have to be kidding me! You, of all people, know that life isn't fair. I learned that early and I learned that hard! And I did it without the cushion of money. How dare you criticise what I do, the choices I've made?'

'I wasn't criticising, I just want you to—'

'Stop talking!' Lex shouted.

She couldn't hear any more, take any more. She felt emotionally battered, not necessarily by Cole but by the old emotions, hurts and truths he'd pulled to the surface. She didn't take time for herself, and had put her life on hold, possibly because she still believed she needed to prove she was worthy of love.

She needed air, she needed space and she desperately needed to be alone.

Lex held up her hands and backed away. 'This was just supposed to be about sex, Cole. Why are we shouting at each other?'

'I'm not the one shouting,' he pointed out, his tone ultra-reasonable. 'And I thought we agreed that we could be friends as well as lovers.'

She held his eyes, her eyes cool. 'One question, Cole.'

He arched one eyebrow, waiting.

'Was deflecting me off the subject of your brother worth this argument?' When he didn't answer her, she spoke again, her voice as brittle as frost-eaten winter grass. 'I'll leave you alone to think about that.'

Lex grabbed a torch from the kitchen drawer and walked to the main building and back, kicking her way through the snow. By the time she returned, she was miserable, freezing and had a pulsing headache. Knowing that she had some pain killers in her bag, she slipped into the master suite, found her bag and the pills, swallowed them down and sat down on the edge of the bed. Would Cole sleep here with her tonight? Would they spend the rest of the trip in silence? Would he simply ignore her, deciding that she wasn't worth his time and energy? Joelle had been the master of the silent treatment and had had a doctorate in making her feel as if she wasn't worth her time and attention after one of their many clashes.

Lex heard his footsteps but didn't look up. He sat down on the bed beside her and his arm snaked around her waist.

'Are you still mad?' Cole murmured in her ear, placing his mouth on the bare skin below her ear.

Yes. No. She was still furious, but more at herself than at him. He'd sliced away the half-truths she'd told herself, and she hadn't liked what she'd seen. She'd been so convinced that she'd recovered from the wounds her mother had inflicted, but she hadn't done as much healing as she'd thought, and she hated that. Hated that the past still had such a hold over her.

She shrugged and couldn't stop herself from leaning into him, soaking up some of his strength. He felt like a barrier between her and the world. At this moment, whatever wanted to hurt her had to come through him.

Lex gave herself a mental shake, telling herself to see things as they were, not as she wanted them to be. They were short-term lovers, as he'd said—friends. It wasn't his job to protect her.

This was all so confusing.

It shouldn't be. He was just a fling, not someone who would be in her life long-term. She had no intention of allowing someone into her heart only to watch them walk away a few weeks or months later, dunking her in a vat of hurt and disappointment. Cole would never be able to put her, and what she needed, first.

Lex ran her hands up and down her face. 'I don't know,' she answered him honestly.

'Fair enough,' he replied, before standing and scooping her up to hold her against his chest.

'What are you doing?' she demanded, wide-eyed.

'Taking you to bed and, after I've made you feel boneless, you're going to take a nap before we eat.'

'I never nap,' Lex told him.

Cole swiped his lips across her mouth. 'You will,' he promised her as he walked her to her side of the bed and lowered her down. 'I'm sorry if what I said pushed your buttons.'

Lex noticed that he hadn't apologised for what he'd said. Why should he, since he was right?

'If I agree with that, will you admit that you changed the subject to avoid speaking about your brother?'

He nodded. 'Yes. I didn't want to talk about him any more, but I still do want you to come to France with me.'

'I thought this would end when we got back to Cape Town.'

'I'm still not promising you anything, Lex, but neither do I think we need to discard each other like last night's takeaways. We're enjoying each other, let's keep doing that.'

She started to shake her head, to tell him she couldn't, that it was impossible, but pulled the words back at the last minute. She was reacting out of habit, because doing something fun wasn't what she did, wasn't something she thought she deserved. She could go to France. Nothing was keeping her here. It was the opportunity of a lifetime. She'd never travelled out of the country and didn't know when she'd next have the chance to use her unstamped passport. Excitement bubbled beneath her skin, skipped into her blood and coursed through her body.

It had been so long since she'd felt excited that she

almost didn't recognise the emotion. But because she was cautious, because a little voice deep inside was screaming at her not to make any impulsive decisions, she lifted her hand to his jaw and told him she'd think about it.

'Good enough.' Cole lay down next to her and pulled the band from her hair, combing his fingers through her bright strands. He stroked his thumb down the cord in her neck and she looked into his warm eyes. 'Can I just say a few more things?'

Lex tensed, wishing he wouldn't. She'd heard enough and had too many thoughts careering around her head. She just wanted to feel.

'Although I do think you neglect yourself, I'm also in awe of you, Lex. I think you are amazing, and I have the greatest respect for you. You are raising your sisters, working, studying, juggling more than a couple of balls in the air and not letting any of them fall.'

Tension seeped out of her body. 'You juggle dozens of balls too.'

'No, sweetheart, my balls are money-related—work. If I drop a ball, I lose money, not a big deal. If you drop a ball, your sisters could be affected, your degree and your second income. Money is easy, people are diffi-cult—complicated. The stakes don't compare.'

Warmth seeped into her eyes and her hand came up to touch his hair, her fingers stroking his scalp. That was the nicest thing she'd heard him, or anyone, say. And she didn't know how much she needed to hear the words until he'd said them.

She felt recognised and seen. Understood. And how strange was it that it was this solitary man, someone so different from her in life experiences, who made her feel affirmed. She'd had so little emotional support, so few people cheering her on, that a part of her wanted to ask him to repeat himself so that she could roll around in the sunshine of his words.

'Thank you for saying that.'

'But you can be pretty scary and damn bossy when you're mad.'

She heard the teasing note in his voice and laughed. How could she go from blisteringly angry to laughter so quickly? Did the 'why' even matter? He was here with her and they were talking—friends again. And lovers.

Talking about loving... Lex used her core muscles to launch herself upwards, her mouth seeking his, her kiss full of thanks, gratitude and a huge hit of want and need.

'I think you should take my clothes off,' Lex instructed, her voice growly with need.

Because he wasn't a saint, and because making love to her was what he most wanted to do, Cole decided that was a fine idea indeed.

'You have the prettiest body,' he told her, pulling her jersey up her ribcage, exposing her pale and lovely skin to his hot gaze. Her bra was plain white, functional rather than pretty, and the thought that he wanted to see her in jewel colours—reds, violets and deep greens—flitted through his mind as he placed his mouth on her nipple and sucked her, fabric and all, into his mouth.

Lex responded to his deep kiss by moaning and trying to wrap her hand around his erection, hampered by the material of his jeans. Holding herself in a half-sit-up position, she pulled his earlobe into her mouth and nibbled on it, sending a warm, fast burst of electricity along every nerve ending he possessed.

'So you like me when I'm bossy, right?' Lex asked, his tone teasing.

'In certain circumstances,' he replied. 'For instance, if you told me to get naked, then I'd listen.'

He saw green fire in Lex's eyes through her half-closed lids. 'Get naked, Cole,' she ordered him.

Eager to play this game, Cole pulled away from her, stood next to the bed and pulled off his jersey, slowly. She beckoned him closer and, kneeling on the bed as he stood, placed her mouth on his sternum, her tongue coming out to touch his hot skin. Cole closed his eyes, his clothes falling to the floor as Lex's clever mouth drifted down across the hard muscles of his stomach, and lower, to where the band of his jeans rested.

He reached down to undo his trousers but Lex smacked his hands away. 'My job,' she told him, her tone suggesting that he not disagree.

He pulled his hands away and their eyes connected as she undid the buttons holding his jeans together.

She looked up at him and Cole's heart flipped over backwards. Damn, she had no idea how sexy she was. He looked down into those eyes that were the exact colour of the nephrite jade Buddha figure he'd bought at auction last year. They were shockingly deep and, like the statue, Lex was rare, special and pretty damn amazing. She was bright, compelling, courageous and massively strong-willed, stronger than she realised and tougher than she gave herself credit for.

He was in awe of her…

In another life, if he'd been another guy, he'd find a way to keep her in his life.

But that was impossible. He couldn't give her any-thing more than sex. Their time together was limited. She was raising a family and he was terrible at relation-ships. He always messed them up by pulling away, by sabotaging them.

But this was the first woman to tempt him into those turbulent waters in over a decade. He had to resist her, had to resist the idea of them. The lines between lust and like were blurring.

Slow down, idiot. Right now. Because, if you don't, you're going to come out of this bloody and bruised.

Lex pushed her hands between his skin and the fabric of his underwear and jeans and tugged everything down. He shed his clothes and, when she reached for him, he shook his head. If she touched him with her lips, if she sucked him, this would all be over very fast indeed. No, he needed to wring pleasure out of every moment they had together.

'My turn to be bossy,' Cole told her, tugging her to her feet. As she stood on the bed in front of him, he stripped her quickly, throwing her clothes to the floor. When she was gloriously naked, he placed feather-light kisses on her ribcage, nibbled her collarbone and dragged his tongue across that sweet spot between her neck and ear. Lex picked up his hand and placed it on her breast, but he wouldn't be rushed. This was his time, so he tickled and teased, tasting her skin on the back of her knee, the arch of her foot. He nuzzled the special space between her thighs, but after a few seconds pulled away to nibble her hip bone, to taste her belly button, to suck on her breasts.

And when Lex's demands became insistent, when her moans deepened, he pulled back and started to explore her lovely body all over again. When she thumped his shoulder with her small fist, when her eyes turned stormy with passion, liquid with need, he placed his mouth on her. That small contact made her orgasm and, wanting her to get off again, he slid two fingers into her and nuzzled her to another high.

Pliant, out of breath and loose with pleasure, she rolled over onto her stomach and lifted her hips, seeming to know what he wanted, how he needed her. He reached for the condom he'd tossed onto the bed earlier, rolled it on and, after widening her knees, slid into her slick warmth and closed his eyes. *Home*, he thought.

He didn't have time to interrogate that thought because he felt Lex push back against him and he recognised the tension in her body. She wanted to come again, and he was fully prepared to take it slow, to make her burn. But Lex had other plans...

Suddenly she was rocking, he was pumping and he heard Lex's scream of pleasure echoing down a tunnel. Her inner walls tightened around him and a stream of pure energy rocketed through him, spinning him away.

Amazing, Cole thought. He tightened his arm around her waist, anchoring her to him, his big body covering hers. They couldn't have a future, but they had this.

And this was pretty astounding.

CHAPTER ELEVEN

ON SUNDAY, JUST over a week after they'd arrived at Rossdale, the weather cleared and they could make their way down the mountain, this time with Cole behind the wheel. Snow still covered the hills but the road was finally navigable. Lex kept her eyes on her side mirror until the ski-lodge disappeared from sight. For as long as she lived, she'd always remember these magical days she spent snowbound with Cole. The ski resort would always hold a magical place in her heart.

She'd never return to this place but she would always remember making love in front of the fire, spending the afternoon wrapped up in a cashmere blanket in Cole's arms and drinking red wine as she watched the snow drift to the ground. Sharing his shower, waking up to him nuzzling her breast with his stubbled cheek and his hand between her legs would be X-rated memories she'd savour.

Returning to her sister-focused life was going to be a lot tougher than she'd bargained for.

Despite knowing their affair had an expiration date, despite constantly reminding herself this was a brief fling and that he wasn't interested in any type of commitment, she couldn't stop herself from wanting more.

She might, because she was a complete moron, just want everything.

Him. For ever.

Lex looked out of the window, feeling the burn of tears in the back of her throat. She didn't know if she was emotional because time was running out or because she was angry at not being able to control her emotions and expectations, to keep her heart in check.

Both, probably.

Cole steered the SUV around the last steep corner and they moved from a dirt road to one covered in tarmac. There were clumps of snow on the grass and a number of trees were buckled and bent from the wind and the weight of the snow. The storm had been unexpected and impressive.

Words that perfectly described Cole.

Cole reached across the console and slid his hand over hers, lifting her knuckles to his mouth and kissing her skin. He darted her a quick look. 'I had the best time with you, Lex. It was a marvellous break.'

For her too. And, despite trying not to let her imagination run riot, she could see them doing it again. And again. Sneaking away for a week here, a few days there to be on their own—him running away from his work, her from her studies and the girls. Without any effort at all, she could see them taking family holidays, with Cole teaching her sisters, and later their own kids, to ski and snowboard.

Instead of being blurry, that mental snapshot was crystal-clear. A dark-haired son and a red-headed daughter, or any combination of sex and colouring. He was the only person she could imagine having a child with, being with, committing to.

The only man she would, could, fall in love with. No,

that was wrong. She already loved him. And, damn, how inconvenient and insane was *that*?

She couldn't handle the implications of her rogue thought and pushed it away, hoping that the feeling would fade. She needed to think of something else, *anything* else.

'Did you get an email back from your brother explaining about Charlie?' Lex asked, thinking about the constant references to Charlie at the lodge.

Cole shook his head. 'No. I don't really expect to. My brother has never been good at giving me what I need.'

After their argument, they'd both avoided the subject of her family and his, choosing instead to get to know each other better, talking about the things new lovers did—art, music, travels and politics. Cole had done some work. She'd found a book to read in the library. He'd skied and she'd tried to. They'd made love.

A lot.

'In some ways, I'm angrier with Sam than I am with my father. Sam could've defied Grenville, he could've chosen to have a relationship with me, but he didn't,' Cole explained, and Lex heard the bitterness in his voice.

'You're assuming that Sam is as strong as you, Cole.'

'What do you mean?'

'I don't think you realise how strong you are. It took enormous guts, determination and self-belief to achieve what you have with no help or emotional support from your family. Maybe Sam simply wasn't good at conflict, or too weak to buck your father's wishes. Maybe he feels intense guilt that he wasn't there for you more.'

'Doubt that,' Cole muttered.

Lex felt a wave of gratitude for having her sisters in her life, particularly Addi. She'd had Addi to steady her, to give her love and support, but Cole lived his life solo.

'Have you decided whether you are coming to France with me or not?' Cole asked, placing her hand on his thigh and holding it down.

Lex looked away and bit her lip. She'd thought that agreeing to accompany him to Rhodes was brave but flying to Europe would be way out of her comfort zone. He was giving her the opportunity to explore another country, and one of the greatest cities in the world. When would she have that chance again? She should say yes on that basis alone.

Honestly, there wasn't a decent reason for her to say no. The girls were still away and Addi would be the first to tell her to take the opportunity, and that she deserved to take some time for herself.

Because she'd experienced massive unpredictability as a child, and wanted a stable life for her sisters and for herself, she'd made a religion of being rigid, of putting her sisters' needs before hers. She was so scared of letting them down—thinking that, in never allowing them to feel insecure and disappointed, she'd heal the wounds her mother and childhood had inflicted on her—that she never allowed any unpredictability to creep into her life.

But life was unpredictable and the ability to deal with change made people resilient and stronger. She wasn't doing the girls, and herself, any favours by being so protective of their hearts and feelings. She wanted Nixi and Snow to live, to gulp down life, but to do that they had to have an example to follow. From Addi they were learning a solid work ethic. Maybe she could teach them to be brave.

She could go with him or spend the weekend in her house binge watching box sets. That sounded so...sad. She didn't want to live a small, sad life any more.

She took a deep breath. 'I'd like to, thank you.'

'Great. Do you have a passport?'

She had a UK passport so there would be no visa issues, which she told him.

Cole squeezed her hand. 'That makes it easier.' He thought for a moment before speaking. 'I need to fly to Mauritius to look at some assets and businesses.'

Seriously, how many businesses did Thorpe Industries own?

'Okay, then I'll arrange for my jet to meet us when we reach Bloemfontein. And, if I leave Cape Town tonight and hit the ground running first thing in the morning, I should be able to complete my business in four days and fly back Thursday morning. We could fly out Thursday evening, spend Friday in Paris and head for Burgundy on Saturday morning.'

He was offering to show her Paris as well. *Oh, wow.* 'Won't you be tired of flying?' she asked.

'Honey, I'm not the one flying the plane,' he pointed out, amused, and laughed when she blushed. 'And I employ two flight crews because I'm always in the air.

'Would taking an extra-long weekend work for you?' he asked.

Uh...yes.

Cole grinned when she gave him her answer and she thought how much younger he looked when his smile hit his eyes, when he looked truly happy.

As for her, Lex felt as though he'd lifted her and swung her around, setting her back on her feet when she was off-balance and giddy. She was going to Paris. She could talk French and test her proficiency in the language. She could see the Eiffel Tower and visit the Louvre. Then she'd hop over to London. She felt breathless, as if her heart was trying to escape, and adrenalin coursed through her system.

Best of all, she'd be with Cole.

But underneath the excitement…oh, so faint but still there…lurked fear, warning her not to become too excited because there was always a chance that he'd disappoint her. Because that was what people did, what she'd experienced over and over again.

But sometimes they didn't. Sometimes people did what they said they would. Cole was too straightforward and too in-your-face honest to play games, to mess with her emotions.

She was going to Europe, and she was allowed to feel excited and thrilled about her first overseas visit.

And about spending more time with Cole.

'You are going to have such a wonderful time and I'm so happy for you, Lex.'

Addi placed her hands on Lex's shoulders and Lex looked at their reflections, so different. For the first time in for ever she didn't compare herself to her gorgeous sister. She looked…well, pretty damn amazing herself.

Earlier in the week, Cole had called and told her he'd managed to complete his business early and that they could fly out mid-Thursday morning if she could meet him at the airport. He'd made a late-night reservation at Mathieu, a three-Michelin-star restaurant on the Boulevard St-Germain. She'd looked up the restaurant online, and it was fancy with a capital F.

Panicking because she had nothing to wear to an exclusive Michelin-star restaurant, or a garden party at a French chateau, she'd called Addi, who'd immediately flown into action.

In a second-hand clothing store off Adderley Street, they found all she needed. She was now the proud owner of a designer little black dress she'd wear to Mathieu tonight, and a couple of classic dresses that were suitable for the French countryside. She was travelling in a long pink pleated skirt with a fitted turtleneck in the same colour. *Pink*—it was a colour she never wore because everyone knew that redheads couldn't wear pink. Or red. Or orange.

Her outfit wasn't blush-pink, or salmon-pink—no, it was flaming pink, a hot pink, the colour of printed sunsets on tourist T-shirts. It was a pink that screamed *look at me!* and stamped its foot if you didn't. To someone who routinely wore black, this shade was a shock to her senses.

But, damn, it looked good on her.

She looked stunning, like herself but not. Bella—a stylist Addi knew from who knew where—had arrived early and spent a long time making her curls straight, then used a flat iron on them until her hair fell past her shoulders. Then she pulled her hair back into a tight, sleek tail, wrapping strands over one another to conceal the band.

Addi watched, fascinated, as she placed a light foundation over her face, evening out the colour of her freckles but not hiding them. Bella showed her how to apply smoky eye-shadow and painted her lips with a natural-coloured lipstick she assured her would last all day.

'You look sophisticated and lovely,' Addi told her. She picked up her phone and snapped a couple of pictures. 'These are going on the family message group. The girls will be beside themselves.'

Addi and Bella left, and Lex closed her suitcase and checked, yet again, that she had everything she needed. She picked up her case and looked at her reflection in the freestanding mirror, cocking her head to the side. She could see this person with Cole in his usual, rich-as-Croesus life. She looked sophisticated and successful, cool and competent. Classy. She didn't look like a curly-haired chauffeur, a harried young woman raising two little girls or a part-time student. She looked like someone had waved a wand and made her…chic.

When Joelle had got her to change her looks, she'd gone to extreme lengths and had continued bleaching her hair and wearing thick make-up. Then, since she'd embraced her natural look, she'd never worn anything but a little mascara and lip gloss. Maybe she could find some middle ground. Straightening her hair every day would be impossible, but maybe she could start wearing tinted moisturiser, a little eye-shadow and this gorgeous shade of lipstick.

As for her clothes, while she wasn't a 'dress up and look smart' kind of girl, maybe she could start wearing something other than black jeans, long-sleeved T-shirts and vintage jackets. She should start introducing a little more colour and variety into her life. She was allowed to experiment with her looks, to dress up or down, to wear make-up or not. She was allowed to swap things around, try something new. It wasn't as if she was hiding behind a thick foundation and bright-blonde hair any more.

She could change her looks without changing herself.

Lex grinned. She was having a bit of a Cinderella moment, but instead of going to the ball in a carriage she'd be flying on a private plane and going to a garden party.

As if she'd summoned him, the doorbell chimed downstairs. Her driver was here.

She slung her bag over her shoulder and grabbed the handle. Her smile split her face as excitement danced up and down her spine.

Lex was about to embark on her truly excellent adventure.

Mr Thorpe, your brother requests your presence in Thailand. He has received special dispensation from the head monk to meet with you Saturday afternoon. He needs to tell you about Charlie. If you miss this opportunity, he does not know when, if ever, he will be able to meet with you again.

Sitting in his car outside Lex's cottage, Cole looked at the email from Sam's lawyer again and cursed. He'd received it as he touched down in Cape Town just an hour ago, earlier than he'd expected. The email was brief, but it felt as if every word was imbued with urgency. So Sam knew who this Charlie was and now felt the need to share the knowledge with him.

Good of him.

Cole was tempted to blow off his brother's request and whisk Lex off to Paris as he'd planned. Man, he'd missed her. He'd missed her laughter, the way she turned to him in her sleep and draped her thigh over his and placed her hand on his heart. He missed her clothes next to his in the wardrobe, the smell of her hair, the way she looked at him, her deep-green eyes glinting with affection and desire.

And he missed the sex. He really missed making love to her.

But if he didn't go to Thailand, if he ignored Sam's request, he'd never know who Charlie was and he knew, somewhere deep down, that whatever Sam had to tell him would fill in many of the blanks, would give him the answers he'd always sought.

He glanced at Lex's cottage, frowning as he tried to work out how to make this work.

He could change their plans, take her to Thailand and leave her on a beach while he visited his brother. But he knew that afterwards he would tell her what had happened between Sam and him, how he felt and what emotions he was experiencing. She'd hold his hand, lean her head on his shoulder and he wouldn't feel so alone.

If she did that, he'd pull the cork from the damn dyke and all his emotions would flood out and drown him. He'd say way more than he should—that he adored her, that he couldn't bear the thought of leaving Cape Town and her behind, that he wanted them to...

What? Have a long-distance relationship? Be his lover? Be his significant other, his girlfriend, his wife... his *something*?

Practically, realistically, they had too many obstacles to overcome. He only needed to visit Cape Town and Port Louis, the capital city of Mauritius, once, maybe twice, more before he'd manage to rid himself of all Thorpe Industries assets and businesses. He could see Lex then, but after those two brief trips he wouldn't be returning to Africa any time soon. He'd been giving his hedge fund and his venture capital business minimal time lately. He'd employed analysts to help him with his workload but he needed to take full control again. He missed his real work, the adrenalin of making massive stock buys, finding new companies to invest in and grow.

And then there was the issue of her sisters. Lex was raising two little girls and it would be disingenuous to suggest that her being the equivalent of a single mum wasn't a factor. If they were together, he'd have to share her time, attention and energy with her younger sisters, and at the very least be a role model to them. He couldn't see himself sharing Lex and living in a noisy house with two young girls when he was so very used to being on his own in his tidy and quiet house.

He'd never had a father, or much of an older brother, so how could he be either to her sisters?

Another obstacle was that Lex's life was here, in

Cape Town. And, while he had all the money in the world to pay for her to fly to see him, or he to see her, he knew that a long-distance relationship, seeing each other occasionally, wasn't something she'd contemplate. And wouldn't having little bites of time with her—a weekend here, a week there—make the times they spent apart harder to endure?

Cole sighed, knowing that he'd exhausted the practicalities and had to get down to the nitty-gritty of what was keeping him from forming a solid attachment to Lex.

Just get on with it, Thorpe, you've played this song before.

A core truth was that he'd made connections with women before and thought he'd met someone special. He'd tiptoe into a relationship but within a few weeks, sometimes a couple of months, he'd always end up feeling trapped, desperate to run.

Right now, he was besotted with Lex, couldn't touch her enough, wanted to make love to her constantly, hated being away from her, felt the need to be near her, talking to her, and having her fall asleep in his arms. He could see her rounded with his child, having a house filled with two little girls and their children running around, loud, messy and full of laughter and love. A house and life that would be the antithesis of his cold and lonely childhood.

But he'd had dreams before—though not this bright and vivid—and knew that feeling like this never lasted. In a month or two—maybe longer, because Lex entranced him like no other woman had before—he'd cool down, pull away. She'd have questions and he wouldn't be able to explain why he felt the need to run.

In his twenties, he'd put his failed relationships down to choosing the wrong woman, timing and mistaking sex for love. Now that he was older, he knew he was the problem, because he wanted something they couldn't give.

And he was doing it again.

Because no matter how much he adored her, how close he came to falling in love with her, she could never give him enough or what he really wanted—love and acceptance. No, that was wrong. She couldn't give him his father's love and acceptance.

Grenville was dead and, no matter how many times he told himself that he was an idiot for wanting something impossible or unachievable, it didn't stop his heart from yearning for it.

And, maybe, he thought that if he hadn't been worthy of Grenville's love then he wasn't worthy of anyone's love and couldn't trust it when he was offered it. Consciously or subconsciously, he might even have decided that, not having been able to interact with his father or have his love, then he'd *become* Grenville—cold, unemotional and soulless—to protect himself against future hurts.

It all sounded a bit weird, a lot crazy, but the truth was that his relationship, or non-relationship, with his father had affected and coloured his relationships with women. It would do the same with Lex.

He had an unhealed wound but that didn't mean that he should create wounds in other people's souls.

No, it was better to walk away now, while their feelings could be harnessed, corralled. It would hurt a little, more than likely a lot, but he was trying to protect her, trying to do the right thing.

That had to count for something, hadn't it? Then why couldn't he make his hand reach for the door and get his body to leave the car?

CHAPTER TWELVE

THE MOMENT SHE wrenched open her front door and saw Cole's hard face, Lex knew she wasn't going to Paris.

Or anywhere.

Despite her heart dropping to her toes, she couldn't help thinking that he looked amazing, taking in his black suit trousers and light-grey jacket, which he wore over a V-necked pale-green jersey. He hadn't shaved for a couple of days and his beard was at the length she loved most, long enough to feel soft, short enough still to be considered stubble.

Lex fought the impulse to throw herself into his arms, to stand on her toes and lift her mouth to his, but his remote expression had her holding back, her hand still on the knob of her front door. She stepped back and gestured for him to come inside, hearing her thunderous heartbeat in her ears.

Please don't disappoint me, Cole. Please don't say the words hovering on your lips.

'Come on in,' she invited.

Cole stepped into the tiny hallway and she saw the heat in his eyes as he took in her bright outfit and her straight hair. He opened his mouth to say something. Was he about to compliment her? Did he like the way she looked? But then he snapped it closed. He jammed his hands into the pockets of his trousers and rocked on his heels.

Right, so he wasn't going to kiss her. Not a good sign.

'Are you okay?' she asked, folding her arms and digging the tips of her shaking fingers into her ribs.

Cole rubbed a hand over his lower jaw. 'Just tired. It's been a long week.'

She waited for him to elaborate, but he looked away from her to examine the many photographs hanging on the wall. The biggest one, dead centre, was a photograph of the five sisters laughing. She couldn't remember when it had been taken, or by whom, but it captured all the love they shared, the enjoyment they had in each other's company. Cole looked at that photograph for a long time before shaking his head and closing his eyes.

Tired of waiting for him to speak, and needing an explanation before she exploded, Lex spoke. 'The weekend is off, isn't it? You're cancelling on me, aren't you?'

He met her eyes. His were a muddy brown instead of their normal topaz, and eventually he nodded. 'Yes.'

She'd expected his answer, had braced herself for it, yet she was still shocked when he confirmed what she suspected. 'Is there a reason?' she asked, forcing the words through her teeth.

Out of the corner of her eye, she saw Addi coming down the stairs and waved her away. This was between Cole and her.

'I need to go to Thailand,' he told her.

Pulling words out of him was like pulling dinosaur teeth out of stone. Where was the laughing man who'd beaten her at Scrabble, the warm-eyed guy who'd brought her hot coffee and kissed her shoulder and neck as she'd waited for the caffeine to kick in? Where had he gone?

'Okay, so I'll come with you to Thailand.' Overseas was overseas, after all.

'Sorry, no.'

Ah, so Cole didn't want her going anywhere with him. Message received.

Her lips pressed together so tightly, she didn't think any blood could reach them and her shoulders were close to her ears. She could visualise her heart shrinking, becoming smaller with each breath she took, and a cold hand held her stomach in a vice-like grip.

Oh, hello disappointment, my old friend. You haven't changed at all.

But she had. She wasn't the timid little girl who'd taken life's punches on the chin, who'd fallen down and then scuttled away. She was stronger, better, older, damn it. Anger, hot and wild, coursed through her system and Lex felt the pressure build up in her head. His behaviour wasn't acceptable. Not now. Not ever.

Don't yell, Lex.

As she knew from Joelle, losing one's temper lessened the impact of the message.

Lex dropped her arms and jabbed a finger into Cole's chest. 'You asked me to go to France with you, you told me to step out of my comfort zone and you encouraged me to be adventurous,' Lex reminded him, her voice sounding brittle. Tears had started to gather in her throat, but she'd be damned if she'd let him see them. He didn't deserve anything but cold fury.

'We've spent the past few days exchanging text messages about what we'd do in Paris, in London, how you wanted to take me wine-tasting in the Pouilly-Fuissé region. Give me a reason for blowing me off, Cole, when I took the huge leap of trusting you, of stepping outside my comfort zone.'

Whatever his reason for cancelling the trip, it was more important than her. She wasn't, in any way, his priority.

'I told you that I've been disappointed by many people in many ways, but I never expected yours to be a name I added to that list.'

Lex didn't drop her eyes from his, and she clocked his regret, but couldn't ignore his determined expression. There would be no talking him out of this, no room for manoeuvre.

It was over. They were done.

All that was left was to say the words and make it official.

Lex's belly twisted into a complicated knot and she felt as if she couldn't pull enough air into her lungs. Another person she loved and adored was about to walk away from her again. Really, she should be used to it by now.

For the first time ever, he didn't know what to say, how to end this. He knew he should tell her that they had no future, but he couldn't make his tongue form the words. 'Lex... I...'

She met his eyes and within those fathomless green depths he saw pain, but also pride. 'You don't need to strain yourself to find the right words, Cole.'

How could he tell her, in the nicest way possible, that this was about him and not her? 'I really do have to go to Thailand,' he told her, wondering if he should just bite the bullet and tell her that he was going to see Sam.

No, he needed to do this alone, to handle this himself. He'd been dealing with the fallout from his family on his own his entire life. If this was the last time he would speak to his brother, and it sounded as if it might be, then he wanted to finish as he'd started—by himself.

Besides, if he let Lex into his thoughts and heart again, he might not have the courage to let her go when they returned. Until he sabotaged their relationship down the line, when he would hurt her far more than he would now.

Admittedly, judging by the pain in her eyes, he was currently doing a great job.

He wanted to howl and beat his fists, but Lex looked dignified and aloof. She glanced at her front door, a silent gesture for him to leave, but he didn't know if he could. Doubt washed over him and he found himself backtracking. 'I need to return in about six weeks.'

She nodded enthusiastically, faking her excitement. 'Yes, sure, of course, I'll meet up with you again! I'll just come running when you call, okay?' she retorted, sarcastic condemnation in her voice.

'Why would I ever give you another chance to disappoint me again, Cole? Another chance to make promises and plans which you'll break with a flimsy excuse?' she demanded. 'Do you really expect me to fall back into line, thrilled to be in the sexy billionaire's bed again?'

Disdain coated her words and Cole felt two feet tall.

'I can't figure out a way for it to work, Lex,' he told her, sounding a little desperate.

'Of course it can't work, Cole, because I would be expected to do all the work. For us to keep seeing each other, I'd have to agree to wait around for you until you could return to Cape Town for a flying visit or until I could carve out time away from work, my studies and the girls.' Her expression was a curious combination of sadness and ferocity. 'And that's assuming that you can make a commitment to me, which I don't think you can. Or even want to.'

He could, *today*. He just didn't know how he'd feel in three months, in six. Would he still be crazy about her, or would he be looking for the nearest exit?

She fiddled with the hem of her jacket. 'Look, even if we decided to try the long-distance thing, I'd quickly run out of patience with that sort of set-up,' she told him. 'I am aware that my circumstances are challenging, that I have more responsibilities than the average woman in her late twenties. But the thing is, Cole, after dealing with a couple of hard knocks I have this crazy notion that I deserve some happy.'

'Of course you do,' he agreed.

'When the time comes for Nixi and Snow to date, I want to teach them not to settle for just anyone, that they are worthy of being more than an option, that they need to insist on being a choice. And I've got to practise what I preach. I need to be your *choice*. I won't be an option.'

She was asking for more than he could give her. 'I'm not good at long-term relationships, Lex.'

'So you say, Cole.' She shrugged, trying for casualness but missing it by a mile. 'But I'm prepared to wait for someone who is, someone who can give me everything I need: love, emotional security, to put me and my needs first. To be his priority. If that guy isn't you, and it obviously isn't, then I'll wait.'

His entire body rebelled at the idea of her with someone else. It felt as though an earthquake were rolling through him. He couldn't give her what she needed but letting her leave his life was harder than he'd thought.

'I think we are done here,' Lex gestured for him to leave. In a fog of confusion and regret, of hurt and relief, Cole walked onto her front step and turned to face her. She looked remote but impossibly lovely.

'I really hope you find happiness, Cole.'

He nodded, wondering how he'd ever manage to do that without her in his life. There was nothing he could say. He felt numb.

He swallowed and forced his tongue to form a series of words. 'I still think you're pretty amazing, Lex.'

'I know you do. You like me and you want me, but you don't trust yourself to love me the way I love you.'

What?

'You love me?' he croaked.

She held his eyes and nodded. 'Yes, of course I do. I love you enough to let you go and I love myself enough to demand more.'

Lex turned away and stepped back, closing the door in his face. He bit his lip to stop himself from calling out to her, from pounding on her door, and forced his feet to head in the direction of his car. He couldn't trust himself, couldn't take the chance...

Couldn't hurt her more than he was already doing.

Lex was out of his life, just as he'd planned.

He never thought that losing her would hurt this much.

Lex and Addi sat at a wooden table overlooking the quaint fishing harbour of Hout Bay, newspaper-wrapped fish and chips in front of them. Addi's iced tea was half-finished and Lex hadn't touched hers. Neither had she managed to lift any food to her mouth.

She could cope intellectually with the notion of Cole not wanting a relationship with her, and accepted that tears were part of her immediate future, although hopefully she'd be done crying by the time the girls returned in a week. But she strongly objected to losing her appetite.

That was a step too far.

Addi broke off a piece of fish, lifted it to her mouth and groaned. 'Man, this is still the best place to eat fresh fish.'

'If you say so,' Lex replied, watching a fishing trawler trundle into port accompanied by a flock of squawking seagulls. The trawler's once-bright hull had faded to a washed-out blue and Lex sympathised. 'Washed out' was a perfect way to describe how she felt.

Not having Cole in her life—the man wasn't even in the country!—had sucked the colour from the world. Sounds felt muffled, everything she put in her mouth tasted like cardboard and her touch was either dulled or her nerve endings felt over-sensitised. And, because she was constantly blinking back tears, her eyesight wasn't operating in tip-top condition either. She was leaving out a sense and didn't have the mental energy to work out which it was.

'Have you heard from him?' Addi asked.

Lex stared at the fisherman who was wrestling a thick rope around a piling. 'No.'

'Nothing at all?' Addi demanded.

'We had an affair. It's over and done with.'

Addi dragged a chip through a pile of tomato sauce. 'Please tell me you used contraception, Lex.'

Lex glared at her. 'I think I learned that lesson from Joelle, Addi. I think we *all* learned that lesson.'

Addi nodded. 'Fair enough.' Addi popped a piece of fish into her mouth before speaking again. 'Jude Fisher offered me a job, with a huge pay rise.'

It took a couple of moments for her words to sink in, for them to make sense. If she understood Addi correctly, then they could stop worrying about money and how they were going to pay the bills when Cole sold off the hospitality sector of Thorpe Industries. Her heart might be broken but at least they didn't have to worry about how to feed, clothe and educate two growing girls.

Lex pulled up a smile. 'That's great, Ads, congratulations.'

Addi pushed her half-eaten portion of food away and twisted her silver ring round and round her finger. Despite having good news, she still looked worried and anxious. Nothing had ever been gained by avoiding a situation, so Lex gathered her courage, pushed her fist into her sternum and met Addi's eyes.

'What's wrong, Addison?'

'I'm just worried about you. I've never seen you so heartbroken.'

Lex wanted to object, to insist that she wasn't heartbroken, but the man she loved didn't love her so, yes, she supposed she was. It was horrible and heart-breaking knowing the person you wanted above everyone else didn't want you.

And, yes, she was having a rough time, but she sensed Addi's anxiety had nothing to do with her and her relationship with Cole. 'Addi...'

Addi's phone lit up with an incoming call, a number Lex didn't recognise, and Addi pounced on it, barking a curt greeting after lifting the device to her ear. Then she stood up and walked away from Lex to stand out of earshot, her lovely face taut with tension as she listened to whatever her caller was saying.

Her sister was keeping secrets, Lex decided, something they'd never done. They'd always shared everything, and knowing that Addi was shutting her out added another layer of hurt onto the ones Cole had painted on her soul.

So far, a broken heart hadn't killed her, but it hadn't made her stronger either. She felt sad, weak and emotionally helpless, mentally drained. But she had to hold herself together to keep her broken pieces from shattering. To keep moving.

She'd always been strong, always managed to keep going, to move forward. This time would be no different.

On Saturday afternoon, Cole sat on a remote beach close to the Cambodian border, sunglasses over his face. The air was hot and muggy and his thin cotton shirt stuck to his back. Hot and irritated, Cole pulled the fabric away from his skin and looked at his watch.

He caught the eye of the Thai waiter and lifted his beer in a silent request for one more. The 'restaurant' where Sam had suggested they meet was no more than a mile from his monastery and comprised nothing more than an outdoor kitchen and two crudely built wooden benches and tables. But Cole was well-travelled enough to know that the best food was to be found in the unlikeliest of places. And, judging by the smell of garlic, chillies and lemongrass coming from somewhere behind him, someone was cooking an amazing fish curry.

Pity he'd lost the urge to eat since leaving Lex in Cape Town.

It was a stunning day, the sea glinting with shades of aqua and tanzanite blue, lazily rolling up the white sand beach. It was hard to believe that just days ago he'd been caught in a snowstorm and had experienced one of the Cape's wettest and wildest winters in history. The sky was a cobalt blue, practically perfect, yet Cole couldn't focus on the view, couldn't think of anything but that Lex should be here.

He'd missed her every second of every day since he'd pushed her away. He thought that he'd be fine, that his heart and soul would reshape themselves into what they'd been before they'd met her but...

No. They were still misshapen and anvil-heavy in his heart. He missed her with every breath he took, with every step he walked. His life no longer made sense without her in it.

Out of the corner of his eye, he caught the flash of an orange robe and he turned to see a tall, slim monk step onto the beach from the jungle, his bald head glinting white under the fierce sun. Cole watched as Sam walked towards him, noticing that his face was thinner and his cheekbones were pronounced.

The urge to walk away was strong. He didn't want to face his brother-that-never-was, but Cole couldn't let this go. He needed to speak to him, find some closure. He needed to repair the wound in his heart and maybe Sam, and his information, would help him do that.

Sam stopped a few metres from him and their eyes collided, so similar. He looked like his brother, like their father, but Cole doubted he'd ever acquire the serenity that he saw in Sam's eyes, nor the contentment.

Not unless he found a way back to Lex.

'Cole, you came,' Sam said, tipping his head to the side, a smile on his face.

Cole stood up and resisted the urge to wipe his damp hands on his thighs. 'Did you doubt that I would?'

Sam gave him a soft smile and sat down on the opposite side of the table. Right, so they weren't going to shake hands or hug. Good to know. He nodded at his beer. 'Want one?'

Sam didn't rise to the bait. 'I'll have a water, thanks.' Without waiting for Cole, he turned to the old man and greeted him in what sounded like remarkably fluent Thai. The old gent's face split into a wide smile. He looked beside himself with joy at the presence of a monk in his establishment. They spoke for a few minutes before the old man scuttled away to get his bottle of water.

Sam looked at Cole and raised his eyebrows. 'So, you found out about Charlie. How?'

'The ski-lodge in Rhodes. Everything carries the name—the pub, the ski runs, the company that owns it. It's the one part of Grenville's business that makes no sense, so I figure that this Charlie must be the reason that he hung on to such a loss-making asset. It's the only entity in Thorpe Industries that's raised questions. And the only one I can't sell.'

Sam looked puzzled. 'I thought you wanted the company. You spent enough money acquiring that block of Thorpe shares. I didn't want anything any more, so I thought it right to give it all to you.'

'I never wanted your damn money or shares, Sam! I wanted your attention, Dad's attention— Look, forget it!' Cole gripped the bridge of his nose in frustration. 'Just tell me who Charlie is, Sam. And, while you're at it, tell me why Grenville hated me so much.'

Sam took a long time to answer and with every second that ticked past Cole felt the tension rising. He braced himself to hear that their mum had had an affair and that she'd fallen pregnant by some man when she'd visited Rossdale. It was the only thing that made sense, that would explain why his father had hated him so. He didn't much care. If anything it would be a relief to know that he wasn't related to Grenville.

Eventually Sam spoke and, when he did, his eyes were dark with emotion. 'Charlie—Charlotte Jane—was our baby sister, Cole.'

I cannot believe that, after ten days of silence, he's texted me to collect him from the Vane!

Um…he owns Thorpe, and you're the company driver.

Sitting in the company SUV in a parking space next to the Vane's impressive entrance, Lex frowned at Addi's message and poked her tongue out at the screen. She hated it when her sister was super-logical, and hated it more when she was right.

Scrolling back, she stared down at the brief message from Cole, simply asking her to collect him at ten from the Vane.

When had he returned to Cape Town? How long was he staying? Could she afford to resign?

The last question was impossibly silly. Her job as the company driver was too good to give up and she'd continue doing it for as long as she could. But remaining professional while driving her one-time lover around, and pretending he was nothing more than her boss when he'd taken ownership of her heart, invaded her dreams and occupied most of her thoughts was going to be a huge ask.

Lex felt the burn of tears in her eyes, pulled her sunglasses off the top of her head and dropped them over her eyes. She couldn't let him see her cry...

Lex sniffed, took a deep breath and told herself, yet again, that she'd be okay, that she wouldn't feel heartbroken for ever. That, hopefully some time soon, she'd feel less sad, less...

Empty.

She was as busy as she'd ever been. The girls were back from their holiday, had started a new term at school and she was preparing for upcoming exams. She'd taken on a new student whose French was abysmal but who was prepared to pay her double her normal tutoring rate and she'd done the occasional delivery and pick-up for Thorpe Industries. But Lex felt like a spectator in her own life, as if she was standing outside of herself and watching herself run around. She was present but also not.

Because, honestly, seventy percent of her brain and all of her heart and soul was focused on Cole—wondering where he was, what he was doing, if he even missed her a fraction of the amount she missed him. Her world was in grayscale, her emotions muted, and she doubted whether she'd ever feel whole again.

She really hoped she would. But when? In two weeks? Two years? Twenty?

Lex saw the doorman step up to the door, her heart rate accelerated and all the moisture disappeared in her mouth. *Right, well, here goes nothing...*

She pulled out of her spot, cursing when the car jerked, and pulled up in front of the entrance, her eyes on Cole as he exchanged words with the doorman.

He wore light-grey trousers and a dark-navy jacket over a white shirt, and she immediately noticed he'd had his hair cut. She couldn't see his eyes because he wore dark sunglasses, but his face looked pale, and the smile he flashed at the doorman held none of its normal power.

He looked wonderful but tense. Was he as nervous at seeing her as she was seeing him? No, that wasn't possible. Cole did billion-dollar trades and invested ridiculous amounts of money in little-known products and business concepts. He was completely confident all the time and didn't tolerate nerves...

He walked over to the SUV and wrenched open the back passenger door. Lex closed her eyes when the scent of his cologne filled the car, remembering how she'd loved to bury her nose in his neck, in that soft place just below his jaw.

Be professional, Lex.

'Thank you for picking me up, Lex,' Cole said, after their eyes met in the rear-view mirror.

'Sure' She shrugged. 'It's my job.'

'How have you been?' he asked, and Lex wondered

if she imagined the crack in his voice or whether she was projecting her jumpiness onto him.

'Fine. You?'

'Fine.'

Lex was quite certain that, within the space of thirty seconds, both their noses had grown two inches. She could see rigidity in his jaw and the tension in his shoulders. Her expression was no doubt grim. They were anything but *fine*.

She didn't bother to contain her sigh. 'Where am I taking you, Cole?'

He reached across and handed her a slip of paper, and Lex plugged the address into the on-board GPS. He wanted her to drive him to Upper Constantia, to a very luxurious area called The Avenues, populated by mansions sitting on huge plots of land.

She started to ask him why he was going to a private address and then remembered that she had no right to pry into his business.

His choice, not hers.

Lex stopped at ten-feet-high wrought-iron gates and Cole leaned between the seats to aim the remote at the control box. As instructed, he pushed the blue button and the gates swung open. 'Follow the driveway and park in front of the house,' he told Lex and grimaced at his croaky voice.

He felt fifteen again, weak-kneed in the presence of his biggest crush. He rubbed his jaw, smoothed back his hair and looked out of the window, automatically clocking the massive oak trees, the huge swathe of lawn and the pretty single-storey, historic Victorian homestead.

Nice. He liked it.

He'd traded tens of billions of dollars, and made some ballsy choices business-wise, but this was his biggest ever gamble to date. For the first time, he felt queasy. He wasn't only gambling with a couple of million pounds—petty change—but with his heart, his future.

What if he'd missed his chance, screwed this all up by letting her down, by not taking her to Europe, for not allowing her to go with him to Thailand? What if he'd missed the boat?

What if...?

His rollicking thoughts were interrupted by Lex stopping the car. Thinking he'd jump out of his skin if he didn't move, he exited the car and walked towards the front door of the house. He was halfway there when he realised that Lex wasn't following.

He stopped, closed his eyes and shook his head. Turning, he walked back to the SUV and jerked open her door. Needing to see her eyes, he gently pulled off her sunglasses and placed them on the dashboard. He stared at her, taking in her glossy curls and her sexy mouth, and didn't miss the trepidation in her deep green eyes. Nobody, least of all him, should make her feel anxious or nervous. He looked into her lovely eyes, still full of hurt, and cursed himself for being a fool.

Walking away from her had been the dumbest move he'd ever made. She was what he needed and, if he wanted her in his life, he was going to have to fight for her. Fight his urges to run, to bail, to protect himself. He'd take anything she would give him, any time she could spare from her busy life looking after her sisters and pursuing her degree.

He was done living alone, being alone. And Lex was the only woman he could imagine being in his life full-time, for ever. Thinking that they couldn't have any barriers between them, he yanked off his sunglasses and tucked them into the inside pocket of his jacket. He held out his hand to Lex.

She looked from his hand to his eyes and back to his hand. 'Why are we here, Cole?'

'I have some things to say. Will you listen?'

She ignored his hand, hopped down from the car and jammed her hands into the back pockets of her pale-blue jeans. She shrugged and looked around. 'Where are we?'

'This property dates back to the late-eighteenth century. It's around five thousand square metres and is one of the biggest in the area. Five bedrooms, a three-bedroom cottage, staff accommodation and an apartment over the four-car garage.' He pointed up and Lex followed his gaze and shrugged.

'So?' When he didn't answer, she threw her hands up in the air. 'Cole, why are you acting like an estate agent? Why am I here?'

He didn't want to have this conversation standing on the driveway, so he took her hand and pulled her around the empty house and onto the entertainment deck overlooking one of the two pools on the property. The house was currently unoccupied, and he'd purchased it fully furnished, so he guided Lex over to a comfortable couch under the veranda roof.

If she agreed to his crazy plan, exploring the house could come later...

Right now, he had a *lot* of explaining to do.

Lex sat down on the couch and Cole pushed back the sturdy wooden coffee-table to make room for their legs. He sat down on the coffee table and rested his forearms on his thighs, inching to touch her.

But that, hopefully, would come later too.

Just say the words. Just get it done, Thorpe.

'I need to tell you who Charlie is.'

Surprise flashed in her eyes and a tiny frown pulled her eyebrows together. It was obvious that wasn't what she'd expected him to say. 'Okay...' She drawled out the word.

'The reason I cancelled our French jaunt was because Sam, my brother, asked for a meeting in Thailand,' Cole explained. 'He wanted to tell me about Charlie.'

'He couldn't email you the information?' Lex asked, sceptical.

'No, and I now understand why.' He swallowed, looked down at his hands, and rubbed the back of his neck. It was still so hard to comprehend, hard to take in.

'Charlie was my sister, Lex.'

He rubbed his hand over his jaw, still having difficulty with the words. 'She was ten months younger than me, and was apparently the centre of our family. A beautiful little girl and utterly adored, especially by my dad.'

Lex wrinkled her nose, trying to make sense of his words. 'I don't understand how you never knew you had a sister.'

He hadn't either and it had taken much convincing from Sam for him to believe that he'd once been a big brother.

'She died when I was very young.'

He felt Lex's hand slide over his knee and he immediately felt calmer, more in control. He wasn't alone, he had someone supporting him. He knew he wanted her, but until this moment he hadn't known how much he *needed* her. Her strength and her calm, her support.

'Tell me what happened, Cole,' Lex said.

'Please know that it wasn't my fault. Sam said it was a freak accident and I was hurt as well,' he gabbled, surprised to know that he could talk so fast.

Lex placed her hands on his face and forced him to

look at her. 'Cole, darling, take a breath and tell me, as simply as possible, what happened.'

Simple. Good idea. Right now, simple was all he could handle.

Cole hauled in a deep breath, nodding once before speaking again. 'The original owner of Rossdale and my father met somewhere and became friends and he invited our family to what was, as Sam explained, quite a rustic place. It was more of a family holiday home than an inn and, apparently, my father fell in love with the place and they visited as often as they could.'

'Go on,' Lex murmured.

'Before it was renovated, it had a steep stone staircase. I was nearly four, Charlie was ten months younger than me. My mum put me and Charlie in an upstairs bedroom for an afternoon nap, but I wanted to play in the snow. Charlie and I left the room. There was a gate at the top of the stairs to keep us from going down the stairs on our own but it wasn't bolted. Nobody knows how it happened, but Charlie fell down the stairs. Sam thinks I tried to grab her and tumbled down after her. She died on impact. I was in a coma for a few days with a brain bleed. I woke up with no memory of the accident. Or her.'

Cole felt as if he was talking about a stranger, about another man who'd had a sister who'd died when he'd been little. How could he not remember anything of this?

'Oh, Cole,' Lex murmured.

'My father blamed my mother for not bolting the gate, my mum said she did. He said I must've managed to open it, but Sam says I wasn't tall or strong enough to do that. But it didn't matter to Grenville—Charlie's death was my mother's fault for not bolting it and my fault for letting her fall. Or for not dying instead of her,' he added.

He heard Lex's sharp intake of breath. 'No, Cole.'

He couldn't stop now. He had to get all of it out. It was the only way to lance the festering wound and put it behind him. 'He was a stone-hard man, someone incapable of emotion, and the little he did have when Charlie died transferred to Sam. He demanded a divorce and my mother agreed to go quietly, provided he never blamed me for, or even told me about, Charlie's death. He agreed because he didn't want anything more to do with either of us.'

'When did he buy Rossdale?' Lex asked.

'About five years after Charlie died. Every three months he'd make an offer, upping it until the owners couldn't refuse the insane money he was offering. Every year or so, around the anniversary of her death, he'd disappear for weeks at a time. When Sam realised he was at Rossdale on his own, drinking himself into a stupor, he challenged him to do something with the place, something that would honour Charlie's life. That's when he threw himself into renovating the property.'

'So, he rejected his own living flesh and blood and blamed you for her death, but remained emotionally connected to Charlie by turning the accident site into a shrine?' Lex asked, sounding incredulous. 'That's… that's so *sad*, Cole. And so selfish and narcissistic. It was all about *him*…his loss and his pain. And it was so easy for him to love Charlie. It didn't require much effort.'

He jerked up his head. 'What do you mean?'

'She died at a delightful age when she was sweet and lovely. She hadn't learned to talk back, to have an opinion, to argue with him or do her own thing. In his head, she was perfect and would be perfect for ever. That's not love, that's a cop-out. It takes courage to accept people with all their faults and foibles and love them anyway. Your father was an emotional coward.'

Of course he was. Cole dropped his head, ashamed that he'd craved Grenville's love and approval. It had taken over thirty years for him to realise his father had been emotionally stunted, an awful person who'd blamed his young son for his younger sister's death.

Because of Grenville, Cole had pushed away people, spent too much time alone and had second-guessed himself every step along the way, and for what? Because he'd thought that if he couldn't have his father, he'd become his father?

He didn't know what had happened that day at the ski-lodge—honestly, he didn't even remember Charlie—but what he knew for sure was that he didn't have it within him to hurt anyone and that her death had been a horrible, horrible, tragic accident.

His father could've grieved for his daughter, loved his wife harder and gathered his sons closer. But Grenville had chosen to distance himself, to perpetuate the pain. And, the longer he'd lived in his cold, acid-tinged shadow, the more like him Cole had become. Cold. Bitter. Lonely.

He was done.

No more. It was time to step into the light. To love and be loved.

Lex lifted her fingers to her mouth and closed her eyes. She said a quiet prayer in Charlie's name.

The little girl who Cole had never known.

Lex did not doubt that Cole's mother had thought she was doing him a favour when she'd hidden the truth from him, thinking that he couldn't handle knowing that his sister had died when he'd lived, and that his father blamed him for her death. But Lex knew children were a lot more resilient than adults gave them credit for and that honesty was always the best way to go. As

Cole had grown up, his mum could've told him what had happened, assured him the accident wasn't his fault and explained that his father couldn't move on.

Cole could've got therapy and a clearer picture of why his father had refused to interact with him.

'I thought that if I couldn't have a relationship with him, then I couldn't have a relationship with anyone,' Cole said, every word coated with pain. 'I've had relationships but I've always cut and run. Because that's what my mum did emotionally, and what Grenville did emotionally *and* physically.'

Lex leaned forward, placed her hands on his knees and rested her forehead on his. 'I'm so sorry, Cole. I'm so sorry about Charlie.' She looked up. 'And you remember nothing about her?'

Cole pulled back and ducked his head. He pulled his hair apart and she saw a long, vicious scar. 'They told me I fell down some stairs, that's all I know. I don't have any memories from before waking up in hospital.'

'I can't believe your brother never told you, especially after both your parents died.'

Cole shrugged. 'Ignoring stuff was what we did. My parents divorced and ignored each other. My sister died and nobody mentioned her again. My family is very good at disconnecting. My brother just walked away from his life, and me, to become a monk.'

And Cole had walked away from her. Yeah, she could believe that it was a family trait. Cole, looking thoroughly miserable, pushed his hand through his hair. '"Just walk away" should be written on our family crest.'

Probably. And wasn't it her luck to fall in love with someone who did exactly what she'd experienced all her life? Could she pick them or what?

She now knew why he acted like he did, why he found it difficult to stick—he'd never been shown how to. But, as sad as his story was, however much she grieved for him, he'd walked away from her once and she wouldn't allow him to do that again. She couldn't take the chance of having her heart stomped on again.

It was her turn to go.

She stood up and raised her shoulders. 'I'm going to go. I need to collect Nixi and Snow from school.'

That wasn't for a couple of hours, but she couldn't stay here and be tortured by what she couldn't have. Seeing him was like backsliding into addiction again— one hit and she was toast. She'd be suffering withdrawal symptoms for days, possibly weeks, now.

'Don't go,' Cole said, his voice breaking.

What was the point of her staying? She was just prolonging the agony. 'Cole…'

'Please stay. Not just for now, but for ever. Please don't walk away from me.'

From a place far away, Lex heard the sound of the car keys hitting the floor and she jammed her hands into the back pockets of her jeans and told her feet to stay where they were. She was not going to run to him and throw himself in his arms.

Not just yet anyway.

'Why not?' she asked quietly. 'How are you going to persuade me to stay?'

If he said money and…stuff…she'd brain him with the rather lovely hand-blown glass bowl sitting on the coffee table behind him.

Cole walked towards her and stopped when they were just inches apart, close enough for her to go up onto her tiptoes and kiss the underside of his stubbled jaw. His hand cradled her face and Lex steeled herself not to react. Yes, her knees wanted to melt, yes, she wanted to kiss him and, yes, she wanted to stand in the protective band of his arms.

But if he couldn't give her what she most needed...

Cole's thumb brushed over her jaw. 'I'm not good at relationships, Lex, but I've been better with you in two weeks than I've ever been with anyone before. Something about you opened up something in me and, while I don't think I'll ever wear my heart on my sleeve as a matter of routine, I will with you. And with any children—yours, ours—that share our house and lives. I refuse to be like him—cold, selfish, alone, bitter. Unloved. Unable *to* love.'

Lex felt a ball in her chest and found she was struggling to take in enough air. She had no idea what to say, even where to start. Then Cole bracketed her face with his hands and he gently, so tenderly, swiped his mouth across hers.

'I love you, Lex, and I want to keep loving you for the rest of my life.'

She closed her eyes, thrilled to her core, infused with a blinding white light of pure joy. But there was still a whisper of doubt...

'Cole, you're saying everything I wanted to hear but—'

'But you are raising your sisters...you have Addi to think of...you have responsibilities,' he interrupted her. 'You also have a degree to finish and a career to start. Fine.'

She held his wrists and raised her eyebrows. 'What does "fine" mean? How can I do that, and have a relationship with you when you live ten thousand miles away?'

He moved his hands to her hips and she noticed that

his eyes had warmed to amber. 'I'm going to relocate and won't travel so much. I'll help with the school runs, I'll help with homework, I'm pretty good at maths...'

She held up her hand, a little overwhelmed. 'Wait, whoa. Are you suggesting that you move in with us?' Their house was tiny and there wasn't room for someone as big and bold as Cole.

'I was thinking that maybe you could move in with me. There's a massive house behind us that I've just bought, sweetheart.' He saw her shock and ignored it. 'If you say yes, then Addi could move into the guest house, your other sister can use the apartment over the garage and the younger girls can live with us and run between their and our houses. We can hire an au pair to look after the girls to free up some of your time so you can get your degree done. Bottom line, I just want to wake up every day in our bed with you in my arms, be in your life.'

Oh, man, that sounded like every dream she'd ever had coming thundering towards her but she still wasn't sure that he knew how much he was taking on. 'Cole, the girls are strong-willed and demanding. They are messy and loud. They fight and cry and are overly dramatic. They will be a constant part of my life for the next ten to twelve years.'

He placed a kiss on her cheek, then on her jaw, and Lex found it hard to think. 'Of course they will. I understand that, in marrying you, I acquire four sisters, two of whom will be moving in with us. I get it, Lex, and I don't care. I would take on a whole orphanage of kids if that's what you wanted.'

Then he shrugged and Lex saw a hint of excitement in his eyes, a smidgeon of terror. 'I didn't have much to do with my brother, and don't remember my sister, so maybe I can share yours.'

He'd never had a family and she could see he was desperate for one. He needed the girly hugs and the drama, to come home to a house filled with love, noise, music and laughter. He needed a family more than he knew. But it still wasn't enough to dispel all her doubt that they could work.

'I'm terrified that in six months, a year, you'll decide that this, us, is too much and that you've made a mistake and you'll walk away,' Lex said, feeling a tiny crack form in her heart. 'I'm scared to take that risk, Cole, but I'm terrified for the girls. I won't have them hurt because you promised to love them and then walked away. I'd risk my heart, but not theirs.'

Cole held her eyes. 'I wish I could stand here and tell you that I'm going to be great at this immediately, Lex. But the truth is that I'll probably be overwhelmed and want to tear my hair out occasionally. But I promise you—I *promise* you—that I won't walk. I won't just wake up one morning and bail. I will stick and I will stay and we *will* work through everything life throws at us. It will be worth it. That I know,' he told her with complete conviction in his voice.

'How? How can you know that?' Lex demanded.

'Because we are better, stronger, happier together than we are apart, sweetheart.'

He was right. She could live a life without him, but it wouldn't be as much fun. Her heart wouldn't be as light and bright as it would be if he was around.

Cole cuddled her closer and rested his temple against hers. 'I've been looking for love my whole life, Lex. And your love is all I need.'

Lex encircled her arms around his waist and reached

up to place her face in his neck, feeling every inch of her settling, sighing, relaxing. Cole was holding her and all was right with her world.

'I love you,' she whispered quietly.

'I love you more, my darling.' He pulled back and pushed her hair off her forehead, tucking a curl behind her ear. Their eyes connected and she saw his throat bob. 'Be mine?'

Every inch of her smiled. 'I have been. I am. I always will be.'

Cole covered her mouth with his, banded his arm around her hips and lifted her up and into him. Lex wrapped her legs around his hips and placed kisses on his cheek and jaw, the side of his nose. 'I think we should call our first child Charlie,' she said.

Cole's smile was sweeter than she'd ever seen it. 'I think that's a very good idea. Shall we start working on that right now?'

Lex laughed. 'I'm brave, but not that brave, Cole. Let's put a baby on hold for a year or two, or three or four.'

He sent her a wicked grin as he walked her into the house, heading for the nearest couch, she presumed. 'You let me know when, sweetheart. I'm always up for the challenge.'

He was. And always would be.

* * * * *

COMING SOON!

We really hope you enjoyed reading this book.
If you're looking for more romance, be sure to
head to the shops when new books are
available on

Thursday 30th March

To see which titles are coming soon, please visit

millsandboon.co.uk/nextmonth

MILLS & BOON®

Coming next month

RETURNING FOR HIS RUTHLESS REVENGE
Louise Fuller

As the door closed, the room fell silent, and just like that they were alone.

His heart was suddenly hammering inside his chest. So, this was it. He had imagined this moment so many times inside his head. Had thought of all the clever, caustic things to say, only now his mind was blank.

Not that it mattered, he thought, anger pulsing over his skin. Sooner or later, she was going to realize that he wasn't going to disappear this time.

Not until he'd got what he came for.

Her eyes locked with his. He felt his heart tighten around the shard of ice that had been lodged there ever since Dove had cast him into the wilderness.

She was staring at him in silence, and he waited just as he had waited in that hotel bar. Only this time, she was the one who didn't know what was happening. Didn't know that she was about to be chewed up and spat out. But she would, soon enough.

"What are you doing here, Gabriel?" Her voice was husky but it was hearing her say his name again that made his breathing jerk.

Continue reading
RETURNING FOR HIS RUTHLESS REVENGE
Louise Fuller

Available next month
www.millsandboon.co.uk

MILLS & BOON

THE HEART OF ROMANCE

A ROMANCE FOR EVERY READER

ODERN — Prepare to be swept off your feet by sophisticated, sexy and seductive heroes, in some of the world's most glamourous and romantic locations, where power and passion collide.

STORICAL — Escape with historical heroes from time gone by. Whether your passion is for wicked Regency Rakes, muscled Vikings or rugged Highlanders, awaken the romance of the past.

EDICAL — Set your pulse racing with dedicated, delectable doctors in the high-pressure world of medicine, where emotions run high and passion, comfort and love are the best medicine.

ue Love — Celebrate true love with tender stories of heartfelt romance, from the rush of falling in love to the joy a new baby can bring, and a focus on the emotional heart of a relationship.

Desire — Indulge in secrets and scandal, intense drama and plenty of sizzling hot action with powerful and passionate heroes who have it all: wealth, status, good looks…everything but the right woman.

EROES — Experience all the excitement of a gripping thriller, with an intense romance at its heart. Resourceful, true-to-life women and strong, fearless men face danger and desire - a killer combination!

To see which titles are coming soon, please visit

millsandboon.co.uk/nextmonth

JOIN US ON SOCIAL MEDIA!

Stay up to date with our latest releases, author news and gossip, special offers and discounts, and all the behind-the-scenes action from Mills & Boon...

 @millsandboon

 @millsandboonuk

 facebook.com/millsandboon

 @millsandboonuk

It might just be true love...

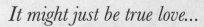